GW01607809

DOCTOR WHO
DALEK OMNIBUS

The Dalek Invasion of Earth
The Day of the Daleks
The Planet of the Daleks

DOCTOR WHO
DALEK OMNIBUS

The Dalek Invasion of Earth
The Day of the Daleks
The Planet of the Daleks

Based on the BBC television serials by Terry Nation and Louis Marks by arrangement with the British Broadcasting Corporation

---

TERRANCE DICKS

W. H. ALLEN · LONDON
A Howard & Wyndham Company
1983

Daleks created by Terry Nation

Phototypeset by Sunrise Setting, Torquay
Printed and bound in Great Britain by
Biddles Ltd, Guildford & King's Lynn
for the Publishers, W.H. Allen & Co. Ltd,
44 Hill Street, London W1X 8LB

ISBN 0 491 03420 2

Contents

DOCTOR WHO
DALEK OMNIBUS

The Dalek Invasion of Earth
The Day of the Daleks
The Planet of the Daleks

THE DALEK INVASION OF EARTH

1

Return to Terror

Through the ruin of a city stalked the ruin of a man. His clothes were tattered and grimy, his skin blotched and diseased over wasted flesh. On his head was a gleaming metal helmet. He walked with the stiff, jerky movements of a robot—which was exactly what he had become.

The robot man moved through the shattered rubble of a once-great city, a fitting inhabitant of a nightmare landscape.

In time he came to a river, a sluggish, debris choked, polluted stream which had once carried great ships. He quickened his pace, sensing that the water would provide the thing he sought—a way to end an existence of misery and pain.

When he came to a gap in the embankment wall, he marched stiffly through it and plunged into the water below. He fell, like a log or a stone, making no attempt to save himself. Dragged down by the weight of the helmet, his head sank beneath the grimy waters. There was something inhuman about the manner of his death—but then, he had not been truly human for a very long time.

Not far away, on the rubble-littered remains of what had been a building site, something very strange happened. There was a wheezing, groaning sound and suddenly a square blue police box materialised out of thin air, light flashing busily on top.

Inside the police box, things were stranger still. There was a large, brightly lit, ultra-modern control room. In the centre was a many-sided control panel, its surfaces covered with a complex array of knobs, switches, levers and dials. From the size of the control room it was clear that the police box must be bigger on the inside than on the outside.

Around the centre console stood an oddly assorted group of people.

The oldest was a man who appeared to be somewhere in his sixties, though in reality he was very much older. He wore check trousers, a frock-coat and a long black tie. He had flowing white hair and a proud, imperious face, with more than a touch of ruthless cunning.

The three others were more ordinary in appearance. There was a young man and a young woman, both somewhere in their twenties, and a dark pretty girl in her teens. All three were casually dressed in the clothes worn on Earth in the last part of the twentieth century.

The young man was called Ian Chesterton, the woman Barbara Wright. Once, though it seemed a very long time ago, they had both been schoolteachers. Led by their curiosity about Susan, the youngest member of the party, then one of their pupils, they had followed her home. To their amazement, they had discovered that she appeared to live in this police box with a mysterious old man known only as the Doctor, who she said was her grandfather. They had been even more astonished to find themselves inside the police box, and to discover that it was a kind of space/time ship, called the TARDIS—a name formed from the initial letters of Time And Relative Dimensions In Space.

Then had begun a series of terrifying journeys through time and space. The TARDIS had many extraordinary qualities, but accuracy of steering did not appear to be one of them. The Doctor's attempts to return them to their own time and place resulted only in an incredible number of unplanned arrivals, sometimes on alien planets, sometimes on Earth, though always at completely the wrong period. They had seen many wonders, and undergone many strange adventures. Such is the adaptability of the human spirit that they had now adjusted to a life of space/time travel. Though they still hoped to see twentieth-century Earth again, their old life had begun to seem more and more like a kind of dream.

Now the TARDIS had made yet another landing. They were all waiting with mingled anticipation and apprehension to discover what lay ahead this time. Moreover, to the Doctor's extreme annoyance, they were all being rather sceptical about his assurances that they were back on Earth, and in the twentieth century.

'Let's take a look on the scanner,' suggested Ian practically.

The Doctor switched on, and they all peered into the viewing screen. The picture was dark and fuzzy, like an old TV set in a poor-reception area. 'Oh dear, oh dear, it's not clear,' said the Doctor peevishly. 'It's not clear at all.' He glared at them accusingly, as if it were all their fault.

'I wonder where we really are,' said Ian thoughtfully.

Barbara sighed. 'Somewhere quiet and peaceful, I hope.' She knew from bitter experience that the TARDIS never seemed to take them anywhere *safe*.

Susan gave her a quick smile. 'Yes, we could all do with a holiday, couldn't we?'

Barbara peered at the murk on the scanner. 'I can't see anything.'

Ian looked over her shoulder. 'Don't worry, neither can I!'

The Doctor indicated sluggish movement on the screen. 'That could be water. A river, perhaps.' Ian gave him a sceptical look, and the Doctor turned away in a huff. 'Susan, perhaps you'll be kind enough to give me the instrument readings?'

Susan was already studying dials on one of the control panels. 'Radiation nil, oxygen and air pressure normal.'

'Normal for where?' snapped the Doctor. He hated any kind of imprecision, especially in matters of science.

'Normal for Earth, grandfather,' said Susan excitedly. 'This is a typical Earth reading.'

The Doctor gave a self-satisfied sniff, as if he'd known the answer all along. 'I don't want to boast, my friends,' he said loftily, 'but that might well be London out there!'

Ian and Barbara exchanged rueful looks. In theory the Doctor's words were true enough. It might indeed be twentieth-century London out there. But on his previous record, it might equally well be some savage alien planet—or the Earth of some completely different age.

Ian braced himself. 'Well, what are we waiting for? Let's go and take a look.'

Barbara agreed. 'Doctor, open the door, please. We'll chance it!'

For a moment the Doctor continued to look sulky. Then he gave one of his sudden charming smiles. 'Yes, of course, my dear.'

He touched the controls, the door swung open and they all went outside.

They found themselves in an open area, surrounded by high buildings. In front the ground sloped down towards a wide river. There were scattered piles of building material all around, bricks, timber, steel girders in enormous stacks. Many of the stacks were partially collapsed—the one nearest the TARDIS was in a particularly perilous state.

There was an ironic gleam in the Doctor's eye as he looked at Chesteron. 'Well, here you are, my boy—home at last. There's the Thames.'

'We've come a pretty roundabout way, Doctor.'

The Doctor nodded. 'And arrived more by luck than judgement,' he said, with one of his disarming flashes of honesty. He looked distastefully at the rubble all around. 'This is a pretty horrible mess, isn't it?'

Barbara nodded in agreement. It wasn't a particularly pretty spot to choose for a homecoming. But at least it was Earth.

'Where do you think we are, Ian?'

'Looks like a building site, down by the Docks. It all seems pretty deserted. We can follow the river into Central London, there'll be people about there.'

Ian and Barbara began making plans to find their homes and friends again. The Doctor watched them, frowning. He ran his hand along the nearest girder, then inspected it. His fingers were covered in thick rust. The Doctor's frown deepened. Building material was valuable. You didn't leave it out in the open to decay unused.

'I wonder which year we're in,' he muttered.

Ian caught the worried tone. 'What's the matter, Doctor?'

'Eh? Oh I was just worrying about the time factor, my boy.'

'After all our travels, we're not going to quibble about a year here or there!'

The Doctor sniffed. For all their recent experiences, these young people didn't realise the dangers and paradoxes in time travel. Suppose they met their own grandparents while they were still children? Or worse still, arrived at a time when all their family and friends were already dead? He kept these gloomy thoughts to himself and said, 'For both your sakes, I hope we're very near to your own time. But bear in mind, we may have arrived in the early 1900s—or in the twenty-fifth century!'

Barbara refused to be down-hearted. 'Well, it's still London. No mistaking that, I can feel it in the air,' she said cheerfully.

Suddenly they realised Susan was no longer with them. She'd grown bored with the conversation of her elders and slipped away. Ian hunted round for her unsuccessfully. Then it occurred to him to look up. Sure enough Susan was far above their heads, scrambling up the pile of girders. 'What do you think you're doing?' he yelled.

'Just having a look around. Can't see a thing from down there.'

Ian was about to order her down when he was distracted by the Doctor who said mysteriously, 'Decay!'

Ian and Barbara stared at him. The Doctor went on talking as if to himself. 'That's the word I was looking for—decay!'

Barbara put a hand on his arm. 'Doctor, what's worrying you?'

'Look at all this! Preparations for some great constructional work. A new bridge across the river, perhaps. Not a small undertaking. Yet all around us is this air of neglect. This place has been abandoned—and for quite some time too.'

Ian could see the force of the Doctor's arguments, but he didn't want to admit, even to himself, that the Doctor might be right. The thought that perhaps they weren't home safely after all was too awful to be faced. 'There's always a lot of mess in construction work, Doctor,' he said unconvincingly.

The Doctor was staring into space, his mind trying to solve the problem on the little evidence available. 'Perhaps, my boy, perhaps,' he murmured. 'And yet . . .'

Barbara shivered. Like Ian, she didn't want her hopes of a safe return snatched away. 'Doctor, you're spoiling it all.'

The Doctor's keen glance went from one to the other of them. 'I'm sorry, my dear. The last thing I want to do is spoil your homecoming. But I think we ought to be wary . . .'

Susan's voice floated down from above. 'I'm nearly at the top now. Still can't see much, though. I'll just go a bit higher . . .'

Enjoying her own daring, Susan continued upwards. Suddenly the girder beneath her feet rocked a little. Nervously she said, 'Oops!'

But the girder steadied again. She worked her way along it and on to the very top of the pile. Balanced precariously, she stared at the view below in shocked disbelief.

Although she wasn't a native of Earth, Susan had lived there with the Doctor for quite some time. She was very familiar with the way that London ought to look. The sight of the deserted, half-ruined city came as as big a shock to her as it would have done to Ian or Barbara.

Susan wondered when they must have arrived. Somewhere in the 1940s, perhaps? She knew London had been damaged in the Second World War—but she couldn't remember hearing that the damage was as bad as this . . . And how was she going to break the news to Ian and Barbara?

She heard Ian calling. 'Susan, be careful! What's it like up there?'

'Doesn't seem to be anyone about,' she called back. 'And the whole city's . . . ' The girder beneath her feet twisted sideways, and Susan lost her footing. She made a desperate grab at the nearest girder but her hand slipped, and she began a bumpy slide down the side of the pile.

The others looked on horrified and helpless, as she tumbled from the pile, landing almost at their feet. Barbara ran to her, kneeling by her side. Susan stirred and muttered, 'Ruined . . . all ruined,' then fell back unconscious. Barbara felt her head with skilful hands. There was a slight trickle of blood on Susan's forehead.

'She grazed her head on the way down but there

doesn't seem to be any real injury. She'll be all right.'

The Doctor looked down at Susan, disguising his very real concern with an air of irritation. 'She will go dashing about,' he said disapprovingly—forgetting that he spent his whole life dashing about on a far greater scale.

Ian helped Barbara to sit Susan up. 'Daft kid,' he grumbled, sounding very much like the schoolteacher he'd once been. 'She's lucky it wasn't worse—'

The Doctor rested a hand on the nearest girder. It was vibrating. 'I'm afraid it is worse,' he said urgently. 'That pile was finely balanced, and Susan disturbed the equilibrium.'

They stared upwards and saw a huge steel girder, balanced see-saw-like across another, tilt slowly to one side. There was a rumbling, grinding sound as the whole pile began to shift. Susan's fall, though minor in itself, had been like the shout that starts an avalance . . .

'The whole lot's going,' yelled Ian. 'Let's get out of here!'

The Doctor had already spotted the only safe shelter—the arched doorway of a half-completed building near by. 'Come on,' he called. 'Over here!' Dragging Susan between them, Ian and Barbara followed him.

From beneath the shelter of the archway they watched the collapse of the pile of girders. It was an impressive spectacle, accompanied by an ear-splitting clang of metal and clouds of dust.

The last girder clattered to the ground and there was a deafening silence. Coughing and choking, the Doctor peered out. 'Everybody all right? Splendid!' He seemed rather exhilarated by the adventure.

'We're all right,' said Ian. 'What about the TARDIS?'

The Doctor smiled complacently. 'How many times must I tell you, Chesterton, my boy, the TARDIS is indestructible.'

The dust was settling now, and the Doctor left the shelter of the arch and began making his way towards the

TARDIS. Suddenly he called in an alarmed voice. 'The ship, Chesterton, the ship!'

Ian ran to join him, then stopped in horror. The police box was still visible—but only just. An impenetrable tangle of twisted steel girders blocked the way to its entrance. The TARDIS was safe right enough—but they couldn't get back inside it.

2

The Roboman

The Doctor began tugging crossly at one of the obstructing girders. Ian came to help him, but they were wasting their strength. Ian shrugged and gave up, stepping back and wiping his hands. 'We'll need help to shift this lot, Doctor. We'd better try and find someone.'

The Doctor didn't move. He stood gazing at the twisted pile of wreckage, rubbing his chin thoughtfully. 'Remember where we are, Chesterton.'

'We're in London—oh, yes, I see what you mean. Why do we want to get into a police box, people will ask.'

'Ironic, isn't it?' The Doctor was still studying the wreckage. 'Now as I see it, this girder here is the main problem. Shift that and we could open the door of the ship far enough to squeeze inside.'

Ian looked at the girder. Luckily it was thinner than the rest. 'I could cut through it with an oxy-acetylene torch.'

'Easier said than done, my boy. One can't just whistle up machinery and tools at a moment's notice.' The Doctor looked at Ian with an infuriating air of expectancy. His manner suggested that he already had the answer to the problem, and was waiting to see if Ian could work it out for himself. Since Ian had a shrewd suspicion that the Doctor had no idea what to do next, he found this attitude particularly annoying. Ian glanced about him. 'That building over there looks like a warehouse of some kind. We might find something in it.

Even a few crowbars would be a help.'

The Doctor shook his head disappointedly, like a teacher whose favourite pupil had let him down. 'I'm impressed by your optimism, my boy. But brute strength will never move that girder. No, a cutting flame is the right answer.'

Ian's temper boiled over. 'I'm sure of one thing, Doctor,' he snapped. 'We won't achieve anything just standing here. And we must be able to get into the TARDIS before we start looking round—just in case we run into trouble.'

The Doctor was quite unruffled. 'Good, good, Chesterton,' he said approvingly. 'A very intelligent observation.' Clearly the favourite pupil was doing better. Ian opened his mouth for a sharp retort, when the Doctor lowered his voice and led him a little further from the two girls. 'I have a feeling, Chesterton, an intuition if you like, that we're not in your time.'

A wave of disappointment swept over Ian, all the stronger because he himself shared the Doctor's suspicions. 'Just a feeling, Doctor?' he asked, hoping against hope.

The Doctor shook his head. 'Consider this, my boy. Here we are by the Thames. We've been here some little while. And what have we heard? Nothing. No sound of birdsong, no voices, no shipping, not even the chimes of Big Ben. Just an uncanny silence.'

Suddenly Ian realised the truth of the Doctor's words. Apart from the noises they'd made themselves, there'd been nothing but dead silence. Now deeply worried, he followed the Doctor back to the two girls.

Susan was trying to stand up, with Barbara supporting her. 'Ow, my foot!' She sank to the ground, looking apprehensively up at the Doctor. 'Sorry about what happened.'

The Doctor sniffed, showing no signs of his relief that Susan wasn't badly hurt. 'Oh, you're sitting up and taking notice, are you?'

'There don't seem to be any bones broken,' said Barbara encouragingly. 'Just a bit of a sprain.'

Susan was still looking at the Doctor. 'Don't be angry. After all, there's no real harm done.'

'Oh isn't there? Just look at all this mess in front of the ship. We can't get in.'

Susan looked as if she was about to burst into tears. Hurriedly Ian said, 'We're going to take a look at that warehouse over there, see if we can find some tools.'

Barbara looked worried. 'Can't we all go?'

Susan tried standing up again, then collapsed with a wince of pain. 'My ankle seems to have got worse. It's all swelling up.'

Ian said, 'I'm afraid that settles it. We'll be back as soon as we can.'

Unhappily Barbara watched Ian and the Doctor move away. She turned back to Susan, who was rolling down her sock. 'That ankle does look swollen, doesn't it? Can you move your toes?'

Susan gave an experimental wiggle. 'Yes, it's fine until I put my whole weight on it. I've just twisted it a bit, that's all.'

Barbara looked towards the river. 'Suppose I go and soak my handkerchief with water for a sort of compress? That might relieve it a bit.'

Susan was already struggling to her feet. 'You're not leaving me here alone, she said determinedly. 'Give me a hand and I can manage to walk.' She put her arm round Barbara's shoulders for support, and they started hobbling towards the water.

By the time they reached the embankment Susan was exhausted. They stopped at the head of some steps leading down to the water and sat on the ground to rest. Barbara looked around. 'It's all too quiet. No traffic . . . this isn't my time, Susan. It can't be.'

Susan managed a smile. 'Well, back to the TARDIS

and off we go again—as soon as we can get the door open.' She saw the sadness in Barbara's face. 'I'm sorry you're not home again after all.' Then she added honestly. 'Sorry for you, but not for me. I suppose I'm selfish, wanting us all to stay together.'

Barbara gave her a consoling hug. 'No, of course not.'

Susan looked at the silently flowing river. 'I think this must be long after your time. We can't expect things to stay as they are. They have to change, don't they?'

'I suppose so,' said Barbara sadly. 'Maybe London's been abandoned. Or maybe they've just done away with noise altogether! You stay there, I'll go down and get some water.'

Barbara made her way down the steps to the river's edge, and took out her handkerchief. By laying face down and stretching her arm, she was just able to dip her handkerchief in the murky water. As she straightened up, something caught her eye, and she jumped back, shuddering.

The body of a man was floating face-down in the water. His clothes were tattered and grimy, and his body seemed thin and emaciated inside them. Some unhappy tramp who'd decided to end everything, thought Barbara—then she noticed the gleaming metal helmet clamped to his head. The body drifted slowly away downstream.

Barbara stood up, half-inclined to drop the water-soaked handkerchief back in the river. But she told herself not to be silly and started climbing the steps.

She was still wondering whether to tell Susan what she'd seen when she reached the top. But there was no one to tell. Susan had vanished. Barbara gazed round wildly. Susan couldn't have walked off, not with that ankle. She must have been taken. Suddenly she sensed a flicker of movement behind. Before she could react, a large, grimy hand clamped over her mouth, and she felt herself being dragged away . . .

The Doctor and Ian had to go round the back of the warehouse before they found an unlocked door. It creaked open to reveal a flight of steps leading upwards into darkness. 'I'll go first, Doctor,' said Ian firmly. He led the way up the stairs. 'Keep close behind me and be careful.'

He heard the Doctor's cross voice behind him. 'I'm not a half-wit, you know, Chesterton.' Ian smiled to himself. It would do the Doctor good to be treated like a child—a taste of his own medicine.

Half-way up the stairs Ian paused and called, 'Hallo! Hallo . . . anybody there?' His voice echoed in the silence and he went on climbing. The staircase led to a long gloomy landing broken up with several doors. The nearest one, on their right, stood invitingly open, and Ian and the Doctor moved inside. Intent on what was ahead of them, neither noticed when a door further down the corridor was pushed slightly ajar by a cautious hand. Through the crack, someone was watching them.

They found themselves in a long high storeroom, empty except for a few scattered crates and boxes, and an old-fashioned roll-top desk in the far corner. Ian looked round. 'Well, there's nothing here.'

The Doctor agreed. 'I'm afraid the place has been abandoned for some time.'

There were shuttered windows on the far side of the room, and Ian threw them open. As the shutters creaked back, sunlight streamed into the dusty room. Ian looked out of the high window, his eyes widening at the panorama of ruined London before him. Below, the river flowed sluggishly through a desert of half-ruined buildings. 'Doctor,' he called. 'Come over here and look!'

The Doctor shook his head sadly at the view. 'Just as I feared. Some unimaginable catastrophe has over-taken London.'

Ian pointed to a square building just across the river.

'Look, there's Battersea Power Station,' he said dazedly. 'It's only got three chimneys. What's happened to the other one?'

The Doctor waved at the surrounding desolation. 'What's happened to all London, my boy? That's the real question.'

The Doctor moved away from the window and began hunting through the desk in search of clues. Suddenly he said, 'Ah,' and triumphantly held up a grimy sheet of paper. 'Well, at least we know the century. This is the remains of a calendar.'

Ian ran across the room and almost snatched the paper from the Doctor's hand. It was a calendar right enough, the familiar pattern of numbered squares. Ian looked disbelievingly at the bold black figures at its head. They read '2164'.

He stared at the numbers, unable to take in what they meant. Slowly realisation dawned. He'd travelled two hundred years into 'his' future.

The Doctor put a consoling hand on his shoulder. 'I'm sorry, my boy, believe me. We must get back in the TARDIS and try again. I'll get you home.'

Ian nodded, unable to speak. The sounds from across the river came as a sudden distraction. 'What's that?'

The Doctor went over to the window. 'Gunfire! This city isn't quite dead after all.'

'Well, we'd better carry on searching. We may find something we can use.'

The Doctor slapped him on the back. 'That's the spirit, my boy.' They started searching the room, rooting through crates and boxes, most of which were empty or filled with useless junk.

The Doctor pulled aside an empty crate to get at the one behind—and a figure slumped to the floor at his feet. 'Chesterton! Over here,' he called.

Ian knelt to examine the body, which had fallen face-upwards. It was a middle-aged man, his body as grimy and neglected as his uniform. Clamped to his head was a strange helmet-like device, a gleaming metal affair fitting round the neck and over the head. Ian looked up. 'He's quite dead, Doctor. What's this metal thing for?'

The Doctor bent to take a closer look. 'Just what I was asking myself. Not for ornament, we can be sure of that.'

'Could it be some kind of surgical device—support for a fractured skull, or broken neck?'

'It's too complex for that,' said the Doctor thoughtfully. 'You know what I think, Chesterton—it's an extra ear, a device for picking up ultra high-frequency radio-waves.'

'A kind of communications system?'

'That—or some method of radio-control . . .'

Ian noticed a couple of objects thrust into the dead man's belt. A truncheon—and a whip. He pulled out the whip, a vicious-looking device with a stubby black handle and long leather thongs, tipped with lead. He passed it over to the Doctor who examined it with distaste. 'Worse and worse. Whoever this chap was, I'm glad we didn't run into him while he was still alive.'

'Any idea what killed him, Doctor?'

'He doesn't seem to be lying quite flat. If we turn the body over . . .' They turned the body on its face. The black hilt of a knife was jutting out from under the left shoulder blade. 'Just as I thought,' said the Doctor grimly. 'He was murdered.'

From outside the room came the sound of a creaking floorboard.

Ian grabbed the truncheon from the dead man's belt and crept stealthily towards the door. He peered out into the corridor. It was empty. The Doctor close behind him, Ian crossed the corridor and pushed open the door of the room on the opposite side. 'Just another storeroom—and it's empty.' They went back into the corridor and Ian looked up and down it. 'The sounds were coming from somewhere out here.' He moved along the corridor and tried another door. It was locked. Ian rammed it with his shoulder, the door burst open, and he found himself shooting into empty space . . . The Doctor quickly grabbed him by his coat and heaved backwards, and they both landed up in a heap in the corridor. Ian scrambled up and looked cautiously out of the door. Once it had led to a wooden staircase running down the outside of the building. But now the staircase was shattered and the door gave on to a sheer drop. Ian helped the Doctor to his feet. 'Well, no one could have gone that way,' he said grimly.

The Doctor dusted himself down. 'Only someone like you would even try,' he replied acidly. 'I suggest we abandon this fruitless search and return to the others.'

It was clear that the Doctor had had enough. Ian was inclined to agree with him. It wasn't very likely they'd find a full set of oxy-acetylene tools lying about waiting for them. And maybe hunting for the unseen killer wasn't such a brilliant idea either. 'All right, Doctor, come along.' Ian turned and led the way back downstairs.

They'd reached the warehouse door, and were about to step out into the open when the Doctor grabbed Ian's arm. 'Chesterton, look!' The Doctor's other hand was pointing upwards. Ian looked, and gave a gasp of sheer incredulity. Drifting low over the ruined buildings, for all the world like a plane coming in to land, was a flying saucer.

Instinctively Ian ducked back. The Doctor muttering, 'Fascinating, fascinating,' stepped out into the open to get a better look. Ian grabbed him and pulled him back into cover.

From the shelter of the doorway they watched the saucer drift slowly downwards. It looked exactly like the classic flying saucer of science-fiction films and drawings, silvery-coloured, oval in shape, and with rows of windows round the exterior. It made a low droning sound as it moved, disappearing behind some buildings.

Ian shook his head wonderingly. 'There were rumours of flying saucers in my time, Doctor. But I never thought I'd see one as close as this.'

The Doctor rubbed his hands together. 'Well, it settles one question. Whatever happened to London was not caused by the people of Earth. That was an interplanetary spaceship, my boy. Earth has been invaded by some other world.'

'Which explains the dead man we found,' said Ian thoughtfully. 'That thing on his head must have been some kind of alien control device. And that gunfire we heard means somebody's still resisting the invaders.' Ian looked at the Doctor in sudden alarm. 'Barbara and Susan! We've got to find them and warn them what's going on.'

They ran back to the TARDIS at top speed. Barbara and Susan were nowhere to be found.

Ian looked angrily round the building site. 'Why will they do it?' he demanded. 'Why must they always go wandering off?'

'Perhaps they heard the gunfire from across the river,' suggested the Doctor. 'Or they might have seen the saucer, and run to hide.'

Ian sighed. 'Well, I suppose we'll just have to look for them.'

They searched the building site without success, then started working their way towards the river. At the top of the embankment steps they found their first clue: a grubby, water-soaked handkerchief.

The Doctor nodded keenly, looking, thought Ian, like a rather elderly Sherlock Homes. 'So far so good, Chesterton, my boy. They came here for water, something frightened them, and they ran off again.'

'Why didn't they run back to find us?'

The Doctor frowned at the interruption to his fine flow of deduction. 'I can't imagine,' he snapped. 'We shall just have to look further afield.'

They turned to leave—and found four uniformed men barring their way. They were ragged, gaunt, emaciated—and each one wore a shining metal device clamped to his head. They held truncheons in their hands.

Ian and the Doctor stood quite still. 'We won't get past them, Doctor,' Ian whispered.

'Then we must go down the steps.'

'Swim for it?'

'What else?'

Ian looked at the Doctor. For all his tetchiness, he was certainly a game old boy. 'All right. They don't seem to have guns. I'll try talking first.' Ian called out a hearty 'Hallo!'. At the same time he and the Doctor began edging their way down the steps.

The four men moved steadily after them. One was a little ahead of the rest. Suddenly he bellowed, 'Stop!' His voice was slurred and dragging, like a record played at the wrong speed. As he spoke he picked up a jagged chunk of masonry, and the other men did the same.

Ian and the Doctor continued their steady retreat. As they neared the water Ian whispered, 'When I give the word, turn and dive!'

'Ready when you are, my boy.'

'Right—now!'

They both turned, and froze in horror. A Dalek was rising from the water and advancing menacingly towards them.

3

The Freedom Fighters

When the flying saucer passed overhead, Barbara and Susan were already fleeing through the ruins of London with a man who called himself Tyler. He was a tough-looking character, burly and middle-aged, and although his manner was curt and brusque, he didn't seem to be hostile.

When he'd grabbed Barbara at the steps, he'd released her almost at once, saying he just wanted to make sure she didn't scream. 'They had their patrols everywhere, and he'd already carried Susan to shelter so she wouldn't be spotted.

He'd taken Barbara to Susan, who was lying under one of the arches of the bridge, confused and frightened. Lifting Susan in his arms, he'd bustled them both on their way, promising to take them to a safe hiding place, and come back later for their friends.

When the drone of the saucer filled the air, Tyler immediately flung Susan and himself to the ground. 'Get down,' he whispered fiercely. Barbara obeyed, though she couldn't resist raising her head to watch the gleaming shape of the saucer glide out of sight. Then Tyler was on his feet again, picking up Susan. Ignoring their questions, he said brusquely, 'We must keep moving, we can talk later. We shan't be safe till we get underground.'

Still carrying Susan, Tyler led the way to the broken entrance of what had once been an underground railway station. He started carrying Susan down the stairs, but she struggled till he had to put her down. 'Wait! What about my grandfather and our friend?'

Tyler shrugged. 'We'll do the best we can for them.'

Susan wasn't satisfied. 'That's not what you said before!'

Barbara joined in. 'You promised you'd get the others. We don't want to be separated.'

'There isn't time to argue,' said Tyler savagely. 'If we stay on the surface we'll all be killed, and then who'll help your friends? Now come on.' They moved on down the steps. Barbara and Tyler supporting Susan between them.

Tyler led the way along dusty silent corridors and onto the platform. Strange posters covered the walls, not the usual announcements of films and plays and exhibitions, but severe-looking official notices in heavy black type. Barbara paused to read one.

PUBLIC WARNING. DO NOT DRINK RAINWATER.
ALL WATER MUST BE BOILED BEFORE CONSUMPTION.

In smaller letters beneath were the words, 'Issued by the European Emergency Commission.'

Tyler reached out and pressed the letter 'O' in 'NOT'. Part of the wall slid back to reveal a tiny gap. A grim-looking young man appeared, rifle in hand. Tyler said, 'OK, David, it's me.' David stood aside and Tyler helped Barbara and Susan through the gap. The door closed silently behind them.

They were in a small tiled ante-room, furnished with a few battered tables and chairs. Barbara guessed it had originally been accommodation for London Transport staff. Susan collapsed thankfully into a chair, rubbing her ankle.

The young man called David looked curiously at the two girls. 'Hallo, then, what have you got here?' There was a faint Scots burr in his voice.

'Found 'em wandering about down by the river. Sitting targets.'

Barbara was annoyed by his scornful tone. 'We've only just got back to London. We didn't know there was any danger.'

Tyler looked incredulous. 'Didn't know? No, I suppose you couldn't have known or you wouldn't have acted so stupidly.'

'Now, listen,' began Barbara angrily, 'you drag us here . . .'

David held up his hand. 'All right, you two, let's not fight among ourselves. Time for introductions. You already know Jim Tyler. My name's David Campbell.'

His friendly smile transformed the grim young face, and Barbara couldn't help smiling back. 'I'm Barbara, and this is Susan.'

'I hope you can cook.'

Barbara gave him a surprised look. 'After a fashion.'

'Good. We're short of cooks down here . . . and my cooking's terrible.'

He turned back to Tyler, his manner serious again. 'One of the Robomen jumped me in the warehouse. I had to deal with him. We'd better stop using the place for storage though.'

Tyler nodded. 'All right. Tell Dortmun.'

Susan had only been half listening to this conversation, but the mention of a warehouse made her look up. 'Are you talking about the warehouse near that building site—beside the river?'

David nodded. 'That's right. Just opposite the old power station.'

Susan tried to get up, then sank down again, wincing from the pain in her ankle. 'Then you must have seen the Doctor and Ian—they went in there.'

'There were two men—but I hid from them. I thought they must be enemies . . .'

An inner door opened and a wheelchair shot through it, halting abruptly. In the chair sat a middle-aged man with a strong deeply lined face. The upper part of his body was muscular and powerful, and he propelled the wheelchair along with big hands gripping the wheels. But his legs were wasted and shrunken, covered by an old army blanket. His voice was deep and commanding, with nothing of the invalid about it. 'Where the devil have you been, Tyler?'

Tyler was obviously used to the newcomer's abrupt manner, and his reply was equally spirited. 'I got delayed. Ran into these two. What are you doing up here? You're supposed to stay below in the operations room.'

'I'm just as active as anyone, and don't you forget it.'

Tyler grinned. 'All right, Dortmun, all right.' Somehow Susan sensed that despite the angry way they talked to each other, these two men were old and close friends.

Dortmun spun the wheelchair to face Barbara and Susan. 'Well, I suppose we can use two more pairs of hands,' he said gruffly.

David winked at Susan, as if telling her not to be too put off by Dortmun's abrupt manner. 'This is Susan. And this is Barbara—she says she can cook!'

'Good!' Dortmun glared at Susan. 'And what can you do?'

Susan grinned cheekily at him. 'Me? I can eat.'

For a moment Dortmun glared at her, then he gave a grim smile. 'Well, mind you leave some for me. David, where do you think you're going?'

The young man was already at the door. 'These two have friends, two men, still on the surface. I know roughly where they'll be. I thought I'd go and bring them in.'

Dortmun considered for a moment—and Barbara and Susan held their breath. Then he nodded. 'All right. But take care—and don't be too long.'

As David passed by her chair, Susan whispered, 'Thank you. Be careful.'

'Don't worry, I'll see you later.'

As David left, Dortmun headed his wheelchair towards the inner door. 'Come along. We'd better get below.' He stopped as he saw Tyler and Barbara helping Susan to get up. 'What's the matter with her?'

Susan hobbled to her feet. 'I happen to have sprained my ankle,' she said sharply. 'Don't worry, I'll manage. I'm just as active as anyone.'

Dortmun gave an approving nod. Clearly he liked people to stand up to him. 'All right, let's get moving.'

He sped the wheelchair through the inner doors, and Tyler, Barbara and Susan followed him.

Ian and the Doctor watched horrorstruck as the Dalek rose slowly from the water and glided along the bank towards them. Instinctively they turned to run. But the nightmarish figures of the metal-helmeted men had moved down the steps to cut off their escape.

The Dalek spoke in the harsh, grating tones Ian remembered from the time-travellers' adventures on the planet Skaro. 'Robomen! Why are these humans wandering freely in a forbidden zone?'

In his slurred, dragging voice the leader of the Robomen replied, 'No explanation.'

'Where is the Robopatrol for this section?'

'Not known.'

'You will take his place until he is found. The human beings will be taken to the landing area.'

'Daleks!' whispered Ian. 'What are they doing here on Earth?'

'Leave this to me, my boy.' The Doctor marched boldly up to the Dalek. 'I demand that you release us at once.'

'We do not release prisoners.'

'Indeed? And by what right do you take prisoners in

the first place?'

'We are the masters of the Earth.'

The Doctor snorted disdainfully. 'Not for long, I promise you.'

The Dalek was both astonished and enraged by this defiance. 'You will obey us or die!'

The threat only made the Doctor more indignant. 'Die? And who are you to condemn us to death? That settles it. Whatever you're up to, I shall pit myself against you and defeat you.' The Doctor folded his arms and glared defiantly at the Dalek. Ian closed his eyes and held his breath, mentally willing the Doctor to shut up. He was all in favour of opposing the Daleks, but he saw no use in getting themselves blasted on the spot.

The Doctor's words seemed to touch off one of those typical speeches, a mixture of threats and boasts, which seemed to be the Dalek's only form of communication with other species. 'We have heard many such speeches from the human leaders. All have been destroyed. Resistance is useless. It must cease immediately.'

'Oh must it? You surely don't expect the people of Earth to welcome you with open arms. Even Daleks can't be that stupid.'

'We have already conquered Earth.'

'Don't you pathetic creatures realise? You'll never conquer Earth, not unless you destroy every living being—'

The Dalek's patience was clearly exhausted. 'Take them! Take them!' it screeched.

Robomen grabbed Ian and the Doctor by their arms and dragged them away. In their ears echoed the angry voice of the Dalek. 'We are the masters of Earth. We are the masters of Earth. We are the masters of Earth . . .'

From his hiding-place nearby, David Campbell watched helplessly as the Doctor and Ian were led away. He had arrived just in time to see their capture. There was little he could do to help them, not with Robomen present in such force. But at least he could find out where they were being taken. Slipping cautiously through the ruins, David began trailing the Robomen and their prisoners.

'Survivors of London. The Daleks are the masters of Earth. Surrender now and you will live. Those wishing to surrender must stand in the middle of any street and obey the orders they will receive. Obey the Daleks!'

The radio went silent. Dortmun crashed his fist on the table, making the set jump and rattle. 'Obey motorised dustbins! We'll see about that! Tyler, come to the office, I want to talk to you.'

Barbara and Susan looked at each other. They were in a long underground room, filled with rows of trestle tables at which people sat quietly working. Some were cleaning or assembling weapons, others were working on radio sets and a variety of technical equipment. One corner was sectioned off into a kind of canteen, where women and girls were preparing food, and in another was the partitioned-off room into which Dortmun had just disappeared. Susan noticed that everyone in the room was tired and grim-faced. The place was obviously the main headquarters of the anti-Dalek resistance movement.

Tyler hesitated a moment before following Dortmun. He called, 'Jenny, come over here a moment, will you?'

A small dark girl got up from the nearest table and walked across to them. She stood before Tyler unsmiling, as if resenting the interruption to her work. 'Well?'

'Two newcomers. See if you can find them something to eat. One of them has a bad ankle.'

The girl looked at Susan and Barbara, no hint of welcome in her face. 'All right.'

Tyler turned to go. 'David will be back soon. I'm sure he'll have news of your friends. He might even have them with him.' He disappeared after Dortmun.

Jenny said briskly, 'Right, who's got the bad ankle?'

Susan held out her foot. 'I have.'

Jenny knelt beside her chair and examined the ankle with skilful but ungentle fingers, ignoring Susan's groan of protest. She straightened up. 'Just a strain, no bones broken. Why haven't you put a cold compress on it?'

'Because I've only just got here,' said Susan spiritedly. She'd no intention of being bullied by someone no older than herself, and she'd taken an immediate dislike to this cold-faced and bossy girl.

Jenny turned to Barbara. 'I'll see to this ankle. You go over there and get some food. While you're at it, put your names down for a work detail.'

Protectively Barbara said, 'Susan won't be able to do much, not till her foot's better.'

'She can work sitting down, can't she? We've no room for useless mouths here.' Jenny moved away.

Barbara glared after her angrily. Like Susan, she didn't take kindly to being bossed about. But she reminded herself that they were dependent upon these people, not only for food and shelter, but for help in finding Ian and the Doctor. It wouldn't do to upset them—at least until Susan's ankle was better. Barbara gave Susan a rueful grin, and went meekly to fetch the food. From inside the little office came the noise of voices raised in anger. No one took any notice. It was only Dortmun and Tyler having another shouting-match. Everyone was used to that . . .

Dortmun slammed his fist on the desk. 'We must attack them, Tyler. We must attack now!'

'That's all very fine. But how? We've got about twenty able-bodied men and women, the rest are old folk, and kids.'

'Ample!' snapped Dortmun defiantly.

Tyler groaned. 'Ample? To attack the Daleks? Remember the wars in the twentieth century, Dortmun, when men with bayonets attacked machine-gun posts?

They got mown down, defeated by superior technology. So would we be . . .'

'Don't lecture me, Tyler!'

'Then don't ask the impossible. You haven't been in the streets for quite some time. The Daleks have increased the Robopatrols, tightened up their security. It's almost suicide to go out there these days.'

Dortmun hammered the arm of his wheelchair. 'All right, I know. I'm in *this*! I send others, but I don't have to go myself!'

Tyler's tone softened. 'I didn't mean that and you know it. Now then, how's this new bomb of yours getting on?'

The distraction worked, just as Tyler had hoped. Eagerly Dortmun wheeled his chair to a table in the corner of the office, where shining glass spheres were set out on a blanket. 'All finished,' he said proudly.

'Have you tested it yet?'

'Tested it? It doesn't need testing, it's perfect. This is the bomb that will destroy the Daleks! Look, here's the casing, the new formula explosive, the detonating device . . .' Eagerly Dortmun began to explain the workings of the bomb on which he had laboured so long.

He was still doing it when David Campbell slipped into the room some minutes later. David had seen Barbara and Susan as he came in, but they'd had their backs turned and he'd been able to slip into the office without their noticing him. Dortmun looked up. 'We're just discussing the next attack, David. How did you get on?'

'I brought back some more tinned food. There's quite a bit left in that department store.'

Tyler nodded. 'All right, I'll send out a foraging party. What about the two strangers?'

'Just as I got to the embankment I saw them being taken away. I followed them part of the way. Judging by the direction, they were taking them to the Heliport Chelsea, where the Dalek saucer landed.'

Dortmun shrugged dismissively. 'Then that's the end of them. Once the Daleks get them inside that saucer, they're done for!'

David thought for a moment. Then he said, 'Not necessarily Dortmun. You listen to me . . .'

4

Inside the Saucer

Guarded by Robomen, the Doctor and Ian were standing in what had once been the Chelsea Helicopter Port—Heliport for short. It was a wide stretch of open tarmac, surrounded by ruined buildings. Towering above them rose the immense gleaming shape of the Dalek spaceship. Together with a group of other prisoners, the Doctor and Ian were being held at the foot of a ramp which led up into the ship. Dalek patrols glided to and fro, guarding the perimeter of the Heliport.

Ian moved closer to the Doctor. 'Why are they keeping us waiting about here?' he whispered.

'I imagine this is an assembly point, my boy. They're going to take all their prisoners on board at once.' The Doctor nodded towards the other side of the Heliport. A group of Robomen were marching two more prisoners to join the main group.

Ian looked round at his fellow captives. They were grimy, ragged and defeated-looking. He turned back to the Doctor. 'I still don't understand all this. The Daleks were destroyed. We were there on Skaro, we saw it happen.'

Sadly the Doctor shook his head. 'The devastation may not have been as complete as we imagined. The Daleks have incredible tenacity, tremendous powers of survival. There may have been other colonies on other parts of Skaro . . .' He looked at the scene around them, the ruined city, the enormous spaceship, the blank-faced, helmeted Robomen standing guard over their prisoners. 'Anyway, however it happened, the Daleks have survived. And they've evolved too.'

Ian studied one of the Daleks as it glided past. 'I see what you mean. These do look a bit different. I wonder if that's got anything to do with their increased power of movement. On Skaro they could only travel in their own metal city.'

'Quite true. But this is an invasion force, remember. They've found ways to adapt themselves to new planets. Something on the hovercraft principle I should imagine.'

By now the two newcomers had been herded across to the main group. They were tough-looking characters, one tall and wiry, the other short and thickset. Ian thought they looked less cowed than the other prisoners. A Dalek glided up to the Robomen guards accompanying them. 'Where are the other members of your patrol?'

In a slurred emotionless voice one of the Robomen answered, 'These men killed them both.'

Angrily the Dalek spun round, its gun-stick pointing at the prisoners. 'What are your names?'

'Bill Craddock,' said the taller man defiantly.

With equal truculence the thick set man said, 'And I'm Mick Thomson. Want to put us in your hall of fame, do you?'

The Dalek's eye-stalk swivelled towards them. 'Craddock and Thomson,' it repeated. 'You will be punished for your crimes. Robomen, continue your patrol.'

The Robomen moved away, and the Dalek addressed the group of prisoners. 'You will remain here without moving until it is time to enter the ship.'

Ian heard the man called Thomson mutter, 'We'll never escape once they get us inside there. I'm going to try something now. Are you with me?'

Craddock glanced around. Daleks were on patrol

everywhere, constantly moving round the edges of their group. 'Don't be a fool, man. You haven't got a chance.'

There was a note of hysteria in Thomson's voice. 'They're not getting me back in their filthy mine.'

A Dalek moved closer. 'The prisoners will be silent.'

Suddenly Thomson shoved Craddock to one side, dodged around the Dalek, and began tearing across the Heliport at full speed. Almost immediately a Dalek appeared to block his path. Thomson changed direction, wheeling to his left, but here too a Dalek was waiting. He dodged desperately to and fro, like a chess pawn threatened by more powerful pieces, but the Daleks were ahead of him at every turn. At last a group of them encircled him—there was nowhere to run. Thomson called desperately to his friend. 'Craddock—help me!'

Instinctively Craddock took a step forward, but the Doctor held him back. 'Don't be a fool! There's nothing you can do. Our time will come.' Such was the confidence and authority in the Doctor's voice that Craddock found himself obeying without question.

They heard a grating Dalek voice. 'Kill him!' Several Daleks fired at once, and Thomson twisted and spun under the agonising impact of the Dalek death-ray. His body crumpled to the ground.

A Dalek moved menacingly back towards the horror-struck prisoners. 'Any further defiance will be punished in the same way. Prisoners will wait until it is time to enter the ship.'

In a corner of the main operations room, David was breaking the news of the Doctor's capture to Susan. He glanced across to the other side of the room, where Barbara was helping to prepare a meal. 'I thought perhaps we wouldn't tell Barbara—not just yet anyway.'

'Oh, but I must,' protested Susan.

'Listen,' said David urgently. 'Dortmun's keen to make an immediate attack on the Daleks. He's got a new type of bomb he wants to test. Now, I managed to persuade him that the saucer would be a natural target. We can put off telling Barbara until the attack is over.'

Susan was beginning to understand what he meant. 'If the attack's a success, there's a chance that Ian and the Doctor will be rescued?'

David took her hand. 'Exactly. And if it isn't—well, they'll just have disappeared. At least there'll still be hope.'

They were interrupted by Jenny, who held out a batch of Roboman helmets to David. 'You wanted these?'

'Yes, I did, thank you.'

'Well, here they are, take them. I've got more important things to do than wait on you.'

'You're a model of patience and charm, aren't you Jenny?'

'I don't believe in wasting time.' Jenny glanced at David's hand, which was still holding Susan's. 'And I don't believe in sentiment, either.'

Her work finished, Barbara came over to them. She looked curiously at the pile of helmets. 'What's all this?'

'An invention of the Daleks,' said David grimly. 'We took them off dead human beings—human beings who'd been turned into Robomen.'

'There aren't that many Daleks on Earth,' explained Jenny, 'so they need helpers. They operate on some of their prisoners and turn them into sort of human robots, radio-controlled by these helmets. David's trying to find some way to block the Dalek transmissions, that's why we're collecting these things.'

David picked up a helmet. 'The Daleks call the operation the Transfer. These helmets here transmit the Dalek orders direct to the human brain—at least for a time. Eventually the effectiveness of the operation wears off.'

Susan looked at the gleaming metal helmets and shuddered. 'What happens then? Do the people become human again?'

Jenny shook her head. 'The process burns out the circuits of the brain. In the end the Robomen go mad and die. They seem to get a sort of suicidal urge. They throw themselves off buildings, into the river . . . That's why the Daleks need so many prisoners—to keep up their supply of Robomen.' David frowned warningly at Jenny, but she went on with her story. 'They take them to their flying saucer and operate on them. Once they've got you on board, there isn't a hope.'

Unaware of the shattering effect of her news on Susan, Jenny moved away. Susan looked at David. Perhaps it was just as well they hadn't told Barbara what had happened to the Doctor and Ian.

'*Move!*'

Obedient to the Dalek voice, the line of prisoners began shuffling up the ramp. The Doctor looked up at the Dalek ship as they moved inside. 'A work of genius, Chesterton.'

Ian was less enthusiastic. 'It's impressive enough. And it looks escape-proof.' The interior of the saucer was built in the Dalek style that Ian remembered from Skaro. Walls, doors, floors and ceilings were all of gleaming metal, everything utterly bleak and functional.

The Doctor rubbed his hands. 'Only on the surface, my friend. There's always a weak point—if you can find it.'

The Daleks were marching them along a curving metal corridor. The leading Dalek stopped, and touched a control. 'The first three prisoners will move into this cell.' The Doctor, Ian and the man named Craddock were the first three in line. The Dalek herded them into a cell and closed the door after them. 'Remaining prisoners—move!' Obediently the line of prisoners shuffled on.

In the control room, a Dalek stood watching the scanner screen. This Dalek was larger than the others, and its casing was a dull jet-black. This was the Dalek Supreme, the Black Dalek, Commander of the expedition to Earth. On the scanner was a view of a prison cell, with the Doctor, Ian and Craddock sitting on the floor, their backs against the wall. The Dalek Supreme touched a control and the hidden camera zoomed in until the Doctor's face filled the screen. 'This is the one?'

Another Dalek replied. 'That is so, Commander. He defied us, spoke of resistance. His words betrayed superior intelligence and determination.'

The Dalek Supreme turned away. 'We shall await the results of the experiment.'

Unaware that he was the subject of a Dalek experiment, the Doctor was chatting to his fellow prisoners, discussing the only subject of real interest—escape. 'I had a good look in that corridor outside. Plenty of scanners about.'

Craddock glanced round the cell. 'Can't see any in here. They may be hidden. What do you make of this thing, Doctor?' He pointed to a semi-transparent crystal box, packed with complex machinery, which was mounted on the wall near the cell door.

'I've a theory about that. I'll investigate it in a moment. Let's continue to survey the general situation.'

'I noticed what looked like a loading bay, Doctor,' Ian contributed. 'It should lead to the ground. There might be a guard outside, though.'

'There will be,' said Craddock gloomily.

'Our task is to escape,' said the Doctor sharply. 'You'll do no good sitting here moping.'

'And you'll do no good fooling yourself,' growled Craddock. 'Once the Daleks have got you, that's it!'

The Doctor shook his head reprovingly, and moved across to the crystal box. He began studying it closely.

Ian said, 'How did all this start—the invasion of Earth, I mean?'

Craddock stared at him. 'Where've you been, on one of the moon stations?'

'Something like that,' replied Ian vaguely. 'I never got the full story.'

Craddock was silent for a moment, then he began to speak in a low, bitter voice. 'The meteorites came first. They bombarded Earth about ten years ago. A freak cosmic storm, the scientists said . . . Then people started dying—some new kind of plague.'

'Germ warfare?' suggested Ian.

Craddock nodded. 'The Daleks were waiting, up there in space, waiting for Earth to get weaker. Whole continents were wiped out. Asia, Africa, America. Everywhere you went, the air smelled of death. The doctors tried all kinds of new drugs, but none of them worked. By now the world was split up into tiny struggling communities, too far apart to help each other. About six months after the plague had begun, the first of the flying saucers landed . . .'

Ian listened in fascinated horror as Craddock went on with his story. The Daleks had flattened whole cities, striking ruthlessly at any sign of resistance. They had captured untold numbers of human beings, turning them into Robomen, discarding them when they died and creating new ones. Other human beings had simply been enslaved, made to toil in the Dalek mines under the whips of the Robomen.

The catalogue of horrors went on, until Ian could bear it no longer. '*Why?*' he interrupted. 'That's the one thing you haven't told us. Why are they doing all this? What has Earth got that they want so much?'

Craddock looked dully at him. 'I don't know, no one knows. But it's something under the ground. They've turned most of Bedfordshire into one gigantic mining area . . .'

The Doctor, who had been only half-listening, turned around impatiently. 'Never mind all this blab about

Bedfordshire. I think I've discovered how this thing works.'

Ian went over to him. 'All right, Doctor. What is it?'

The Doctor pointed to a small metal rod clamped into a holder beside the box. Fixed next to it was a lens with a handle, looking like a pocket magnifying glass. 'Just hand me that, will you, my boy?'

'I wouldn't touch it,' warned Craddock.

Ian looked at the Doctor, who beamed infuriatingly at him. Carefully Ian took out the rod and handed it to the Doctor. 'There you are. Now what?'

'First, an experiment.' The Doctor moved the rod close to the transparent box. As if in sympathy, a similar but much larger metal rod inside the box began to move. 'You see, it's magnetic.'

'Marvellous,' said Craddock sarcastically. 'How does it help us?'

'And why's the box here at all?' asked Ian. 'What do the Daleks use it for?'

The Doctor nodded approvingly. 'An excellent question, my dear chap. Now, suppose you were a Dalek shut in here, how would you get out?'

Craddock frowned. 'Push up the door?'

The Doctor shook his head reproachfully. 'A Dalek has no hands, only a sucker. They rely on brain, not brawn.'

Ian looked at the crystal box, the lens and the metal rod. 'Are you telling me this set-up is some kind of key?'

'Precisely. All we have to do is open the box and use the key. Now then, pass me that lens, will you?'

Ian handed it over, examining the handle. 'You know I think you're right, Doctor. This thing is obviously made for a Dalek to hold.'

The Doctor gave him an encouraging smile. 'You're a good lad, Chesterton, you really do try hard. Now we must find the correct refractive index, or the box will probably explode.'

The Doctor began moving the lens about near the top of the box. Craddock watched him sceptically. 'Refractive rubbish,' he muttered. 'You don't think the Daleks would leave the key in here for us to find.'

'They have only contempt for human intellect,' said the Doctor sharply. 'And if all their prisoners are like you, I'm not so sure they're wrong . . .' The Doctor started muttering abstruse calculations to himself. 'Did you ever do applied three-dimensional graph geometry at your school, Chesterton?'

Ian shook his head. 'Only Boyle's Law.'

'Let's boil down this problem then, shall we?' Chuckling at his own excruciating pun, the Doctor added, 'Cover your eyes gentlemen, this may be nasty.'

Craddock shook his head scornfully. 'I suppose it'll turn into a great big pumpkin or—' He broke off in astonishment. The lid of the crystal box had sprung silently open. 'Hey, it's a flaming miracle.'

Ian slapped the Doctor on the back. 'Doctor, sometimes you amaze me!'

'Only sometimes?' The Doctor chuckled. 'Now, all we've got to do is find the way to use this bar . . . it'll be something to do with static electricity, I imagine. Now, if I push the bar in the box back with this one . . .'

Craddock looked at the two bars. The one in the Doctor's hand was tiny, the one in the box large and heavy. 'You're going to push *that*—with *that*?'

'Exactly. And since similar poles repel, and both bars are magnetic . . .'

The Doctor moved the small bar close to the large one. Immediately the large bar slid back—and the cell door moved smoothly upwards.

Craddock looked admiringly at the Doctor. 'You're a genius!'

The Doctor waved a deprecating hand. 'Oh it was nothing, nothing at all . . . Now let's get out of this infernal flying machine and find Susan and Barbara.'

They ran out into the corridor and straight into a waiting group of Daleks and Robomen. The Black Dalek dominated the group. 'He has passed the escape test. Take him.' Robomen grabbed the Doctor and dragged him away. Others held back Ian as he tried to follow. He turned angrily to the Black Dalek. 'What are you going to do with him?'

The toneless Dalek voice replied, 'He will be robotised.'

5

Attack the Daleks!

The voice of the Dalek Supreme seemed to shake the little radio set. 'Rebels of London. This is your final warning. Leave your hiding places. Show yourself in the open streets. You will be fed and watered. Work is needed, but in return the Daleks offer you life. Continue to resist and we will destroy London. You will all die, the males, the females, the young of the species. Rebels of London, come out from your hiding places.'

The radio went silent. Dortmun gestured exultantly at the pile of shining glass grenades. 'We'll come out all right—with these. We don't need to hide any more, we can make *them* run.'

Barbara looked round the operations room, which was packed with grim-faced freedom-fighters. Dortmun had called a meeting to listen first to the Dalek speech,and then to make one of his own. 'We'll answer their ultimatum for them—tonight. We're going to make a frontal attack on their flying saucer. Now *we* have the superior weaponry. One success and people will hope again. One victory will set this country alight. Then Europe, then the world. That's all we need—one victory!'

There was a roar of enthusiasm. Jenny's sceptical voice cut through it. 'How do we get within throwing range at the Heliport? The Daleks guard the perimeter—and they can fire long before we're near enough to use the bombs.

Tyler didn't care for opposition. 'This will be a surprise attack, at night.'

Jenny wasn't convinced. 'The surprise will be over when the first bomb is thrown.'

Barbara jumped up. 'I've got it! You can use *these*.' She pointed to the pile of Robomen helmets at the back of the room. 'Some of the men can disguise themselves as Robomen. The rest can be prisoners they're bringing in. You'll be able to get right into the middle of the Heliport before they suspect!'

Tyler picked up one of the helmets and put it over his head. 'It'll work,' he said slowly.

Dortmun smiled grimly. 'Yes. It'll work. Let's prepare for the attack.'

Barbara, David and Susan crouched in a ruined house, overlooking the edge of the Heliport. The open area before them was brightly lit, the gleaming shape of the flying saucer towered above them. Patrolling Daleks moved silently around the perimeter.

All three were carrying satchels full of grenades. David tapped his meaningfully. 'Sure you've got it straight? As soon as Tyler and his attack group move in, we start chucking these.'

The two girls nodded. There was nothing to do now but wait. Susan rubbed her ankle, hoping it wouldn't let her down. Though still a little sore, it was almost better. She'd been determined not to be left out of the attack . . .

Inside the saucer the Doctor had been taken to a small room packed with intricate electronic machinery. Its central feature was a long table. Above one end was suspended an elaborate helmet-like device from which projected two metal prongs. For what seemed a very long time the Doctor was subjected to a variety of measuring devices which had recorded his blood pressure, his temperature, the electrical activity of the brain, and indeed his total physical condition. The robotising process was elaborate and time-consuming, and the Daleks did not care to waste it on subjects who might ruin everything by dying on them. At last the battery of tests was complete, and a Dalek scientist droned, 'Prisoner suitable subject for operation. Take him to the table.'

Two Robomen bustled the Doctor over to the table and stretched him out on it. Before he could move metal clamps were applied to hold him in place. His sleeve was pushed back and he felt a prick in his right arm. Immediately a numbing paralysis spread over his entire body.

The Doctor discovered he was unable to move a muscle. But although his body was immobilised, his brain was fully alert. Surely there was something he could do . . . Surely something would turn up to save him. Or was this really the end, after all?

The Doctor lay quite still on the metal table. Dalek scientists glided around him, making final adjustments to the machinery that was designed to turn the Doctor into their helpless slave.

In the ruined house, David suddenly tensed. A dispirited-looking group of prisoners was being marched to the bottom of the saucer ramp, under the charge of a squad of Robomen. David drew a deep breath. 'Here they come. Get ready.' He took a grenade from his satchel, and prepared to throw. Roboman-helmet weighing heavy on his head, Tyler marched his squad of fake Robomen, with their equally fake prisoners, straight towards the ramp. The nearest Dalek guard moved up to him. 'Stop. What are you doing?'

Tyler made his reply in the slow dragging tones of the Robomen. 'I am taking the prisoners into the ship.'

'Wait. In which area were these prisoners captured?'

Tyler answered at random. 'Sector Four.'

'No patrol was ordered in Sector Four.'

Tyler did his best to bluff. 'New orders were given by the Dalek Supreme.'

Before the Dalek could reply there came the dull crump, crump, crump of exploding grenades from all around the Heliport. Barbara, Susan and David, and several other groups of freedom-fighters, hurling grenades at random from widely different points, tried to create the impression of an attack from all sides. Forgetting Tyler, the Dalek guard began to scream, 'Attack warning. Attack warning!'

A siren started blaring from inside the ship. Daleks were rushing around in all directions. In his Roboman voice Tyler shouted, 'I will take the prisoners into the ship.' He marched his party quickly up the ramp.

Daleks were all round the perimeter of the Heliport now, firing in the direction of the explosions. But since the attackers were so few in number, and well spaced out, they were very hard to find.

A Dalek sped close to the building in which David and the girls were hiding, firing almost at random. David yelled, 'Get down!' and swept the two girls to the floor. The blast of a Dalek ray-gun sizzled through the open window and set fire to the wall above their heads. A man ran past the window then dropped screaming as the Dalek fired again. David struggled to his feet. 'Right, that's it. They must be inside by now. Time for us to pull back.' They ran from the blazing building and disappeared into the darkness.

Tyler and his men dashed along the metal corridors of the Dalek ship. 'Right,' called Tyler, 'spread out. Free as many prisoners as you can before you use the bombs.' One of the freedom-fighters began blasting open the door of the cell which held Ian and Craddock.

The noise of battle came only faintly to the robotising room, and the Dalek scientist continued his work undistracted. Suddenly a harsh voice blared from a hidden speaker. 'We are under attack. Report to main ramp. General alert. Report to main ramp.'

Obediently the Robomen and the Dalek scientists began filing from the room. The last Roboman was about to leave when a Dalek scientist stopped him. 'The prisoner is already prepared. You will remain and supervise the operation.' The Roboman touched a control. The robotising machinery started to hum and throb with power. The pronged, helmet-like device began to descend, coming closer and closer to the Doctor's head. Just as the prongs seemed about to sink into his forehead Tyler dashed into the room and wrenched the helmet device to one side. It blew up in a shower of sparks. The Roboman ran forward, there was a brief struggle, and he dropped with Tyler's knife between his ribs.

Another freedom-fighter ran in. Tyler called, 'Baker! Help me get this man off the table.' They unfastened the clamps and lifted the Doctor clear. He slumped limply in their arms. Tyler made a quick attempt to bring him round and then gave up. 'No good, you'll have to carry him. See if you can get him clear.' Baker began dragging the Doctor from the table. A Dalek voice blared from the speaker. 'All reserve Robomen into action. Destroy the invaders!'

From a new hiding place behind a ruined wall. David, Susan and Barbara surveyed the scene. Fires were blazing all round the perimeter of the Heliport. The Daleks had now abandoned the search for their elusive attackers and were retreating back to their ship. Barbara gripped David's arm. 'Tyler's going to be trapped inside the ship! Are those bombs of Dortmun's really any use against Daleks?'

Susan said, 'I didn't see the bombs stop any Daleks. But there's too much smoke to see what's going on.'

David said nothing. He too had his doubts about

Dortmun's bombs.

Jenny came tearing towards them, pausing only to hurl a grenade at the Dalek ship. David seized on her arrival with relief. 'Jenny, take these two back to HQ. I'm going to see if I can get Tyler out of that ship.'

As David ran off, Jenny said, 'I'm not playing nurse to you two. I'm going with David.' She looked scornfully at Barbara and Susan. 'I should have thought you'd have wanted to come too. After all, your two friends are in there.'

Barbara looked at her in astonishment, then turned to Susan. The look on Susan's face told her the whole story. 'You knew. You knew all along.'

Susan was shamefaced. 'We didn't want to worry you before—'

Barbara was already running towards the Dalek ship. Susan followed, and caught her by the arm. 'Barbara where are you going?'

'To help David find Ian and the Doctor. We've got to get them out of there.' Pulling free of Susan's grasp, Barbara ran off.

Susan turned to find Jenny looking at her. 'Well, are you coming?'

'I suppose so, though what good *we* can do . . .'

Jenny wasn't listening. 'We'll do no good if we don't try. Come on, this way.'

Jenny ran off and Susan, still hobbling a little, did her best to keep up with her.

By now Tyler and his men were already rushing down the ramp, bringing with them all the released prisoners they could find. Ian was somewhere near the back of the confused bunch of men.

At the foot of the ramp, the Daleks were waiting to meet them. They fired into the crowd at point-blank range, and men screamed and dropped all around. Tyler shouted, 'The bombs. Use the bombs!' He pulled a grenade from his satchel and hurled it at the nearest Dalek. There was an explosion, a blaze of flame, and a cloud of smoke. Then, through the drifting smoke, Tyler saw the Dalek moving inexorably towards him, quite unharmed. Dortmun's bombs were a failure. Tyler yelled, 'Scatter all of you. Run! The bombs are no good!'

Freedom-fighters and escaping prisoners began to run in all directions. Remorselessly the Daleks pursued, shooting them down. Since he'd been at the back of the escaping crowd, Ian was still on the ramp when the battle started. He got a grandstand view of the unequal struggle. He saw the useless bombs exploding all around, producing flame and smoke, but doing very little damage. Two freedom-fighters tipped a Dalek on to its side by main force—only to be themselves blasted down by more Daleks. Suddenly, he saw a familiar face appear out of the darkness. 'Barbara,' he yelled desperately. 'Barbara, get back!' Barbara saw him and waved then she disappeared, swept up by the milling crowd.

Ian jumped down from the ramp, just as the ramp itself began retracting with a hum of power. Two Daleks appeared round the curve of the Dalek ship, their gun-sticks trained on Ian. The lifting of the ramp had left a small gap between the base of the ramp and the ship itself. Instinctively Ian flung himself into the gap—just as the ramp started to come down again, closing the opening and trapping Ian inside the Dalek ship. Gun-sticks blazing, Daleks poured down the ramp . . .

Barbara shielded her eyes from the smoke, dodged the blast of a Dalek gun-stick, and stumbled straight into Jenny. One glance at the disaster and chaos around them had convinced Jenny that the attack was hopeless. She grabbed Barbara's arm and started dragging her away. 'Come on. We're getting out of here.'

Barbara pulled away from her. 'But Ian's there—I saw him on the ramp. And where's Susan?'

'We got separated. I think she's with David. They'll

both have to take their chances. There's a way through the sewers. If you don't come now, you'll get killed.'

Without waiting for a reply, Jenny ran off. After a last agonised glance at the spaceship, Barbara ran after her.

In the control room of the Dalek ship, the Black Dalek watched the scene outside the saucer on a scanner. The screen showed a confused picture of blasting Daleks, exploding grenades, and falling freedom-fighters. The area around the saucer was littered with the crumpled bodies of those who had failed to escape.

The Black Dalek transmitted orders to those outside. 'The enemy are retreating. Recapture as many prisoners as possible. Block all exits from the area. Find the enemy attackers and exterminate them.'

Tyler was ushering the last of the survivors down an open manhole cover, in an alley behind a burning building. 'Hurry,' he shouted. 'They'll be here soon.'

He was just about to duck down the manhole himself, when he heard pounding footsteps. He hesitated, then yelled, 'Come on, over here . . . Quickly!'

A man tore round the corner of the building, hesitated for a moment then started running towards Tyler. Seconds later a Dalek appeared in pursuit. It fired immediately, and the man screamed once then dropped to the ground. Tyler disappeared down the manhole like a rat into its hole, pulling the cover over his head.

The Black Dalek turned away from the scanner screen. 'The attack has been defeated.'

His number two came forward eagerly. 'Many prisoners have been recaptured. Most of the attacking rebels have been killed or wounded. Only a very few are still at large.'

There was cold fury in the voice of the Black Dalek. 'Find them. Find all survivors and destroy them. They must be exterminated!'

In a ghastly chorus, the surrounding Daleks took up their leader's chant. 'Exterminate them! Exterminate them! Exterminate them!'

6

The Fugitives

The freedom-fighters' operations room was almost empty. Jenny was bathing a cut on Barbara's head with a wet cloth, while Dortmun looked on in gloomy silence. There was no one else. The rest must have been captured or killed, thought Barbara wearily. She looked up at Jenny. 'You're sure you didn't see what happened to Susan? She was with you the last time I saw her.'

Jenny's voice was gruff. 'I told you. She caught up with David—we were going to look for you. Then there were all those explosions, and I just lost sight of her.' Barbara sighed, and Jenny's voice softened at the sight of her unhappy face. 'Don't worry, she may still turn up. There, your head's fine now. Just a scratch.'

There came the sound of movement from the corridor outside. Barbara looked up hopefully—but it was Tyler who came into the room.

'Your bombs are useless, Dortmun.'

The man in the wheelchair looked up. 'How many were killed?'

'It was a massacre. We didn't stand a chance.'

'How many?'

Tyler sighed. 'I don't know. Almost all of them, I think. A few got away before the Daleks sealed the area, one or two got out through the sewers . . .' He picked up a rucksack and started to fill it with supplies.

Barbara said dully, 'The Doctor and Ian were in the

saucer. I saw Ian . . . just for a moment . . .' her voice faltered, then she regained control. 'What about the Doctor? Did you see any sign of him?

'There was an oldish man,' said Tyler slowly. 'We found him in the Robotiser Chamber. Baker got him clear of the ship, but after that . . .' He shrugged, then turned to Dortmun. 'We'll have to get out of London.'

'Why? The Daleks have never looked for us down here.'

'That was before we attacked their precious flying saucer. We've stirred them up now. They'll search every inch—destroy every inch.'

'But I must stay here. I need to work on my bomb.' He looked up at Tyler appealingly. 'It only needs a little more work, the principle is sound . . .'

'Forget your bomb. It's a waste of time.'

'It's the answer. It's the only answer . . .' There was a mad obsessive determination in Dortmun's voice.

'And who's going to use it for you?' asked Tyler. 'Me? These two girls here? Use your intelligence, man.'

Jenny joined in. 'Tyler's right. London will be too hot for us now.'

'If we could just stay a few days longer,' persisted Dortmun.

Tyler shook his head decisively. 'No, I'm going to see if I can find any more survivors, then I'm heading North.'

Barbara got to her feet. 'Can I come with you? If Ian and the Doctor did escape, we might find them . . .'

Tyler shouldered the rucksack. 'I'm sorry, but you'd slow me down. I've got to go alone. Good luck.'

Barbara called, 'If you do see any of my friends . . .' But Tyler had already gone.

Jenny said, 'We must get out of here too.'

Dortmun looked at them with sudden eagerness. 'There's the other HQ. People will be gathering there—your friends too, maybe. I can go on working on my bomb—there's a laboratory there . . .'

'Dortmun, *please—*' began Jenny.

Dortmun was beyond reason. 'That's it, we'll go to the Transport Museum.' He looked hopefully at them. 'It means crossing London, going over one of the bridges . . .'

Barbara sighed. 'All right, we'll come with you.'

Dortmun spun his wheelchair, and headed for his office. 'I'll just get my things together. You'd better pack some supplies.'

Jenny moved closer to Barbara, and said in a low voice. 'We'd stand a lot more chance on our own.'

'Maybe. But he won't stand any chance without us. You needn't come—if you don't want to.'

Jenny hesitated, then shrugged. 'Might as well. Maybe Dortmun's right . . . people might start collecting at the other HQ.'

By the time they had loaded two more rucksacks, Dortmun came out of the office, a satchel slung over his shoulder. 'We'd better be moving. It's nearly light now.'

He headed his chair for the door. As she followed him, Barbara said, 'Do you really think my friends might end up at this Museum?'

Dortmun nodded vigorously. 'It's possible. Yes, it's distinctly possible.'

Possible, but not very probable, thought Barbara wearily. In her heart she feared she would never see her missing friends again.

The Black Dalek was addressing his aides. 'Orders from Dalek Supreme Command. Rebels must be totally crushed. An intensive search of London is to be made. If necessary the city will be totally destroyed.'

'Do you intend to remain in the city?' asked the second-in-command.

'No. The ship will now take me to the mine workings in the Central Zone.'

'We have recaptured many escaped prisoners.'

'They will be put to work in the mine. Feed and water them. They must be strong in order to work.'

'I obey.'

The second-in-command began issuing orders into a communications network. Dalek and Robomen patrols would cover all central London, seeking out and destroying rebel hiding places.

The Black Dalek swivelled to face the spaceship's flight operators. 'Prepare ship for lift-off!'

Although the Daleks didn't know it, there was at least one escaped prisoner who was still free, and still on the ship. After his dive into the hatch below the ramp, Ian had found himself in a service tunnel somewhere in the bowels of the ship. Wriggling between humming and throbbing Dalek machinery, he had gradually worked his way back to the upper levels. Immediately he headed for the robotiser room, in the hope of finding the Doctor.

He slipped inside, glancing with a shudder at the central table and sinister electronic apparatus suspended above it. The place was completely empty, no Doctor, no Daleks.

He heard movement in the corridor outside and ducked behind a bank of instruments. Two men came into the room. One was slight and wiry, with curly black hair. Behind the first man, holding him in a painful armlock, was a tall figure that Ian recognised immediately.

He stepped from his hiding place. 'Craddock!'

Releasing his prisoner, Craddock swung round. His face was expressionless, and there was a gleaming metal device on his head. His voice was slurred and dragging. 'You are to be robotised.'

Ian backed away. 'Craddock—it's me . . .'

Craddock lurched forward and grabbed Ian's arm, trying to bend it behind his back. Ian struggled desperately. Although his movements were slow and clumsy, the robotised Craddock seemed abnormally strong, and quite impervious to pain. A savage blow to his ribs produced only a grunt, and there was no slackening in the steady pressure on Ian's arm.

Ian decided to use skill rather than strength. Grabbing Craddock by sleeve and coat, Ian twisted round, bent and sent his opponent hurling over his shoulder in a judo throw. Craddock crashed to the floor, with enough force to stun any normal man. But Craddock was no longer normal. He scrambled immediately to his feet and advanced on Ian, hands outstretched. Despairingly Ian realised he was fighting not a man but a machine—a machine that couldn't be hurt, would never get tired and never give up . . .

As Craddock's hands closed on Ian's throat, the wiry man joined in the struggle. He threw himself on Craddock, gripped the helmet-device with both hands, and ripped it from Craddock's head. The results were immediate and dramatic. Craddock let out a series of terrifying screams, his hands clutching his head. His body flopped to the floor and thrashed frantically like a stranded fish. His back arched in a final convulsion and he went limp and still.

Ian got up slowly, rubbing his throat. He examined Craddock's body. As he'd expected, the man was quite dead. He looked at the wiry man and held out his hand. 'Thank's for the help—my name's Ian.'

The other returned the handshake. 'Larry. And thank you. I was on my way to ending up like him.' He nodded towards the body on the floor. 'He caught me hiding in one of the storerooms. I smuggled myself on board quite a while ago.'

'You did what?'

'This saucer makes periodic trips to the mine workings in Bedfordshire. My brother's one of the slaves there. I'm going to find him and get him out.'

'So you're hitching a lift with the Daleks? You don't

choose the safest way to travel, do you?'

Larry grinned. 'Maybe not. But it's the quickest. What about you? What are you doing here?'

Quickly Ian explained how he'd been captured by the Daleks, freed during the raid, and trapped in the ramp housing straight afterwards. 'I'm looking for the friend who was captured with me,' he finished. 'Though I'm not even sure if he's still on board. There's a chance he got away during the raid.'

Larry started dragging Craddock's body towards the wall. 'We'd better put this down the disposal chute. They'll start hunting for us if it's found in here.'

Ian helped Larry to drag the body to a hatch set in the far corner. Larry slid back the hatch-cover, and immediately they felt a powerful suction dragging them towards the opening.

Between them they wrestled the body into the hatchway. Immediately the force of the suction snatched it down the chute. Larry slid the cover back into place. 'Right, we'd better get out of here and find somewhere safer to hide.'

Suddenly there was a hum of power, and a steady vibration all around them. Ian put a hand on the wall to steady himself. 'Looks as if you might get your trip to Bedfordshire after all. I think we're taking off!'

In the Control Room, the Black Dalek ordered, 'Maximum repulsion. Set course for mine workings in Central Zone.'

The Dalek spacecraft lifted slowly from the Heliport which was still littered with the bodies of those who had died in the attack. It rose smoothly into the air and began skimming northwards over London, just as dawn was breaking.

From their hiding place, Susan and David watched the saucer disappear from sight. Susan wondered if the

Doctor and Ian were still on board, or if they'd managed to get away during the raid. She had only a confused and nightmarish memory of her own escape. Daleks firing into the crowd of freedom-fighters and escaping prisoners, the screams of the dying, the roar of the explosions, sheets of flame and clouds of smoke. Somewhere in all the confusion David had grabbed her hand and pulled her clear. They'd escaped from the area just before the Daleks sealed it off, and they'd been stumbling through the ruins ever since. At last they'd arrived in the cellar of a ruined house, and here they'd stopped to rest. David explained it was one of the freedom-fighters regular hiding places. Although the house above it was in ruins, the cellar itself was warm and dry. It was furnished with battered old beds and chairs, and there were even stores of food, water, weapons and ammunition. A flight of steps led up from the cellar into an alleyway between rows of ruined houses.

From the cellar doorway, Susan saw the flying saucer disappear over the rooftops. 'Does that mean the Daleks have gone?'

David shook his head wearily. 'The saucer comes and goes regularly, ferrying prisoners to the mines. There are still plenty of Daleks and Robomen on the ground.' Suddenly he broke off. 'Get down—there's a patrol coming.'

They ducked back inside the cellar. Despite David's warning Susan couldn't resist peeping round the door. Two Daleks were gliding along the alleyway above them. Alert and supicious, their eye-stalks swivelled to and fro, scanning all around them. Susan shrunk back inside the cellar, closing her eyes. After a moment, David touched her gently on the shoulder. 'It's all right—they've gone. We'll give them time to get well clear and then move on.'

'Move on where?'

'We'll have to try to get out of London, join up with one of the other groups.'

From the alleyway came the sound of pounding footsteps. A Dalek voice grated, 'Stop! Surrender or you will be exterminated!'

The footsteps faltered then ran on. There was a scream of 'No . . . no . . .' and the crackle of a Dalek gunstick. Then silence.

Susan shuddered and threw herself into David's arms. 'Why did we ever come here,' she said hysterically. 'Why, why? If only we could get back in the TARDIS and just go away . . . I'm sure the Doctor would let you come with us . . .'

David said sadly, 'You get away if you can. But I can't.'

'Why not?'

'This is my world. My Earth. I can't just leave it, clear off somewhere else.'

Susan looked at him wonderingly. 'I've never felt like that about anywhere. I left my own planet when I was very young, and we've been travelling ever since. I've never really belonged anywhere.'

David looked seriously at her. 'Someday you ought to stop travelling and really arrive somewhere—Get down, someone's coming.'

'Daleks?'

'Don't think so. Human footsteps. Could be Robomen . . .'

Pushing Susan down into cover, David crouched in readiness at the bottom of the stairs. He slipped something from his belt, and Susan saw light glinting on the blade of a knife.

They waited as the dragging footsteps came closer . . .

7

Reunion with the Doctor

Susan cowered back as a monstrous, deformed shape appeared at the top of the steps. The huge misshapen figure began to descend the stairs . . . As it came nearer, Susan realised she was looking not at one man but two, one carrying the other on his shoulders. And the man being carried was the Doctor!

Joyfully she ran forward calling, 'Doctor, it's me, Susan!'

David meanwhile had recognised the other man. He put his knife away, and helped the newcomer to lower the Doctor's body to the ground. 'Baker! Are you all right?'

Baker grunted with relief as he lowered the Doctor's body. 'I'm OK. Worried about him, though.'

The Doctor was very still. His eyes were wide open but he seemed unable to move or talk. Susan looked anxiously at Baker. 'What is it? What's the matter with him?'

'Daleks drugged him. Should be beginning to wear off by now.'

The Doctor stared up at them. Slowly, very slowly, his lips moved and he said, 'Susan . . .' Susan hugged him in happy relief.

Shrugging aside Susan's thanks, Baker told them of the disastrous aftermath of the attack, of how he'd managed to get the Doctor away early on. 'We were lucky. I think most of the others were killed or captured.'

'What will you do now?' asked David. 'Do you want to join up with us?'

Baker, a burly, taciturn character, was clearly something of a loner. 'No, the bigger the group, the bigger the risk. I'll make for the Cornish coast. Not so many Daleks down there.'

David handed over a flask and a packet of food. 'Here, take these. You'll need them.'

'What about you?'

'We'll manage. Plenty of food stored here—and not many left alive to eat it.'

Baker took the supplies and made for the cellar door. 'Thanks. I'm off then. Good luck.' He disappeared up the stairs, and they heard his footsteps moving along the cobbles of the alleyway.

Suddenly a metallic voice shouted, 'Halt!'

David ran to the top of the steps and peered out. He could see Baker half-way down the alley. A Dalek had appeared at the other end. Baker spun round. A second Dalek was blocking the alleyway behind him.

As both Daleks advanced towards him, Baker dropped his rifle and raised his hands. The second Dalek screeched, 'Exterminate!' Both Daleks fired at once. Caught in the double blast, Baker twisted in mid air and died immediately. His body dropped to the ground. For a long moment the two Daleks scanned the alley with their eye-stalks. Then they glided silently on their way.

Shaken, David crept back to Susan. 'The Daleks just shot him down, wouldn't even let him surrender. They must have decided to kill everyone on sight.'

Susan was cradling the Doctor in her arms, getting him to drink a little water. 'Where can we go, David? What can we do?'

'Dortmun set up a second Command HQ—in the old Transport Museum. If your friends have survived, that's probably where they'll make for. There are supplies there too, bombs and weapons. Dortmun had quite a laboratory . . .'

The Doctor groaned and started to sit up, and Susan helped him into a chair. 'How are you feeling now?'

The Doctor spoke with surprising clarity. 'The Daleks paralysed my body and my will power, but not my mind. Really a most interesting experience.' He flexed his legs and found he could move them a little. 'It's wearing off, though. Wearing off fast.'

Susan hugged him again. 'You just have a good rest. As soon as you feel better, we're going to go and find Barbara.'

For Barbara and Jenny, the long journey across London was fraught with danger. Although it was now broad daylight, the fact that Dortmun was in a wheelchair meant they had to keep to roads and paths in fairly good repair, and prevented them from using the safe routes across the rubble and through the sewers. Time and time again they had to shove the chair into some doorway for cover, and crouch motionless while a patrol of Daleks glided by.

Most dangerous of all was crossing the river. They had decided to use Westminster Bridge, since that part of Central London seemed fairly free of Daleks. They had almost reached the bridge itself when Jenny called, 'Look out!' and they rushed into a shop doorway for cover. Barbara never forgot the sight that met her eyes when she peeped out. A patrol of Daleks gliding over Westminster Bridge, their sinister shapes profiled against the ornately decorated façade of the Houses of Parliament. It made an unforgettably symbolic picture. The squat metallic shapes of the alien invaders stood out against the building that represented so many centuries of human progress and tradition—a tradition the Daleks had ended with brutal abruptness. They watched in silence as the Daleks filed over the bridge and disappeared.

Dortmun nodded satisfied. 'There shouldn't be

another patrol for a while. Come on, let's try to get across while we can.'

They pushed the wheelchair across the bridge and through the deserted streets of Belgravia without running into any more Daleks. The Civic Transport Museum was housed in an elegant exhibition hall, in a quiet side street.

Dortmun led them to a back entrance in a mews, and produced a key that opened a locked side-door.

They found themselves in a shadowy darkened hall, rather like a huge bus garage. All around stood vehicles of various kinds, roped off with explanatory placards near by. There were milk-floats, taxis, old-fashioned open-topped buses, dust-carts—all the many kinds of vehicles that are part of the life of a big city. Some of the vehicles had still been in use in Barbara's day, and she wondered what had replaced them in this future age. Had Londoners ever solved their traffic problem? If they hadn't, thought Barbara, remembering the empty streets, the Daleks had certainly dealt with it for them.

At the back of the hall were various rooms intended for Museum staff, including a workshop where Dortmun had established his laboratory. He made for it immediately, forgetting the two girls in his anxiety to get back to work on his one obsession—the creation of a bomb that would destroy the Daleks. Jenny disappeared too, scouting the area for signs of the enemy.

Several hours later, Barbara was prosaically employed in boiling a kettle in one corner of the hall. Behind a small screen she'd found a tiny kitchen alcove. There was a table and a gas-ring, a packet of tea in one of the cupboards, and an unopened tin of milk. The logical thing to do seemed to make a cup of tea. The typically English response to any crisis thought Barbara with a smile as she poured water into a chipped china teapot.

A side-door flew open and Dortmun propelled himself towards her. The satchel over his shoulder was once more filled with gleaming grenades. 'It's finished,' he announced triumphantly. 'I've boosted the explosive charge. The problem is to crack the Daleks' outer casing. It's made from a metal called Dalekenium.'

Barbara looked doubtfully at the grenades. Would they really work this time? Dortmun had been just as confident before the disastrous raid on the Dalek flying saucer. She passed him a cup of tea. 'This Dalekenium . . . could that be what they're mining for in Bedfordshire?'

'I doubt it. I imagine they mine Dalekenium on their own planet.'

'Then what are they looking for? Oil maybe? Some other metal?'

Dortmun shook his head. 'They could have picked on a hundred planets to find those things. But they're after something . . . Something buried deep in the heart of Earth.'

Footsteps echoed through the great hall as Jenny came towards them. 'I've checked over the whole building,' she announced. 'Not a sign of anyone. But I think the Dalek patrols have been here—and I know some of our people have.'

Barbara poured her some tea. 'How can you be so sure?'

Jenny pointed to a mysterious symbol scrawled on a wall nearby. 'That's one of our message-signs. It means some of our people have been here and moved off towards the south coast. Don't blame them either. London seems to be swarming with Daleks.'

Dortmun frowned. 'You think they've landed another force in London?'

'You saw for yourself. We were lucky to make it here through the streets. If things go on building up, we haven't a chance. We'll have to move on.'

Barbara's heart sank at the thought of another pointless, dangerous journey. 'Where can we go? What's the good of just running all the time?'

Jenny looked coldly at her. 'We're surviving, aren't we? That's what counts.'

Dortmun patted his satchel of grenades. 'We'll all survive. Now I've got this new-formula explosive . . .'

Barbara looked despairingly at her two companions: Dortmun obsessed with perfecting the bomb that had become his reason for living; Jenny thinking only of running and hiding like some hunted animal. They needed someone who could look at the problem with a wider perspective. Barbara spoke her thoughts aloud. 'I wish the Doctor were here.'

Jenny looked surprised. 'He's just an old man, isn't he? What could he do?'

'He happens to be a brilliant scientist. He could think—which is more than the rest of you seem to be doing!'

'A scientist, you say?' Dortmun was immediately interested. 'I'd like to discuss my work with another scientist. If only we knew where he was . . .'

'I've been thinking about that, trying to put myself in his place. I'm sure he'd be intrigued by those mines in Bedfordshire. He'd want to take a look at them.'

Jenny said brutally, 'If he's still alive.'

'Of course he's still alive,' said Barbara angrily.

'Why? What's so special about your Doctor? He doesn't wear some invisible shield, does he?'

Dortmun spoke with sudden authority. 'Jenny! Go and take another look around.' As Jenny moved sulkily away, Dortmun said apologetically, 'She's not really callous, you know. She's been fighting the Daleks for most of her life.' Barbara nodded understandingly and he went on. 'I'd like to try to find your friend the Doctor and give him this—it's the notes for my bomb.' He handed her a tightly folded bunch of papers, scrawled over with notes and incomprehensible diagrams . . .

Barbara looked at the papers in astonishment. 'Why can't you give them to him yourself?'

'I can, I can . . . if we ever meet. But meanwhile I'd like you to take care of them. I'm not exactly mobile like this am I? If something happened, I'd like my work to go on.'

For all his bitterness, thought Barbara, no one could deny Dortmun's courage. Crippled, defeated, hunted, his one thought was to go on fighting. She took the papers and laid them on the table. 'All right, I'll look after them if you like. But I'm not leaving you . . .'

Dortmun gave one of his rare smiles. 'Thanks. Now then, if you'll round up Jenny, we can set out for those mines . . .'

Barbara didn't have to go far to look for Jenny. There were stairs on the other side of the hall, and Jenny came running down them, her footsteps echoing. 'Daleks! I saw them from an upper window. They're all over the place.'

Jenny's voice rang out across the hall. Near by, Dortmun heard it, and came to a sudden decision. Clutching the bombs on his lap, he wheeled his chair towards the main doors.

Barbara and Jenny missed him as they ran down the other side of the hall. Barbara stopped in astonishment when she saw Dortmun wasn't where they'd left him. Jenny looked round. 'Where is he? He can't have gone outside, he wouldn't be so stupid.'

Barbara saw the papers on the table. 'Look, he's left the plans—but he's taken the bombs. I think he's gone to try them out!'

There was an echoing crash from the front of the hall. Daylight streamed in as the main doors were flung open. They turned and saw Dortmun in the doorway, heard his voice raised in defiant challenge.

'Daleks! Where are you, Daleks?'

The group of Daleks outside the Museum's main door seemed frozen in astonishment as Dortmun appeared in the doorway. To be defied and attacked was a new experience for them, and they hesitated, fearing some trap.

Dortmun wheeled himself forwards straight at the nearest Dalek. When he was close enough he hurled the entire satchel of grenades. There was a shattering explosion, and a sheet of flame. A corner of the building collapsed, and Dortmun and his Dalek enemy disappeared beneath the rubble. Daleks milled about in confusion, shouting 'Emergency! We are being attacked!'

Picking up Dortmun's papers, Barbara pulled Jenny back into the shadows. 'They'll be here any minute. We've got to hide!'

Daleks moved cautiously into the hall, eye-stalks scanning the exhibits on either side. One of them trained its gun-stick on the waxwork of a milkman, posed stiffly beside his float. 'Halt! Who are you?' The waxwork, naturally enough, didn't move. Another Dalek examined it more closely. 'It is a sub-cultural effigy. Proceed with the search.'

Methodically the Daleks continued to search the hall. Barbara and Jenny retreated before them, dodging from one antiquated vehicle to another. Despairingly, Barbara realised they were being driven into a corner. The Daleks moved closer and closer, tightening the circle around the two girls . . .

The Doctor was staggering determinedly to and fro across the cellar, working off the remaining effects of the Dalek drugs. His face was grim and set as he fought to ignore the shooting cramp-like pains in arms and legs. Susan watched him in concern, realising the Doctor was quite likely to go on till he dropped. She caught him by one arm, and gently led him to a chair. 'Easy does it. That's enough for a first try.'

Thankfully the Doctor stretched his aching limbs. 'I never realised walking could be so exhausting. The numbness is most certainly wearing off though. I shall be able to travel in a short while.'

'Good. David says we should move North, join up with the resistance groups there.'

Susan saw at once that she'd made a mistake. The Doctor frowned and said sharply, 'My dear child, I don't care what that young man says. I make the decisions, and I think it best that we return at once to the TARDIS.'

'But we can't even get inside. David says London's swarming with Daleks. We'd never even get there alive.'

The autocratic side of the Doctor's nature came to the fore. 'Are you questioning my authority, child?'

'No, but David says . . .'

'David says, David says,' mimicked the Doctor savagely. 'You seem to trust this young man's judgement more than you do mine!'

With a shock Susan realised the Doctor was quite right. Somehow she had grown to rely on David, to trust his judgement in every crisis. She felt safe when they were together. That was why she didn't want to leave him. Perhaps there were other reasons too . . .

Returning from his scouting expedition, David heard raised voices, and listened to the last stages of the argument. He paused at the head of the cellar steps, realising he would have to move carefully. He was getting very fond of Susan, and he didn't want them to be separated. He ran down the steps into the cellar. The Doctor and Susan were glaring at each other, and scarcely seemed to notice him. David ignored the tension in the atmosphere. 'I didn't even get as far as the river. There are patrols everywhere. We'll never make it to the Museum.'

The Doctor snorted. 'I take it you're saying it would be impossibly dangerous to go back to the river too?'

David nodded. 'I'm afraid so. There are Daleks in this area of course, but not nearly so many.' He grinned reassuringly at Susan and turned back to the Doctor. 'I wanted to ask you— what would you suggest as our next move?'

The Doctor sat bolt upright. 'Me? Why do you ask me?'

'You're the senior member of the party, sir. Naturally, I'd like the benefit of your superior experience.'

The Doctor beamed. Clearly this young fellow David was a sensible chap after all. He considered carefully. 'Well, if you really want my advice . . . I think we should head North, join up with some of the resistance groups there. I'm very keen to see what the Daleks are up to in this mine of theirs!'

Susan flung her arms round the Doctor and hugged him. 'Grandfather! Oh, Grandfather!' The Doctor returned her hug, winking at David over her shoulder. 'My dear child, what *is* all the fuss about?'

The Commander of the Dalek ground forces glided into the control room of the London base. 'Message from Dalek Supreme, now *en route* for mining area. Report on the destruction of rebel hiding places.'

The Dalek engineer gestured with his sucker towards an illuminated wall-chart. 'Destruction is proceeding. Rebel hiding places in areas one to three destroyed. Areas four to eight now in flames. Proceeding to lay charges in vicinity of suspected rebel hideout in area nine.' The sucker indicated a spot on the map . . .

Two Daleks glided along the alleyway outside the basement in which the Doctor and his friends were hiding. Between them they pushed a small trolley on which stood a large metal canister. Dials and switches were set into the canister lid. One of the Daleks touched a control and the canister began emitting a steady electronic bleep.

Leaving the trolley just at the head of the stairs, the Daleks turned and glided away. From somewhere in the distance there came the noise of an explosion.

Susan looked up at the sound of the distant rumble. 'What was that?'

'The latest Dalek tactic,' said David grimly. 'Blockbuster bombs. They destroy whole sections of the city at a time. Anywhere the Daleks think we've a hideout, they just blow up the entire area.'

The Doctor was on his feet. 'Shouldn't we be on our way, my boy? If they suspect you've a hideout in this area . . .'

Susan shivered. 'Must we? I don't like the sound of those explosions—and there may still be Daleks about.'

David put an arm round her shoulders. 'All right, we'll hang on a little longer. But the Doctor's right, we must go soon.'

A needle flickered on the detonation dial of the canister outside. The electronic bleep quickened as countdown entered the final phase . . .

8

The Mine of the Daleks

Suddenly the Doctor held up his hand. Susan stared at him. 'What's the matter?'

'Listen!'

In the silence the electronic bleep sounded clearly. It was speeding up, and getting louder. The Doctor and his companions ran out of the basement. They stopped in horror at the sight of the gleaming metal canister at the top of the steps. 'What is it?' whispered Susan.

David's face was grim. 'One of the Dalek blockbuster bombs.'

Susan tugged at his arm. 'Quick, let's get clear . . . run!'

David didn't move. 'No use. That thing's due to go off any moment. There's no way we could get out clear of the range of the blast.' He stood staring at the bomb as if paralysed by horror.

'In that case we'd better dismantle the thing,' said the Doctor briskly. He ran nimbly up the steps and leaned over the canister, studying the controls set into its top. 'Now then, this dial with the needle is the time mechanism. The red area at twelve o'clock signifies the detonation point, I imagine.'

David looked over his shoulder. 'So when the needle reaches the red, that will be it?'

The Doctor nodded. 'Help me prise the front off this thing, will you, my boy? I must destroy the timing control.'

David produced his knife and thrust it into the join between the main body of the canister and its lid. He heaved with all his strength—and the knife blade broke in two.

'I need some kind of a lever,' snapped the Doctor. 'Look around, both of you. A nail, a piece of metal, anything will do.'

Obediently David and Susan began searching the rubble. The Doctor went on working with the broken blade but without much success. The stub of the blade was too thick to go in the crack. He tossed it aside. Susan found a twisted piece of iron. 'How about this, Doctor?'

'Too big. There must be some way we can get in . . . some tool.'

Suddenly David said, 'Acid! Those bombs of Dortmun's—the detonation mechanism is acid-based. Maybe we could burn through the casing.'

The Doctor nodded eagerly. 'It's a chance. Let's have one of them here. Quickly now!' David ran down into the cellar, reappearing almost immediately with his bomb-satchel. He ran back up the steps and handed the Doctor one of the fragile glass spheres.

The Doctor took it from him, and held it carefully on the top of the canister, just over the point where he estimated the timing mechanism to be. 'Pass me your piece of iron, Susan. Now, if I can manage to release the acid without detonating this bomb . . .' Using the iron as a hammer, the Doctor gave the sphere a carefully measured tap, like a man cracking a boiled egg with a spoon. A crack appeared in the sphere and a colourless liquid started to trickle out. As it ran over the lid of the canister it smoked.

'Look,' whispered Susan. 'It's starting to burn through . . .'

A patch of the metal was beginning to crack and crumble. The Doctor jabbed cautiously with the piece of iron, and the metal flaked and crumbled away. 'Splendid! Now your knife again, young man.' Feeling like the assistant surgeon at an operation, David passed the Doctor the broken knife.

The Doctor glanced at the detonation dial. The needle was now only a fractional distance from the red zone, and the bleep was rising even higher. But the Doctor's face was calm and his hand steady as he jabbed at the delicate mechanism with the improvised tool.

'Now, if I remove the fuse . . .' Carefully he lifted out a small section of the bomb's 'works' . . .

Suddenly the bleeping stopped. The needle on the detonation dial became still, and the Doctor leaned on the canister for support as he drew a deep gasping breath . . .

The Daleks finished their search of the Transport Museum and assembled outside. 'There are no more rebels in the building,' announced the patrol leader in confident tones. 'We shall continue the search elsewhere.'

The Dalek patrol moved away, leaving behind them a pile of rubble which entombed one of their number and the rebel leader Dortmun.

Inside the museum, Barbara and Jenny crept from the vintage corporation dustcart in which they'd been hiding. Although it was an unglamorous hiding place it had proved quite effective. The Daleks had searched all round the parked vehicles, but hadn't bothered to look inside any of them, perhaps not understanding the purpose of these alien machines.

Barbara peered out of the still-open front door. 'They've gone. But there's no saying they won't be coming back. We've got to get away from here.'

'How? With Dalek patrols everywhere, we'd be shot down as soon as we set foot in the streets.'

'Then we won't set foot.' Barbara waved her hand.

'With transport all around us, why should we have to walk?'

Ignoring Jenny's protests that the whole scheme was crazy and would never work, Barbara started checking over the vehicles in the hall. Some were too clumsy and antiquated, others too slow, and she settled at last on the sturdy corporation dustcart in which they'd hidden.

A search of the garage attached to the Museum produced tools, a foot-pump, and best of all, half a dozen cans of petrol under a tarpaulin. Soon Jenny was pumping up the dustcart's tyres while Barbara checked over the engine. She'd run her own little car in her teaching days, and had learned the basics of car-maintenance just to save on garage bills. Jenny collapsed, out of breath, and Barbara lowered the bonnet of the dustcart. 'All right, let me take a turn.'

'What's the engine like?'

'Fine as far as I can see. They're usually pretty well maintained in this sort of place. I imagine they used to drive them out occasionally, for parades and exhibitions.'

'Surely the Daleks are bound to hear when we start the engine?'

Barbara stopped pumping, and gave the tyre an experimental kick. 'There, that'll do.' She disconnected the pump. 'We'll just have to chance the noise. It'll still be better than walking.'

Jenny was pessimistic. 'You realise we won't get very far in this old thing?'

'Probably not,' said Barbara patiently. 'But at least it will give us a start out of London.'

'Anyway, do you even know the way to Bedfordshire.'

'Yes, of course . . .' Barbara hesitated. 'At least, I used to.'

'What does that mean?'

'Things may have changed. I'm not sure how much damage the Daleks have done.'

'Just wait till you see it,' said Jenny, with a kind of

gloomy relish.

Barbara sighed. There were times when she could have wished for a more cheerful companion. Once again her thoughts turned to Susan and the Doctor. What were they doing now? And Ian . . . What had happened to him?

Crouched in an empty storeroom, Ian and Larry were talking in low voices. Both were tense and watchful. There had recently been a change in the note of the spaceship's engines, and Ian was convinced they would soon be landing. Would they be in Bedfordshire as he hoped? More important, would they be able to get off the ship without being recaptured?

Larry was talking about his missing brother Phil, and his determination to find out what the Daleks were doing. 'Phil got himself sent to the mines on purpose. He reckoned if we knew what the Daleks were doing we'd stand a better chance of defeating them.'

Ian nodded abstractedly, his ears alert for more signs of a landing. 'I suppose that makes good sense.'

'Phil sent back just one message from the mines. He'd worked out some kind of theory . . . he reckoned the Daleks were drilling to reach the magnetic core of the Earth . . .'

A sudden jolt sent them reeling across the storeroom, and Ian lost interest in Larry's brother and his theories. 'We're down,' he said excitedly. 'Now, how do we get out of here?'

Larry nodded towards the corner of the room, where there was the usual disposal chute. 'Only one way out. Through there. As soon as we get out, make for cover. I'll go first.'

Larry moved over to the chute, but Ian moved in front of him. 'You realise we've no idea what's out there?'

Larry pushed him aside. 'Only one way to find out.'

He flung open the hatch-cover, swung his legs over the

edge, and was immediately sucked away by the powerful down-draft. Ian hesitated for a moment. But Larry was right, there was no alternative. They'd never make it down the ramp. He swung his legs over the hatchway and followed Larry. Immediately the suction swept him away. He was whizzing through darkness, sliding down what felt like a giant drain pipe. Suddenly the pipe came to an end and Ian found himself flying through open air. He landed with a thump on solid ground, rolled over on his shoulder and came up running, heading for the shelter of a clump of bushes ahead. He flung himself into the midst of them—and landed on top of Larry, who'd obviously followed exactly the same route.

As soon as he had his breath back, Ian gasped, 'Where do you reckon we are? Is it Bedfordshire?'

Larry parted the bushes. 'Take a look.'

Ian peered through the leaves, and gasped in astonishment. The saucer had landed on what looked like the biggest mining area in the world, an immense muddy valley torn out of what had once been wooded English countryside. It was dotted with mine-shaft entrances at regular intervals. There were earth-moving machines all around, some of Dalek origin, others obviously commandeered from the humans. Rows and rows of little shacks dotted the site, giving it the air of a mining camp in gold-rush days. A gleaming metal pylon dominated the area with beside it, a crater like an extinct volcano.

The enormous site was swarming with activity. Slave workers trudged to and fro in long lines, guarded by metal-helmeted Robomen with whips and guns. Here and there Daleks glided up and down on tours of inspection. Ian felt a new respect for Larry's missing brother and his theories. The Daleks were engaged in some colossal undertaking. Surely it held the answer to the mystery of their presence on this planet—and perhaps, the key to their defeat. He turned to Larry. 'You'll have quite a job, finding your brother in this lot.'

'I'm going to have a darned good try. Come on, let's get on to the site. With any luck we can mingle with the slave workers.'

Making no attempt at concealment, Larry started marching across the site. Ian trudged beside him, hoping they looked like a couple of industrious workers on some errand for the Daleks. They certainly looked as ragged and hungry as the rest of the slaves.

They reached the shelter of a huge excavating machine and paused to survey the activity around them. 'If we can get a chance to grab one of these blokes going by,' whispered Larry, 'we can ask him for news of my brother.'

The familiar hated tones of a Dalek voice rang out. 'Section Beta Zero. Parade for robotisation selection at hut thirty.'

'I think we ought to find better cover,' muttered Ian. 'There's a bit too much going on around here.'

A voice spoke from behind them. 'And who are you two?' They whirled round. A thin-faced middle-aged man had just come round the corner of the excavator. He was as ragged-looking as the rest of the slave workers, but at the same time he had an air of natural authority about him. He looked at them impatiently, waiting for their answer.

Larry looked defiantly at him. 'Never mind about us. Who are you?'

'My name's Wells. I'm a section leader. Why aren't you with your work detail? It makes trouble for all of us if you dodge your share of work.' They didn't reply, and he looked more closely at them. 'Escaping, are you? I suppose you know there are Robomen just the other side of this machine?' He reached under the machine and grabbed a pile of picks, tossing some to Ian and Larry. 'Grab these—and leave the talking to me.'

A Roboman appeared round the side of the machine. He stopped, looked searchingly at them and spoke in the familiar slurred voice. 'Who are these two men?'

'I took them from a work detail,' said Wells quickly. 'I needed them to collect more tools.'

'Which work detail?'

Wells waved an arm vaguely. 'I don't know, somewhere over there.'

Ian and Larry stood quite still as the Roboman came closer and looked at them with his dead eyes. 'They must attend for robotisation.'

Wells shook his head. 'They're needed on their work details. I'll take them back with me.'

'No. They must attend.' The Roboman moved closer to Ian. 'Why do you wait? Move!'

Slowly, very slowly, Ian and Larry began walking away. The Roboman turned to Wells. 'You. Come here.'

Slowly Wells walked across to him. As soon as Wells was close enough the Roboman swung his arm in a brutal arc, clubbing Wells to the ground with the butt of his gun. Wells collapsed face down in the mud, moaning and clutching his head.

Emotionlessly the Roboman said, 'In future, refer all decisions to your masters.'

Ian ran across to Wells and helped him to his feet. After a second's hesitation, Larry ran to join him. Between them they got Wells to his feet, blood streaming from a gash in his forehead.

The Roboman suddenly realised what was going on. 'What are you doing?'

Ian said furiously, 'You can't just leave him like this.'

'Do not disobey orders.'

'Get some other orders!' said Ian contemptuously. Between them Ian and Larry took Wells across to the shelter of the nearest hut.

The Roboman stood quite still, and made no attempt to pursue them.

They laid Wells on the table, and Ian wiped away the blood with his handkerchief. After a moment Wells struggled to sit up. 'I'm OK. Sorry I got you into that—it was all I could think of.'

'We should be thanking you,' said Ian. He ran over to the window and looked out. The Roboman was still standing quite still. Then he nodded his head abruptly, as if in response to some unheard voice. Gun at the ready, he began marching towards the hut.

The Roboman stepped through the doorway. Wells was sitting on the table, and Larry stood beside him. That was the last thing the Roboman saw. Ian stepped from behind the door and clubbed him down with a savage swing of his pickhandle.

Wells got shakily to his feet. 'We'll have to get out. The Daleks always know when a Roboman is attacked. It cuts off the radio-link. Pick up some tools and try to mingle with one of the working parties. This place is so big there's a chance they'll lose you in the crowd.'

Ian nodded and picked up a couple of picks, passing one to Larry.

'What about you?'

'I know a good hiding place not far away. I've got to stay in the area, I'm meeting Ashton here later.'

'Someone important?' Ian guessed that Wells was one of the leaders of whatever resistance movement existed in the mines.

'Ashton's a rat,' said Wells dispassionately. 'He smuggles in extra food, and sells it to us for whatever we can raise—rings, jewels, anything people have got hidden away. He's useful though. That extra food has saved quite a few lives.' He looked curiously at Ian. 'I still don't know about you two. Are you trying to break out?'

Ian grinned. 'Believe it or not, we're breaking in. Larry here's looking for his brother, and I'm looking for a friend of mine. I want to take a look around as well, see what the Daleks are up to.'

'You must be mad,' said Wells simply.

'Maybe. Look, whatever happens we'll want to get out

of here sooner or later. Will this Ashton smuggle us back to London?'

'Maybe—for a price. Meet me back here when it gets dark—should be safe again by then. I'll tell you what he says.'

Ian shouldered his pick. 'Right, we'll see you later. Come on, Larry, it's time to go down the mine.'

All three slipped quietly out of the hut. They trudged through the mud and attached themselves to a file of slave workers heading towards one of the mine entrances. No one seemed to notice them. Ian guessed that the sheer scale of the enterprise made it impossible for the Daleks to keep tabs on all their slaves.

As they headed into the darkness of the mine, Ian suddenly wondered what on earth he was doing. Larry had a definite mission—to find and rescue his brother. But Ian had only the vaguest of plans. First he wanted to look for the Doctor. Knowing the old chap's insatiable curiosity, Ian thought it was a fair bet that the Doctor would come to see what the Daleks were up to. And if he didn't find the Doctor, he'd gather as much useful information as he could, then return to London and take up the search for his companions there. As a scheme it was somewhat on the vague side. But Ian felt a curious sense of excitement as he trudged into the darkness. Somewhere in the depths below lay the secret of the Dalek invasion of Earth. If he could find out what it was, he might yet have a hand in their defeat . . .

9

Dangerous Journey

Barbara swung the starting handle of the dustcart. The engine coughed, spluttered, then began to turn over. She withdrew the handle and climbed behind the wheel. Jenny finished flinging back the main doors and jumped in the cab beside her. Slowly the dustcart rumbled out of the Museum where it had stood for so many years.

As they came into the street, Jenny glanced briefly at the pile of debris covering Dortmun. A single hand projected from the rubble . . . she looked hurriedly away. 'I wonder why he did it?'

Barbara drove cautiously through the empty streets. 'Mostly because he just wouldn't give up.'

'It was senseless,' said Jenny harshly. 'He threw his life away.'

'Depends how you look at it, doesn't it?'

'You've got some romantic idea about this resistance business haven't you? There's nothing heroic about dying uselessly.'

'Does it occur to you that Dortmun sacrificed himself to save us, to draw off the Dalek attack? If he hadn't we probably wouldn't be alive now!'

They drove on in silence for a while. Suddenly Jenny shouted, 'Look out—Dalek!' A Dalek had appeared at the end of one of the side turnings. Barbara put her foot down, and the Dalek disappeared from view as they sped past.

Jenny looked back nervously. 'Do you think it saw us?'

'Even if it didn't it must have heard the noise.'

'Then we're really in for trouble. It'll send a message ahead . . .'

Barbara increased speed. 'We'll worry about that problem when we come to it.'

They came to it very quickly. A turn in the road revealed a line of Daleks stretched across their path. 'What shall we do?' shouted Jenny. 'Jump for it?'

Barbara stamped on the accelerator. 'No! Hold tight, I'm going through!'

Roaring and rattling, the old dustcart sped straight for the line of Daleks, scattering them like skittles. Barbara was vaguely conscious of hitting one head-on, sending it flying through the air. The dustcart lurched as she ran over another one, crushing it beneath the heavy wheels. A Dalek blast sizzled past the open window and then they were through, the line of Daleks scattered in confusion behind them. One or two blasts were fired after them, but Barbara swung the dustcart round a corner and they were safely out of sight. Jenny was bouncing exultantly in her seat. 'We went straight through them, we went straight through them!'

Barbara smiled in satisfaction. 'I enjoyed it too. We can't go on much longer in this thing though. They'll really be after us now.'

On the flight deck of the Dalek spaceship, a message was received from central ground control. 'Rebels travelling north in motorised vehicle. Have broken through Dalek cordon. You will intercept this vehicle and destroy!'

'I obey. Give position of rebel vehicle.' The saucer prepared for take-off.

They were driving along a quiet country lane when suddenly a low droning filled the air. Jenny stuck her head out of the open window and craned her neck to gaze up above. 'It's the Dalek saucer, coming in low!'

Barbara nodded, grim-faced. 'All right. Jump for it Jenny— now! I'll follow you.'

Jenny flung open the door and jumped, rolling over and over on the dusty road. Barbara saw thankfully that the road stretched dead ahead of them. She decreased speed slightly, adjusted the steering wheel carefully, then opened her door and jumped clear . . . She rolled over as she hit the ground, flinging herself desperately to the side of the road.

High above in the control room of the Dalek ship, a scanner showed the old vehicle trundling along the lane like some bright orange bug. The Dalek commander said, 'Target located. Destroy!' Another Dalek reached out and touched a control . . .

A ray shot from the hovering ship and bathed the dustcart in a glow of light. Seconds later it exploded in a cloud of flame and smoke.

The commander sent a message back to central control. 'The rebel vehicle has been located and destroyed.'

The Dalek ship glided higher and sped on its way back to the mines.

From the roadside ditch, Jenny and Barbara looked regretfully at the blazing remains of the dustcart. Both had jumped clear at the last possible moment. It was Barbara's hope that the Daleks would believe they had died in the flames and call off the hunt. She got to her feet. 'Come on, Jenny, time to move. It's still a long way to Bedfordshire.'

Susan tramped wearily along behind David, wrinkling her nose at the ripe mixture of smells that floated up from the murky waters below. They were following the course of the main sewer, walking along a sort of tow-path beside an underground canal.

'David,' she called. 'Can't we rest for a moment?'

David's heart softened at the weariness in her face. 'Yes, of course we can.'

Susan sank thankfully to the ground. 'How long do we stay down these sewers?'

'Just as long as we can. It's smelly, but its safe!'

Something tinkled by Susan's foot and she held it up. 'Look—a cartridge case.'

David took it and examined it. 'Could be Robomen—though they don't usually come down here.'

'Some of your friends then?'

'Not necessarily. We're not all allies, you know. There are people about who just think of their own survival. They'd kill you for a few scraps of food.' David tapped his rifle. 'This isn't much use against Daleks, but it will keep anyone else away.'

Suddenly they heard footsteps. A shadow moved down the tunnel towards them. David raised his rifle. 'All right, who are you?'

The shadow stopped. 'David? Is that you? It's me, Tyler.'

David jumped up and ran forward, overjoyed to see his old friend again. Tyler explained that he'd abandoned his search for other guerilla bands, and decided to go North on his own. 'Did they manage to find that Doctor chap?' he asked.

David nodded. 'He's back there. We left him to rest while we made sure it was all clear ahead!'

'You'd better get back to him. There are renegades about down here, I scared a couple off with this.' Tyler brandished his rifle.

Susan held up the cartridge. 'Did you shoot at one?'

Tyler looked. 'That's mine all right. I wasn't shooting at renegades though.'

'What then?'

'Alligators.' He saw Susan's look of horror and smiled grimly. 'Quite a lot of animals escaped from zoos after the invasion. Most of them died off. But the big reptiles flourished—down here.'

Susan jumped to her feet. 'Come on, David. Let's get back to the Doctor!' She had immediate visions of alligators creeping up to the Doctor's dozing form.

Tyler said, 'Better let me scout ahead, just in case. You two follow.'

David nodded, and Tyler moved away.

Susan called, Mr Tyler, you haven't any news of our other friends?'

Tyler said curtly, 'Barbara got back to HQ with Dortmun. I left her there—that's all I can tell you.' He disappeared into the darkness. David and Susan waited a few minutes then followed him down the tunnel.

Somehow during their journey he drew further ahead of them, gradually disappearing from sight. They came to a main junction in the tunnels and David stopped. 'This is where we left the Doctor.' He called out, 'Doctor? Tyler?' There was no reply.

'There are these ladders to upper and lower tunnels. Susan pointed. 'Maybe they took one of those.' She moved across to a ladder and began to climb down. 'Mr Tyler? Grandfather, are you down there?'

There was a rusty creaking sound from Susan's ladder. David yelled, 'Be careful,' but he was too late. The top end of the ladder pulled away from the wall and pivoted round on its lower fastening. Susan clung on desperately, and found she was suspended just a few inches over the water. She heard David's voice. 'Hang on! I'll come and get you.' He leaned over, trying to pull her back.

Susan's eyes were fixed on the rushing flood beneath her. Surely there was something moving? To her horror she saw a squat shape gliding nearer. A long jaw lined with savage teeth appeared from the murky water. Susan screamed as the alligator's teeth clashed within inches of her dangling foot.

The alligator dropped back into the water and turned for a second try. Its jaws opened . . .

A bulky shape appeared above her, there was the crack of a rifle. Tyler fired straight into the open mouth of the alligator and it dropped back into the water with a coughing roar. Seconds later Tyler and David had grabbed the ladder and dragged it and Susan back to safety. She collapsed into David's arms. 'Where's Grandfather?'

Tyler pointed upwards. 'Don't worry. I got him to one of the upper levels. It's not really safe down here.'

Susan looked at the murky water and shuddered. 'I believe you.'

David put an arm round her shoulders. 'Don't worry, you'd probably have given the poor old chap indigestion!'

They started to climb the ladder after Tyler.

It lay curled and asleep on one of the throbbing machines. The machine was warm, and it didn't care for the cold on this planet. Suddenly it quivered and woke. Its keen hearing had picked up voices . . . human voices. And humans meant food. It slithered from the machine and began sliding quietly through the darkness.

Ian stopped moving and listened intently. 'I tell you I heard something. A sort of slithering noise.'

Larry peered into the darkness. 'Which direction?'

'I'm not sure. It seemed to come from all round . . .'

They stood waiting tensely. Their exploration of the mine had not proved a great success. Security was tighter than Ian had imagined, and all the deeper levels were closely guarded. He'd been unable to pick up any real clues as to what was going on here. Nor had they found any trace of the Doctor, or of Larry's brother. Most of their time had been taken up with dodging the constantly patrolling Robomen and their Dalek masters. Now they were back where they'd started, close to the hut where they'd parted from Wells. But this time it was dark—and something very nasty was hunting them through that darkness.

A huge shapeless bulk slithered towards them, making a kind of screaming roar. They jumped back. A Dalek searchlight cut through the darkness, and Ian and Larry flung themselves down. Ian caught a glimpse of a hideous bloated shape, slithering off into the darkness. The searchlight passed by and they picked themselves up. Larry was trembling violently. 'Ian, did you see? What was that thing?'

'Search me. Luckily for us it doesn't seem to like the light. Come on, let's get under cover.'

They ran to the little hut and threw themselves inside. Ian closed the door and turned round. Larry was standing absolutely still. From the shadows a man was covering them with a rifle.

'Now you can turn round and go out again,' said a cold sneering voice. The man stepped forwards into the moonlight which shone through the window. He wore a soft hat and heavy raincoat, not old and ragged but new and of good quality. His face was round, even a little plump, not gaunt and thin like the slave workers. Suddenly Ian realised who the man was. 'I take it you're Ashton?'

'How do you know that?'

'Wells told us. We came to meet you.'

'You're lying. You came to steal my food. Now get out.' He jerked the rifle barrel towards the door.

Ian didn't move. 'With that thing out there?'

'It didn't see you come in—it needn't see you go out.'

From outside came the roar of the creature that was roaming the darkness. Ian decided he wasn't going outside again whatever happened. The thing was to keep talking. If he could get close enough to jump the man . . . Edging a few inches nearer Ashton, Ian said, 'Maybe we can do business together. I want to get back to London.'

'Indeed?' Ashton seemed intrigued. 'And why can't you just die here?'

'I'm not planning to die anywhere yet. I've got friends

in London and I want to find them. Can you get me there?'

'Of course I can. For the right price.'

'And what's the right price?'

'As much as you can afford. I'll take anything. Stones, precious metal, jewellery, rings . . . I'm not particular . . .'

'I'm afraid I don't have very much in that line.'

Ashton smiled coldly. 'Then goodbye. I do hope you avoid the Slyther on the way back.'

'We're not leaving.'

'No?' Ashton raised the rifle and worked the bolt. Ian tensed himself to spring . . .

Suddenly the door opened. 'Ashton? It's all right, these two are friends of mine.' Wells slipped into the hut, closing the door behind him.

Ashton lowered his gun. 'You came up with the character references just in time. You've got the goods?'

Wells produced a bundle of objects tied in a handkerchief. He opened it and Ian saw a pathetic collection of wedding rings, cuff-links, ear-rings, bracelets . . . whatever valuables the inmates of the mines had managed to hide. Ashton examined it. 'Not much—but it'll have to do.'

From a corner Ashton produced a small sack, and tossed it across to Wells. 'There you are, then. Now why don't we all have something to eat, boys?'

Wells hefted the sack. 'This has to go round a lot of people. I'll share with my friends here—but you're not included, Ashton.'

For a moment Ashton flushed, but he forced a sneering smile back on his face. 'Don't worry. I've brought my own.' He produced a silver hip-flask, pushed the top off with his finger and took a swig. The whole operation was performed one-handed. The other hand still held the rifle, and it was still pointed in their direction.

Ian looked across at Wells. 'Know all the best people, don't you?'

Wells was checking the contents of the sack. 'I told you—he's our only source of real food. You can hardly survive on the slop the Daleks dish out.'

The weird howl echoed through the hut. Ian looked up. 'What is that thing out there?'

'We call it the Slyther. The Black Devil keeps it as a sort of pet.'

'The Black Devil?'

Impatiently Ashton joined in. 'Where've you been—Fairyland? The Black Dalek. Otherwise known as the Dalek Supreme. He's the big boss Dalek.'

'And what's this Slyther thing doing roaming about loose? Is it on guard?'

Wells nodded. 'In a way. There's a curfew, see? The Black Dalek turns the thing loose to deter people from wandering about at night. It wanders round in search of food.'

The howl rang out again. 'What kind of food?' asked Larry nervously.

It was Ashton who answered the question. 'People,' he said simply. 'The Daleks can always spare it a slave or two. They've got plenty more.'

Wells fished out two tins of spam and two tins of peaches, tossing one of each to Ian and Larry. 'Here, we can spare you these. No, don't argue. Take it, you'll need it.' He fished out two tins for himself and produced a can-opener.

They made a strange, uneasy, meal in the darkened hut, digging the food from the cans with their fingers. Ashton watched them sardonically, taking the occasional swig from his flask. He passed the time checking through the little hoard of jewellery. 'You're a fool, Wells,' he said conversationally. 'There's enough here to buy you a passage out of this place. I could take you to nice empty countryside, plenty of food . . . Why don't you forget your ridiculous resistance movement, look after yourself?'

Wells swallowed his last half-peach and drained the juice from the can. 'I'll get out . . . when everyone gets out.'

'Suit yourself. Some people never learn.'

Larry slipped a signet ring from his finger and tossed it to Wells. 'Here, this is for our supper.'

Wells stowed the ring away. 'I'll take it too, if you don't mind. It'll help to buy the next lot from our greedy friend here.'

Whether it was the sound of their voices or the scent of the food they were eating, they never knew, but something led the Slyther to their hut. Suddenly there was a shattering roar and the door burst open. *It* was there filling the doorway. They cowered back as the terrible bulging shape slithered towards them . . .

10

Trapped in the Depths

Ian saw a vast lumpy blob of a body, powerful flailing tentacles, two tiny deep-set eyes shining with malice . . . Moving incredibly fast, the creature lurched towards them.

It was Ashton who saved their lives, though he was only trying to preserve his own. It was his last good deed, perhaps the only one in his misspent life. The rifle was still in his hand, and instinctively he raised it to his shoulder and began blazing away at the Slyther. He succeeded only in attracting its attention. The horrible creature paused for a moment then began rolling swiftly towards him. He fired again and again with no result. Ashton was still screaming when the creature flowed over him and engulfed him entirely.

Ian didn't like to leave even Ashton to the mercy of the Slyther, but it was dreadfully clear that there was nothing they could do for him. 'Quick,' he yelled. 'Now's our chance,' Leaving the Slyther to its feast, Ian, Larry and Wells ran from the hut into the darkness outside. Immediately they were caught in the beam of a Dalek searchlight. 'Scatter!' yelled Wells, and they all split up, Wells running one way, Larry and Ian the other. From behind them came the screaming roar of the Slyther as it abandoned Ashton to pursue the rest of its prey.

Ian and Larry struggled to the surface of a low mound of earth. In its centre was a crude mine shaft, a deep round hole. A wooden derrick straddled the hole, and from the derrick hung an enormous iron bucket, obviously designed for carrying earth.

They paused, wondering whether to run round the excavation or go back—when the Slyther appeared over the top of the mound, rushing towards them at amazing speed.

Ian acted without thinking. He took a flying leap through the air, clutched the side of the earth-bucket and scrambled inside. Larry hesitated, took a look at the approaching Slyther, and followed his example. Ian grabbed him and hauled him inside the bucket.

Howling with rage the Slyther ranged to and fro on top of the mound, its prey just out of reach. 'It's still after us,' shouted Ian. 'I hope it can't jump!'

Larry grabbed Ian's arm. 'It's going to try!'

Larry was right. The Slyther somehow gathered itself, then flew through the air in a tremendous leap. It landed on the edge of the bucket and began scrambling over the side.

Terrified by the thought of being trapped inside the bucket with the voracious monster, Ian and Larry fought like demons. They heaved and kicked and punched at the Slyther's flabby bulk, shoving it out of the bucket with maniacal fury, dodging the flailing blows from its enormous tentacles. A last desperate heave sent it over the edge. With a long final scream, the monster disappeared. There was a squelching thud as it struck the edge of the crater, then screaming in rage and pain it slithered off into the darkness . . .

For a moment Ian and Larry crouched in the bucket, panting for breath. Then Larry gasped, 'Come on, let's get out of here.' He started to climb the side of the bucket, but Ian held him back. 'No—someone's bound to have heard all that racket. Let's just stay here till things quieten down.'

In the mine control room deep below the surface a Dalek engineer was studying his work-chart. He turned to his assistant, 'There is no work party in shaft nine. Why?'

The assistant consulted another chart. 'The section is completed. A labour force is now being assembled for clearing operations.'

'Work must proceed to schedule. There must be no delay.'

'All will be ready. I shall now lower the waste bucket into shaft nine.' The assistant touched a control.

Ian listened cautiously. Everything seemed silent. 'It's all clear now.'

'Might as well take a chance,' agreed Larry. 'Can't stay here all night.'

There was a shuddering, a clanking sound—and Ian and Larry felt the bucket jerk into sudden movement. 'What's happening?' yelled Larry.

'Hold tight,' shouted Ian. 'We're going down!' And so they were. Slowly the bucket clanked down into the darkness below.

'I must say this is a nice state of affairs,' announced the Doctor peevishly. 'All this time and we're still hiding in sewers.'

David grinned, well used to the Doctor by now. 'Better to hide down here, Doctor, than be caught by the Robomen. As soon as Tyler says the coast is clear we can travel on the surface again.'

They had climbed up from the deeper parts of the sewer system and were now in a stone-walled antechamber directly below street level. A ladder led up through a manhole, and Tyler had just gone ahead to see if it was safe for the rest of them to emerge.

There was a scrambling sound and Tyler shot down the ladder, rifle in hand. Susan looked up hopefully. 'Is it clear?'

'It is not,' announced Tyler grimly. 'Ran straight into a patrol. I couldn't get under cover, they came after me.'

David grabbed his rifle. 'How many?'

'Just two of them.'

Tyler started back up the ladder. 'David and I will deal with them, you stay under cover.'

'Just a moment,' said the Doctor mildly. 'Wouldn't it be better to—er, lure them down here? If they succeeded in communicating with their fellows and summoning reinforcements . . .

Tyler shook his head ruefully. 'I suppose if we stick together long enough I'll learn to do what you say the first time. All right, David, you draw them in. Don't shoot unless you have to, ricochets might get one of us.'

David climbed up the ladder, emerged through the manhole, and ran a little way into the street. The Robomen saw him immediately and wheeled round in pursuit. They raised their guns, but David had already disappeared down the manhole.

Crouched in the corner of the little chamber, the Doctor and Susan waited. David and Tyler were also waiting, one each side of the ladder. The first Roboman came to the top of the ladder, paused, then slowly began to descend. As soon as he was down, Tyler grabbed him round the throat and pulled him to the floor.

The second Roboman more cautious, paused halfway down the ladder. David grabbed his feet and pulled him down. The two men collapsed in a wildly struggling heap. The Roboman's gun went off, but luckily the shot went up through the open hatchway. Quickly David raised his rifle and used the butt to club the Roboman into unconsciousness.

The Doctor went over to Tyler, who was methodically choking the life out of his victim. 'That will do, Tyler,' he said sharply. 'I never countenance the taking of life unless my own is directly threatened.' The astonished Tyler let go of the Roboman who slumped unconscious to the floor. The Doctor made his way to the ladder. 'Now then, let's be on our way to this mine, and then we shall discover how to deal with the Daleks. We'll leave these poor creatures to their own devices. David, you lead the way, my boy. Come along, everybody.' Very much in command, the Doctor bustled his party up the ladder.

Barbara and Jenny were tired and footsore by the time they came to the little cottage in the forest. It was nearly dark now, and there was an ominous rumbling in the sky, with occasional lightning flashes. They'd cut across country, keeping off the roads for greater safety, but now night was coming and they were lost somewhere in thick woods.

Jenny looked at the cottage. 'It seems deserted. What do you think, shall we try it?'

Barbara hesitated. There was something sinister about the tumbledown old cottage. It looked curiously like the witch's house in some fairy tale. She told herself she was being over-imaginative. 'Well, there's a storm coming on. We'd be much better off under shelter.'

They moved cautiously up to the front door. Suddenly it swung open and a hag-like old woman dressed in rags stood glaring at them, a lantern held over her head. Jenny jumped back with a scream, and Barbara thought wildly that perhaps it was a witch's house after all . . .

The old woman snarled, 'What do you want?'

Barbara made her voice calm and reassuring. 'We're lost. We were looking for shelter.'

'Just the two of you?' The old woman gave a sudden cackle of a laugh. 'Tired are you?'

'Yes . . . yes, we are.'

Jenny looked at the old woman uneasily, 'Barbara, I think we should be moving on.'

The smaller, equally ragged figure of a younger woman appeared beside the first in the doorway.

'Dogs'll get you,' it piped suddenly.

'Dogs?' Barbara echoed nervously.

The old woman took up the chorus. 'Terrible beasts. After the plague they formed a pack. They hunt travellers. You'd better come in.'

Reluctantly Barbara and Jenny stepped inside. The cottage was dirty and primitive, like something out of the Middle Ages. A bed, a stove, a rickety table and some battered wooden chairs were all the furniture of its single room. Barbara looked at the two women who stood nodding and smiling. It was clear from their close resemblance that they were mother and daughter. Barbara told herself that she was wrong to feel repelled by them. They were poor and ignorant, that was all, and small wonder in this horrible world the Daleks had made.

'Where are you making for?' asked the old woman suddenly.

Barbara sank into a chair, suddenly realising how tired she was. 'The Dalek mines. We have friends there. We're trying to find them.'

The younger woman shook her head dolefully. 'Nobody ever gets away from the mines. You'll be caught yourselves.'

The old woman nodded. 'You're lucky you got this far—and found us. Patrols pass here all the time.'

Jenny was still suspicious. 'Then how is it you're still free. They must know you're here.'

The old woman cackled. 'Oh, they know all right. But we can't harm them.'

'We helps 'em,' piped up the younger one.

The old woman scowled at her, swiftly changing to a smile as she turned back to Barbara. 'We make clothes for the slave workers,' she explained. 'We're more use to them doing that than we would be in the mines.'

'How do you manage for food?'

'They give us a bit from time to time, payment you might say. We go hungry most days though.'

Even Jenny was won over by their sad faces. 'We've got

a little food with us,' she said gruffly. 'You can share it if you like.'

The old woman gave a toothless grin. 'Why thank you, my child. We've little to offer in return, but if you like you can sleep here for the night. We can make up a bed in that corner, you'll be comfy enough.'

There was another rumble of thunder, and rain began lashing down. Barbara realised she couldn't face going out again. 'Thank you,' she said wearily. 'We'll stay the night if we may.'

Jenny unpacked the meagre supplies—apples, a tin of meat, some rather stale biscuits. The old woman put out some plates, four battered tin mugs and a jug of water.

Barbara noticed that the younger woman was wrapping herself in a heavy hooded cloak. 'Where are you going?' she demanded.

'I have to go out to deliver these clothes.'

'In this weather?'

The old woman sighed. 'Daleks don't care about the weather, my dear. We have to keep up our quota—and these are late already.'

'What about those dogs you told us about?' asked Jenny.

'She follows the patrols,' explained the old woman.

The younger nodded eagerly. 'That's right, I follow the patrols.'

'She'll come to no harm,' said the old woman soothingly. 'She's done it often enough before. Now why don't we sit down and enjoy our meal? The girl will have hers when she gets back.'

Jenny shared out their food with scrupulous fairness, putting aside a portion for the younger woman, and they sat down to eat.

Barbara and Jenny ate the scanty meal in tired silence, but, the old woman was excited and talkative. She plied Barbara with questions about London. 'What's it like now, dearie, still as wonderful?'

'I'm afraid not. The Daleks have destroyed quite a lot of it.'

'Destroyed? Well, I never! When I went it was all so pretty. The shops and the moving pavements . . . and I went to the Astronauts' Fair . . .

The old woman rambled on about her once-in-a-lifetime day trip to London, and all the wonderful things she'd seen. Barbara's head began nodding. It was pathetic really, she thought, she should feel sorry for the poor old thing. But somehow she still felt uneasy. The old woman was nervous too, glancing constantly at an old alarm clock on a shelf, and looking out of the window. Probably worrying about her daughter.

Suddenly bright light flooded into the room as the clearing outside was lit up with a blazing searchlight. Jenny screamed as the cottage door smashed open. In the doorway stood a Dalek, flanked by Robomen guards. 'Both of you will follow me. Do not try to escape or you will be exterminated!'

Stunned, Barbara and Jenny stood up and gathered their few possessions. How had the Daleks found them so easily? The thin figure of the daughter dodged round the Dalek and scuttled to her mother's side. She held out a little sack. 'Look, ma. There's bread, and oranges and sugar . . .'

The old woman chuckled. 'Good, good. I knew they'd give us food if we told them.'

Impatiently the Dalek shouted, 'Move!'

As Barbara and Jenny were marched out of the cottage, the other two women were excitedly rummaging through the sack. The older one looked out of the window as the Robomen led their captives away. 'Such a pity,' she muttered. 'Still, they'd have been captured anyway, in the end.' Eagerly she sucked the juice from her orange. She hadn't tasted an orange for years and years . . .

The giant wastebucket clanked down through the darkness on a seemingly endless journey, taking its human cargo deeper and deeper into the Dalek mine. Ian supposed he shouldn't complain, since he'd wanted to get into the mine anyway. But he hadn't bargained on travelling this way. He heard Larry's nervous voice from the darkness beside him. 'How long do you think we've been going down now?'

'Must be nearly twenty minutes.'

'It's getting warmer, isn't it?'

'Yes . . . pressure's increasing too, my ears are popping.'

Larry shuddered. 'I'd rather be dead than work down here.'

'I hope we don't have to make the choice!'

'We're stopping,' said Larry excitedly. 'We must be nearly at the bottom.' He craned his head over the side of the bucket. 'Look—lights, just below!'

Ian saw a huge open space, the junction of several earth-walled tunnels supported by wooden pit-props, lit by dim working-lights. Piles of earth and rock were everywhere. 'Let's get out of here, before this bucket tips over and chucks us out.'

They clambered on to the rim of the giant bucket. This was by no means an easy job, since the bucket tended to tip with the movement of their weight. Ian wriggled over the edge, hung by his hands and dropped. The fall was a long one, but he landed unhurt in a pile of soft earth.

Larry wasn't so lucky. He landed with a thud right beside Ian, but when he tried to get up he groaned and clutched his leg. 'It's my knee. I hit it on the bucket coming down.'

Ian looked round. 'We must hide for a bit till you can walk. It's too open here. Come on, put your weight on me.'

He helped Larry away from the open area and into one of the side tunnels. They crouched in the semi-darkness, resting thankfully.

After a few minutes Ian said, 'How's the leg?'

Larry straightened it, and gave another groan. 'Seems to be stiffening up. I don't think I'll be able to walk.'

'Don't worry. We'll stay here for a while.' Ian looked out of the tunnel and into the main area. There were lots of tunnels leading off, enormous piles of earth and stones, and that was all. 'This mine doesn't make sense to me. All they seem to be digging is rocks. I suppose they could be processing ore somewhere.'

'You remember what my brother Phil said—the Daleks want to tunnel through to the magnetic core of the Earth.'

'But why? What are they up to?'

Larry shrugged. 'You can't tell much from here. This is only a sort of clearance area. Perhaps the important work's going on somewhere else.'

'You may be right at that.' Ian felt a surge of impatience. It was maddening to be so close to the Daleks' secrets without learning more. 'Larry, would you be all right if I went to have a look around?'

'Yes, sure.'

Ian got to his feet and moved out of the tunnel into the main area. He chose the largest of the tunnels leading off, and made his way along it. Soon he heard voices and movement coming towards him, and ducked behind a pit prop for cover. Cautiously he peered out. A procession of gaunt ragged men and women was stumbling along the tunnel, driven by the whips of Robomen guards. They clutched a variety of containers, and some carried picks and shovels. Ian turned and ran back to Larry.

'Lie low and keep quiet. There's a crowd of workers and Robomen coming this way.'

Larry and Ian watched from hiding as the workers flooded into the central area. The huge bucket in which they'd travelled down suddenly dropped the rest of the distance to the ground, tipping over on its side.

Immediately workers began carrying earth and rocks from the piles and tipping them into the bucket. They worked at a feverish pace and the whips of the Robomen lashed out at anyone who slowed down or stumbled.

A Roboman spoke briefly to one of the slaves who collected a small group of workers. The Roboman started leading them across the area and into the tunnel in which Ian and Larry were hiding. Gun in hand, he marched straight towards them . . .

11

Action Underground

A few yards from Larry and Ian, the Roboman halted his party, and set them to work on the nearest rockpile.

Ian put his lips to Larry's ear and whispered, 'We'll have to move back! They're clearing this whole section . . .'

Desperation gave Larry the power to overcome the pain in his twisted knee. Ian helped him to his feet and they started edging their way deeper into the tunnel.

Larry's foot slipped, and he fell back against the tunnel wall with a moan of pain. The Roboman left his workers and ran towards them, covering them with his gun. 'Halt!'

Ian and Larry stood quite still. The Roboman stared intently at them. Ian guessed that the robotising process reduced the human mind to the lowest level, capable of giving and receiving only the simplest of commands. Finally the Roboman worked things out. 'You are not in the working party. Who are you?'

Larry gripped Ian's arm in a painful grip. 'It's Phil,' he whispered. 'Ian, it's my brother Phil.' He moved closer to the Roboman, staring into his face. 'Think, Phil. You must remember me. I'm your brother, Larry. *Remember me!*'

There was no change in the Roboman's voice or expression. With the same painful slowness, he came to another conclusion. 'You are runaways.'

'Angela,' said Larry desperately. 'Remember your wife, Angela. I can take you to her.'

'You must both be punished. I shall take you to the Daleks. Follow me.'

The Roboman turned, taking obedience for granted—and immediately Ian jumped him. The Roboman fired at once but Ian shoved the gun barrel upwards and the blast hit the ceiling. They wrestled fiercely for possession of the weapon. Once again Ian realised the inhuman strength of the Robomen, their total imperviousness to pain.

Helplessly Larry watched Ian and the Roboman roll over and over, finishing up almost at his feet. His back to Larry, the Roboman wrenched free of Ian and stood up. He levelled the gun at Ian's still prone body—and with a scream of 'No, Phil, no!' Larry launched himself at his brother's back, ripping the Roboman helmet from his head . . .

The gun exploded again, missing Ian and bringing rock down from the wall. The Roboman screamed and convulsed, collapsing in his death agony. Sobbing, Larry held the body in his arms. He knew he hadn't really killed his brother. The Daleks had done that a long time ago, when they'd taken away his humanity.

Stunned and shocked, Ian scrambled to his feet. Larry was still clutching Phil's body, tears streaming down his face. Behind them in the main area an alarm signal was ringing out, and there was a confused shouting.

'Come on, Larry, run!' shouted Ian. 'Here, I'll help you . . .'

Larry shook his head. 'You run, Ian, while you've got the chance. They'd only get both of us . . .'

From the tunnel behind them came a voice shouting 'Halt!' A Dalek was at the end of the tunnel, a Roboman behind him. Ian flung himself to one side and the Roboman fired a long raking blast. Larry's body jerked convulsively, and he collapsed on top of his dead brother.

Ian turned and ran into the darkness of the tunnel. Behind him he could hear the Dalek's blaring voice. 'Emergency, emergency in shaft nine. Seal all exits! Emergency!' Ian ran blindly on into the darkness.

The Doctor stood on a wooded hill overlooking the Dalek mine-workings, his face solemn. He studied the shafts, the machinery, the immense ordered pattern of activity for a moment longer, then returned to his companion. 'Thank you, Mr Tyler, I've seen all I need to see.' They turned and made their way back through the wood.

As they walked back to their little camp, the Doctor mused how often there seemed to come a period of tranquillity in the time of greatest danger. After their fight with the Robomen in the sewer, they'd had a surprisingly peaceful journey to Bedfordshire. They'd even travelled by road for a part of the way in an abandoned car that Tyler had managed to get working.

It was certainly an idyllic scene that met them as they returned to the camp. They'd established themselves by a little stream, and David had produced fishing gear from his pack and started to fish. Clearly he'd been successful, for Susan was frying trout over a small fire, while David himself could be seen coming downstream with another fine fish in his hand.

The Doctor watched smiling as David crept up behind Susan and suddenly thrust the fish over her shoulder. Susan screamed and jumped up. David caught her in his arms, and kissed her. Astonished, Susan stood quite still. The Doctor cleared his throat very loudly, and made a deliberate crashing noise as he came through the bushes.

The two young people jumped apart and David babbled, 'Ah, yes, there you are, Doctor. We were, that is, I was just . . .'

The Doctor looked at the sizzling frying pan. 'Yes, I could see something was cooking,' he said drily. He looked closely at Susan. How deeply was she involved with this young man? For some time now the Doctor had been aware that Susan was fast growing up, and that their wandering way of life posed problems that would one day have to be faced . . . Still, time enough for that later on. First they had to solve the problem of the Daleks. Unless that was dealt with, they'd none of them have a future to worry about.

The meal was the most enjoyable one they'd had for quite some time, and the Doctor's instincts told him it might be even longer before they got another. The food was simple enough, fish, biscuits, the remains of their tinned fruit. Tyler even produced some long-hoarded coffee from his pack. It was jet black, milkless and sugarless, but still delicious.

As they sat round sipping it, David asked, 'Now you've actually seen the Dalek base, Doctor, what do you think?'

'Well, young man, it's quite obvious to me that these mine workings are the centre of their entire operations.' He gave Tyler a reproving glare. 'I really can't think why you didn't focus all your resistance efforts down here.'

Tyler grunted. 'That's all very well Doctor. We've been fighting the Daleks wherever we could. Fighting to stay alive mostly!'

David came to his support. 'We assumed they were just mining for Earth's minerals, looting the planet.'

'No,' said the Doctor decisively. 'These workings hold the answer to the one question that is of any importance to you. *Why* are the Daleks here?'

David looked puzzled. 'Why? Surely they're here because they've invaded us? It's as simple as that.'

'Indeed it isn't, young man. It goes much deeper. The Daleks have no interest in Man as such. He's just a work machine, an insignificant specimen of life scarcely worth conquering. It doesn't matter to the Daleks whether you live or die.'

'All right,' said David. 'Suppose you're right, Doctor. What are the Daleks up to?'

'I'm not quite sure yet, my boy. There must be something about this planet, something no other planet can offer. It's nothing near the surface, or they'd have collected it and gone. Instead there they are, burrowing like metal moles, deep into the Earth's crust!'

Tyler scratched his head. 'I'm no scientist, Doctor, but surely . . . if they penetrate the Earth's crust they'll cause an enormous earthquake—something nobody will survive?'

'That is so—unless they've found some way of controlling the flow of living energy.' The Doctor looked round the little group. 'The Daleks are daring to tamper with the forces of creation—and we must dare to stop them!'

There was a moment of silence. The Doctor's words had made them all aware of the tremendous issues they were facing.

Suddenly the Doctor stood up. 'Time to pack up camp and be on our way,' he ordered. 'We have a great deal to do.' No one questioned the order. Once again, the Doctor had taken charge.

Ian ran on through the darkness until he saw a glimmer of light ahead. He slowed down and went more carefully. The tunnel widened ahead, and joined up with several others. Rows of slave workers were filling their buckets and emptying them into wheeled trucks, which others pushed away. Robomen stood on guard and occasionally a Dalek moved past. It all looked very familiar, and suddenly Ian realised why. He'd stumbled upon another clearing area, a point where the endless debris from the Dalek's drilling was collected and hauled to the surface. Ian looked along the line of workers. A tall, dark-haired woman was emptying a bucket of rocks. Ian gave a silent gasp of astonishment. It was Barbara. He started creeping nearer . . .

Barbara and Jenny had been toiling for hours now, and Jenny was beginning to crack up. She was carrying yet another basket of rocks to the wastebucket when she stumbled and fell, spilling most of the painfully gathered rocks. She crouched by the overturned basket, almost sobbing in despair. 'It's no good, Barbara, we're beaten. We'll never get out of here, never.'

Barbara knelt to help her. 'Steady, Jenny, that's no way to talk. We wanted to get to the mine and here we are.'

'But there's nothing we can do.'

'We can get this bucket filled for a start,' said Barbara practically.

Already a whip-carrying Roboman was moving towards their part of the mine. 'Move,' he shouted. 'Continue with your task.'

Barbara went on tossing rocks into the basket. 'We can try to find their main control room. That's what the Doctor would do.'

Jenny sniffed. 'And what do we do then?'

'I don't know, Jenny, but at least we could try to do something. If we don't succeed, we'll just end up back here.'

From his hiding place near by, Ian saw one of the Robomen address a crouched over slave worker. 'You! Collect more containers from the nearest storage section.'

The man straightened up, and started moving towards Ian. To his joy he saw it was Wells, the man who'd helped him and Larry earlier. As Wells passed his hiding place Ian hissed softly. 'Wells, it's me, Ian.'

Wells pretended to have trouble with his shoe, bent to fix it. 'Ian? Should have thought you'd have been out of here by now.'

'That tall girl over there—I know her. See if you can get a chance to speak to her. Tell her I'm here.'

Wells picked up the last bucket. 'I'll try. But I've got to get the buckets first.' He trudged off along the tunnel and Ian settled down to wait for his return.

On the work line, Jenny was still objecting. 'They'll never let us get near their control room.'

Something crackled inside Barbara's coat as she bent down for another rock. 'Jenny, I've just realised. I've still got Dortmun's notes.'

'A lot of use they are!'

Barbara suddenly lost patience with Jenny's pessimism. It was time to act. A Dalek was coming towards them. Deliberately Barbara straightened up and stepped out in front of it. The Dalek stopped, eye-stalk swivelling round in astonishment. 'Continue work.'

Barbara stood her ground. 'I have important information for you. Rebels are planning a revolution against the Daleks.'

The Dalek's reaction was immediate. 'There will be no revolution. The Daleks are masters of Earth.'

'You don't understand. This is no ordinary uprising. They have scientists working with them.'

'You are lying. It is a trick.'

'No. I have proof.' Barbara held out Dortmun's notes.

The Dalek scanned the first page. 'These contain details of the acid bomb used in the unsuccessful attack on the Dalek spaceship.'

'There's more,' said Barbara quickly. 'We know the names of the rebels, the places where they plan to attack.'

'You will tell me immediately.'

Barbara shook her head. 'No, I must speak to someone in authority. You'll have to act at once on what I tell you, and it's all very complicated.'

The Dalek paused, considering. Barbara held her breath. Then the Dalek spoke. 'Very well. I will take you both to the Dalek Supreme. If you are lying you will be killed. Follow me.'

The Dalek set off down the tunnel, Jenny and Barbara

following behind.

Ian watched all this from hiding, not really understanding what was going on. Wells came back down the tunnel, loaded with buckets. 'All right. Take some buckets, and follow me. I'll try to get you to your friend.'

'Too late. The Daleks have just taken her off.'

'They've probably taken her to the control room for questioning.'

'Then that's where I'm going. Just you point me in the right direction. Come on! Give me some of the buckets.'

Ian stepped out boldly behind Wells, and walked along the line of workers handing out buckets. The Robomen didn't seem to notice him. Wells took him to the far end of the line and pointed. 'That tunnel at the end there, runs towards the control area. Good luck.'

Wells turned back towards the line of workers, and Ian ran off down the tunnel.

Very soon the nature of the tunnel started to alter. Earth and rock walls gave to metal. There was better lighting and the hum of powerful machinery nearby.

At the end of the tunnel was an open door, and through it Ian could see a long room lined with banks of strange machinery and complex control panels. Daleks glided to and fro, tending the instruments. Ian crept quietly to the door and slipped inside.

The place was so enormous, the Dalek scientists so absorbed in their many tasks, that Ian found it easy to slip from machine to machine and work his way to the centre of the area. He saw no sign of Barbara. What he did see was a circular hole in the centre of the area, about the size of a large well. From the concentration of Daleks and instruments around this spot, something very important was going on. Ian crept closer, looking for a good hiding place, near enough to allow him to eavesdrop.

Facing him, and just on the edge of the area was a curious container, rather like half of a giant metal egg. Cables ran into its top. It was partly filled with machinery, but there was just room for Ian to duck inside and crouch down out of sight. He was near enough now to hear the voices of the Daleks as they moved busily around their instruments.

He saw the Daleks in the group wheel round as a large Black Dalek approached. 'Give me your report.'

'The main drills have penetrated the final strata. We are within four miles of the Earth's outer core.'

'When will the final breakthrough occur?'

'As soon as the slave workers have finished clearing the top of the fissure, we shall put into position the penetration explosive. The charge is already prepared in the capsule.'

The Black Dalek addressed those around it, rather like a professor delivering a lecture to students. 'The charge will be timed to detonate in the fissure in the Earth's crust. The fissure will expand and the molten core will be released. We will then control the flow until all the gravitational and magnetic forces in the Earth's core are eliminated. I shall now announce to Dalek Earthforce the near completion of Project Degravitate.'

The Black Dalek moved across to a communications console.

Ian listened eagerly. He had arrived at a crucial moment, just as the secret of the Daleks' plans was to be revealed. He heard the voice of the Black Dalek once more, this time echoing through a whole series of loudspeakers. Clearly the announcement was being relayed over the entire control area.

'This is the Supreme Controller. Our mission to Earth is nearly completed. We were sent here to remove the core of his planet. Once the core is removed we shall replace it with a power system. This will enable us to pilot the planet anywhere in the Universe. All that remains is to put into position the penetration explosive capsule. Daleks controlling this device will now report.'

There came another voice. 'The device is ready.'

'Capsule to closed position.'

Inside his hiding place, Ian's mind was reeling at the sheer audacity of the Dalek plan. To steal an entire planet, to steer it around the Universe as a moving base for conquest . . . No doubt something about the structure of Earth had made it exactly the kind of planet the Daleks needed. They weren't taking anything *from* Earth—they were stealing Earth itself!

Lost in thought, it took Ian a moment too long to notice that something was happening. The container in which he had hidden was gliding across the floor. Another identical metal shape, its opposite half, was moving towards it. The two halves clicked together to form a giant metal egg, shutting Ian inside.

The capsule glided across the control room floor until it was suspended above the central well. The overhead cable was paid out and the container slowly descended into the bombshaft.

The Black Dalek's voice rang out in triumph. 'Once the capsule has been guided into position, it will be released. It will travel to the fissure in Earth's crust and then explode.'

The penetration explosive capsule was on its way—and Ian was trapped inside.

12

Rebellion!

Inside the capsule Ian was struggling frantically. The metal container was completely sealed, the only possible exit a small hatch in one side. Ian set his back against one side of the capsule and kicked frantically at the hatch with his heels. The capsule swung violently to and fro on the end of its cable.

Suddenly it jerked to a halt.

In the control room above there was pandemonium. A panic-stricken Dalek scientist reported, 'Capsule oscillating violently, due to operation of unknown forces. Descension mechanism has ceased to function.'

The Black Dalek was in a fury. 'Recover capsule and re-check immediately.'

'Descension mechanism now jammed. Capsule must be drawn up manually. Alert Robomen working party. Emergency!'

Soon the capsule began moving upwards again, more slowly now, as a party of sweating Robomen heaved on the cable. It was still spinning to and fro as Ian inside kicked frantically at the hatch.

In the control room a Dalek scientist announced 'Capsule now arrived at sub-station immediately below this level. Still vibrating violently.'

The Black Dalek decided to take no chances. 'Arrest capsule at sub-station. Ascertain cause of breakdown.'

The capsule jerked to a halt, just as Ian finally kicked

the hatchway open. He peered out of the hatch. He was at a point where an intersecting tunnel cut at right angles across the vertical shaft. Down that tunnel a Dalek was speeding straight towards him.

Ian jumped from the capsule and looked round for an escape. There was only one way to go—down.

A coil of rope lay amidst a jumble of timbers at the edge of the shaft. Ian tied the rope round a pit prop, threw the other end into the shaft and started climbing down.

The Dalek arrived at the shaft and spun round angrily, puzzled by the disappearance of its prey. Then its eye-stalk swivelled on to the knotted rope. It fired at the beam and the rope blazed and snapped in two . . .

Ian began whizzing down the smooth metal shaft, scrabbling desperately at the sides. The edge of another tunnel flashed by and he flung himself forward frantically. He hit the edge with an impact that drove the breath from his body. Painfully, Ian pulled himself up into the lower tunnel. With the last of his strength, he crawled slowly away into the darkness. Half-way down the tunnel he slumped forward, unconscious.

Barbara and Jenny heard the Dalek Supreme's announcement while they were waiting in the outer control area. Like Ian they were astonished at the scope of the Dalek scheme. Soon they were taken to the centre of the control area and ordered to wait until the Black Dalek was free. It was clear by the number of Daleks bustling about, and their evident agitation, that there was some kind of crisis.

Barbara looked curiously at the opening to the bomb shaft. No doubt this was where the penetration capsule had been lowered. She whispered to Jenny, 'See if you can get to one of the control panels and do some damage. I'll try to hold their attention.'

She could hear agitated Dalek voices. 'Dalek unit reports human being discovered in capsule. Human fell down bomb shaft in attempt to escape.'

The Black Dalek was still issuing orders. 'Every error must be corrected. The penetration explosive must strike the fissure correctly if we are to extract the molten core. Are all slave worker tasks completed?'

'Only final clearance remains.'

'Once clearance is completed, you will confine all slave workers below ground level. When the molten core breaks through they will be completely exterminated.'

Completely unmoved by this order to commit mass murder, the aide moved to the communications console. 'To all Robomen. Herd all human slaves to lower galleries as soon as clearance is complete!'

Jenny looked at Barbara in horror. 'Did you hear what they're planning to do?'

Barbara was thinking furiously. 'That's where they control the Robomen . . .'

'Maybe we can put it out of action,' said Jenny eagerly.

'Better than that—we can use it.'

A Dalek guard ordered them forward, driving them to stand before the Black Dalek. 'Here are the humans who reported an imminent revolt.'

The Black Dalek scanned them. 'Speak!'

Barbara held out Dortmun's notes. 'This is the bomb—'

'We are not interested in the bomb. Give information on planned revolt.'

Barbara racked her brains for a sufficiently colourful story. 'Well, it's planned to start quite suddenly, like the Indian Mutiny.'

'We have already conquered India.'

Barbara rattled on, ignoring the interruption. 'I'm talking about Red Indians of course, in disguise, like the Boston Tea Party. General Lee and the Fifth Cavalry will attack from the North while Hannibal's forces move in from the Southern Alps—'

While the bemused Daleks were listening to this historical mish-mash, Jenny made a sudden dash for the communications console. Immediately a nearby Roboman grabbed her—but the diversion gave Barbara her chance. She ran to the console. 'Attention all Robomen. You will attack the Daleks. Attack the Daleks—'

Like a huge metal dodgem car, the Black Dalek shoved Barbara aside. 'Cancel last order. Resume normal operations.'

The order given, the Black Dalek swung menacingly towards Barbara and Jenny. An aide came forward, 'They were lying to trick us. Shall I exterminate them?'

The Black Dalek considered for a moment. 'No. Hold them here for interrogation. I will deal with them later. There is still much to be done!' Moving to the communications console, the Black Dalek began issuing a further stream of orders.

'Spaceship will hover above main crater, ready to evacuate all Dalek personnel. Repair capsule and descension mechanism. Return capsule to main control—'

As they were marched away, Barbara whispered, 'Sorry Jenny.'

'What for? It was a marvellous try—and it nearly worked.'

Their Roboman guard shouted, 'Silence!' Robomen smartly grabbed Barbara and Jenny and manacled them to clamps on a nearby pillar. All around the bustle of Dalek activity continued.

At the edge of an enormous crater, David and Susan were waiting while Tyler and the Doctor crawled round the rim of the excavation.

'Any idea what they're up to?' asked David.

Susan shook her head. 'The Doctor never explains anything. He'll tell us when he's ready.'

David sighed, 'Well, whatever it is, I just hope it works. The Doctor seems to be our only hope.' He paused. 'Susan—if we are successful—what will you do?'

'Go on travelling with grandfather, I suppose, moving from place to place . . .'

'Wouldn't you like to belong somewhere? Like here—with me?'

Susan looked at him in distress. 'Please, David, don't ask me that. I just don't know.' She looked at his unhappy face. 'I'm sorry, David, really . . .'

They moved apart as the Doctor and Tyler came back to them. The Doctor rubbed his hands together briskly. 'David, my boy, have you any of those bombs left?'

'Just three, I think.'

'That will be sufficient. Now, you see that radio mast over there with the cables leading away? I want you and Susan to destroy it. Use the bombs; you can detonate them from a distance with your gun. Off you go—and don't stop to pick flowers on the way.'

As David and Susan scrambled away, the Doctor turned to Tyler. 'I don't think they'll run into any trouble—but I can't say the same for us! We're going down this crater. Come along!'

The Doctor started scrambling rapidly down the steeply sloping sides. Tyler shook his head in reluctant admiration, and started climbing after him.

Ian was never sure how long he'd been unconscious but it couldn't have been very long. He came to, suddenly, in the darkness of the lower tunnel, his mind still full of the Daleks' terrible plan. If there was only something he could do to frustrate them . . . He had just one advantage. He was still very close to the shaft down which the bomb capsule must pass. If he could only stop or divert it . . .

Ian walked slowly back along the tunnel to the bomb shaft. He peered upwards, to where the light shone down from the Dalek control room. They'd hauled the bomb-capsule back up by now. Soon they'd have it repaired, and ready to drop. Released from its cable it would plummet down the bomb shaft, into the fissure and then explode. Unless . . .

Just as there had been on the level above, there was a pile of timber close to the end of the tunnel. Ian looked thoughtfully at the heavy planks. Heaving and struggling, he dragged a plank off its pile and laid it like a bridge right across the bomb shaft. He pulled out another plank, and another . . . Some time later, his work completed, Ian ran back up the tunnel. He was looking for a way through to the upper levels. If his plan worked, the tunnel he was in now would soon be a very unhealthy place.

Tyler and the Doctor stood by a massive metal door let into the side of a tunnel. The Doctor was rubbing his chin. 'Since it isn't guarded, there's probably a photo-electric alarm . . .'

He examined the lower edge of the door. 'Ah yes, here . . . and here. One to trigger the alarms, one to open the door. Now I need something shiny.'

Tyler produced his knife. 'Will this do?'

'Excellent.' Using the shiny blade of the knife as a mirror, the Doctor reflected the light beam of one cell into the other. 'By glancing one beam onto the other, we open the door and neutralise the warning system . . . so!' There was a crackle of electricity, a shower of sparks and the door sprang open.

Tyler scratched his head. 'I'll say one thing, Doctor, life with you is never dull!' They passed into the Dalek Base.

Manacled and helpless in the control room, Barbara and Jenny watched as the re-checked capsule was swung out over the bomb shaft. The Dalek Supreme ordered, 'Commence lowering capsule!'

The huge metal egg, this time without a human

passenger, was lowered slowly down to the bomb shaft.

The Dalek scientist moved to a control. 'Am releasing capsule—now!'

The penetration explosive capsule dropped only a short distance further down the bomb shaft, before it hit the wooden barrier constructed by Ian. Deflected from its intended path, the capsule rolled down the side-tunnel, hit the earth wall, then stopped, hidden in the darkness.

Proudly the Black Dalek announced 'The Capsule is on its way to the core of this planet. When it reaches its destination it will detonate automatically. We shall go to the edge of the mine workings for greater safety. We shall remain in the Dalek spaceship until we are certain it is safe to return. All Daleks will now evacuate this base.'

Barbara gave Jenny an agonised glance. The Dalek plan looked like succeeding after all. And they were being left behind—to die.

13

Explosion!

Tyler and the Doctor jumped back into an intersection, as a long line of Daleks moved down the corridor ahead of them. Tyler popped his head out. 'That was a near one.'

The Doctor nodded. 'They seem to be on the move. Let's go to where they've come from.'

Jenny and Barbara were still struggling with their manacles when Tyler and the Doctor made their way into the now deserted control area. The reunion was excited and ecstatic. 'My poor Barbara,' said the Doctor indignantly. 'Mr Tyler, help me to get these things off.' Tyler set to work on the manacle locks with his knife, and soon Barbara and Jenny were free again.

Briefly Barbara explained what she'd gathered about the Dalek's plan. The Doctor seemed unsurprised. 'I thought it would be something like that. I'm working on a scheme to circumvent them. Now, let me see if I can work this scanner.'

The Doctor swiftly adjusted controls and a little screen in front of him sprung to life. It showed various shots of the mines, then suddenly a picture of Susan and David laying bombs around the base of an enormous radio mast. 'They're trying to blow up the mast and so fracture the outer cable ring,' explained the Doctor.

Jenny was none the wiser. 'What good will that do?'

'You know the Daleks communicate by a sort of radio network? Well, if the radio-link is suddenly broken it will give them a most tremendous shock. A kind of brainstorm. It should immobilise them completely, at least for a while . . .

A Dalek voice crackled from a nearby speaker. 'Interference to scanner settings in main control area. One Dalek unit will return to investigate!'

Tyler ran to the doorway. 'There's a Dalek coming along the corridor now!'

On the screen David and Susan continued their task with maddening slowness.

From the doorway Tyler called, 'Doctor—the Dalek's nearly here!'

He ran back to join them at the scanner. Seconds later a Dalek glided into the control area.

The Doctor stood quietly at the scanner, ignoring the approaching Dalek completely.

On the screen they saw David and Susan finish laying their charges, and retreat to a safe distance. David raised the rifle to his shoulder, then a flash filled the screen. When it cleared they saw the radio mast toppling slowly to the ground.

The Doctor beamed triumphantly, turned round—and saw the Dalek heading straight towards him.

Tyler tried to pull him aside. 'Run, Doctor, it hasn't worked.'

The Doctor shook him off, and stepped directly in front of the Dalek, hands clutching his lapels.

The Dalek said, 'Halt! Who *aaare* . . .'

Its voice seemed to wind down, and trail away into silence. The Dalek stopped moving.

Tyler gave a huge sigh of relief. 'You certainly took a chance.'

'Science, my dear chap, not chance. It took a little time for the effect to be felt, that's all.'

'What will you do now, Doctor, stop the bomb?'

After this latest display, Tyler was quite prepared to believe the Doctor could do anything.

'All in good time,' replied the Doctor calmly. 'I'm not sure how long this little shock will hold the Daleks. We must find some more permanent way of dealing with them.'

Barbara said excitedly, 'The Robomen, Doctor. That console controls them. I tried ordering them to attack the Daleks, but they caught us. Let me try again.'

The Doctor gave an assenting wave of his hand and Barbara rushed to the console. 'Robomen, this order cannot be countermanded. Attack the Daleks! Destroy them!'

The Doctor stepped up to the console. 'Slave workers—here is your freedom. Use it. Destroy the Daleks.' He turned away from the console, rubbing his hands with glee. 'Now come along all of you. Let's see what happens!'

They walked along the corridor towards the mining area. Soon they heard a clamour and a shouting, the ringing of metal on metal. They turned a corner to find a seething mob of slave workers and Robomen battering and smashing at a Dalek with pails and picks, until it was no more than a hunk of twisted metal. The crowd rushed past them, obviously searching for more Daleks to destroy.

A grimy ragged figure dashed out of the crowd and caught Barbara in his arms, hugging her till she was breathless. 'Ian,' she cried delightedly. 'Ian!'

'Bless my soul, it's young Chesterton!' said the Doctor. 'Where did you spring from, my boy?'

Ian shook the Doctor's hand like a pump handle. 'Doctor! I might have guessed you were behind all this. Just listen to them!'

From all over the mine came the sound of exultant shouting, the roar and clamour of battle. The Doctor smiled. 'The people of Earth are fighting back at last.'

They made their way back to the control room, exchanging a babble of congratulations, explanations and recitals of all their different adventures.

The Doctor listened gravely as Ian told of his attempt to deflect the bomb. Ian crossed to a chart on the wall which showed the bomb shaft plunging down to join the fissure in the Earth's crust. He put his finger on the chart. If this contraption works, the bomb's jammed here—just a couple of levels below us.'

'A brave scheme, my boy,' said the Doctor, 'But not without its perils to the rest of us. The bomb won't release the Earth's core as the Daleks had hoped, but there will be the most tremendous explosion in a very short time!'

'How long have we got, Doctor?'

The Doctor crossed to the bomb control area. 'If I read these dials correctly—something in the order of ten more minutes!'

Barbara ran to his side. 'Can you switch it off to delay the explosion?'

The Doctor shook his head. 'The bomb was intended to explode deep within the Earth's core, remember. The detonation device is automatic—and self-contained.'

'Then we've got to get out of here!' said Tyler urgently. 'And we've got to get everyone else out too!'

The Doctor went over to the communications console. 'The public address system will still be working. It's on a separate circuit.' He cleared his throat and spoke into it. 'Robomen and slave workers. This mine is about to explode. You must make for the surface and leave the area immediately. Never mind the Daleks. Leave them to their fate. I repeat, this mine is about to explode. Leave the area immediately.' He turned to the others. 'We've done all we can. It's time to look to our own safety. Follow me. We'll go out the way I came in!'

Swiftly the Doctor led them out of the control area along the corridors, out into the tunnel, and finally in a last frantic scramble up the sloping sides of the crater. They found Susan and David waiting for them at the top. 'Don't talk—run!' ordered the Doctor breathlessly, as they joined the crowds fleeing desperately from the mine.

They witnessed the end of the Dalek invasion of Earth from the hill overlooking the mine area. The place looked like a disturbed ant-hill, long lines of people streaming away from it in all directions. The Dalek spaceship hovered over the main crater, but made no attempt to attack, waiting no doubt for the results of the experiment.

As the last few escapers fled from the mine there was a low subterranean rumble . . . It grew steadily until, suddenly, the whole of the mine workings erupted in a great belching cloud of smoke and flame. The noise was shattering, and they all dropped to the ground, hands over their ears. All except the Doctor, who stood watching the holocaust with keen scientific interest.

The incredible noise ended at last, dying down to a low, constant rumble. They looked up to see a huge mountain of earth, the crater on its top belching smoke and flame. 'Quite a sight, eh, Mr Tyler,' said the Doctor. 'An active volcano in England!'

Jenny looked upwards. 'What happened to the Dalek spaceship?'

'Totally destroyed,' said the Doctor with satisfaction. 'I saw it. They were caught in the first up-blast of the explosion.'

Jenny stood looking at the sky. Barbara put an arm round her shoulders. 'It's all right, Jenny, it's over . . .'

'Over,' said Jenny quietly. Barbara saw tears streaming down her cheeks. Suddenly she realised—in all their adventures together, it was the first time she'd ever seen Jenny cry.

14

The Farewell

It took them a very long time to make their way back to London, the riverside, and the building site where the TARDIS had been trapped so long ago. So many people wanted to congratulate them, to hear the story of their adventures and final triumph. But they arrived at last, and now the Doctor stood looking on in quiet satisfaction while a willing gang of Tyler's men cleared the last of the girders away from the TARDIS door.

London was already a very different place from the ruined city in which they'd arrived. There were people in the streets again and even a few cars, and boats on the river. Everywhere was a spirit of hope, the sense of life starting again. London was being reborn before their eyes.

Tyler stood beside the Doctor and looked round at the bustling scene. 'It's a pity Dortmun isn't here to see this. Dortmun and lots of others like him.'

'It's up to you to build their memorial,' said the Doctor quietly. 'A new London, a better Earth. I'm certain you'll succeed.'

The TARDIS was clear at last. Tyler nodded towards it. 'There's your police box, Doctor. And I won't ask questions. As far as I'm concerned you're welcome to every police box in London.'

The Doctor smiled. 'This one will do, thank you.' A sound rang out, a sound once familiar to every Londoner, one that had been missing for a very long time—the chimes of Big Ben. Tyler smiled contentedly.

The Doctor left him listening happily to the chimes, and scrambled down to Susan. She was sitting on a beam of timber, absently toying with her TARDIS key, which hung as usual on a chain around her neck. 'All alone, child?' he asked gently.

Susan smiled. 'I've already let Barbara and Ian into the ship. I was just—thinking.'

The Doctor sat down beside her. 'Hasn't been much time for that recently. I'm afraid you must blame me—I seem to have a nose for trouble.'

Susan gave him an affectionate hug. 'You know I wouldn't blame you for anything, Grandfather.'

They sat in silence for a while. Several times the Doctor seemed about to speak, and then changed his mind. Susan seemed plunged in a fit of abstraction. Suddenly she stood up and said, 'Ah well—' then broke off, wincing.

The Doctor jumped up too. 'Susan, you're hurt . . . '

Susan stood on one foot. 'No, I'm all right. I just trod on a sharp stone.' She held up one shoe to reveal a gaping hole in the bottom. 'The journey to the mines wore them out completely.'

The Doctor took the shoe from her, pursing his lips. 'Dear me. Still it's nothing to worry about. I'll soon mend it for you.'

Susan smiled at him affectionately. The funny thing was that he was quite serious. It was typical of the Doctor that he was quite as willing, and as able to repair a worn-out shoe as he was a damaged spaceship computer. 'It's all right, Doctor, I've got plenty more pairs in the TARDIS.'

The Doctor frowned. 'That reminds me, I'd better go and check up on the ship.' He gave Susan a pat on the head and wandered off, the shoe clutched in his hand.

Susan was still sitting on the beam when David came quietly up to her. He sat beside her, his arm round her shoulders.

'Susan, stay with me,' he pleaded.

'David, I can't! I don't belong on your world or in your time.'

'I love you, Susan. I'm asking you to marry me.'

'I have to stay with grandfather. He's old now, he needs me. Please—don't ask me to choose between you.'

David took a deep breath. 'You told me once you'd never really belonged anywhere. That's what I'm offering you now, Susan. A place and a time of your own.'

Susan stood up and started limping towards the TARDIS. There were tears in her eyes. 'Goodbye, David. I'm all right. I just trod on a nail.' She limped off towards the waiting police box. As she moved away she said quietly to herself 'But I do love you, David. I do . . .'

The Doctor stood at the TARDIS console, still holding Susan's shoe. Behind him Ian and Barbara stood hand in hand. They knew the dilemma the Doctor was facing, but there was nothing they could do to help.

Suddenly the Doctor stood very erect. He put Susan's shoe down carefully, reached for a particular control-switch and slammed it over, hard.

Susan had almost reached the TARDIS when its door closed in her face. She took the key from round her neck and tried to open it. Nothing happened. 'Grandfather,' she screamed. 'Grandfather!'

Suddenly she heard the Doctor's voice. 'Susan, please listen. I've safety-locked the door—you can't get in.'

Inside the TARDIS the Doctor could see Susan's puzzled face looking at him on the scanner. Gently he said, 'All these years I've been taking care of you—and all the time, you really felt you were taking care of me . . .'

He heard Susan's voice. 'But I belong with you . . .'

'Not any more, Susan. Your future is with young David, not with an old buffer like me.' He saw that David had come to join Susan, his arm around her. 'Look after her, David, my boy. Be kind. Work hard both of you. You'll find that life on Earth can be an adventure too.'

For a moment the Doctor's voice faltered, then he recovered himself. 'Now then, both of you, no regrets. And look to the future. Remember, both of you, love's the thing. That's what really counts. Goodbye. One day I'll come back. One day . . . Goodbye . . . '

Susan and David stepped back, as the dematerialisation noise began, and the TARDIS disappeared.

Quietly David said, 'He knew, Susan. He knew you could never leave him. That's why he left you.'

As David took Susan in his arms the TARDIS key slipped from her fingers, and lay disregarded on the ground. Susan made no attempt to pick it up because she knew she wouldn't be needing it again.

Inside the TARDIS the Doctor turned away from the scanner with a sniff. He glared at Ian and Barbara, as if daring them to comment. When they said nothing, his face broke into a smile. 'I'll get over it,' he said briskly. 'Bound to happen one day. Now then, I really must get you two home again. Right place *and* the right time, eh? Let's see what we can do!'

As the Doctor leaned over the console, his fingers moving over the controls, Ian gave Barbara a nudge. 'I wonder where the old boy will land up this time!'

'I'd be willing to bet you it's not Earth,' she whispered.

Through the space time vortex, the TARDIS sped on

its way. The Doctor still had two faithful companions, and many more adventures lay before them.

THE DAY OF THE DALEKS

1

Terror in the Twenty-second Century

Moni sat up and looked around cautiously. The enormous dormitory was packed with sleeping forms, drugged into total exhaustion by hours of brutal physical toil. One or two murmured and twisted and cursed in their sleep. A man screamed, 'No, no, please don't . . .' and then his voice tailed off into the mutterings of a nightmare. Moni saw that it was Soran. He had been beaten by the guards that morning for failing to meet his work-norm. Soran was weakening daily. He wouldn't last much longer.

Somehow the incident seemed to give Moni courage. It was for Soran that he was fighting, Soran and thousands like him, who would die in the work camps from the brutal beatings, or worn out after years of grinding labour, unless . . . unless . . . Moni threw back the coarse blankets and swung his feet to the floor. There was nothing unusual in his being fully dressed. The dormitories weren't heated and most of his fellows slept fully clothed against the night cold. Vaguely Moni remembered having heard of a time when men had special clothes to sleep in—called py-something or other. His mind could scarcely imagine such luxury.

Moni fished his boots from beneath his pillow. He'd put them there automatically the night before. The boots were made of new strong plastic, and in the work camps nothing valuable was safe unless it was within touching distance. Tucking the boots under his arm, Moni moved silently across the room towards the door. His bare feet made no sound on the rough concrete floor.

Once in the compound, he paused in a patch of shadow to pull on the boots, then crept silently along the edge of the outer wall. Taking off his tunic, Moni uncoiled a thin plastic rope from round his waist. He took the crude grappling hook from his pocket, tied it to the rope and swung the grappling hook at the row of spikes on top of the wall. It fell short and landed back at Moni's feet with a metallic scrape. Moni froze in terror. He glanced towards the doorway of the guards' quarters. Surely they must have heard. But there came only the rumble of guttural inhuman speech. The compound was supposed to be patrolled at all times, but the guards were careless and idle. On cold nights like this they kept to their quarters, huddling round the roaring fires in the iron braziers, stuffing down slabs of coarse grey food that their masters provided.

Moni hurled the grapple again, and this time his luck was in. It caught firmly on the spikes and, after testing it with a tug, Moni climbed quickly up the rope, his tunic between his teeth. Once he was on top of the wall it would make a rough pad to protect him from the spikes. Awkwardly he bestrode the wall, pulling the rope up beside him and freeing the grappling hook. He lowered the rope to the other side of the wall, dropped his tunic after it, and then jumped down, landing with a thud that jolted the breath out of him. Quickly he put on his tunic, and hid rope and grappling iron beneath it. He set off swiftly down the endless concrete road through the rubble.

Moni had covered several miles before his luck ran out. He was just turning the corner of one of the many ruined buildings when an enormous hairy hand reached out from the darkness and plucked him off his feet. The hand slammed him against the remains of a brick wall, making him gasp out loud. Moni flinched, as a burning brand was thrust uncomfortably close to his face. As his eyes became accustomed to the light he could just begin to pick out the hulking shape of the creature that had captured him. Nearby was a small campfire with other giant forms huddled round it. Moni cursed his luck. He had run into one of the roving patrols, camping out in the ruins. From the campfire, a guttural voice said, 'Bring!' Moni's captor shambled back towards the fire, dragging Moni after him like a rag doll. Moni let himself hang limp, making no attempt to resist. He had no wish to be torn to pieces. Against human beings he might have stood a chance, but these guards were not human: these were Ogrons.

Thrown sprawling at the feet of the patrol, Moni looked up at the hulking shapes looming over him in the firelight. Often as he had seen them before, the Ogrons never failed to terrify him. Creatures somewhere between gorilla and man, they stood almost seven feet in height with bowed legs, massive chests and long powerful arms that hung almost to the ground. Their faces were perhaps the most awful thing about them: a distorted version of the human face, with flat ape-like nose, small eyes glinting with cruelty, and a massive jaw with long yellow teeth. But the Ogrons had one quality which gave Moni a glimmer of hope, even now: for all their savage ferocity and primitive strength, they were very, very stupid.

Moni scrambled to his feet. Forcing himself to speak slowly and calmly, he said, 'I am a section leader of Work Camp Three. I am needed to replace a section leader of Work Camp Four, who has been taken ill.' He looked round the circle of Ogrons to see if his story was being believed. The Ogrons looked at him impassively. Did they believe him? Had they even understood what he was saying? In the same calm, flat voice Moni said, 'The order for my transfer came direct from your masters. If I am delayed they will be very angry. They will be angry with *you*.'

This time his words had some effect. It was almost comic to see the looks of alarm on the brutal Ogron faces. The one thing which could strike fear to the hearts of these terrifying creatures was the mention of the even more fearsome beings who were their masters.

The leading Ogron gestured into the darkness with a massive hairy paw. 'You go. Go quickly.' Moni turned and ran into the darkness.

It took him another hour of hard, dangerous travel before he reached his destination. He crossed a patch of waste ground. The moonlight showed weeds flourishing over the shattered foundations of a house. Shifting the concealing rubble, Moni found and then lifted a hidden trap-door and dropped down into the darkness. He landed at the head of a still-intact flight of steps. Cautiously he moved down them until his eyes picked out a little patch of light at the bottom. It was shining beneath the edge of a closed door. Moni moved quietly to the door and rapped out a complicated series of knocks. After a moment the door creaked open. Boaz stood facing him, blaster in hand. 'All right, Boaz, it's me,' said Moni.

Boaz's voice showed the strain he was feeling. 'You're late . . . we didn't know—'

Moni interrupted him. 'Ran straight into an Ogron patrol. Managed to talk my way out of it. The others here?' Boaz nodded, and Moni followed him into the cellar.

Anat and Shura were huddled round the charcoal fire that blazed in a makeshift brazier. Moni glanced quickly round the room. It was his first visit to the HQ of this particular cell, but they were all much the same. In every city there were hidden rooms like this. Places to store arms and food. Places to meet and talk and plan. Places where men and women met with one burning desire in common—to take back their planet from the alien beings who had stolen it.

Patrolling Ogrons carried out an unending search for these hide-outs. Sometimes they found one: Ogron boots kicked in the door and the little group of plotters inside were ruthlessly destroyed. But for every cell that was wiped out, another and still another sprang up to replace it.

Moni looked round at the three eager faces. Boaz, dark, scowling and intense; fiercely brave, but too highly strung, too ready to act without thinking. Shura, the youngest, full of a fiery idealism. Finally, he looked at the girl, Anat. Slim, dark and wiry, with close-cropped hair, Anat was still beautiful, in spite of the rough work-clothes she was wearing. Here was the real leader, Moni thought, with her fierce courage, a passionate hatred of the enemy, and cunning and caution that made her wait until the best moment to strike.

Anat spoke first. 'Something's happening, Moni. What is it? You wouldn't have called this meeting without good reason. We don't often have the honour of meeting one of the Central Committee!'

Brisk and to the point as always, thought Moni approvingly. He said, 'You're right, of course, Anat. Something has happened. Something big, and it involves you all.' He paused for a moment, collecting his thoughts. 'You know the kind of thing we've been doing up till now—isolated bits of sabotage, sometimes big, sometimes small. But pinpricks, no more than that.'

Boaz burst out: 'Pinpricks? Is that what we've been fighting and dying for? As long as we go on hitting them, at least they know they haven't beaten us.'

Anat put a restraining hand on his arm, 'Let him talk, Boaz. He knows the value of our work.'

'Of course,' said Moni quickly, 'any act of resistance is valuable in itself but we can't go on for ever like this. They can't stop us but we can't really hurt them. We're all losing sight of the big objective because we're too concerned with the day-to-day struggle!'

Anat said, 'Is there an alternative?'

Moni nodded. 'There may be—now. The scientists and historians of the Central Committee have come up with a plan. It's dangerous, maybe suicidal, but it offers a chance to free the entire planet. It calls for a special mission, carried out by just a handful of us. I have recommended you three for the final assault team—that is, assuming you all three volunteer.'

Anat leaned forward urgently, the glow from the fire illuminating her thin face. 'We volunteer. All of us. You know that without asking. Now, tell us the plan.'

Moni paused for a moment looking round at their eager faces. He might well be about to send them all to their deaths. He said, 'I can only give you a brief outline now. Like the rest of you, I have to be back in camp before morning. But I can tell you this much: we want to attempt to send you back through time . . .'

The Controller of Earth Sector One pushed aside the remains of an excellent meal. Appreciatively he drained the last of his drink—real wine in a real china cup! Few men on Earth enjoyed such luxury in these times. He repressed a twinge of unease at the thought of those of his fellow humans who were less fortunate, those in the work camps. They would be draining their bowls of gruel about now, desperately licking the bowls clean to see that not a scrap of food was wasted . . . Before leaving the room the Controller paused before a mirror, smoothing back his thinning hair and adjusting the tunic on his shoulders. More luxury, he thought. The same basic tunic as the others, of course, but cloth! Real cloth, none of your plastic! He picked up the sheaf of reports he had been working on through dinner, and sighed. He knew how much he was envied and hated. People didn't realise that his rank had its duties too. The constant unremitting work. And now he had to make his report to Them. Something They wouldn't care to hear, what's more.

Bracing himself, the Controller left his private dining room and strode along the endless corridors of Central Control. Scurrying human slave workers made way for him deferentially. But it was a different story when he reached the doorway leading to the innermost HQ. The door was flanked by Ogron guards, and as he tried to enter, one of them shoved him away with a hairy paw. The Controller strove to retain his dignity.

'You know who I am. Chief Controller of this entire sector. You will show me the respect I am entitled to.' The Ogron looked at him impassively, and the Controller's shoulders drooped in defeat. He knew that the Ogron saw him as just another human. A slave, like all humans. He said dully, 'You don't understand. I must make a most important report—to your masters.' Unconsciously copying the tactics of Moni the night before, the Controller added, 'They will be angry if you do not let me enter.'

The Ogron grunted, 'You—wait!' Leaving its fellow to guard the Controller, it went inside. After a moment it returned and said, 'Come now.'

The Controller went through into the antechamber and then waited. Silently a panel slid open in front of him and he entered the inner chamber.

It was a small, completely bare room with a raised ramp at one end. After a moment another wall-panel slid open and a gleaming metallic creature glided through. Its eye-stalk swung round to look at the Controller, who bowed respectfully. This, after all, was the Black Dalek, one of the supreme rulers of the planet Earth in the twenty-second century.

In its grating metallic voice, the Black Dalek said, 'Report!'

The Controller tried to restrain the quaver of terror in

his voice. 'I have been studying the recent reports of resistance activity. It has reached a peak in recent weeks. I think they are planning some major operation against you.'

The Black Dalek said, 'The humans you refer to as the resistance are criminals. They are enemies of the Daleks. You will find and destroy them.'

The Controller sighed. It was always the same: the flat, toneless command to do the impossible. The Daleks seemed to have no conception of the courage and cunning of the resistance, nor, for that matter, of the lumbering stupidity of the Ogrons they expected to catch them. He struggled on. 'There has been one particular feature of the recent wave of activity. Several recent thefts have involved papers or equipment dealing with your research into time travel.'

For a moment the Black Dalek did not reply. When it spoke, its grating voice seemed to be pitched a few degrees higher. The Controller shuddered. This, he knew, was a sign of anger. The Dalek said, 'We shall maintain a continuous scan upon the Time Vortex. If the humans attempt to travel in time, we shall track them down and destroy them.' The Black Dalek's voice rose higher still, as it chanted the threat of destruction that was the Daleks only creed: 'They are enemies of the Daleks. All enemies of the Daleks must be destroyed. Exterminate them! Exterminate them! Exterminate them!'

2

The Man Who Saw a Ghost

Suddenly, in the clump of trees that huddled close to the side of Austerly House, an owl hooted. The UNIT sentry swung round, his Sterling sub-machine gun at the ready. Then he went on with his lonely patrol, grinning at his own nervousness. Mind you, he thought, a night like this was enough to make anyone jumpy: the wind howled eerily in the trees, black clouds streaked past the full moon, so that pitch darkness alternated with bright moonlight. And all the time, he heard the mysterious night noises of the countryside. The sentry was a Londoner. He would have been far happier guarding somewhere where there was a bit of life—pavements and street lights and people passing by.

He marched along the gravel path that bordered the house. He glanced up at the rows of windows. All dark—except for one, where light showed through a gap in the curtains of the ground-floor study. Nobody could say the old boy wasn't a worker, thought the sentry. Past midnight and still at it. The sentry remembered what the Brigadier had said at the briefing meeting.

'The international situation has taken an ugly turn. There is a very real possibility that the events in the Near East will escalate into a full-scale conflict. We may well be on the verge of World War Three. The peace of the world depends on the success of the coming conference. And the success of that conference depends on one man—Sir Reginald Styles. His safety is in your hands.'

The peace of the world . . . thought the sentry. It was a big responsibility for one tall, grey-haired old man. No wonder the old boy was a bit tetchy. Still, Sir Reginald would be safe enough with sentries all round the house, more at the main gate, and patrols in the grounds. With a final glance at the study window, the sentry turned and began to retrace his steps.

As he disappeared from view round the corner of the building, there was a curious shimmering in the air. Suddenly a man appeared. One moment he wasn't there, the next he was. He wore dark combat clothing—tunic, trousers, and boots. A massive hand-gun was holstered at his side. He had no badges or military insignia, but looked like a soldier . . . perhaps some kind of irregular, a commando or a guerilla.

The man flattened himself against the side of the building. Then he began to edge cautiously towards the lighted French windows of the study.

Inside the study all was silent except for the ticking of the clock and the scratching of Sir Reginald's pen. He was preparing the notes for his speech at the coming conference. 'It is therefore vital,' he wrote, 'that the Chinese Government accepts the assurances . . .'

Sir Reginald stopped writing and looked up. Had there been something at the window? A tapping, a scratching, as if the latch was being slid back? No, there was nothing. It was all this security nonsense making him jumpy. How could he work with soldiers clumping round the house? He began writing again. '. . . accepts the assurances of good faith . . .'

The sound came again. Sir Reginald stood up . . . maybe one of the sentries was trying the window. Sir Reginald called, 'Who is it? Who's there?' No answer. He strode to the French windows and threw them open.

Facing him was a youngish man in some kind of guerilla uniform. The man was holding an enormous pistol, trained straight at Sir Reginald's head. It was many years since Sir Reginald had been a soldier, but the old reflexes still worked. He flung himself upon the man, dragging down the gun arm. He hung on desperately as the guerilla thrust him back into the room. The two men reeled about, sending the lamp crashing from the desk. They tripped and fell over a chair, smashing it beneath them. Sir Reginald hung on to his attacker's gun arm with both hands, desperately trying to get control of the weapon. There could only be one end to the unequal struggle: Sir Reginald was well in his sixties, the guerilla young and strong. Pinning the old man beneath him, the guerilla slowly brought his gun round to aim at his victim's head. Despite all his efforts, Sir Reginald saw the muzzle of the gun pointing straight at him. He could see and feel everything with a strange clarity, as if it were happening in slow motion. The circle of the gun barrel looked enormous. Above it he could see the guerilla's face twisted with savage hatred. He could even see the man's knuckles begin to whiten as his finger tightened on the trigger. He wrenched at the guerilla's sinewy wrist with both hands, but it was as firm as a rock. His hands were slipping. Then, incredibly they were empty. The whole figure of his opponent shimmered, then vanished. As the study door was flung open Sir Reginald found himself flat on his back wrestling with thin air.

A UNIT Corporal helped Sir Reginald to his feet: he was trembling with shock. Miss Paget, his secretary, went to him. 'Sir Reginald, what happened? Are you all right?'

Sir Reginald looked at her wildly. 'Attacked me . . . he attacked me. Tried to kill me!'

One of the patrolling sentries stood outside the French windows. The Corporal rapped, 'See anyone?'

The sentry shook his head. 'Came running when I heard the noise, Corp. No one came through there.'

The corporal turned back to Sir Reginald. 'Who attacked you, sir? Who did you see?'

Sir Reginald said slowly: 'He vanished . . . disappeared into thin air . . . like a ghost . . .'

Brigadier Alastair Lethbridge-Stewart swung his highly polished boots onto the top of his desk, tucked the telephone receiver under his chin, and waited for the Minister to stop yammering in his ear.

The Brigadier glanced at the headlines on the front page of *The Times*: 'NEAR EAST CRISIS—WAR LOOMS.' If it happened he'd apply to be posted back to his regiment. It would be nice to wear the kilt again. The Brigadier realised that the voice in his ear had stopped. He said, 'Er, quite, sir. Quite.' The yammering started up again. The Brigadier sighed, interrupting politely but firmly.

'I have the reports in front of me now, sir. The sentry outside the house heard sounds of struggle and ran towards the French windows. The sentry inside the house also heard the noise and ran through the study door. Except for Sir Reginald himself, the study was empty.'

There was a further outburst on the other end of the phone. The Brigadier replied, 'No, sir, I was not proposing to ignore the matter!' Since he had in fact been proposing to do exactly that, he had to pause and rack his brains for a moment before going on. Then inspiration came.

'As a matter of fact, sir,' said the Brigadier, lying magnificently, 'I was about to pass the matter over to one of my top men.' The Brigadier allowed a hint of reproach to creep into his voice—'I was just on my way to brief him when you called . . .'

Inside the laboratory of the Scientific Adviser to UNIT everything was still. Mysterious tangles of elaborate equipment straggled over the benches. The solid blue shape of an old police box stood incongruously in one corner. Suddenly the police box began to give out the most agonising groaning sound. It vibrated, shaking the whole laboratory and rattling the retorts and test tubes. The groaning reached a peak, there was a loud bang, the door of the police box burst open, and a tall, lean man shot out of the police box in a cloud of smoke. He slammed the door behind him, cursing fluently in an obscure Martian dialect.

The laboratory door opened. A very small, very pretty girl came in. Quite unsurprised, she slapped the coughing Doctor on the back, gave him a glass of water, and opened the laboratory window to let out the smoke.

'Foiled again, Doctor?' asked Jo Grant sympathetically.

The Doctor nodded, sipping his water gloomily. 'It's maddening. I'm so nearly there. If I could only cut out their primary override on the dematerialisation circuit.' He picked up a sheaf of notes and studied them gloomily.

Jo looked at him affectionately. Sometimes the Doctor seemed to think she understood the most difficult scientific theories as easily as he did himself. At other times he had an infuriating habit of carefully explaining that two and two made four.

When she had first joined UNIT, Jo Grant had assumed that the Doctor's story of travelling in Time and Space in a police box called the TARDIS (the initials stood for 'Time and Relative Dimensions in Space') was some kind of joke. Recent experiences had changed all that. The TARDIS, temporarily 'grounded' by decree of the Doctor's mysterious superiors, the Time Lords, had suddenly started working again, and Jo had found herself caught up in adventure on another planet in the distant future. With this in mind, she said, 'I thought the TARDIS was working again!'

'My dear Jo, the TARDIS was being operated by

remote control by the Time Lords . . . just because they wanted me to do their dirty work for them!'

'But if it works for them—' Jo persisted.

'I don't want it to work for them,' said the Doctor irritably, 'I want it to work for me. No one's going to use me as an interplanetary puppet.'

Suddenly, an inspiration seemed to strike him. 'Of course! Now why didn't I think of that earlier.'

Leaping up, the Doctor dashed back inside the TARDIS. Through its open doors Jo could see that he was bent over the central control column, making careful adjustments to the instruments. As he did so the laboratory door opened. Jo looked up and to her utter astonishment saw the Doctor standing in the doorway.

Amazed, she looked back inside the TARDIS. There was the Doctor still bending over the console. She looked back at the door. There was the Doctor standing looking at her. But there was an even bigger shock to come. Another figure appeared from behind the Doctor. She was looking at herself.

The two Jo Grants looked at each other in mutual astonishment. Then the Doctor, the one in the doorway, spoke.

'Good grief! Oh yes . . . yes, of course. I remember now.' He gave Jo his familiar charming smile. But she could only gaze back at him thunderstruck, as he said reassuringly, 'Now don't worry, my dear. I know you're alarmed, but . . .'

He was interrupted by the appearance of the Doctor from inside the TARDIS. But this Doctor shared none of Jo's astonishment. He looked at his other self with a sort of mild curiosity. 'Oh no! What are *you* doing here?'

The new arrival rubbed his chin and said apologetically, 'Don't worry, I'm not here . . . that is. . . well in a sense I am here, but you're not there. It's all a bit complicated to explain . . .'

The Doctor cut his other self short. 'Well, this

won't do at all, will it? Can't have two of us running about.'

'Don't worry, old chap,' said the second Doctor cheerily. 'It'll all be—'

And then he vanished in mid-sentence, the second Jo Grant with him. The remaining Doctor gave a satisfied nod, and headed back inside the TARDIS.

'Now just a minute, Doctor,' Jo protested. 'What was that all about?'

'I'm afraid I must have overloaded the temporal circuitry, Jo. Must have produced a localised distortion.'

Jo looked at him, still baffled. The Doctor chuckled. 'Very funny thing, Time. Once you start tampering with it, the oddest things happen.'

Jo said, 'But there was another me—and another you. Where did they go?'

'Back into their own time stream, of course. Or do I mean forward?'

Jo made a final protest. 'But Doctor . . .'

The Doctor waved her aside reassuringly. 'Don't worry, my dear. Just a freak effect. Now I really must get on.'

He was just about to re-enter the TARDIS when the door opened once more. Jo looked up in alarm, but this time it was only the Brigadier.

'So there you are, Doctor. I need your help.'

Jo could see that the Doctor was not very pleased by this new interruption. She braced herself for the inevitable clash.

'I'm sorry, Brigadier,' said the Doctor curtly. 'I happen to be extremely busy.'

'So am I, Doctor. Now then, you've heard of Sir Reginald Styles?'

'No,' said the Doctor flatly. He picked up his notes and began to study them.

Jo said helpfully, 'Isn't he the chief British representative at the United Nations?'

'That's right, Miss Grant. And he's the key man in the latest summit conference.'

The Doctor looked up. 'My dear Brigadier, I'm a scientist, not a politician.'

With an exasperated sigh the Brigadier retorted, 'If you weren't always tinkering with that wretched contraption of yours, perhaps you'd realise just how bad the international situation has become.'

'You humans are always squabbling over something,' remarked the Doctor pointedly.

'This particular squabble looks very like ending up in a Third World War.'

There was real anxiety in the Brigadier's voice. The Doctor's attitude changed at once. 'As bad as that, old chap?'

The Brigadier sank down on to a laboratory stool. 'The whole thing flared up in the Near East. But really it's a sort of three-cornered quarrel between Russia, America, and China. Spheres of influence, that sort of thing.'

'And Britain arranged for this summit conference,' said Jo, 'so that the three big powers could meet and sort it all out.'

'Exactly, Miss Grant. But at the last moment the Chinese refused to attend. Without them the conference can't even start. Sir Reginald Styles is due to fly to Peking in a few hours' time. The Chinese trust him. There's just a chance he may be able to persuade them to change their minds.'

Tossing aside his sheaf of notes, the Doctor said, 'All right, Brigadier. You've convinced me the situation's serious. Where do I come in?'

'Styles has started acting oddly. Last night he claimed someone tried to kill him at his home. This morning he denies the whole thing. You see the problem, Doctor. If Styles doesn't fly to Peking, the conference may fail. But how can we let him go if he's cracking up?'

'Suppose he isn't cracking up?' said Jo. 'Suppose his story's true?'

'That's just it. According to my men, no one was there. No one could have been there.'

Briefly, the Brigadier recounted the events of the previous night.

The Doctor looked thoughtful. 'From what you say of Styles, he's not the type to invent or imagine things. So obviously something happened. The question is what? Did Styles say anything more—last night, I mean?'

The Brigadier shrugged. 'Apparently he just babbled something about a ghost.'

In a clearing in the woods near Austerly House there was a sudden shimmering and distortion in the air. Then a man appeared! One moment he wasn't there, the next he was. He wore the tough, serviceable clothes of a guerilla, and there was a massive hand-gun holstered at his side.

The man looked swiftly around him. He heard movement nearby, and with a swift, practised movement flung himself to the ground, rolling into the cover of a patch of bracken. Seconds later the boots of a UNIT patrol passed within inches of his head. When the patrol had gone on its way, the man got to his feet. He began to move cautiously through the trees towards the house. Then, directly ahead of him, came another shimmering in the air. Three huge forms materialised, blocking his path. The guerilla's mind filled with panic. Ogrons! They had pursued him from his own time.

Abandoning any attempt at silence, the guerilla turned and ran away from the direction of the house. He heard the sound of the pursuing Ogrons as they crashed through the woods behind him. He knew he could outrun them, at least for a while. Their huge hulk made them slow and clumsy. But he knew, too, that the Ogron's endurance was almost limitless. When he was utterly worn out and breathless they would still be lumbering after him. And if they caught him . . . instant death—if he was lucky; otherwise, capture, and a return to his own time zone for interrogation by the Daleks.

The guerilla burst from the edge of the woods into open park land. The going was easier here. Easier too, for his pursuers. They were still behind him. Just ahead a high wall marked the edge of the grounds. With a desperate spurt of speed he ran towards it. The three Ogrons appeared behind him in close pursuit.

Meanwhile a third group had joined the chase. Sergeant Benton of UNIT had been outraged to have the peace of a routine patrol disturbed by what sounded like a herd of elephants crashing through the woods. He led his patrol at a fast trot towards the sound. As they ran they unslung their Sterling sub-machine guns.

The fleeing guerilla reached the wall and hurled himself at the top in a desperate, scrabbling leap. For a moment he hung by his hands from the top of the wall, then, slowly and painfully, managed to heave himself over.

Benton and his patrol emerged from the woods just in time to see the guerilla drop down out of sight. They watched in amazement as the pursuing Ogrons swarmed over the wall with ape-like ease and also disappeared from view. Benton yelled, 'After them!' adding to himself, 'Whatever they are.' The UNIT patrol sprinted for the wall and began to scale it.

The guerilla was panting and gasping now, beginning to slow down. Getting over the wall had cost him time, and the Ogrons were very close. Across the field in front of him he could see a fenced-off strip of land running parallel to the road. Two steel rails ran along the centre of it. Of course—a railway! Some primitive twentieth-century transport system. Not far away the rails disappeared into a dark archway. A tunnel. He could hide in its darkness, use the time transmitter and get back to his own time. He was almost within reach of the tunnel mouth when his foot twisted on a stone. He crashed to the ground, half-stunned.

With a savage roar of triumph the pursuing Ogrons were upon him. He struggled to rise but his leg gave way beneath him. The huge hairy hands of the Ogrons reached out for him and a massive blow smashed him to the ground.

Benton and his patrol came running up. 'Give 'em a warning shot!' snapped Benton. A burst of machine-gun fire rattled over the Ogrons' heads. One of the Ogrons drew the strange, massive pistol from the holster at its side and fired back. There was a sharp electronic buzz, and the man next to Sergeant Benton simply disintegrated. He vanished, as though his whole being had exploded into fragments.

'Take cover!' yelled Benton, and the UNIT soldiers hurled themselves to the ground, rolling into whatever shelter they could find. A burst of fire hammered into the Ogrons. The creatures staggered under the impact of the bullets but did not fall. At a sign from their leader they fled into the darkness of the tunnel mouth, leaving the crumpled form of their prisoner behind them.

The UNIT patrol dashed up to the tunnel. 'One of you look after him,' ordered Benton, indicating the unconscious guerilla. 'You two, cover the other end of that tunnel. Whatever those things are, we've got them bottled up.' Cautiously, with guns at the ready, Benton and his men advanced into the blackness of the tunnel.

3

The Vanishing Guerilla

In Sir Reginald's study at Austerly House the Doctor, the Brigadier, and Jo Grant were hearing an account of the events of the previous night. Miss Paget, Sir Reginald's secretary, was a thin, sharp-featured woman in her fifties, the perfect picture of the top-ranking senior secretary. It was obvious that she was devoted to Sir Reginald, and had been very shaken by his strange behaviour.

'Please go on, Miss Paget,' said the Doctor in his most reassuring voice.

'I think that's everything, really. Sir Reginald *said* someone attacked him. But there just wasn't anyone there.'

'And he definitely used the word "ghost"?'

'Oh yes. I was quite struck by it. You see he's always been very scornful of—'

Miss Paget stopped talking as though she'd been switched off. Sir Reginald marched into the room. He looked round angrily. 'What's going on here?'

'These gentlemen are from UNIT,' said Miss Paget.

'And who asked them to come here? We've got enough soldiers cluttering up the place as it is.'

Miss Paget's voice was shaky but determined. 'I asked them, Sir Reginald. Because of what happened last night.'

'Nothing happened last night,' said Styles icily.

Crushed, Miss Paget was silent. The Brigadier said

firmly, 'there does appear to have been *some* sort of incident, Sir Reginald.'

Sir Reginald was obviously not used to being contradicted. He looked as if he might explode at any moment.

Tactfully, Jo Grant said, 'Perhaps if *you* could tell us what really happened, Sir Reginald?' She gave him her most charming smile.

Sir Reginald was too well mannered to storm at what appeared to be a mere child. Wearily he said, 'I was working late—must have nodded off at my desk. I knocked over the lamp, scattered all my papers. I woke up a little confused. I was picking up my papers when Miss Paget and the sentry came in. All a lot of fuss about nothing.'

Sir Reginald wasn't used to lying and he did it very badly. Jo couldn't help feeling sorry for him as he gazed fiercely around, trying to hang on to his dignity. The Doctor, meanwhile, had wandered over to the French windows and seemed to be studying the pattern of the carpet. The Brigadier persisted, 'But you did mention ghosts, Sir Reginald.'

'Did I? Must have been having a bit of a nightmare.'

The Doctor said gently, 'What about these marks here?' He pointed downward, 'Muddy feet, Sir Reginald. Someone was here.'

'Must have been the sentry.'

The Doctor shook his head. 'According to Miss Paget the outside sentry didn't come into the room.'

Sir Reginald blustered, 'Are you accusing me of lying, sir?'

Hastily the Brigadier cut in, 'You've obviously been under a good deal of strain, sir. Were you feeling at all unwell last night?'

Sir Reginald snapped. 'Felt and feel perfectly well. Now, if you'll excuse me, Brigadier, I really can't afford to waste any more time.' He turned to Miss Paget.

'Where's that car? I'm due at the airport in twenty minutes.'

'It's waiting for you now, sir.'

Jo saw the Brigadier look quickly at the Doctor. She sensed the unspoken question. The Doctor said, 'Then we mustn't detain you further, Sir Reginald. Allow me to wish you every success in your mission.'

For a moment Sir Reginald seemed taken aback. Then with a brief nod of farewell he turned and left the room, Miss Paget scuttling behind him. Captain Yates, the Brigadier's number two, appeared in the doorway. 'Call for you on the RT, sir. Sergeant Benton.'

As the Brigadier went out into the hall, Jo turned to the Doctor. 'What was all that about? Something did happen last night, didn't it?'

The Doctor nodded.

'Then why did Sir Reginald say that it didn't?'

'My dear Jo,' said the Doctor gently, 'whatever happened was so extraordinary that Sir Reginald can't believe it. He thinks he's been having hallucinations.'

'So why doesn't he admit it?'

The Doctor sighed. 'If you were about to begin an important mission would you want to admit you'd been seeing things?'

'I see,' said Jo brightly. 'So that's why you pretended to believe him.'

'Nothing else to be done. He's been shaken up, but he's still perfectly capable. And at the moment this little planet of yours needs his talents very badly.'

The Brigadier appeared in the doorway. 'Doctor, Miss Grant, will you come with me, please? There's been some kind of shooting incident just outside the grounds.'

As Jo, the Doctor and the Brigadier came down the steps at the front of Austerly House they saw Sir Reginald's limousine drawing away. The Brigadier looked after the car for a moment, strain and anxiety plain on his face. Then he bustled Jo and the Doctor into the waiting jeep. Captain Yates started the engine and they shot off, gravel spurting from beneath their wheels.

Five minutes fast driving brought them to the road near the railway tunnel. An anxious-looking Sergeant Benton was waiting for them.

'Morning, Sergeant Benton,' said Jo cheerily. But Benton was too worried to give her more than a quick nod.

'This way, sir,' he said, and led them across the fields to the tunnel.

On the way he told his story to the extremely sceptical Brigadier. Eventually the Brigadier interrupted, 'Let me see if I've got it straight, Benton. This chap appeared from nowhere, and these other—creatures were chasing him?'

Benton said, 'That's right, sir. Sort of ape-like they were. Like stone-age men, or gorillas.'

'I see. Gorillas wearing clothes and carrying guns?' drawled the Brigadier.

Benton nodded dumbly.

'Then where the blazes are they, Sergeant Benton? You said you had them trapped in the tunnel. Presumably you captured or killed them all?'

Benton swallowed hard. 'Well no, sir. We had men going in from both ends. The two patrols bumped into each other. The tunnel was empty.'

'You saw them go in, you sealed off both ends, and the tunnel was empty?' said the Brigadier incredulously.

Again Benton nodded. 'Some kind of trap-door,' said the Brigadier hopefully. 'Maybe a secret passage?'

Benton shook his head. 'We checked, sir. Every inch. It's just a plain, ordinary railway tunnel. Not even used any more. This line was shut down years ago.'

The Doctor was bending over the unconscious man in guerilla's clothes. 'This chap's in a pretty bad way. Concussion, I think. He should be in hospital.'

'Ambulance is already on it's way, Doctor,' said

Benton. 'We'll get him to the UNIT sickbay.

The Brigadier picked up the strange-looking gun lying by the guerilla's side. 'What do you make of this, Doctor?'

The Doctor examined it curiously. 'It's a new one on me, Brigadier. But at the moment I'm rather more interested in this. It was hidden inside his tunic.'

The Doctor held out a small black box with control knobs set into the top. Jo thought it looked like a rather superior transistor radio.

'Some kind of signalling device?' suggested the Brigadier.

The Doctor shook his head. 'As a matter of fact, Brigadier, I think it's a rather primitive form of time machine.'

There was the rhythmic blare of a siren, and they saw a UNIT ambulance driving along the road. It stopped. Two men jumped out carrying a stretcher. The Brigadier turned to Sergeant Benton. 'See him into the ambulance, Sergeant. You'd better travel with him. Take a couple of men with you. I want him kept under constant guard.'

Benton saluted, waved over the ambulance men, then started to transfer the wounded guerilla to the vehicle. The man was muttering and groaning as they lifted him on to the stretcher.

'Do you think he'll be all right, Doctor?' asked Jo.

The Doctor was still absorbed in the strange black box. 'Oh I think so, Jo.'

'As soon as he recovers consciousness,' said the Brigadier grimly, 'he'll have quite a few explanations to make.'

The Doctor looked up. 'No doubt. Meanwhile, we've found two very interesting clues. That gun of his, and this machine. Let's get back to the laboratory, Jo. I think I'd like to run one or two tests . . .'

The office of the Controller of Earth Sector One was not a pleasant or comfortable place, just bare gleaming metal walls and floor, and a plain functional desk. But to the Controller himself it was evidence of his power and rank. Few humans enjoyed such space and luxury. But after all, he reminded himself, he was the supreme authority in that part of Earth once known as England. Supreme after the Daleks, of course . . .

Coldly, the Controller studied the Ogron guard. There was a cutting edge in his voice when he spoke. 'You have failed in your mission.'

The Ogron shook his head vigorously. There was almost a tremor in the thick guttural voice as it replied. Ogrons could master human speech only with difficulty, and their vocabulary were very small.

The Ogron growled, 'No, Controller, we did not fail. We found the enemy and destroyed him.'

'You were told to capture him alive. He was needed for interrogation.'

'Human soldiers came. We had to return to this time zone.'

Wearily, the Controller wondered if the Ogron was telling the truth. The creatures were so savage that it was difficult to persuade them to take prisoners. Their instinct was to kill anyone they got their hands on.

'Then you are sure the rebel was dead? If the twentieth-century humans captured him alive, he could tell them much.'

Therc was a flicker of fear in the Ogron's tiny red eyes. It grunted, 'The enemy is dead. We killed him.'

The Controller rose from behind his desk. 'I want an intensified effort by all your patrols. These rebellious criminals must be found and destroyed! If not—the Daleks will be displeased. They will punish you. Now go!'

The Ogron lumbered from the room. The Controller sighed. For years now the criminal rebels—guerillas they called themselves—had been resisting the rule of the Daleks. Never more than a pitiful handful of them. Yet, in a way, that handful seemed immortal. As soon as one group of resistance fighters were tracked down, another sprang up. With their pitifully tiny resources, their cellar hide-outs and their home-made weapons, they took on all the might of the Dalek technology. Naturally, the rebels could never win. But it also seemed they could never lose. The Controller was forced almost to admire his fellow humans. They were wrong, of course. Hopelessly misguided. But such courage! Such persistance and cunning in the face of impossible odds! With qualities like these it was easy to see why the race of Man had once been a great one. The Controller sighed again. But ultimately it was all for nothing. Eventually the rebels would lose the unequal fight. They would suffer the fate of everyone who opposed the Daleks. They would be exterminated.

With a deliberate effort the Controller turned his attention back to his duties. The production figures for Work Camp Three were below the norm. If they did not improve the Daleks would be angry. The Controller began to study the sheaf of production reports on his desk.

As the Brigadier strode into the UNIT laboratory he was astonished to see Jo Grant hauling a large stuffed dummy across the laboratory. She propped it up in a chair at the far end of the room and stood back, looking at her work in satisfaction.

'Bit early for Guy Fawkes' Night, Miss Grant,' said the Brigadier.

Jo turned at the sound of his voice. 'The Doctor wanted it. Don't ask me why. How's that poor man you found?'

The Brigadier shrugged. 'Benton's with him in sickbay now. Chap's still out cold, apparently. Will be for some time.'

The Doctor emerged from the TARDIS, the guerilla's gun in one hand, the black box in the other. 'Then we'll just have to wait till he wakes up, won't we?' His tone was brisk and cheerful. Jo saw that he was thoroughly enjoying the task of grappling with this new problem. She couldn't help feeling glad that he'd found something to take his mind off the endless and seemingly hopeless struggle to get the TARDIS working again.

'Splendid, Jo. Just what I wanted. Most life-like, isn't it, Brigadier?'

The Brigadier studied the drooping dummy without enthusiasm. 'Yes, very nice. May I ask what it's in aid of?'

'I thought you might like a little practical demonstration. Now then, if you'll all step this way.'

The Doctor led them to a position by the door. At the opposite end of the laboratory, the dummy slumped grotesquely in its chair. The body was made from an old pair of army denims stuffed with newspapers. It had a crude grinning face on the pillowcase with lipstick.

'Now, Jo, Brigadier,' said the Doctor, 'I think you'd better stand behind me—just in case.' He raised the guerilla's gun, and aimed it at the dummy.

'Steady on, Doctor,' said the Brigadier hurriedly. 'Just in case of what exactly?'

The Doctor looked over his shoulder. 'In case I've mistimed the setting, of course. In which case we might lose most of the wall.'

The Brigadier was outraged. 'Now just a moment! This building happens to be Government prop—'

But he was already too late. The Doctor had resumed his aim and activated some kind of trigger. There was a high-pitched electronic buzz. Chair and dummy simply vanished! The Doctor gave a satisfied nod.

The Brigadier walked slowly to the other end of the laboratory. There was absolutely no sign of either chair or dummy. He looked at the gun in the Doctor's hand. 'What the blazes is that thing, Doctor?'

The Doctor put the gun down on a laboratory bench.

'Quite an effective little weapon, isn't it?'

The Brigadier looked grim. 'According to Benton those ape-creatures were carrying exactly the same kind of weapon. He lost one of his men. No trace of the body afterwards.'

The Brigadier's voice was angry. Jo knew how much he worried about the safety of the men under his command. To lose even one soldier was a considerable blow.

Gingerly, Jo picked up the alien weapon. It looked something like a cross between a revolver and a blunderbuss. It was heavy, and she needed two hands to hold it.

'What is it, exactly, Doctor?' she asked. 'I mean, how does it work?'

'Basically it's a form of ultrasonic disintegrator.'

Jo tried to translate the Doctor's reply into something she could understand. 'You mean it's some kind of ray-gun?'

The Doctor took a deep breath. 'Er, well, yes, Jo. Sort of . . . The point is, it's an extremely sophisticated weapon. Far more advanced than anything yet developed on Earth. Er—I don't think you'd better point it like that.'

Jo realised that she was aiming the gun straight at the Brigadier. Hastily she put it back on the bench.

The Brigadier said, 'You say it wasn't made on Earth? You mean it came from another planet?'

The Doctor shook his head. 'I've just done a metallurgical analysis: it proved conclusively that the metal from which this gun was made was mined here on Earth.'

Jo was puzzled. 'But you said it couldn't have been made on Earth.'

'Not at the present time, Jo.'

'Kindly stop talking in riddles, Doctor,' said the Brigadier irritably.

The Doctor walked to the other end of the bench and picked up the black box. 'Do you believe in ghosts, Brigadier?'

'Do let's be serious.'

'I am serious, I assure you. Perhaps I used the wrong word: not so much ghosts as apparitions—creatures that appear and disappear.' He studied the box, turning it round in his hands. 'You see we usually think of ghosts as coming from the past. But what about ghosts from the future?' He looked from Jo to the Brigadier, smiling gently at the sight of their baffled faces.

Jo said slowly, 'You said that thing was some kind of time machine . . .'

The Doctor picked up the little machine and began fiddling with the controls. 'That's right. But I think it must have been damaged when the man fell. I can't seem to get it to . . .'

But even as the Doctor spoke, the machine seemed to come to life. It gave a sort of low him. A curious shimmering effect filled the air around it.

The Doctor shouted, 'Good grief, it's working! Stand back both of you!' Frantically he jabbed at the control knobs.

In the UNIT sickbay not far away Sergeant Benton sat beside the unconscious guerilla's bed. The guerilla, now wearing a pair of hospital pyjamas, was twisting and muttering, drifting in and out of a kind of coma. Not long ago he had suddenly shouted in fear, then slumped back into unconsciousness. For the moment he was relatively quiet. Benton's head began to nod as he was lulled by the peace of the little room. Suddenly Benton jerked awake. A strange shimmering seemed to fill the air. Benton looked on in utter amazement as the guerilla simply faded away. The shimmering stopped and the bed was empty. Benton found himself pulling back the sheets and peering under the pillow as if he expected to find the man hiding. Then he pulled himself together. The bloke was gone and that was that. Benton sighed. Guess who'd have to try and explain that to the Brigadier . . .

The Controller of Earth Sector One stood in the Temporal Scanning Room. All around him was the strange and mysterious machinery of the Daleks, keeping continuous watch on the Time Vortex, that mysterious void where Time and Space are one. Girl technicians moved silently about the room. The Controller thought to himself that there was something strange and inhuman about them. They seemed completely emotionless, dedicated to the machines they served. He turned to the girl beside him and said, 'Why did you send for me?'

The girl indicated a faint flickering pulse on one of the screens in front of them. 'A time transmitter is in operation in the twentieth-century time zone.'

The Controller felt a sudden excitement. This could only mean more resistance activity. This time, perhaps, he could trap them. He said, 'Can you fix the Space Time co-ordinates?'

Coldly the girl said, 'I will try. The trace is very faint.'

Her hands flickered quickly over the controls on the console in front of her. Slowly the pulse on the screen flickered and died.

'It's no use, Controller. Transmission has stopped. I think a transference has taken place but it is not possible to be specific.' Her voice was flat and unemotional. She was simply reporting a fact.

The girl's indifference only increased the Controller's feeling of anger and disappointment. Sharply he said, 'Continue scanning. Next time, I advise you to be more efficient or it will be the worse for you.'

The girl was completely unimpressed. In the same emotionless voice she said, 'Everything possible was done. We shall continue scanning. If further transmissions take place you will be informed.' She turned away and returned to her duties.

The Controller looked after her furiously. Then he sighed, accepting defeat, and left the scanning room.

In the UNIT laboratory the Doctor put the machine down with a sigh of relief. 'It's all right. The thing's gone completely dead again.'

'But it was working,' Jo said anxiously.

The Doctor sighed. 'Oh yes. Unfortunately it was accidental. I still don't know how or why.'

The telephone rang and the Brigadier snatched it up. 'Yes? All right, Benton, what is it?' The Brigadier's voice rose to a sort of strangled yelp. 'What! He did *what*, Benton?'

The Brigadier listened a moment longer and said, 'All right, Sergeant, I believe you. Yes, I'll tell him.' With a mighty effort he put the phone down slowly and gently. 'That was Benton from the sickbay. You may be interested to know, Doctor, that at exactly the moment you started tinkering with that wretched machine our guerilla friend shimmered, and vanished—just faded away out of his hospital bed.'

'Now that is interesting,' said the Doctor. 'What's more it proves I was right. The thing's definitely a time transmitter. Somehow I managed to shoot the poor chap back to where he came from.'

The Brigadier gave him an exasperated look. 'I'm glad you find it interesting, Doctor—but it's not particularly helpful, is it? When that man vanished our chance of finding out what's going on vanished with him.'

'Don't be so pessimistic, old chap. This business isn't over yet, you know.'

'It isn't?' said the Brigadier gloomily.

'I very much doubt it. You see, I don't think those behind it have achieved their objectives yet. So they're bound to try again.'

'Try what again?'

'I'm not sure about the *what*, Brigadier, but I think I know the *where*!'

The Brigadier said, 'Well, I suppose that's something.'

'Everything that's happened,' the Doctor went on, seems to centre round Austerly House. And whoever tried to harm Styles is certain to try again.'

'But he isn't even there! He's in Peking by now.'

'That's right. So the place will be empty.' The Doctor turned to Jo, who had been looking on in puzzlement. 'Well, Jo, how about it?'

'How about what?'

The Doctor smiled. 'How do you fancy spending a night in a haunted house?'

4

The Ghost Hunters

Once again the wind whistled eerily in the trees round Austerly House. Once again a nervous sentry jumped at the sudden hoot of an owl. And once again one solitary window was illuminated, that of Sir Reginald Styles' ground-floor study.

Inside the study, however, things were very different. Instead of Sir Reginald toiling over his papers the elegant figure of the Doctor lay sprawled at his ease in an armchair by the blazing log fire. On a little table beside him stood a heavy silver tray. It held knives, plates, glasses, a little basket of biscuits, a bottle of wine and a very large Stilton cheese. The little black box, the time machine, stood on the table next to the tray.

Jo Grant stood beside the Doctor's chair. The Doctor looked up at her.

'You know, Jo,' he said thoughtfully, helping himself to a large slice of cheese, 'you can always be sure of one thing with politicians, whatever their political ideas: they always keep a well-stocked larder.'

Jo looked at the loaded tray with an air of some disapproval. 'I'm not sure that you really ought to help yourself like that,' she said dubiously.

'Nonsense, Jo. You heard what Miss Paget said. We're to consider the place our own.' The Doctor took another bite of cheese by way of underlining the point.

Jo looked around uneasily. In spite of the warmth and comfort of the firelit study she was very much aware that the rest of the big, old house was dark and empty. And outside the house itself was the black night, with strange noises coming from the gloomy woods. Of course, Captain Yates, Sergeant Benton and armed UNIT patrols were guarding the house. But that hadn't helped Styles. He'd still been attacked.

Jo shivered. 'I wish you hadn't sent all the servants away.'

The Doctor poured himself a glass of Burgundy. He held up the glass to admire the rich red colour of the wine. 'Had to be done, Jo. How can you expect ghosts to walk in a house full of people?'

Jo shivered again and the doctor stopped his teasing. 'Look, there's really nothing to worry about. Have a piece of this delicious cheese.'

'No thanks, Doctor. I don't seem to be hungry right now.' Jo came and perched herself on the arm of his chair.

Munching away at his cheese, the Doctor said indistinctly, 'Really ought to eat something, it's liable to be a long night.'

Jo said, 'I know. That's what I'm worrying about.'

Outside the house the wind howled, and it was starting to rain. Captain Yates stood in the shelter of the main doorway and watched the wind thrashing about in the tree-tops. Sergeant Benton hurried around the corner of the building and joined him. Benton's army waterproof was spotted with big drops of rain.

'Everything quiet, Benton?'

'Yes, sir, quiet as the grave.' Benton shuddered, wishing he'd found a more cheerful expression.

'Right, carry on.'

Benton saluted and plunged back into the darkness.

Throughout the grounds little patrols of armed men moved quietly through the pitch-black night, exchanging prearranged signals and passwords.

There were no sentries around the abandoned railway tunnel. It was some way from the house, and it hadn't struck the Brigadier that there was any point in guarding it.

Inside the darkness of the tunnel there came a faint glimmering and glowing. Three figures materialised one by one. First the girl, Anat, leader of the resistance cell that Moni had visited at such peril. Next Boaz, scowling with grim determination. Finally Shura, young and eager, trembling with nervous excitement. All three were loaded down with equipment.

Once all three were materialised Anat produced a tiny light-cell. Dimly it illuminated the rough brickwork of the tunnel. Boaz said exultantly, 'We made it, Anat. We made it!'

Swiftly they began to unload the heavier equipment. Shura found a hiding place for it, a crevice in the wall of the tunnel. He covered the equipment with loose rubble, and looked up excitedly. 'Well, this is it!'

Anat was more cautious. 'The place *looks* right. But the tinest error in the temporal co-ordinates and we may be too soon. Or too late.

Shura said, 'There's no chance of that. We'll succeed this time.'

'We've got to,' said Anat grimly. 'Now listen to me, both of you. You heard what Moni said before we left. We're the last chance. Two others have tried before us and failed. The Daleks are getting closer all the time and they can track our equipment. If we fail we'll be lucky to get back to our time zone alive. And we'll have lost the chance of defeating the Daleks.'

Boaz said, 'We won't fail, Anat.'

'We mustn't,' Shura added eagerly.

Anat said, 'We'll make our way to the house. You've all memorised the old historical maps?' The others nodded. She went on, 'Remember, it'll be very different outside the tunnel. You'll see fields, roads, houses with people in them. The kind of world we should have had. The kind of world we can still have if we succeed. Are you both ready?' Again the two men nodded. 'Then we'll make our way to the house. There'll be army patrols, but we'll avoid them.'

Boaz said fiercely, 'If they try to stop us . . .' He patted the holstered gun at his side.

Anat cut in, 'Don't forget, they are not our enemies. We have only one enemy. The man we have come to kill.'

Swiftly and silently the three guerillas slipped out of the tunnel and began moving across the fields to Austerly House.

The Doctor took another appreciative sip of his Burgundy. 'Ah, yes. A most good-humoured wine, this. A touch of the sardonic, perhaps, but not cynical. A truly civilised little wine, one after my own heart.'

Jo looked at him impatiently. 'Do stop chuntering on, Doctor.' She got out of her chair and moved to the door. 'I'm going to the kitchen to make myself a cup of tea.'

The hallway was empty and dark. There were suits of armour by the staircase and a stuffed stag's head stared glassily at her from the wall. Everything looked strange and sinister in the gloom.

Jo was making for the kitchen when suddenly the massive front door began to creak. She tried to call to the Doctor but her voice seemed to have gone. Terrified, she crouched against the wall as the door swung open. A huge figure loomed in the doorway. With a sigh of relief Jo realised it was Sergeant Benton.

In the darkness outside, the three guerillas had come to the high wall surrounding Austerly House. Working with trained efficiency, they climbed it and dropped to the other side. All three froze into cover, face downward. Their dark combat clothes blended perfectly into the woodland floor. The boots of a UNIT patrol passed by within inches of them. Once it had moved away they got up. Slowly they began to work their way towards the house. They moved in utter silence—just like ghosts.

Jo said indignantly, 'Sergeant Benton! You took years off my life, creeping about like that.'

'Didn't want to disturb the Doctor. What's he up to anyway?'

'Nothing very much. He's either tinkering with that black box you found, or carrying on like a one-man wine-and-cheese society!'

At the mention of food and drink Benton cheered up. He was a big chap and he needed a lot of fuel to keep him going. He leaned forward confidentially. 'Couldn't spare me a bite, could you, Miss Grant? I'm famished.' He did his best to look undernourished.

Jo said, 'You wait here.' She marched back into the study. The Doctor had cut himself another piece of Stilton and poured out another glass of wine. He was contemplating them with anticipation when Jo entered and took both plate and glass from his hand.

'Jo!' he said protestingly.

'All in a good cause, Doctor.'

The Doctor watched her disappear through the door. He sighed, and reached for the cheese knife.

Benton beamed as Jo put the plate and glass on a hall table beside him. 'You've saved my life, Miss.'

He was just reaching out when a familiar voice said, 'And what do you think you're doing, Sergeant Benton?' Captain Yates stood in the main doorway.

Benton straightened up to attention and saluted. 'Just checking up, sir.'

'I see, Sergeant. Then perhaps you'd like to check up on number two patrol?'

Benton said, 'Yessir.' With an anguished glance at the little table, he disappeared into the darkness.

Mike Yates seemed to notice the plate and glass for the first time. 'Why, Jo, how very kind of you!' He swigged down the wine and popped a piece of cheese into his mouth.

Jo looked at him severely. 'Mike Yates, that was mean.'

'R.H.I.P.,' said Mike indistinctly, his mouth full of cheese.

Jo looked at him blankly. 'Come again?'

'R.H.I.P.,' he repeated. 'Rank Has Its Privileges.' He gave her a smile, and followed Benton out into the night. Jo went back to the study.

The Doctor looked up. 'So what was all *that* about?'

'Oh nothing. Just feeding the troops.'

The Doctor nodded approvingly. 'Quite right. I remember saying to old Napoleon, you know, Boney, I said, always remember this: an army marches on its stomach.'

Jo sniffed. 'Well, Mike Yates certainly does.' A gust of wind rattled the window panes and she looked up nervously. 'Doctor, did you mean what you said to the Brigadier about ghosts?'

The Doctor smiled, 'I also said there were different kinds of ghosts.'

After a moment's silence Jo said, 'I never got that cup of tea!' Once more she set off for the kitchen.

The Doctor picked up the black box and began to examine it for the hundredth time. Restlessly he turned it over and over in his long fingers. He slipped off the back and began to peer at the maze of alien circuitry inside. 'Thing's a complete botch-up,' he grumbled to himself. 'Shouldn't work at all but it does. Or did. Must be a booster somewhere, or you wouldn't get the power.' Muttering to himself, he bent absorbedly over the little box.

At a signal from Anat the three guerillas burst from the bushes. They knew that their moment of greatest danger would come in crossing the little patch of open ground between the the bushes and the house itself. Just as they were completely in the open a two-man UNIT patrol rounded the corner of the house.

For a split second the soldiers peered at the dim figures before them. One of the soldiers snapped, 'Who goes there? Give the password.'

When there was no answer the UNIT men raised their guns. But Boaz and Shura were already shooting. There was a high-pitched electronic buzz, and the UNIT patrol vanished, totally disintegrated.

Anat gave an anguished look at her two fellow guerillas. But she knew there was nothing else they could have done. This mission had to succeed, even at the cost of innocent lives. She gave Shura a quick signal. He moved to the French windows. Anat and Boaz slipped through the front door of the house.

In the study the Doctor gave up the time machine in disgust. It seemed he could do nothing to make it come to life again. He slammed it down on the table. Immediately, it began to give out a low hum, and the swirling shimmering effect appeared very faintly around it.

The Doctor looked at the device in amazement. 'Hey, Jo,' he called. 'I've got it working again. Come and see. Jo, where are you?'

Jo heard the Doctor calling her from the kitchen though she couldn't hear what he was saying. Still, it might be urgent. She abandoned her tea-making and headed back to the study.

Shura peered through the gap in the curtains. To his utter amazement he saw a time machine standing on the table. And it was operational! The one thing that was certain to bring the Daleks and their Ogron killers down upon them!

Shura crashed his booted foot against the lock of the French windows. They flew open, and he shot into the room amid a shower of glass.

The tall man had been standing in the doorway but he whirled round with amazing speed at Shura's entrance.

Shura had temporarily forgotten that he had come to kill this man. He only wanted to turn off the time transmitter before the Daleks picked up the signal. But before he could even speak an amazingly long leg shot out and kicked the gun from his hand. Shura dived desperately for the time machine. But the tall man obviously mistook this for an attack.

He dodged, reached out, and Shura found himself gripped by long steely fingers. Somehow he was spun, twisted and sent crashing into the wall. He slid to the floor half-dazed. The one thought in his mind was that the man must, *must* be made to turn off the time transmitter, which still pulsed away.

In the Temporal Scanning Room the Controller of Earth Sector One peered eagerly at the screen. The tiny pulse was very faint. He turned to the girl technician beside him. 'This time, you must fix the co-ordinates.'

'We are attempting to do so now, Controller!' A panel

in the far wall slid open. A squat, black metallic figure glided towards them. Its eye-stalk swung round onto the Controller, and the harsh, metallic voice grated, 'What is happening? Re-port.'

The Controller said, 'We have located a time transmitter operating in the twentieth-century zone. We're fixing the co-ordinates now.' He shot a quick look at the impassive girl technician beside him and hoped desperately that his words were true. Hastily he went on, 'Security patrol are standing by.'

The Black Dalek swivelled round, turning its eye-stalk towards the faint pulse on the screen. The Dalek voice rasped, 'Whoever is operating the time transmitter is an enemy of the Daleks. They are to be exterminated.' Once again the voice rose almost to a shriek. 'Exterminate them! Exterminate them! Exterminate them!'

In Sir Reginald Styles' study Shura struggled desperately to his feet. He pointed to the pulsating time transmitter and croaked, 'Please turn it off. You must turn it off or they'll kill us all!'

The tall man hauled Shura to his feet and dumped him down in an armchair. 'To be quite honest I don't think I can turn it off. I'm not even very sure how I turned it on. Now then, my friend, I want to ask you one or two questions.'

From the doorway a girl's voice said, 'Get away from him.'

The Doctor turned from his captive. He saw a thin, dark girl in guerilla costume. Next to her another guerilla, a man. He held Jo Grant firmly in front of him, a gun at her head.

Obediently the Doctor moved away. The girl went straight to the time machine and with a few complex manipulations of the controls managed to turn it off.

In the Temporal Scanning Room the Controller's heart sank as he looked at the blank screen. He turned to the girl technician, hoping against hope. Perhaps there had still been time to trace the transmission.

The usually impassive technician's voice held a tremor of fear as she said, 'I'm sorry. We've lost the trace.'

The Black Dalek swung round on her angrily. Then it swung back to the Controller. The Dalek gun was pointing straight at him. The Controller knew that he might well be blasted into extinction then and there. The Daleks had no mercy on those who failed them. He stood perfectly still, not daring to breathe, trying not to even think. There was a long and terrible silence. Then the Black Dalek turned and glided out of sight.

5

Condemned to Death!

With an air of grim satisfaction the guerillas surveyed their prisoners.

Jo stood motionless, still held by Boaz, who had grabbed her in the hall. The Doctor leaned his shoulders against the mantelpiece and looked round the room. He appeared utterly calm and relaxed, yet Jo could see that his eyes were bright and alert, his long thin body poised for instant action.

The Doctor nodded towards Boaz and said mildly, 'I think you might let the young lady go. She's scarcely likely to harm you.'

Boaz suddenly felt rather foolish holding his gun to the head of such a very small girl. He let her go. She gave him an indignant glare and walked across to the Doctor.

Ignoring Jo completely, Anat walked towards the Doctor, gun in hand. She looked up into his face. 'So you're the man. Outwardly so innocent-looking, yet capable of such terrible crimes. Who would ever know?'

The Doctor gave her a puzzled look. 'I'm sorry, young lady, but I haven't the faintest idea what you're talking about.'

Anat snapped. 'Silence! You have done enough talking. It is time for your execution.'

Jo looked at the girl appalled. Why would anyone want to execute the Doctor? She felt the girl was working herself up into a kind of frenzy—as though she couldn't quite face the idea of killing in cold blood.

The same thought had occurred to the Doctor. The girl wasn't a natural killer but she had it within her to shoot him down in certain circumstances. In a deliberate attempt to lower the emotional temperature he said, 'Execution? Don't I even get a trial?'

Anat said, 'We have our orders.'

'No doubt. But whose orders?'

'That does not concern you.' Anat stepped back. 'Boaz, Shura!'

All three guerillas trained their guns on the Doctor. Desperately, Jo threw herself in front of him. 'Please, leave him alone. He's never done anyone any harm.'

Gently, the Doctor took Jo by the shoulders and moved her out of danger. Then, quite undisturbed by the three gun muzzles pointed at him, he said, 'Young lady, may I say one thing?'

'A last-minute speech of repentance?' said Anat contemptuously.

'Not exactly. You see I rather think you're making one terrible mistake.'

'And that is?'

'A simple question of identity. You think I'm Sir Reginald Styles, I imagine?'

'Of course you're Styles.'

'Ah, but that's the mistake, you see. I'm not Styles at all.'

Anat looked at him scornfully. 'Very feeble, Sir Reginald. Is that the best you can do? You answer Styles description. You're in his house.' She indicated the tray. 'You drink his wine and eat his food. But you're not Styles.'

Once again the three guerillas raised their guns. Jo was frozen with horror. She remembered the dummy she had made, the way it had shimmered and vanished. She tried to rush forward again but Boaz caught her and threw her into an armchair, holding her down with his free hand.

'I admit that it does all sound a little implausible,' said the Doctor calmly, 'but perhaps you'd care to look at the newspaper on that table.'

Anat moved to the table and picked up the newspaper. It was last night's evening paper. The headline read: 'STYLES FLIES TO PEKING IN TALKS CRISIS'.

'There's even a picture of him,' said the Doctor cheerfully. 'As you can see we're not really very alike.'

Worried, Anat looked at the headline, the picture of Styles, and then back at the Doctor. 'If you're not Styles why are you here?'

'Believe it or not, I was waiting for you.'

Boaz, who had been listening with increasing impatience, raised his gun. 'We're wasting time, Anat. Here, I'll do it.'

Anat knocked the gun aside with surprising force. 'I command this mission. We are soldiers, not murderers. Now get outside, I want you to keep guard.'

For a moment Boaz didn't move. Then he nodded and moved to the door.

Anat turned back to the Doctor. 'Now then, suppose

you answer my question sensibly. How could you be waiting for me? You couldn't have known we were coming.'

'Oh, but I did. You tried to kill Styles once. It was logical to assume you'd try again.'

'And you deliberately took his place? Why?'

'Because I wanted to talk to you. To discover *why* you want to kill Styles. To find out where you came from, and equally important—when.'

Anat looked up sharply. That last remark showed familiarity with the idea of time travel. Suddenly Boaz burst into the room. 'Soldiers! Coming up the path.'

Anat said, 'We must hide. Bring them!' and she pointed to the Doctor and Jo.

Quickly the guerillas hustled their captives out into the hall. The crunch of army boots could be heard coming up the path. Anat looked round. There was a big wooden door beneath the staircase and a flight of steps leading downwards. 'Down there,' she ordered.

Pushed by the three guerillas, Jo and the Doctor stumbled downwards into the darkness. They heard Anat hiss, 'You are both covered by our guns. One sound and you will be dead.' The little group huddled silently in the darkness.

Sergeant Benton and his patrol looked round the empty hallway. He called, 'Doctor! Jo! Where are you?' There was no reply.

Benton said to the soldiers, 'Take a look in the other rooms.' The soldiers clattered off, scattering through the house.

Benton spotted the door under the stairs and pushed it open. He found a light switch and pressed it. A single grimy bulb illuminated a flight of wooden steps leading down to a whitewashed cellar. Row upon row of wine racks stretched away into the darkness. Benton yelled, 'Anyone down there?' There was no answer.

Only a matter of inches away from him a silent group

crouched behind the massive cellar door. Jo and the Doctor could feel the cold metal of guns pressing against their foreheads. Benton paused uneasily. Something didn't feel right . . . Then he heard Captain Yates calling him. He turned out the light and closed the cellar door.

Yates was standing in the hallway, his face grave. 'Number two patrol failed to report in, Sergeant Benton. They seemed to have vanished.'

Benton said, 'So has the Doctor, sir. And Miss Grant. The study window's smashed open and there seems to have been a struggle. You reckon they've been kidnapped?'

The soldiers came back into the hall. One of them said, 'We've checked every room, Sarge. Whole place is empty.'

Yates looked at his watch. 'It'll be light before long. We'll make a full-scale search of the ground and check with all the other patrols. Someone must have seen something.' He turned and led the way out of the house.

When the noise of the soldier's departure had faded away Anat pressed the light switch again. She looked down the steps into the cellar and said, 'This will do for the moment. Tie them up and gag them!'

Boaz and Shura shoved the Doctor and Jo down the steps. Anat went out into the hall, back into the study, and peered cautiously out of the window. Dawn was very near now. There were already pale streaks of light in the east. Dimly, Anat could see the woods and lawns of Austerly Park. She gazed at the peaceful landscape with a kind of wonder. Then she looked around the study. For the first time she realised that she had actually journeyed into the past. The comfort and luxury of old houses, well-furnished rooms such as this, had long been things of the past when Anat was born. She reached out and touched the softness of the velvet curtains.

The entrance of Boaz and Shura recalled her to the realities of her mission. They were not here to enjoy Earth's past but to change its future.

Boaz said, 'They'll be no trouble for a while.' He turned to Anat with a hint of challenge in his voice. 'Well, what happens now?'

'I'm going to ask for fresh orders. The whole situation has changed.' She produced the little sub-temporal voice transmitter from her tunic and spoke into it. '*Mission intercept to base . . . mission intercept to base . . .*' There came only a crackling. Anat shook her head. 'It's no good. There's some kind of disturbance in the Time Vortex.'

Shura said, 'Why don't I go back to the tunnel, Anat? The big booster transmitter's there. That'll get through.'

Anat thought for a moment. 'All right. Tell them what's happened. Ask them for a prediction on Styles. They may be able to look up the date of his return here. Now hurry, it'll be light soon.'

Shura slipped out of the French windows and faded away into the darkness.

Anat sunk into a chair, realising for the first time how tired she was. Boaz looked down at her and said, 'Surely it's obvious what we should do?'

'Is it?'

'We're here now. Actually in Styles' house. We wait till he returns and then kill him.'

Anat looked at him wearily. 'And suppose Styles doesn't return? How long do you think we can stay here undetected. What about those two down in the cellar?'

'They might come in useful as hostages.'

'And if they don't? If they become a danger to us?'

Boaz shrugged. 'Then we kill them.'

Down in the cellar the Doctor was wiggling his neck and chin in the most amazing manner. With a last desperate twist he managed to free the gag from his mouth and chin. 'Ah, that's better,' he exclaimed with a sigh of relief.

'Mmmmm,' said Jo indignantly. 'Mmm mmmm mmmmm mm?'

The Doctor regarded her thoughtfully. 'I'm not at all sure I shouldn't leave you like that. It's very peaceful.'

There came a fresh outburst of indignant 'mmm's' from Jo, and the Doctor rolled over to her. After a bit more effort he managed to pull her gag away with his teeth.

Immediately Jo burst out, 'Doctor! Who are these people? Why do they want to kill Styles? Where do they come from?'

The Doctor said, 'One thing at a time, Jo. And it's not where but *when*. In terms of technological progress I'd say they're about two hundred years ahead of your time.'

'The twenty-second century?' said Jo.

'Visiting the twentieth,' said the Doctor thoughtfully, 'on a special mission through time to find a certain politician and kill him. But why?'

'You're the one with the answers, Doctor.'

'Well, for a start, they're not criminals.'

'Oh, aren't they?' said Jo indignantly. 'They were going to murder you, remember.'

'The word they used was "execute". They're political fanatics. I think they've come here to try and change history. And that's a fanatical idea.'

The Doctor was quiet for a moment, then said, 'Let me have a go at getting your ropes off, Jo. At least it'll help to pass the time.'

The Controller stood watching as Dalek scientists supervised the installation of a massive and complex piece of equipment in the Temporal Scanning Room. He turned and spoke to the Black Dalek at his side. 'We are maintaining a constant watch upon the Time Vortex. If we detect a transmission that continues long enough and strong enough we shall certainly be able to trace it to its source.'

The Black Dalek intoned, 'All enemies of the Daleks must be tracked down and destroyed.'

The Controller said, 'This new equipment . . . I am not quite clear as to its purpose.'

'Since you are unable to capture the criminals unaided the science of the Daleks will help you. This is the Magnetron. If the time transmitter that was traced is used again anyone so doing will be diverted in the Space Time Vortex and materialise here.'

'But only if that particular machine is used?'

'It is necessary to set the Magnetron to the frequency of a particular transmitter.' The Black Dalek's answer sounded almost sulky.

The Controller wasn't very impressed. *If* one particular time machine was used they *might* be able to capture the person using it. Since the resistance fighters knew that all transmissions risked being traced it was highly unlikely that the machine would be used again. But the Controller knew better than to express his doubts. Humbly he bowed his head.

The Black Dalek said, 'It is likely that the criminals will have returned to the spatial co-ordinates where the first criminal was located. You will despatch another security patrol to that place and time zone.'

The Controller looked up sharply. 'With respect, is that wise?' he asked. 'If they are seen . . .'

The Dalek rounded on him fiercely, its voice rising to a pitch almost of hysteria, 'Do not dispute with the Daleks! The function of the human is to obey!'

Again the Controller bowed his head, and followed the Black Dalek from the room. The Daleks were becoming frightened, he thought. Fear could only have one result—to make them even more ruthless than before. And that meant harshness and oppression for Earth. As he followed the Black Dalek along the endless corridors of Central Control his mind was busy.

What were the resistance guerillas up to in the twentieth-century zone? What did they hope to achieve that the Daleks were so desperate to prevent? The Controller entered his office and gave the orders that would despatch a patrol of Ogrons back to the railway tunnel where the first guerilla had been found.

It took Shura a long time to reach the tunnel. He was helped by the fact that he was alone instead of one of a group of three. But it was beginning to get light now and the grounds were alive with UNIT troops.

For a long time Shura hid in a tree near the outer wall. When at last the patrols had finished searching that particular area he dropped down from his tree and began to scale the wall. At the last moment he was spotted. He heard a shout of alarm as he dropped down on the other side of the wall and sprinted for the tunnel. He guessed the soldiers would follow him.

Once inside he paused to get used to the darkness. He fumbled his way along to the hidden cavity where he had stowed the equipment. Moving aside the two heavy Dalekenium bombs, he fished out the big transmitter and started to use it. '*Mission intercept to base . . . mission intercept to base . . .*'

But even the powerful transmitter picked up only crackling and static. There was obviously some kind of massive disturbance in the Space Time Vortex, thought Shura. Maybe some new invention of the Daleks—their time travel technology was constantly improving.

He was about to try again when a massive foot stamped down on the transmitter, smashing it beyond repair. Shura looked up to see an Ogron grinning savagely down at him. The Ogron hauled him to his feet and smashed him against the tunnel wall. His gun was ripped from his holster before he could use it.

Shura was young and strong and he fought desperately. But like any human being he was helpless against an Ogron's strength. The Ogron gripped him in a savage bear hug, then hurled him to the ground. As he tried to rise, a booted foot smashed him savagely in the ribs. He rolled away desperately as the Ogron kicked again.

Shura had one advantage in the unequal struggle. He guessed the Ogron didn't want to kill him. Or rather, it wanted to but had been ordered instead to take him alive. The beating-up was merely a way of relieving its frustrations at being deprived of the pleasure of destroying him. Shura rolled towards the cavity and groped inside. Next to the bombs was a spare disintegrator pistol. As the Ogron reached for him again Shura rolled and came up with the gun in his hands. He fired, and the Ogron was blasted into nothingness.

Shura sank down against the side of the tunnel wall, gasping for breath. He took stock of his injuries: several ribs were broken for sure, and one arm. There must be other Ogrons about, he thought muzzily. He wouldn't survive long if they found him. There was only one possible hiding place.

Scrabbling aside the rubble with his good hand, Shura enlarged the cavity they had used as a cache. He dug out a space big enough to lie in, pulled the ruined transmitter and the gun in after him, and then covered the supplies and himself with rubble.

Minutes later other Ogrons came lumbering along the tunnel. Shura heard shouts and then shots. He heard the Ogrons muttering briefly in low guttural voices. Then there was the familiar hum of a time transmitter. Shura guessed that the Ogrons had been spotted by the UNIT troops and were returning to their own time zone. Soon he heard more human shouts and the sound of army boots.

Shura should have been found by the army patrol. But the UNIT troops had already had one experience of chasing Ogrons into the tunnel and finding it empty.

Perhaps, too, they weren't too keen to linger long in the tunnel just in case those gorilla things hadn't all gone. The soldiers rushed in quickly one end and out the other.

Shura heard one of them call, 'No good, Corp, they've faded away again.' That shout was the last thing Shura heard for quite a while.

Battered and exhausted, suffering not only from his wounds but from the strain of the last few hours, he felt himself drift into a state of unconsciousness. Soon, curled up in his nest of rubble, bombs and pistol clasped to his chest, Shura was fast asleep.

Anat and Boaz waited for Shura's return with increasing unease. Both jumped when the telephone began to ring. Although neither had seen or used a telephone before, they knew well enough what it was.

They stared at it helplessly, wishing it would stop. But the ringing went on and on. Anat reached a hand out towards the phone. Boaz snapped, 'Leave it!'

'They'll be suspicious if no one answers,' said Anat desperately. She came to a decision. 'Those people in the cellar. Bring them up.'

Boaz dashed from the room and Anat waited for what seemed an agonisingly long time. Still the telephone kept up its unending ringing and ringing.

Boaz came back into the room, herding Jo and the Doctor before him with his pistol. Anat said, 'Untie him.' Boaz cut the ropes from the Doctor's wrists and pushed him towards the phone. 'Answer it,' said Anat. 'Tell them everything's all right,' Boaz held the gun to the Doctor's head.

Slowly the Doctor picked up the receiver and said, 'Hello?'

'Sorry to bother you so early,' said the Brigadier. 'Been up all night with this conference crisis.'

'That's all right, Brigadier. As a matter of fact I've been up all night myself.'

'Ghost-hunting, eh?' The Brigadier chuckled. 'Anything happen?'

Anat moved her head close to the Doctor's so that she too could hear what the Brigadier was saying.

'Nothing happening,' responded the Doctor calmly. 'Everything's very quiet here.'

'Jolly good. Thing is I had some kind of garbled report from Yates and Benton that you'd vanished. They looked in the house and couldn't find you. Said the place was deserted.'

The Doctor said, 'Did they? Oh yes, must have been when we were down in the cellar. Did I tell you old Styles has a fascinating collection of wines?'

'Now listen, Doctor, you're absolutely sure everything's all right at that house? Because Styles is coming back there tomorrow night. He is taking the main delegates to his house for an informal preliminary conference.'

Boaz and Anat exchanged exultant glances. Before anyone could stop him the Doctor said, 'I'm not sure that's wise, Brigadier.'

Boaz thrust the gun closer to the Doctor's head. Anat gave him a look of warning.

'Oh really? Why not?'

The Doctor didn't reply.

After a moment the Brigadier said, 'You're sure everything *is* all right, Doctor?'

Speaking clearly and distinctly, the Doctor said, 'I assure you, Brigadier, there's nothing to worry about. Tell Styles that. Tell the Prime Minister. And, Brigadier, be particularly sure to tell it to the marines.' Hoping that his knowledge of twentieth-century slang was accurate, the Doctor put down the phone.

At UNIT HQ the Brigadier turned to Yates and Benton. 'You were right. The Doctor's in trouble. I think he's been made prisoner. We're going back to Austerly House right away.' He paused at the door. 'Oh, and send a message to the patrols. They're to keep the house surrounded but they're not to go inside.'

Anat and Boaz were jubilant. 'He's coming here!' exclaimed Anat. 'Sir Reginald Styles is coming here! We can carry out out our mission.'

'Of course,' said Boaz, 'the conference *is* here tomorrow night. Our dates were right after all.'

'You certainly showed a remarkable ability to predict the future,' agreed the Doctor, 'though I suppose it's not so remarkable really since our future is your past.' Boaz and Anat were scarcely listening to him.

Nor was Jo. Before the guerillas had brought them up from the cellar she and the Doctor had practically succeeded in getting the ropes off her wrists. Although the Doctor's wrists had been tied he had still been able to use his fingers, and by standing back to back he had been able to untie most of the knot. Now Jo was finishing the job herself. Suddenly she was free. And no one seemed to be worrying about her.

The Doctor made a second attempt to talk to Anat. 'Isn't it about time you told me what you think you're up to? Why do you imagine that killing Styles will make any difference to the future you come from?'

Anat said, 'It will make every differencc.'

'Styles isn't a bad man. At the moment he's doing all he can to stop a world war . . .'

'You believe that?' said Anat. 'You really believe that?'

'Most certainly.'

'Then I've got some rather startling news for *you*. Your friend Styles isn't trying to stop a war—he's going to start one . . . unless we can stop him.'

Jo dashed across the room and picked up the time machine. She raised it threateningly above her head.

'Right,' she snapped, 'you can both drop your guns.'

Anat and Boaz made no move to obey her.

'If you don't do as I say,' said Jo determinedly, I'm going to smash this machine to bits. You'll be stranded here forever. You'll never get back to your own time.'

The Doctor said, 'Jo, you've got it all wrong . . . Put that machine down before it starts working again.'

Jo ignored him. Looking at Boaz and Anat she said, 'I warn you, I mean it.'

Anat sounded almost sorry for her. 'My dear child, we don't need that machine. We have others of our own.'

Jo looked at her uncertainly. 'You're just bluffing.'

'I assure you I am not,' said Anat. 'Now put that machine down and stop being silly.'

To Jo's amazement the Doctor said, 'Jo, do as she says.'

Confused, Jo gripped the machine tighter. Unconsciously her fingers tightened over the control knobs. Suddenly the machine hummed into life. A shimmering effect filled the air around Jo's body. She felt herself in the grip of some terrible force drawing her away—and before the Doctor's horrified gaze Jo, still clutching the time machine, just faded away and vanished . . .

6

Prisoner of the Daleks

Jo Grant was twisting and turning in a sort of strange misty nothingness. Soon she lost all sense of up or down. Over and over, round and round she went. All the time she could feel the tug of powerful forces that seemed to be pulling her apart. She felt sick and dizzy and terrified.

Just when she could bear it no longer all the different pulls seemed to combine. She felt herself being drawn steadily in one particular direction.

Gradually it seemed that she was becoming more solid, more real. The misty nothingness was fading away . . . she was in a real place again. She could feel a solid floor beneath her. It was cold and metallic.

Cautiously, Jo opened her eyes and looked around her. She was in some kind of control room, surrounded with gleaming alien machinery. Towering above her was a group of huge, ape-like creatures with savage cruel faces. They carried guns, big pistols like those used by the guerillas. The guns were all pointing straight at her.

The Doctor called, 'Jo! Jo!' but it was too late. She had completely vanished. He turned to Anat. 'What's happened to her?'

Anat's look was almost sympathetic. 'The machine was faulty. She's probably been disintegrated, dispersed for ever into the Time Vortex.'

Boaz said, 'That's if she was lucky.'

'And if she wasn't?' said the Doctor grimly.

Again the look of sympathy from Anat. 'If the machine was still working it's possible that she'll be re-embodied in our time.'

'Believe me,' Boaz added ominously, 'she'd be better off dead.' He indicated the Doctor with his pistol. 'What do we do with him?'

'Put him back in the cellar. Tie him up again.'

While Anat covered him with her gun Boaz put the ropes back on the Doctor's wrists. The knots were cruelly tight. No chance of undoing them again, thought the Doctor.

When the binding was finished Boaz stepped back. 'All right, get moving.' The Doctor ignored him and looked at Anat. 'There's nothing you can do to save my friend? Nothing at all?'

Anat shook her head. 'Believe me, I'm sorry. But she brought it on herself. We didn't want to harm anyone unnecessarily.'

Boaz came up to the Doctor and jabbed the gun in his ribs. 'Now listen, you! Anat may be soft-hearted but I'm not. As far as I'm concerned you're just a nuisance and I'd as soon kill you. Now get back to that cellar.'

It was obvious that Boaz meant what he said. The Doctor went out of the study and into the hall. Boaz opened the cellar door and shoved him down the steps.

The Doctor lay in darkness on the cold stone floor. For a moment a wave of despair washed over him. It seemed that the guerillas might well succeed in their plan to kill Styles and start another war, though why should they want to do that? The Doctor sighed. And now Jo was gone, perhaps dead, perhaps stranded in some alien and terrifying future.

It wasn't in the Doctor's nature to give up for very long. Surely the Brigadier had understood his message? Anyway, the one thing you could always do was try. Patiently the Doctor began to work on the ropes that bound his wrists.

Guarded by two of the ape-like monsters, Jo Grant was being marched along a series of endless, gleaming metal corridors. From time to time they passed shabbily dressed men and women bustling about on mysterious tasks. The place was like an anthill, thought Jo. Everyone seemed cowed and terrified, standing aside rapidly and showing no curiosity at the sight of Jo.

They reached a sort of office and Jo was thrust into a chair. Behind a desk sat a thin, dark man with a haggard, haunted face.

The two monsters took up a position behind Jo's chair. The man waved them away. 'You can go now.' For a moment they didn't move. The man said again, 'Go!' They turned and lumbered from the room.

The man smiled at Jo. 'They're only servants, you

see. And so stupid! Nothing to be frightened of really.'

Jo said, 'What are they?'

'A kind of higher anthropoid. They used to live in scattered communities on one of the outer planets. They make useful servants.'

For a moment Jo had a ridiculous picture of one of the hulking gorilla-things coming in with a tea tray. She giggled. 'Servants? What do they do?' she asked.

'We use them as a kind of policeman, or rather to help the police.'

'I see,' said Jo brightly. 'You mean they're sort of police dogs?'

'Exactly. They are very faithful, very loyal.'

Jo was beginning to feel less frightened. The explanation did make the creatures less terrifying. After all, people had used guard dogs for ages, and it was the same thing really. And the man seemed to be friendly enough.

'Look, I know it sounds silly, but could you please tell me where I am?' she said.

'You're at Central Control in Sector One. In fact, I'm the Controller of the Region.' There was pride in the man's voice. His rank was obviously important to him.

'Yes, but where? What planet?'

The man seemed puzzled. 'Why, Earth of course. Where else?'

'But it's all so different,' said Jo helplessly.

'That's because you've travelled in time. You see, this is the twenty-second century.'

For a moment Jo's head reeled. The Controller said reassuringly, 'Don't worry. We can get you back to your own time. Is that what you want?'

Jo nodded eagerly. 'Yes, of course.'

The Controller sat back in his chair. 'First I'd like you to tell me everything that happened to you before you found yourself here.'

The Controller sat back and listened as the girl told her story. He congratulated himself on his handling of the situation. It had been obvious from the start that the girl was no guerilla. But her possession of the time machine meant she must have been in contact with them, probably quite innocently. And her story was bearing out his theory.

When Jo had finished, the Controller sat back for a moment, trying to digest the flood of new information. He wished his knowledge of twentieth-century history were better. What was so important about this man Styles?

Jo said, 'The really worrying thing is that the Doctor is still their prisoner.'

Her heart sank as the Controller said solemnly, 'I'm afraid your friend is in very great danger.'

'But why? They know now he's the wrong man.'

The Controller's face was grave. 'You don't know these people as I do, Miss Grant. I've spent years trying to track them down. They've been responsible for the most terrible crimes. And if anyone gets in their way they're totally without mercy.'

Jo remembered the burning fanatical eyes of the three guerillas. She shuddered. 'I can well believe it,' she said.

The Controller leaned forward across his desk. 'Now, we may be able to mount a rescue operation to save this friend of yours. But we'll need your help.'

'Yes, of course. Anything at all.'

'We know where the criminals are holding your friend. We have maps that show where Austerly House once stood. But equally important is the *when*. Can you remember exactly what time they arrived?'

Jo nodded. 'Just after midnight.'

'Yes, but the date, the month, the year?'

Puzzled, Jo told him. The Controller gave a sigh of relief. 'Excellent, I'm sure we'll be able to help your friend. Now I must ask you to excuse me. I must start arranging the rescue expedition at once.'

'And you'll take me with you, get me back to my own time?'

The Controller came from behind his desk and took Jo's arm. 'Naturally, naturally. Now I'm sure you're tired, hungry and thirsty. We have special refreshment suites for honoured guests. Let me take you to one . . .'

He paused at the door. 'When the criminals transferred to your time, did they arrive near the house itself?'

'I doubt it,' said Jo. 'The UNIT guards would have seen them.'

'Have you any idea where they did arrive? Some kind of hide-out in your time, perhaps?'

Jo frowned. 'There's an old railway tunnel near the house. That's where we found the wounded man and the time machine. They could have hidden in there. It's a very long tunnel and completely abandoned.'

'A tunnel?' said the Controller. 'Excellent. Now come with me. I'll let you know as soon as there's any news.'

A few minutes later the Controller stood once more before the Black Dalek.

'I have won her trust completely. Thanks to me we now have the information we need.'

The Controller knew that there would be no word of praise for his success. Daleks spoke only to condemn failure. Their servants were expected to succeed, or pay the penalty.

The Black Dalek said, 'The criminals are using the tunnel as a transfer point. We will prepare an ambush in the twentieth-century time zone.'

'Security forces are standing by,' the Controller said quickly. 'If you wish I will take charge of things myself.'

The Black Dalek swivelled his eye-stalk towards him. With a tinge of contempt in the metallic voice it said, 'This expedition is too important to be entrusted to a human. Some of us will accompany you. The expedition will be led by the Daleks!'

7

Attack of the Ogrons

Boaz looked out cautiously from behind the curtains. 'There are patrols all round the house but they don't seem to be coming near it.'

Anat said, 'Well, why should they? They think the place is empty, apart from the Doctor and that poor girl.'

Boaz turned away from the window. 'They're bound to send people here before Styles comes back. I know from the history books—such a man will have many servants.'

Anat shrugged. 'It's a big house. We'll find somewhere to hide. In the attics perhaps, or down in the cellar with our prisoner.'

'Yes, of course,' said Boaz. 'Or we could take the servants hostage. We only need to survive until Styles arrives. Once we kill him we either escape or die. Doesn't really matter which, does it?'

Anat looked at him with concern. She wondered how much longer Boaz would be able to stand the waiting. He could only bear it by screwing himself up to a pitch of fanatic dedication. Her own nature was calmer, more determined. She bitterly regretted the deaths they had caused—the girl, the UNIT patrol. But she accepted them as a necessary part of the price that must be paid if they were to succeed. In the same way she accepted that her own death might well be a part of that price.

Suddenly there came a familiar sound. They rushed to the window.

Ogrons were materialising outside the house. Boaz

raised his gun and blasted the first one before it had time to get its bearings. Anat joined him at the window.

For a while it was a kind of grim target practice. An Ogron would materialise, look round, and be instantly shot down, vanishing as fast as it had arrived. But they couldn't get rid of them all. Others were materialising out of their line of fire and coming to join the attack.

The air was full of the savage buzzing of the disintegrator guns. Soon the rattle of machine-gun fire was added to the din.

Boaz said exultantly to Anat, 'It's the soldiers!'

UNIT patrols began to arrive, opening fire on the Ogrons. The soldiers tried to form a protective line in front of the house.

The UNIT soldiers fought at some disadvantage. The weapons of the Ogrons were far more effective. It took a full clip of machine-gun bullets to kill an Ogron. Anything less and the monsters just went on fighting, roaring with rage and pain but hardly even slowed down. But one direct hit from an Ogron pistol could blast a UNIT soldier into extinction.

Boaz and Anat, shooting from the now shattered French windows, had disintegrator guns of their own, and the atomic power packs built into the handles were practically everlasting. But they were only two and the Ogrons outnumbered them badly.

In the cellar the Doctor heard the sound of battle and speeded up his attempt to escape. By flailing his legs about he had managed to upset a whole rack of wine bottles. They had fallen to the floor in a crash of broken glass. Now the Doctor was rubbing his bonds against the jagged end of a broken bottle.

A UNIT soldier blazed away at the nearest Ogron. Roaring, the creature sank slowly to the ground. The soldier reached for a new clip of bullets but before he could fit it another Ogron blasted him into oblivion at close range. The Ogron swung its gun onto another soldier but Anat disintegrated it with a shot from the window.

Boaz yelled, 'The soldiers can't hold them!'

Anat saw that it was true. The UNIT forces had lost too many men. Before long the Ogrons would break through the protective cordon and get into the house. Anat saw that defeat was just a matter of time. 'We'll have to get back to the tunnel,' she shouted. She took a final shot at an Ogron and ran from the room.

Boaz waited a moment longer, firing from the window to cover her retreat. Then he too turned to go, only to find himself facing a very angry Doctor, covered with dust and cobwebs and bleeding from several cuts on the wrists.

Before Boaz could even speak the Doctor was upon him. A long arm reached out and Boaz went hurtling across the room, his gun skidding across the floor before he had a chance to use it.

As the Doctor moved to pick it up a voice said, 'Keep still.' He felt the cold metal of a gun barrel on his neck. Anat was in the doorway. She said to Boaz, 'Out—get to the tunnel!' and he rushed from the room. Anat gave the Doctor a sudden shove and turned to run after Boaz. As she did so there was a shattering crash and an Ogron burst through the French windows, smashing the few remaining panes of glass in the process.

At once the Doctor grappled with the Ogron, trying to get hold of its gun. The creature's strength was enormous and the Doctor strove in vain to wrench the gun from the hairy paw. At the same time he fought to restrain the creature's other hand from grasping his throat. The Doctor knew he could never match the immense strength of his opponent. Instead he applied the judo principle of turning an enemy's strength against him. Giving way before the Ogron's rush, the Doctor rolled onto his back, shoved his feet into the Ogron's stomach and sent it flying. The top of the Ogron's head thudded into the wall and the creature slid to the ground, stunned. The Doctor tried to get its gun but the weapon was still tightly gripped in the hairy paw. He remembered Boaz's dropped gun, scooped it up, and ran after the two guerillas.

The Doctor ran along the passages of the old house, through the kitchens and into a paved courtyard. He ran through a back gate and found himself on the gravel path at the rear of the house.

Quickly working out his bearings, he decided to make for the tunnel. Something told him that the only hope of rescuing Jo was to stay with the guerillas. Two Ogrons ran round the corner of the house, cutting off his retreat. The Doctor raised Boaz's gun and fired. There was a buzz and the Ogron exploded into nothingness. He turned the gun on the other Ogron and fired again, but nothing happened. The thing was jammed, or empty. The Doctor hurled the gun at the monster's head but missed. The Ogron grinned savagely, showing its yellow fangs. Slowly it raised its gun, enjoying the moment . . .

The Doctor braced himself, wondering what it would be like to be disintegrated. There was a noise of an engine, and the Ogron turned to face a new enemy.

The Brigadier came roaring round the corner in a jeep. Before the Ogron could fire, the Brigadier drove straight into it, sending it flying through the air. Then he slammed on the brakes.

As soon as the Ogron hit the ground it was up again, charging the jeep. Coolly, the Brigadier snatched up his Sterling from the seat beside him and emptied the full clip of bullets into the Ogron. Rocked back on its heels by the impact, the Ogron staggered, then slumped to the ground.

The Brigadier jumped down from the jeep, stepped over the Ogron's body, and walked up to the Doctor's grimy and bleeding figure.

'Are you all right, Doctor? What the blazes have you been up to?'

The Doctor gave him a weary grin. 'I'm fine—thanks to your most timely intervention.'

'Then perhaps you'll explain what's going on,' said the Brigadier sternly. 'What are these creatures?'

'I'll try to explain later,' said the Doctor. 'At the moment I'm in a bit of a hurry.' To the Brigadier's indignation the Doctor jumped into the jeep and shot off.

'Come back, Doctor! Come back at once!' the Brigadier yelled. But the only response was a cheery wave as the jeep disappeared out of sight.

The Doctor sped through the grounds of Austerly House and along the road that led to the tunnel. As he came in sight of it he saw Anat and Boaz running across the fields towards the tunnel mouth.

The Doctor took the jeep as close to the tunnel as he could. Then, abandoning it, he ran across the fields after the two guerillas.

Once inside the tunnel he was in almost total darkness. He groped his way forward cautiously. Ahead he could hear the echoing footsteps. The footsteps stopped. A tiny point of light glowed in the distance. The Doctor made his way towards it.

A strange humming noise came from behind him and he turned round. In the darkness a kind of glowing circle had appeared from which was emitted an eerie light. Within the circle a shape began to form. It was a shape the Doctor knew only too well, that of his oldest and bitterest enemy. A Dalek was materialising in the tunnel!

In a moment the process was completed. Still glowing with the same sinister light, the Dalek swivelled round its eye-stalk as if getting its bearings. The Doctor froze, flattening himself against the tunnel wall. Behind the Dalek, Ogrons were beginning to materialise.

As if it sensed the Doctor's presence the Dalek spoke. The familiar grating, metallic voice said, 'Stop! You are all enemies of the Daleks. Surrender, or you will be exterminated!' The Dalek began to trundle down the tunnel towards him.

8

A Fugitive in the Future

Again the Dalek voice echoed through the darkness of the tunnel. 'You are all enemies of the Daleks. Surrender at once or you will be exterminated!'

The Doctor realised the Dalek hadn't seen him at all. It was addressing the guerillas. Somehow it must know they were in the tunnel. He turned and ran on at full pelt through the darkness towards the tiny glowing point of light.

As he got nearer he saw that the light came from a little torch-like device held by Anat. She and Boaz stood side by side, hands joined. Each held a pulsating black box in the other hand. The two time machines were pulsating rhythmically and already the shimmering effect was beginning to build up.

As the Doctor ran up to them Anat screamed, 'Get back!'

Almost out of breath, the Doctor gasped, 'There's a Dalek . . . more Ogrons . . . in the tunnel behind me!'

The two guerillas turned. They saw the Dalek and the Ogrons bearing down on them. The Doctor pointed the other way. From that direction another Dalek, with Ogrons in support, was approaching. 'You're trapped,' said the Doctor.

The shimmering effect of the time field grew even stronger. Anat yelled, 'Get back! If you're caught up in the time field you'll be taken with us!'

The Doctor had no intention of being left behind . . . not with Daleks and Ogrons arriving from both sides. Instead of arguing, he wrapped his arms around Boaz in a determined bear-hug. The guerilla tried to break free but the Doctor couldn't be budged. It became clear that wherever Boaz was going the Doctor was going with him.

As their pursuers converged upon them the little group shimmered and faded from sight. Like Jo Grant before him the Doctor found himself twisting and twirling in the Time Vortex. Since he was used to time travel he was much less frightened than Jo had been. He couldn't help thinking that time travel by this method was very different from time travel in the TARDIS. It was like comparing a trip in a luxury liner with going over Niagara Falls in a barrel.

Still holding grimly on to Boaz, the Doctor became aware that the Vortex was fading away. They were back in the real world. With a sudden jolt the Doctor found himself on firm ground. Letting go of Boaz, he looked round. They were still in a tunnel but a very different one, more modern in design.

The two guerillas were checking equipment and stowing away their time machines. Anat said, 'We warned you.'

The Doctor was looking around with interest. Only a single rail ran along this tunnel. They were in a part of a monorail system. Probably built some time in the twenty-first century and by now abandoned. Anat followed his glance. 'This may come as a shock to you,' she said gently, 'but you've travelled in time.'

The Doctor gave her a quizzical look. 'My dear young lady, I'm probably rather more familiar with time travel than you are.'

The guerillas started to move away. The Doctor said, 'Wait. Those Daleks we saw—where did they come from?'

Anat looked at him curiously. 'You know of the Daleks?'

'Indeed I do. You might say we're very old enemies. What are they doing on Earth in this time zone?'

Anat said flatly, 'They've ruled the Earth for almost two hundred years.'

'And if you knew about the Daleks you're a fool to have come here,' said Boaz.

'I came to find Jo Grant. As long as there's a chance that she's alive . . .'

Boaz said, 'Come, Anat, it's dangerous to stay here.'

'Please,' said the Doctor, 'how do I set about finding her?'

Boaz said, 'that's *your* problem!' He made another attempt to pull Anat away.

She hesitated. 'We can't just leave him to fend for himself.'

'I can,' said Boaz. 'Now, are you coming or not?'

Hurriedly Anat whispered to the Doctor, 'If the Daleks have got her she'll be at Central Control. But don't try to rescue her, it'd be suicide.'

Suddenly Boaz yelled, 'Run, Anat!' More Ogrons and Daleks were rushing at them out of the darkness.

The guerillas turned and ran. The Doctor ran too. This new set of tunnels was a complete maze with openings in every direction. Here and there the tunnel roof was broken away so that patches of daylight lit up the gloom. The Doctor took a wrong turn and ran almost straight into an Ogron patrol! He turned and ran back with Ogrons pounding close behind him. As he turned into the opening of yet another tunnel he saw a patch of light gleaming above him. In the half-light he looked around and saw some kind of hand-rail. The Doctor leaped for it and found himself hanging onto a maintenance ladder bolted to the wall. He clung there while the Ogrons ran past below him. Then, deciding that up was as good a direction as any, he started climbing the ladder.

It led up to a rusty trap-door. The Doctor managed to get his shoulder under it and shoved hard. Reluctantly the trap-door creaked open. Cautiously the Doctor poked his head out and wriggled through the trap-door into daylight.

All around him was a scene of complete and utter desolation. Every inch of the countryside, as far as he could see, seemed to have been built up till not an inch was left, then methodically hammered down. A sea of rubble stretched before him. Here and there a wall or two was still standing.

The Doctor fished a tiny instrument from his pocket. It was a sort of miniaturised Geiger counter. He tested the rubble around him. The little instrument began a subdued clicking.

The instrument was registering minute traces of radioactivity. Atomic war had brought about this ruination. The radiation had faded as time went by.

The Doctor climbed a little hill of rubble and looked around him. In the distance a group of buildings stood out from the desolation. They were stark and ugly, made of rough concrete. They looked bleak and functional with nothing attractive or welcoming about them. They looked—there was only one word for it—'Daleky'. The Doctor sighed. Unattractive as the buildings were they made a point to aim for. There must still be people left on Earth. Perhaps someone would help him. He began to pick his way through the rubble.

The Controller of Earth Sector One was talking for his very life. After the latest failure to capture the guerillas he had been summoned to appear before the High

Council of the Daleks, the supreme ruling body of the planet Earth.

He stood, isolated in a pool of light, in a long, bare metallic room. It was completely featureless except for the raised area at the end. Here the dreaded Black Dalek and its superior, the even more powerful Golden Dalek, stood, with other Daleks grouped around them.

Briefly, the Controller ended his report. 'Security guards combed the tunnels, both here and in the twentieth-century time zone. Nothing and no one was found. Our forces had to leave the twentieth-century zone because of increased opposition from the human soldiers.'

For a moment there was silence. Then the Golden Dalek said, 'You have failed the Daleks. You will be punished.'

The Controller knew that appeals for mercy would be useless. He decided to speak his mind. At least he could die with dignity. 'Am I responsible for this failure? Ogron security guards carried out the mission. And was it not led by the Daleks themselves?' There was a stunned silence. Not for more than a hundred years had any human dared question the authority of the Daleks. The Controller went on, 'The Ogrons are stupid and clumsy! They are useless for operations of this kind. As guards in the work camps, perhaps . . . but definitely not for anything that calls for intelligence or initiative!'

There was a note of uncertainty in the voice of the Black Dalek, 'The Ogrons are loyal servants of the Daleks.'

'No doubt. But it takes humans to deal with humans. Now, if you would allow me to recruit *human* security guards . . .' (The Daleks used humans mostly for manual labour and simple administration.)

The Black Dalek said, 'Humans are treacherous and unreliable.'

'Not all humans,' replied the Controller, a little

amazed at his own daring. 'I have served you loyally all my life.'

The Golden Dalek spoke again, 'Do not dispute with the Daleks. Obey without question. The hunt for the enemies of the Daleks must be carried on unceasingly. All enemies of the Daleks will be exterminated.'

The Controller sighed. He hadn't really expected any concessions. He was being turned away with the usual propaganda. At least he was still alive.

The Black Dalek said, 'Is your report concluded?'

'Except for one thing. It seems likely that a human returned from the twentieth-century time zone with the guerillas. According to the patrols it must be the man the girl spoke about. She called him "the Doctor".'

He turned to leave. The Black Dalek's voice rose almost to a shriek—

'Stop! Doc-tor? Did you say, Doc-tor?'

The Controller was astonished at the strength of the reaction. The word 'Doctor' was pronounced jarringly in two syllables, and he could almost feel the hate in the Dalek's voice.

Now the Golden Dalek joined in, pronouncing the Doctor's own name with the same venomous intensity. 'The one known as the Doc-tor is not human. He is the supreme enemy of the Daleks. He must be found and exterminated.'

Now the other Daleks took up the chorus. As the Controller left, their voices rang in his ears. 'Exterminate him! Exterminate him! Exterminate him!' But there was something different about those voices. They held some quality the Controller had never heard before and as he walked from the council hall he recognised it. The quality was *fear*. For the first time in the Controller's experience of them the Daleks were actually afraid.

The Doctor had been travelling for many hours across the ruined landscape. Progress was slow. There were no roads to speak of and the Doctor avoided those he saw. He had to be constantly alert for Ogron patrols and always ready to shelter in a ruin or a ditch. Once he had lain for what seemed ages in the cellar of a wrecked house while a resting Ogron patrol sat almost on top of him, chomping food from their pouches and talking in low guttural voices. At last they had moved on and he had been able to go on his way.

Now he had reached the edge of the enormous building which he had seen shortly after emerging from the trap-door. A high stone wall ran around it, with savage spikes at the top. Although the Doctor didn't know it, a resistance leader called Moni had climbed that wall a few nights before. Looking for an easier way in, the Doctor moved along the wall cautiously. He passed what looked like a kind of lamppost. But on top of it was not a lamp but a monitor lens. The Doctor unwittingly activated it when he passed through its field of vision. It swung round to follow him as he moved by.

On a screen somewhere inside the building a little spot of light began to move, recording the Doctor's progress. A girl technician leaned forward and spoke into a microphone. 'Alert, alert, intruder detected by outer wall. Description corresponds to that of wanted man known as the Doctor.'

'Allow him to enter the area and then surround him. He must be captured alive.'

The Controller himself gave that final order. He knew the Daleks would probably prefer the Doctor to be killed on sight. But he was anxious to meet the man who could actually produce fear in the Daleks. He wasn't sure why he felt like this. He only knew that he had to meet and talk to the Doctor before he let the Daleks dispose of him.

The Doctor meanwhile had found a small door in the

wall. He was busy picking the simple electronic lock with the aid of his sonic screwdriver. Soon he had it open and had slipped inside. He found himself inside a large bare concrete yard which gave on to a number of barn-like buildings. Automated trucks on rails rumbled into them. The trucks were filled with crushed rock, obviously some kind of mineral ore.

He slipped across the courtyard and peered inside one of the long low buildings. An endless conveyor belt ran right across it. Ragged, thin workers were standing beside the belt, sorting through the mineral ore with their bare hands. Others were staggering from the trucks to the belt with rock-filled baskets, keeping the conveyor supplied. The sorted ore moved off in another set of trucks; the rejected rocks were carried away and dumped onto another belt which took them out of sight. Ogron guards with whips stood by the workers. There was also a human guard who seemed to be in overall charge.

The Doctor watched the whole process with horror and indignation. The minerals arrived, were sorted, and were carried away. The whole process went on endlessly and could obviously have been carried out entirely by machines. Probably the Daleks found it simpler and cheaper to wear out human beings instead, the Doctor thought angrily.

A thin old man stumbled and dropped his basket. Instantly, the human guard's whip cracked across his shoulders. The Doctor was quite unable to stop himself. He leaped from his cover and next second the guard found himself flying through the air. He landed with a thump inside one of the trucks. The workers at the conveyor belt stopped working in astonishment. The Ogrons drew their guns.

Then a voice called, 'No!' It was the human chief guard climbing shakily out of the truck. 'The orders were to take him alive. And you needn't be gentle about it!'

Two Ogrons closed in on the Doctor. He ducked under the grip of one and sent it spinning into its fellow. Both Ogrons fell. The Doctor sprinted for the door. Beside it stood two more Ogrons. They fell on him savagely and within minutes the Doctor was beaten into unconsciousness. The Ogrons dragged him away. The human chief guard turned to the workers. 'Get on with your work—unless you want some of the same.' Hastily, they went back to their tasks, the Ogrons standing over them with their whips at the ready.

Moni slipped across the rubble and down the flight of stairs. It was dangerous to risk a daylight meeting but the situation was urgent. As far as he knew, this hide-out was still secure. If Anat and the others had escaped . . .

He rapped out a complicated series of knocks on the door and to his relief the door was opened. Boaz was there, pale and weary. Beside him was Anat. Moni glanced round the cellar. 'Where's Shura?'

Anat said, 'We lost him. He went to contact HQ and never returned. They must have got him.'

Boaz said angrily, 'We were nearly caught getting back here ourselves.'

Moni listened silently while they told the story of the failure of their mission. He said, 'There's a girl being held prisoner at Central Control—she must be the one you're talking about. Can she tell them anything?'

Anat said, 'She knows we want to kill Styles. She can tell them that.'

Moni sighed wearily. Everything seemed to be going wrong. The mission had been a shambles from the start.

Anat asked, 'What about the man—the one who came back with us? Have they caught him yet?'

Moni shook his head. 'Not yet. But it's just a matter of time . . .'

9

Escape from the Ogrons

Jo Grant pushed her plate away with a sigh of pleasure. 'No more, please. I couldn't eat another thing.'

The Controller leaned forward with a wine bottle. 'A little more wine?'

'No, honestly, nothing. It was a terrific meal.'

Actually, thought Jo, it hadn't been all that hot . . . coarse bread, tough meat and a mish-mash of strange vegetables. And she didn't think the Doctor would have thought much of the wine.

'I'm glad you enjoyed it,' he said. 'Few people eat so luxuriously these days.'

Jo thought he had a strange idea of luxury. She smiled and said nothing. 'Nowadays,' the Controller went on, 'we have to get most of our main food elements from pills and tablets.' The Controller sat back and smiled at her. 'Do go on telling me about your friend the Doctor.'

'I don't think I can tell you anything more,' said Jo frankly. 'We've covered just about everything.' And indeed they had. The Controller seemed fascinated by the Doctor and had asked question after question about him.

'You really don't know what he was doing before he joined this UNIT organisation?' asked the Controller.

'No idea,' said Jo firmly. 'No one knows very much about the Doctor, he's a very mysterious character. Look,' she went on hurriedly, 'please don't think I'm ungrateful but you did say something about rescuing the Doctor and getting me back to my own time.'

The Controller said, 'It isn't easy, you know. Our scientists are working on the problem.' He paused. 'As for your friend the Doctor, well, there's something I haven't told you. There's a reason to believe that he followed you to this time zone.'

Jo was overjoyed. 'That's marvellous! Do you know where he is?'

'I'm afraid not. He was travelling with the criminals. No doubt they kidnapped him. We're carrying out a search for him this very moment.'

A girl entered the room, bowed to the Controller and handed him a note. He waved in dismissal and she scuttled away. He opened the note, looked up at Jo and smiled. 'Good news, Miss Grant. Your friend the Doctor has been found. I'm going to fetch him now.'

Jo jumped up. 'Can I come with you?'

He shook his head. 'That isn't advisable. But don't worry, I assure you he's safe and well.'

At that particular moment the Doctor was in a bare metal cell, feeling on the very contrary both unsafe and unwell. He was at the end of a very long and gruelling interrogation. The purpose seemed to be to get him to admit that he was in some kind of resistance movement. The guard hoped to impress his masters by producing a confession by the time they arrived. But despite some brutal handling the Doctor wasn't co-operating.

Again the guard yelled, 'Tell us who you are!'

'You'd never believe me,' said the Doctor wearily.

'Name your contacts in the criminal resistance movement.'

'Haven't got any.'

'What are you doing here?'

'Looking for a girl called Jo Grant. How many more times?'

'As many as it takes to get the truth out of you. Shall I hand you over to our friends here? They don't get much fun.' The guard indicated the two Ogrons holding the Doctor down in his chair. The hairy paws were gripping his shoulders with brutal force.

'Poor fellows, that's too bad . . . but I'm not in the mood for games.'

The cell door opened and a small plumpish man entered. He wore plain dark clothing, with a civilian rather than a military look.

'Any progress?' he enquired.

The guard said, 'He's not being very co-operative.'

'How unwise of him. Perhaps I can persuade him. The rest of you wait outside.'

The guard looked rebellious for a moment. 'I said outside!' the newcomer repeated with an edge to his voice. At a nod from the guard the Ogrons released the Doctor and trooped out of the cell. The Doctor wriggled his aching shoulders. What next he wondered.

The plump little man started to say, 'I am the manager of this work camp, and I advise you . . .' But as soon as the cell door closed behind the Ogrons, he changed his tone. He leaned close to the Doctor and hissed, 'Which group are you with?'

The Doctor sighed. 'Don't you start. I've just been telling your hairy friends—I'm not with any group.'

The manager's voice was frantic, 'You don't understand. I'm in the resistance myself. I want to help you. Now, who sent you here? What were you supposed to do?'

Angrily the Doctor said, 'Nobody sent me! I am *not* a spy *or* a guerilla. I'm simply trying to find . . .'

But the little man wasn't listening. As the cell door started to open he grabbed the astonished Doctor by the collar and did his best to shake him.

'You're a spy! Admit it, you're a spy!'

The new arrival entered the cell and said severely, 'Stop this at once! Why is this man being treated like this?' He turned to the Doctor and said, 'My dear

Doctor, please permit me to apologise. I'm the Controller of this Sector. You're an elusive fellow, you know, I've had quite a job tracking you down.'

Gingerly, the Doctor rose to his feet. 'I'm glad you finally succeeded!'

By now he was beginning to feel that he must have broken into a madhouse.

'I've been looking forward to meeting you for some time. Miss Grant has told me so much about you.'

'Jo Grant?' said the Doctor eagerly. 'She's safe?'

'Safe and well and longing to see you again.' The Controller turned to the guard. 'See that the Doctor is taken at once to the guest suite at Central Control. I'll join you there later, Doctor.'

Deciding to make the most of his new status as an honoured guest, the Doctor said simply, 'Thank you,' and allowed himself to be ushered from the cell.

Once the Doctor had gone the Controller said, 'Perhaps we might go to your office, manager?'

The manager was deferential. 'Of course, Controller. This way.'

As they walked along the manager said, 'Excuse my asking, Controller, but who was that man? Why is he so important?' They reached the manager's office and went inside.

'That's no concern of yours,' said the Controller. 'What does concern you is the recent drop in production figures for this work camp. You are becoming too soft. As from next month your work targets will increase by ten per cent.'

'It's impossible, Controller. I can't do it!'

'Shall I replace you with someone who can?' asked the Controller coldly.

'I'm sorry. I'll do the best I can.'

'That's better. We'll consider this a friendly warning, shall we?'

'You're very kind, Controller.'

With a farewell nod the Controller left the room. The manager waited for a while, looking out across the work compound. Then he closed the door, unlocked a drawer in his desk and produced a tiny communicating device. He spoke softly, 'ZV 10 to Eagle, do you connect?'

The crackling voice came back at once. 'This is Eagle, ZV 10. We connect. What is your message?' (Eagle was the emergency channel of the resistance, manned 24 hours a day.)

The manager said, 'Time is short. I think they suspect me. Today a man was captured in the grounds. The Controller himself came to fetch him. I don't know who he is but he's important.'

'Do you know why he's important?'

'Negative. Check with your source at Central Control. Ask them why—'

The manager broke off short as his office door was smashed open. An Ogron stood in the doorway, the human security guard behind him. There was no time to conceal the communicator. Its tinny voice said, 'ZV 10 this is Eagle. Do you connect?'

Deliberately, the manager smashed the communicator to the ground. He waited hopelessly as the hands of the Ogron reached out for him . . .

In the guest suite at Central Control the first rapturous greetings were over. The Doctor was listening to Jo's account of life in the twenty-second century with more than a little suspicion.

'Honestly, Doctor, it's not so bad. I quite like it here. Everyone's been very kind, not like those nasty guerillas . . .'

The Doctor rubbed his chin. 'I'm glad you're being treated so well, Jo. I met some people earlier today who were anything but kind I can assure you.'

The Controller entered in time to hear this remark. 'Now be fair, Doctor. That was a regrettable error, which I put right as soon as I could. You mustn't jump to conclusions.'

The Doctor's manner was distinctly cool. 'Better than jumping to the crack of a whip from some security guard. Tell me, do you run all your factories like that?'

The Controller smiled. 'That isn't just a factory, Doctor. It is a rehabilitation centre for hardened criminals.'

The Doctor was unimpressed. 'Including a large proportion of old men and women?'

'I can assure you,' said the Controller, 'life on this planet has never been more efficiently or more economically organised. People have never been happier or more prosperous.'

The Doctor snapped, 'Then why do you need so many guards around? Don't the people like being so happy and prosperous?'

Jo Grant had been listening to this conversation with increasing dismay. Reproachfully she said, 'You're being a bit unreasonable, Doctor. The Controller only wants to help us.'

'Does he now?' said the Doctor. 'I wonder why?' Turning back to the Controller he said, '*I* find it rather surprising that, with a few rather remarkable exceptions, the human population of this planet seems to lead a life below the level of a dog. It makes me wonder who really rules this Utopia of yours.'

Jo had never seen the Doctor so angry before. The Controller seemed to wither at the sound of the cutting voice. He said haltingly, 'I'm afraid I must leave you. I have work to do. If you'll excuse me, Miss Grant.' The Controller turned and almost stumbled from the room.

Jo looked after him, worried. 'You shouldn't have spoken to him like that, Doctor. You don't know the whole picture.'

'Neither do you, Jo. Don't you see, Earth has become a slave planet. That man's no more than a sort of superior slave himself. Humans don't rule their own world any longer.'

Jo felt completely baffled. 'Then who does?' she asked.

'The most evil, ruthless life-form in the cosmos—the Daleks!' said the Doctor. 'Now just you listen to me.'

He told Jo all he had learned of the true state of affairs in the twenty-second century. Jo was horrified. 'Then why is he being so nice to us?'

'They want to get information. It's an old technique. They've tried the hard treatment. This is the soft. I don't think I want to wait till the hard comes round again.'

Jo shivered, 'Nor do I.'

The Doctor said, 'I got myself captured deliberately. I thought they'd put us together. But now I've found you we need to get away from here!'

Jo lowered her voice. 'There's a guard in the corridor outside.'

The Doctor said softly, 'Don't worry, Jo. I can deal with him.'

The Controller strode down the metal corridors towards the innermost Dalek HQ. He could still hear the sound of the Doctor's scornful voice. Well, he'd tried to help the man, tried to treat him decently. Now the Daleks could take over. They'd been right all along, it was a waste of time being considerate to such criminals. With thoughts like these the Controller tried to drown the memory of the Doctor's accusing voice. But it was no good. In his heart he knew that everything the Doctor had said was true.

Jo Grant stood in the middle of the guest suite and screamed just as loud as she could, 'Help! Help! Please help me!'

The Ogron guard lumbered through the door and stood looking at her suspiciously. All it could see was the small human girl jumping up and down and screaming. No danger there. It made no attempt to draw its pistol. It stood staring at Jo in amazement as she shrieked, 'Help! Help!'

The Doctor stepped from behind the door and delivered one of his celebrated Venusian karate chops. In theory the Ogron should then have slid quietly to the ground. Unfortunately it did no such thing. The nervous system of the Ogron race is very resistant to shock and is also protected by layers of incredibly tough muscle. As a result the Ogron turned round slowly and snarled at the Doctor, rather as though he'd stepped on its toe.

Somewhat taken aback the Doctor yelled 'Hai! Hai!' and delivered three more devastating blows—left hand, right hand, left foot—guaranteed to pulverise any life-form in the universe. The only result was that it irritated the Ogron even further. It advanced on the Doctor roaring with rage and the great hairy paws reached out and grabbed him. Before the Doctor could dodge, the Ogron hands were locked round his throat. The pressure of the mighty arms sent him slowly to his knees. As consciousness started to slip away the Doctor thought that this was a useful lesson: never underestimate an opponent. Unfortunately it looked like being the last lesson he would ever learn.

At this point Jo Grant took a hand in things. She jumped on the table, snatched up a full wine-bottle and smashed it down as hard as she could on the top of the Ogron's head. The result was instant and dramatic: the bottle shattered and the Ogron collapsed on top of the Doctor, out cold, wine trickling down its face.

The Doctor wriggled from underneath it, rubbing his throat. 'Thank you, Jo,' he said a little hoarsely.

He remembered the Ogron he had sent crashing into a wall, back in Austerly House. 'Top of the head seems to be their only weak point.' He grinned at Jo. 'Seems a terrible waste of wine, though. Come on, we'd better get moving.'

They moved out into the metal corridor, not running, but walking briskly as though they had a perfect right to go wherever they were going. The people they passed ignored them. In this world of the future it was safer to mind your own business.

A buzzer sounded and Jo looked up at the Doctor in alarm. He shook his head, telling her not to worry. Suddenly the corridor seemed to fill with people all going in one direction. Jo and the Doctor let themselves be carried along with the tide.

Lost in the bustling crowd, they were swept into a big lift which then went down and down for a long time, then out they emerged onto a sort of wide entrance hall. Through the big main doors they could see daylight.

The hall was very congested. They followed the crowd out through the doors. A second crowd was trying to get in. 'Shift-changing time,' whispered the Doctor in explanation.

There were Ogron guards at the door but their only interest seemed to be in keeping the crowd moving with guttural yells and occasional blows from their whips. They obviously didn't see the crowd as individuals at all and the different clothes and appearance of the two fugitives seemed to pass unnoticed.

In the Inner HQ the Controller was reporting the Doctor's capture to the Black Dalek. He finished his story and waited. Surely this would bring at least a word of praise.

For a moment the Dalek was silent. Then it grated, 'Your description of the Doc-tor does not tally with our files. Repeat.'

Puzzled, the Controller described the tall lean man with the shock of white hair. 'Do you mean this isn't the man?' he asked.

The Dalek said, 'Evidence indicates that the Doc-tor has changed his appearance.' It turned to a Dalek at a control console and said, 'Immediate visual display of suspect!'

The Dalek at the console said, 'I obey.'

It touched a control knob and a screen lit up showing the guest room suite. It was empty except for the Ogron now struggling slowly to its knees . . .

For a moment the Dalek seemed stunned. Then the Black Dalek screeched, 'Emergency! Emergency! The Doc-tor has escaped! Sound the alarm!'

The Dalek at the console touched another control and a strident alarm began to blare out. The Dalek said, 'The Doc-tor has escaped. Alert all security units. He must be found and exterminated.'

The Black Dalek intervened, 'No! We must capture him alive. We will use the Mind Analysis Machine to discover if this *is* the Doc-tor.'

The Controller shuddered. He had seen captured guerillas after they had been under the Dalek's Mind Analysis apparatus—shambling idiots, with all their intelligence drained from them. Death would be better than that.

The Dalek at the control console spoke into its microphone. 'Cancel previous instructions. The Doc-tor and the girl are to be captured alive and taken to Mind Analysis area.'

Jo and the Doctor were crossing a wide busy compound. Doorways on the far side led to long halls where crowds of people were standing in line to get bowls of grey unappetising stew. At the end of the compound was a huge main gate. Through its bars they saw the familiar vista of endless rubble.

The gates were standing slightly open but there were more Ogron guards on duty. Unlike those at the doors of the building, they were scrutinising keenly all those who went in and out, checking passes and permits. Jo realised that getting out of the building was one thing; getting out of the entire compound was going to be much harder. Which way should they go? They would never get through that main gate. There seemed no point in going back into the main block either. Sooner or later someone would notice them and ask questions.

The Doctor said, 'Look, Jo,' and drew her attention to the main gate. An extraordinary vehicle was jolting across the rubble. It looked like a sort of giant tricycle. It had enormous balloon tyres and their purpose was obvious: the odd-looking vehicle sped over the rubble as easily as if it were on a paved highway.

The tricycle shot through the gates and into the compound. The Ogron security guard riding it parked it near the gates, jumped off, and clattered up some stairs, carrying some kind of despatch box.

The Doctor looked at the tricycle with interest. 'Useful little vehicle, that,' he murmured. 'Specially developed for crossing all that rubble.'

Jo looked up at him, alarmed by the gleam in his eyes. 'Now, Doctor . . .' she said, warningly.

A strident alarm began to blare out through the compound. The Doctor yelled, 'Come on, Jo, I think that's for us.' Dragging Jo behind him, he ran across the compound to the parked tricycle. He jumped into the driver's seat, and Jo perched up behind him. It took the Doctor only a moment to work out how to use the simple controls. With a roar of power the machine shot through the main gates past the astonished guards and out across the sea of rubble.

Jo hung tightly to the Doctor as the tricycle sped across the ruined landscape. The little vehicle seemed to be able to cross virtually anything, and they flashed over ruined buildings, occasional bits of road and once even the scrubby and patched remains of a field.

All around was nothing but destruction and desolation, with here and there the jutting towers of the Dalek compounds breaking the horizon. The Doctor pulled up at the top of a little hill and looked round. Three or four more giant tricycles ridden by Ogrons were coming fromthe compound they had just left.

'Can't we outrun them?' asked Jo. 'We've got a good start.'

'We might,' said the Doctor. 'But what about those— and those?' He indicated the other compounds in front of them. From each one was speeding a group of more tricycles.

'We're surrounded!' said Jo anxiously. 'What are we going to do, Doctor?'

'Only one thing we can do,' said the Doctor cheerfully, 'give them a run for their money. Ever wondered how the fox feels, Jo? Hold tight!'

Jo closed her eyes and hung on to the Doctor as hard as she could. The rest of the journey was a nightmare. She saw it in glimpses as she opened her eyes from time to time, only to close them again hurriedly. The Doctor did incredible things with the giant trike, weaving it in and out of the rubble and the ruins. Jo could have sworn that once they drove up the side of a house and dropped down the other. They zoomed along the tops of walls, leaped over gaps in the ruins, and ploughed through weed-choked ditches. But every time Jo opened her eyes the circle of their pursuers was drawing in closer.

In a final desperate effort to break through the cordon the Doctor drove straight off the edge of a small cliff of rubble. The trike shot through the air and Jo screamed as they landed, bounced, and then crashed into a tangle of broken timbers. There was a jarring impact, and then silence.

The Doctor said gently, 'Open your eyes, Jo. It's all over.'

Jo looked around. Their trike, its handlebars buckled, was jammed in a pile of timbers, wedged far too tightly to move. Around them was a circle of grim-faced Ogrons, guns in hand. The Doctor sighed, 'Well, it was fun while it lasted.'

10

Interrogation by the Daleks

'Rescue him? Why should we risk our lives to rescue the Doctor?' In the guerillas' underground cell Boaz stared at Moni in disbelief.

Moni's voice was low and urgent. 'I tell you we *must*.'

Anat said, 'Why?'

'When the work camp manager reported the Doctor's capture he said he was important to the Daleks in some way.' Moni paused. 'He couldn't tell us any more. They must have got him just afterwards. He was executed this morning.'

Anat sighed. The plump, frightened little man had been an old friend of hers. Thanks to his position he had been one of their best agents. But she was used to such losses. They all were. She said, 'Go on.'

'I checked with our contact at Central Control,' Moni continued, 'she's a clerk on the Controller's personal staff.'

'And what did she tell you?' asked Boaz. 'What's so important about one man?'

'It seems the Doctor is a sworn enemy of the Daleks. He's fought and defeated them in the past.'

Anat murmured, 'Did he say he'd encountered them before.'

'According to our contact the Doctor is the one man the Daleks actually fear. Don't you see how important that makes him—to us? He must know a tremendous amount about them. If anyone can help us he can.'

'Why should he?' asked Anat. 'He's no reason to be grateful to us. We threatened to kill him.'

Moni said, 'That was all a misunderstanding. If we rescue him he'll owe us something. And if he hates the Daleks as much as we do he's bound to be on our side when we explain.'

Boaz looked dubious. 'An attack on Central Control. It's suicide. A lot of us will be killed even if we succeed.'

'But it will be worth it,' said Moni urgently. 'Look, I need you two because you know the Doctor by sight. Well, what do you say?'

Deep inside the Central HQ of the Daleks the Controller looked on impassively as the Doctor was strapped to a long low table by Ogron guards.

The walls of the little room were lined with strange alien equipment. Dalek scientists monitored control panels. A giant screen filled the whole of the fourth wall.

Once the Doctor was totally immobilised the Ogrons strapped a silvery helmet over his head. Leads from the helmet ran to the equipment nearest the screen. When all was ready the Ogrons stepped back. At a nod from the Black Dalek a Dalek scientist operated some controls. The screen lit up but only a fuzzy swirling nothingness could be seen.

The Dalek scientist said, 'He is deliberately suppressing his thoughts.'

'More power,' ordered the Black Dalek. The hum of power rose higher and higher. Still the swirling clouds on the screen did not change.

The Black Dalek said, 'You will admit your identity. Who are you?'

As the power rose yet higher a face began to appear on the screen. An old man with a sharp querulous face.

There was a note of triumph in the Black Dalek's

voice. 'It is the face of the Doc-tor as we knew him on Skaro. Confess! Confess!'

The Controller saw the Doctor's face distort with the effort of his mental resistance. But it was in vain. Slowly the first face disappeared and a second one took its place. This showed a younger, dark-haired man with a humorous, rather comic face. 'That is also the Doc-tor.' The voice of the Black Dalek rose to a shriek of triumph. 'You *are* the Doc-tor. You are the enemy of the Daleks! Now you are in our power! You will be exterminated! You will be exterminated! You will be exterminated!'

Every Dalek in the room aimed its gun-stick at the Doctor's helpless form.

11

The Raid on Dalek Headquarters

The Black Dalek and his aides gathered round the table to which the Doctor was tied. Their guns were swivelled round to aim at the Doctor. It was obvious that he was to be executed on the spot.

The Controller stepped forward and shouted, 'Stop!' The Daleks swivelled round to face him.

The Black Dalek said, 'Be silent.'

'To kill him now would be a mistake,' said the Controller firmly. 'Don't you see? He can give you valuable help.'

'The Doc-tor is an enemy of the Daleks. How can he help us?'

'He's been in contact with the resistance groups. We

know that. Don't you see? He may well be the brain behind them.'

The Black Dalek seemed to consider for a moment. 'You have proof of this?'

'We know that he's been working with them,' said the Controller urgently. 'Why else did he break into the work camp? It must have been to make contact with the manager—a leader of the resistance who has just been executed. Why did he take that risk? Perhaps there is some new plan to attack you.'

The Black Dalek turned to the Dalek scientist. 'Continue to operate the Mind Analysis Machine. We shall force the truth from his mind.'

The Controller pointed to the Doctor. He was limp and unconscious, his head lolling back against the restraining straps. 'Look at him. You've practically had to kill him just to establish his identity. He'll die before he tells you anything more.'

Again the Black Dalek considered. 'What is your plan?'

'Let me interrogate him.'

'Why should you be more successful than the Daleks?'

'I understand how his mind works. I can gain his confidence. Bring pressure on him through the girl.'

There was a moment's silence. Pressing home his advantage, the Controller said, 'When I've finished with him we'll have enough information to smash the whole resistance network.'

The Black Dalek swung round to the Ogrons and indicated the Doctor. 'Release him.'

The Ogrons unstrapped the Doctor from the table and dragged him to his feet. The movement seemed to revive the Doctor. Slowly his eyes opened. He looked at the Daleks all round him.

When he spoke his voice was low and determined. 'I've defeated you before. I defeated you on Skaro. I defeated you here on Earth, too.'

The Black Dalek's voice was triumphant. 'The Daleks have discovered the secret of time travel. We invaded again. We have changed the pattern of Earth's history.'

Defiantly the Doctor said, 'You won't succeed, you know. In the end you will always be defeated.'

'You have been defeated, Doc-tör! The Daleks' empire will spread through all planets and all times. No one can withstand the power of the Daleks.'

With the triumphant sound of the Dalek voice ringing in his ears the Doctor was dragged from the room.

In the guerillas' underground hide-out there was a scene of quiet activity. Guns were being cleaned and assembled. Little packs of plastic explosives were being made up. They were getting ready to raid Dalek Headquarters.

Boaz looked round the cellar. It was strange to see new faces in the place that he had shared with Shura and Anat all this while. Another three-man cell had been called in to make up the assault party.

The leader was Mark, a short stocky man, with hands scarred from years of work in the Dalek mines. It was said that he'd escaped by strangling an Ogron guard. Looking at those broad tough hands as they assembled a disintegrator gun, Boaz could easily believe it.

Then there was Zando, a round-faced red-headed lad, with an expression of mild innocence. He looked too young and timid to be a guerilla—a fact which had often saved his life.

Finally Joab, a shy and timid man, who was expert with all forms of explosives. Boaz watched as he rolled a batch of plastic Dalekenium compound into balls the size of a man's fist.

'Steady on,' he protested as Joab slapped the plastic around like baker's dough. 'Isn't that stuff pretty unstable?'

Joab gave a shy grin. 'Only when it hits a Dalek.' In

this form Dalekenium exploded on impact with a Dalek outer casing.

Boaz crossed to where Moni and Anat were studying a map. Moni was joining their group to replace the missing Shura. He would lead the expedition.

Moni and Anat seemed cheerful and confident as they planned possible routes. Boaz looked at the others in the little cellar. 'You'd think they were planning a day's outing,' he thought bitterly. 'In a few hours' time some, perhaps all of us, will be dead. And why are we risking our lives? To rescue some mysterious character who'd probably refuse to help anyway.

'And to think we had him as our prisoner,' thought Boaz with continuing bitterness. 'If we'd known he was so important we could have brought him here in the first place.'

Moni folded up the map. 'Well, that's it then. Everybody ready?' There was a murmur of assent. 'We'd better get moving. Time is short.'

Boaz packed up his equipment and followed them from the cellar. Well, Doctor, he thought, you'd better be worth it.

Back in the guest suite the Controller was watching in astonishment as the Doctor made a rapid recovery. When he had been carried from the Mind Analysis Machine the Doctor had seemed broken and exhausted. Now with a little food and wine, and a chance to rest, he was almost his old self again. So much so that he was paying very little attention to the Controller's efforts to convince him that he should co-operate with the Daleks.

'My dear chap,' the Doctor was saying a little impatiently, 'how can I possibly tell you what I don't know myself?'

'But you were in contact with the guerillas,' the Controller persisted.

'Not from choice,' Jo chimed in indignantly. 'They were going to kill him.'

The Controller turned his attack to Jo. 'Can't you see, I'm trying to help him? I've already saved his life.'

'True enough, old chap, and I'm grateful,' said the Doctor, 'but wasn't that just so that you could impress your Dalek masters by getting information out of me?'

The Controller was silent. To be truthful he wasn't sure of his own motives. Certainly that had been part of the reason. But he had also felt a strange reluctance to see the Doctor killed. He tried again. 'Unless you give me information about the resistance—the names of their leaders, the location of their hide-outs, their future plans—the Daleks will destroy you.'

The Doctor took another swig of wine and said coolly, 'I don't doubt it.'

The Controller looked curiously at him. 'You value your life so little?'

'On the contrary, I value it enormously. But the Daleks will try to kill me whatever I tell you. They've had it in mind for years.'

'But if you co-operate with them—'

'As you co-operate with them?' The Doctor looked at the Controller with a kind of pity. 'You really think it possible to co-operate with the Daleks?'

'They can be reasonable,' said the Controller defensively. 'They value my services.'

'They tolerate you,' said the Doctor. 'They allow you to live as long as you're useful.'

The Controller said angrily, 'I am a senior government official!'

'You're a slave,' said the Doctor simply. 'A slave who has a few privileges in return for helping to oppress his fellow slaves.'

Suddenly the Controller yelled, 'Be silent!' And Jo saw that he was literally shaking with emotion.

There was a moment's quiet. Then the Controller

spoke in a low hoarse voice. 'You don't understand,' he said. 'No one can understand who doesn't know about those terrible years. Towards the end of the twentieth century a series of devastating wars broke out. There were long periods of nothing but destruction and killing. Nearly seven-eighths of the world's population were wiped out. The rest lived for a long time in holes in the ground, starving, reduced to the level of animals. The entire planet was in ruins.'

Jo and the Doctor were silent, overcome by the horror of the picture he had drawn. Then Jo said softly, 'And that's when the Daleks took over?'

The Controller replied, 'There was no power on Earth to resist them.'

'So Earth became a giant factory,' said the Doctor. 'All the wealth, all the minerals, carried away to Skaro.'

'But why do they need to do all this?' asked Jo.

The Doctor looked grim. 'Because the Dalek empire is continually expanding. They need a constant flow of raw materials for their war machine. And the planet Earth is particularly rich in minerals.'

The Controller nodded. 'Everyone who is strong enough works in the mines. The rest work in factories, sorting and grading the ore, helping to build weapons for the Daleks. As you say, we're all slaves.' The Controller rubbed his hands over his eyes. It was years since he had allowed himself to think thc truth, let alone speak it out aloud.

Jo said, 'How did you come to work for them?'

'Everyone has to work for the Daleks,' said the Controller simply. 'This is better than the mines or the factories.'

'Is it?' said the Doctor. 'Is it really?'

The Controller tried to defend himself. 'I've used my position to help others. I've gained concessions, even saved a few lives.'

'Wouldn't you have helped more by using your skills

to lead the fight against the Daleks?' said the Doctor.

The Controller sighed. 'It's hopeless . . . no one can fight the Daleks.'

'That's not what the guerillas think.'

'A handful of fanatics . . . most of them killed off already. Believe me, there's nothing they can do to change things.'

In a small courtyard at the back of Dalek HQ, an iron hatch began to slide open. Moni, Anat, Boaz and the other three guerillas emerged. They looked around them. The courtyard was narrow, dark and windowless. On one side an archway gave on to a bigger courtyard. On the other a low ramp ran up to a metal door set into the side of the main building.

The group clustered around Moni, who indicated the metal door. 'This exit is hardly ever used. It's reserved for the Daleks. The door will be locked.'

'We'll open it,' said Joab, fishing out a pack of plastic explosive.

'Up the stairs, along the corridor and we're there,' said Moni. 'It's the nearest exit to the guest suite. Boaz and Anat come with me . . . the rest of you hold this courtyard. We have to go back the same—' He broke off as an Ogron came into the yard. It reached for its pistol but immediately Zando tripped it and Mark smashed it over the head with his gun. The Ogron fell without a sound. Moni said, 'Well done.'

Zando grinned. 'We've had a lot of practice.' Anat and Moni moved towards the ramp.

Seconds later it seemed that the little expedition was doomed before it began. Two Ogrons, guns in hand, rushed through the archway from the next courtyard. At the same moment the metal door opened. A Dalek came through it and glided down the ramp, heading straight for Anat. Its gun swung round to cover her.

Zando and Mark and Joab all fired through the little

archway at once, blasting the Ogrons out of existence.

At the same time Boaz grabbed the ball of plastic explosive dropped by Joab. He ran straight at the Dalek menacing Anat and slapped the explosive on to its outer casing. There was a tremendous explosion and Boaz and the Dalek disappeared in a cloud of smoke.

Anat turned blindly to Moni. 'That stuff's designed to explode on contact. He must have known.'

'He knew,' said Moni, 'but it doesn't always go off when you throw it. He wasn't taking any chances.' He shook her roughly. 'Now come on! Do you want him to have died for nothing?'

Moni and Anat rushed through the open door and up the stairs. The second group stayed behind as arranged. Zando and Mark kept up a steady fire through the archway while Joab lobbed balls of plastic explosive.

They were in a good position but hopelessly outnumbered. They couldn't hope to hold out for very long.

In the guest suite the Controller continued his vain attempt to convince the Doctor that he should furnish information about the guerillas. 'Think what you like of me,' he said wearily, 'but I did save your life. I won't be able to keep you alive unless you give me something to tell the Daleks.'

'I simply don't have any information,' said the Doctor, 'and quite frankly I wouldn't give it to you if I had.'

Suddenly there came the thump of plastic explosive and the high-pitched buzz of disintegrator guns.

The Controller leaped up in alarm. He looked round wildly as the sound of firing came nearer. 'Guards!' he shouted 'Guards!' A figure dashed through the doorway, gun in hand. But it wasn't an Ogron guard. It was Anat.

With her was a man they didn't know. He looked at the Controller. 'No use calling for your guards, my friend. They're all dead.'

Anat said, 'Doctor, Jo, are you all right?' Before they

could answer she went on, 'You've no reason to trust me but please come with us. We need you to help us fight the Daleks. This is Moni, one of our leaders.'

The Doctor said, 'Come on, Jo.' They made towards the door.

Suddenly the Doctor stopped. The other guerilla, Moni, was aiming his gun to shoot down the Controller. 'And as for you . . .' he was saying.

The Controller stood motionless, waiting. The Doctor said, 'No!'

Moni looked at him in astonishment.

'Killing him won't do any good,' said the Doctor, 'he's not the real enemy.'

Moni said, 'But he's helped them. If you knew of the blood on his hands . . .'

The Doctor replied, 'They'd always have found someone. Leave him.'

Anat called, 'Moni—let's go.' Reluctantly Moni lowered his gun. Jo, the Doctor and the two guerillas sprinted down the corridor. The Controller stood perfectly still where they had left him. He was stunned, unable to grasp what had happened. He could scarcely believe that he was still alive.

12

Return to Danger

Wrapped in an old blanket Jo Grant huddled close to the wood fire in the brazier. She sipped gratefully at a tin mug full of steaming herbal tea. She looked round the cellar curiously. It was a grim enough place yet the firelight gave it a homely look. She preferred it to the shining metallic luxury of the Dalek quarters.

The Doctor sat next to her. He too was sipping tea. There was a constant buzz of conversation between the Doctor, Moni and Anat who were gathered round the fire. Jo knew that three more guerillas had been lost in the rescue. One had been killed fighting a Dalek. Two others had sacrificed themselves to cover their retreat.

Jo's mind drifted back to their escape. Everything had happened so quickly. She and the Doctor had followed the guerillas down corridor after corridor and then down a flight of endless steps. Eventually they had emerged into a courtyard. There had been shooting and the thud of explosives, yells and roars and clouds of smoke.

Then they'd all crawled through a little hatchway and along narrow tunnels. Finally they'd crossed what seemed like miles of rubble, stopping to hide from Ogron patrols. At last they'd ended up here.

Jo tried to concentrate on the conversation going on around her but kept nodding off. Dimly she was aware that they were talking about Sir Reginald Styles.

The Doctor was saying, 'But how do you know all this? How do you know Styles was responsible?'

'There were still history books,' said Moni impatiently, 'even after the catastrophe. We know.'

Anat took up the story. 'You see Styles only pretended to be working for world peace. Really he wanted power for himself.'

The Doctor took another swig of his tea. 'So you're saying that this conference he called was a trick?'

'Exactly that,' affirmed Moni. 'He managed to lure all the leading delegates to his house.'

The Doctor said, 'I was told that he was planning a sort of preliminary conference, just before I, er . . . left Austerly House.'

'Once they were at the house,' said Moni, 'there was a

tremendous explosion. The house was completely destroyed. Styles was killed with the others.'

'That wasn't very clever of him,' commented the Doctor.

Moni said, 'Obviously he must have set a bomb. Perhaps he mistimed the fuse.'

'There were charges and counter-charges,' said Anat, 'and of course the conference was finished. Soon after that war broke out. First with conventional weapons, then with atomic. Thereafter a succession of wars led us to this—' She waved her hand round the cellar.

Moni nodded in agreement. 'And after that the Daleks came and took over what was left.'

The Doctor stared thoughtfully into the fire. 'So you decided to go back in time and intervene in your own history . . . to kill Styles before he managed to carry out his plan?'

'That's right,' said Moni.

'We stole the plans of time machines from the Daleks. We stole parts and equipment, and managed to build machines of our own.'

Anat joined in. 'At first things didn't go too well. The transference was unstable. People appeared for a while in your time and then just faded away.'

'That explains the ghost that Styles saw,' said Jo. 'And the man who vanished from the UNIT sickbay.'

The Doctor nodded. 'Then you three turned up—which is more or less where I came in. By the way, what happened to the other one? That young chap . . .'

Anat frowned. 'Shura? He simply vanished. We think an Ogron patrol must have got him.'

Moni said, 'Somehow the Daleks learned what we were trying to do. They sent Ogron security guards back into your time to stop us. Shura probably ran into one of them.'

The Doctor looked round the circle of intent faces. 'There's one thing you still haven't told us. Why did you go to so much trouble to rescue us.' He looked quzzically at Anat. 'After all, our first meeting wasn't very friendly.'

Anat said, 'I'm sorry about all that, Doctor. At first we thought you were Styles. When we found out that you weren't you were just a nuisance. Our mission had to succeed at all costs.'

The Doctor looked across at Moni. 'You still haven't answered my question. Why did you rescue us?'

Moni leaned forward. 'We learned later that you were an old enemy of the Daleks, that you'd fought and defeated them before. Surely you'd help us beat them here?'

The Doctor said, 'If I can—certainly. What do you want me to do?'

Moni said urgently, 'You can succeed where we failed Doctor. We want you to go back to your own time and kill Styles!'

There was a good deal of bustle and activity around the tunnel near Austerly House. The area was floodlit by spotlights and by the headlights of army jeeps.

Captain Yates stood before the Brigadier's jeep with some odds and ends of guerilla equipment. There was food, the shattered booster transmitter, and a stubby looking cylinder with controls set into it.

'We found this stuff in a sort of hiding place, hollowed out beneath some rubble, sir.'

The Brigadier looked at the odds and ends, and grunted. 'This all?'

'Yes, sir. No sign of anyone or anything else.'

The Brigadier sighed. He had spent a very long day clearing up after the battle at Austerly House and carrying out a search of the area. Now he had extended the range of his search as far as the tunnel. Except for this bundle of odds and ends there had been absolutely no results.

Equally useless had been the Brigadier's efforts to convince the powers-that-be to abandon the idea of a conference at Austerly House. As was often the case in UNIT operations the Brigadier's reasons were too fantastic to be believed. In addition there was an embarrassing shortage of evidence. The disintegrator guns used by both Ogrons and guerillas destroyed all trace of their victims. Even the bodies of Ogrons killed by bullets had mysteriously faded away. All the Brigadier could produce to support his story were the signs of battle in Styles' study and the fact that numbers of his own men had vanished.

A sceptical official from the Ministry had looked at Styles' wrecked study and muttered disapprovingly about 'vandalism.' Squads of painters and decorators had worked hard all day to repair the damage and now even *that* evidence was gone.

The main obstacle though was Styles himself. At present he was in London greeting the other delegates as they arrived. And he was firmly opposed to any change of plan. Arranging the conference, he said, had been a delicate, almost impossible business. The slightest change in plan might arouse suspicion in the delegates and send them rushing home again.

The Brigadier could see the old boy's point. And the prize of world peace no doubt justified the risks. But it still left the Brigadier with the problem of trying to protect the conference.

There was the roar of a motorbike and a despatch rider halted by the jeep. The Brigadier took the offered message and tore it open.

'Well, that's it, Mike. No change in plans will be considered. Styles and the other world leaders will arrive first thing tomorrow.' He crumpled up the signal in disgust.

'All we can do is keep searching, Mike. Constant patrols at all times. We'll extend the radius of the search.

I want a completely safe area all round the house and grounds. Oh, and keep a heavy guard on this tunnel. It seems to be the centre of things.'

'What about this lot, sir?' asked Captain Yates, indicating his finds from the tunnel. The Brigadier poked the collection with his cane. 'Be careful, sir!' said Yates in alarm. 'The cylinder looks very much like a bomb.'

'Oh, send it all back to UNIT HQ. The Doctor might like to look at it—*if* we ever see him again.' The Brigadier started his jeep and drove back towards the house. Yates dumped his finds in the back of a UNIT truck. He wondered if the Doctor would ever turn up to examine them. Jo Grant, too, come to that. Mike shook his head wearily and went back to organising the search.

The Brigadier and Captain Yates didn't know it but two important items were missing from their find in the tunnel. The most important was Shura himself. Then there were the things he was carrying, stuffed into a bulky parcel inside his tunic: a disintegrator pistol—and a Dalekenium bomb.

After the noise and shooting of the Daleks' failed ambush at the tunnel Shura had drifted off into more uneasy sleep. When he awoke his condition was worse rather than better. His exhaustion, his wounds, the long spell in the cold damp tunnel had sent him into a high fever. When he awoke he was almost delirious. Only one thought filled his mind: the others had gone, abandoned him! But he himself must complete the mission. He must get back to Austerly House and kill Styles.

Just as darkness began to fall he had emerged from his hiding place, limping along slowly, like a wounded animal. He came out of the tunnel into the cool night air and stood gasping for a moment. Then he lurched across the fields towards the house. Just as he reached the edge of the field he heard the noise of soldiers coming towards him. He stumbled into a ditch and lay still, covering himself with leaves and bracken. He heard the sound of army vehicles as they parked on the road. Men jumped out, there was a clatter of booted feet, shouted orders. Footsteps thudded by him within inches of his head.

When it was quiet Shura got to his feet and staggered on leaving the little cluster of vehicles behind him.

Although he didn't realise it this was Shura's greatest stroke of luck. As the Brigadier's men were spreading outwards from the house he was moving towards it. Once he'd passed through the line he and the searchers were moving in opposite directions.

It took him a long time to get into the grounds. He was too weak to climb the wall so he went round to the main gate and waited. The gate was guarded. Shura waited patiently under cover until a UNIT lorry drove up. While the sentry was checking the driver's pass Shura somehow scrambled over the tailboard and inside the lorry. It was full of food and drink, cases and cases of it. Sir Reginald and his guests had to be well fed. Shura hastily added a loaf of bread and a bottle to the bundle inside his tunic.

The lorry soon jolted to a halt at the back of the house, and Shura jumped out, slipping into the shadows as the driver came round to unload. The kitchen door stood open but there were lights on and he could hear the sound of voices.

Shura moved along the side of the house, looking for a way in. His boots clanged on metal and he looked down. At his feet was a round manhole cover. Shura fished a knife from his pocket and managed to prise it up. Unhesitatingly, he took off his tunic, made a bundle of all his possessions and lowered them through. Then he swung his legs into the dark circle and slid down. He found a foot-hold on something lumpy and shifting. Reaching up again through the hole he dragged the cover back into place. Minutes later a UNIT sentry came round the corner. His boots clanged on the manhole cover just as Shura had it back in place.

Shura fished a light cell from his pocket and looked around him. He was in a cellar filled with lumpy black stone. He remembered his history. Of course, coal! They used to burn it for fuel . . .

Shura's incredible luck had served him well again. It was almost as though he was meant to succeed . . . as though fate was co-operating with him. Austerly House had long ago been converted to oil-fired central heating. But the old coal cellar, and the remnants of the coal, were still there. Nobody ever came to the cellar now.

Shura hollowed out a nest for himself in the coal and settled back. He knocked the top off the wine bottle and took a swig, then stuffed handfuls of bread into his mouth.

Under the influence of the wine and the fever that possessed him he was floating aloof and carefree above the world. Everything was going well. When Styles arrived he would kill him. The mission would be completed. In the pitch blackness of the coal cellar, gun and bomb clutched to his chest, Shura felt calm and happy. All he had to do now was wait.

Jo woke up with a start from her doze by the guerillas' fire. Something was happening in the cellar. Voices were raised in excitement. The Doctor was on his feet, pacing about the room.

'Don't you see, man,' he said, 'you're asking me to commit murder! How can I agree to do what you want?'

Anat said, 'We're asking you to kill one man—and to save many more lives.'

'It's still murder,' said the Doctor stubbornly.

'Isn't it justified,' insisted Moni, 'if it would save the human race from the Daleks?'

'Ah, but would it?' said the Doctor, resuming his pacing about. 'Would it?'

Anat looked at him in puzzlement. 'We've told you how it all happened.'

'And suppose your history books got it wrong? Oh, not the basic facts but their interpretation of them?' He turned to Moni. 'Won't you return us to our own time? Now we know the facts there may be other things we can do to help you.'

'Doctor, please,' said Moni. 'The relationship between our time zone and yours is fixed. A day has gone by here, a day has gone by in your time. Soon it may be too late. Won't you promise to help us? We'll send you back if you'll give us your word to kill Styles.'

'My dear chap,' said the Doctor, 'I'm completely with you as to the ends but I can't accept your choice of means. And more than that, something feels wrong about the whole idea . . .'

Jo yawned and stretched. Everyone looked round when she spoke up. 'The thing that puzzles me is that I just can't believe in Styles as a ruthless mass-murderer. I mean, he got a bit stroppy but basically I thought he was quite a nice old boy.' She yawned again.

The Doctor swung round on her enthusiastically. 'That's it, Jo. That's it! Just what was worrying me . . . that's what I feel, too!' He turned to the guerillas. 'Styles is a *good* man—vain, arrogant, pompous, if you like, but underneath it all, good. He really does want world peace, I'll swear it. He couldn't have caused that explosion.'

Anat said, 'Then who did?'

'Let me see that book of yours again,' said the Doctor. Anat passed him the tattered book. Worn almost to pieces by constant handling it was obviously one of the guerillas' greatest treasures. He peered at the faded print and began to read aloud. 'The explosion in the cellar was of such shattering force that it was suspected that a small atomic bomb had been used. But later tests showed no trace of radioactivity. It was charged that the Government had developed some new and deadly "clean" form of atom bomb. This was strongly denied, and no such bomb was ever used in the wars that followed.'

The Doctor closed the book. An incredible idea was beginning to form in his mind. 'An explosive unknown *at that time*,' he said softly. He looked at Anat. 'And one of you didn't get back from your mission!'

'That's right—Shura. He went to try and contact base. We never saw him again.'

The Doctor said thoughtfully, 'What sort of equipment did you take to the twentieth century?'

Anat said, 'Usual battle gear: disintegrator guns, booster for the sub-temporal radio, food supplies, explosives . . .'

The Doctor stopped her. 'Explosives?'

'We took two Dalekenium bombs. Just in case . . .'

'What did they look like?'

'Stubby black cylinders, about so big.' She gestured with her hands. 'Small but tremendously powerful. We stole them from the Daleks!'

'I don't remember ever seeing you with these bombs,' said the Doctor. 'When you were at the house, did you have them with you?'

'Shura hid them for us in the tunnel when we arrived. We didn't have time to pick them up on our way back.'

'Exactly,' said the Doctor. 'Shura hid them in the tunnel where he went to make his attempt to call base. And Dalekenium is a clean explosive. All the power of the atom but no fall-out!'

'Well yes, but . . .' Anat stared at him in horror. 'No Doctor. It's impossible.'

The Doctor said remorselessly, 'It all fits. An explosive unknown on Earth at that time . . . Shura, abandoned, wounded perhaps, but determined to carry out his mission . . . and Styles returning to the house with the other delegates,'

The Doctor looked round the circle of horror-struck

faces. 'Don't you see? You want to change history. But you can't. You're part of it, trapped in a temporal paradox. Styles didn't kill all those world leaders. He didn't start the wars that led to the Dalek conquest. *You* did. You did it all yourselves!'

13

The Day of the Daleks

Once again the Controller stood before the High Council of the Daleks.

The Black Dalek, the Golden Dalek and their aides surrounded him, menacing and threatening . . .

Dully he listened to the accusing voice of the Golden Dalek. 'You have failed the Daleks. The Doc-tor has escaped.'

'He will be recaptured,' said the Controller. 'I swear it.'

'He must be found and destroyed.'

Wearily the Controller said, 'I am sure he will attempt to return to his own time zone. When he does, and if the guerillas are helping him, they will use the old monorail tunnels. It gives them a fixed reference point near Austerly House in the twentieth century. I can set another ambush—fill the tunnels with guards.'

The Black Dalek said, 'If you fail us you will pay with your life. This is your final chance.'

The Controller turned and walked from the room.

He returned to his office and summoned Zeno, his senior assistant, a sharp-featured, ambitious young man. Briefly, the Controller gave instructions for the ambush.

'I leave the whole thing to you. Don't trouble me with details.'

Puzzled, but happy at a chance to distinguish himself, Zeno returned to his own office. A few moments later his good mood was shattered when he received a summons to appear before the Black Dalek. Hurriedly he made his way to the inner HQ, where he waited trembling until the Black Dalek appeared.

Zeno looked at the Dalek in awe and horror. Though he had worked for the Daleks all his life it was very seldom that he actually saw one. Particularly one of this exalted rank. The Daleks ruled by proxy and were seldom seen.

The Dalek said, 'We are not satisfied with the loyalty and efficiency of the Controller. It may be necessary for you to replace him!'

Zeno bowed, 'I'm sure that you know best,' he said.

'You will observe him closely during the coming operation. Then you will bring us your report.'

It was still dark when Jo, the Doctor, and the two guerillas made their way across the rubble. Jo was very tired now. She stumbled several times and the Doctor steadied her with a hand on her arm.

She could remember the hours of argument that followed as the Doctor tried to get the guerillas to accept his theory . . . their final reluctant acceptance. Jo hadn't followed all the ins and outs of the argument; all she knew was that at last they were going home, away from this horrible world of Daleks and Ogrons, back to their own time.

Moni halted at the tunnel entrance. 'This is it, Doctor. Anat will take you to a point that is equivalent to the railway tunnel in your own time. Then you'll be transferred. Goodbye and good luck.'

Moni shook hands briefly and turned back. The rest of them plunged on into the darkness. Anat led the way, flashing a little light-cell occasionally to give them their bearings. They plodded on for what seemed an endless time, through the tunnels. At last Anat said, 'We're here!' She shone round her light and the Doctor recognised the point of his first arrival. Anat produced a time machine. 'It's already set. All you need do is press the operating button.' She, too, shook hands. 'Goodbye, Doctor. I hope you're right about it all. Do what you can for us, won't you?'

She was about to hand over the machine when they were all caught in the beam of a fierce spotlight. A voice said, 'Stay where you are, all of you!'

Ogron guards appeared all round them.

The Controller walked forwards. 'It has ended as I said it would, Doctor. No one can defeat the Daleks. It is madness to oppose them.'

The Doctor walked up to the Controller. He spoke in a low urgent voice.

'I can free this whole world from their rule. I know what happened, how they were able to conquer this planet. I can set Earth's history back onto its proper path. Are you going to stop me?'

In an agonised voice the Controller said, 'If only I could be sure . . .'

The Doctor said, 'You spoke of the war, the suffering, the starvation . . . I can stop that from ever happening. *We* can stop it! Will you help me?'

'You saved my life,' said the Controller slowly. 'You could have let them kill me. And now you offer freedom.' He turned to the surrounding Ogrons and said, 'Go! I will deal with these criminals alone! Go, I tell you!' Confused, the Ogrons shambled back into the darkness.

The Controller turned back to the Doctor. 'You go, too. Go quickly!'

The Doctor beckoned to Jo. She ran to join him. He looked at Anat. She shook her head. 'I'll stay in my own time, Doctor. Besides, the machine will only transport two.'

Swiftly the Doctor activated the machine. The glow of the time field surrounded the two figures. Slowly Jo and the Doctor began to fade away.

Zeno came running down the tunnels, armed Ogrons at his heels. He bellowed, 'Stop! Stop them!' But it was alredy too late—Jo and the Doctor had vanished.

Zeno looked at the Controller. 'You have let them escape. You will pay the penalty for this, Controller.' He turned to Anat, 'And so will you.'

But Anat's gun was already in her hand. She shot out the spotlight and disappeared into the darkness. Zeno made a determined grab for the Controller. To his surprise the Controller was standing quite still. He made no attempt to escape.

Anat ran swiftly through the dark tunnel. She slipped easily through the milling crowds of Ogron guards, shooting out any spotlight that appeared. The Ogrons panicked and fired wildly, killing each other in the process.

Anat came to the point where the Doctor had left the tunnels. The maintenance ladders were an old and familiar escape route. She climbed nimbly upwards and emerged into the fresh air.

She stood for a moment looking over the sea of rubble, the only world she had ever known. There were streaks of light in the east. Dawn was breaking. If the Doctor succeeded it might be a new dawn for all of them. If not, she could always go on fighting. She began to clamber across the rubble, towards the hide-out.

After the same mind-twisting voyage through the Time Vortex Jo and the Doctor found themselves back in the railway tunnel of their twentieth century. 'All right, Jo?' queried the Doctor. She nodded. 'Come on then. There's very little time.'

They ran out of the darkness of the tunnel and cannoned straight into Sergeant Benton, who was in charge of the tunnel guard. 'Jo! Doctor!' he yelled. 'Where have you two been?'

'No time for explanations!' snapped the Doctor. 'What's happening at the house?'

Benton looked at his watch. 'Delegates will be arriving for the conference at any moment. Styles is there already. Wants to make an early start.'

'We may still be in time then,' said the Doctor. 'Lend me a jeep, Sergeant, I've got to get over there right away.'

Benton shrugged. 'I've got to stay here. The Brigadier wants this tunnel guarded. Help yourself, Doc!' He indicated a jeep parked on the road nearby. The Doctor made for it at a run.

Jo said helplessly, 'Hello and goodbye, Sergeant.' She set off after the Doctor.

For the last time the Controller of Earth Sector One stood before the Dalek High Council. Somehow he seemed a different man. His shoulders had lost the cowed slump of slavery and he was free at last from fear since he had nothing now to lose. He listened quietly while an eager Zeno made his report.

The Black Dalek swung round on the Controller accusingly. 'You will be exterminated! You are a traitor to the Daleks.'

Its gun-stalk swung round to cover him. So, too, did the guns of the other Daleks.

The Controller's voice was calm as he said, 'Oh no. I have been a traitor to humanity all my life. But not any more.'

The Black Dalek shrieked with rage, 'You will be exterminated!'

The Controller smiled. 'Who knows? I may even have helped to exterminate *you*.'

The smile was still on his face when the blast from all the Dalek guns caught him. His body twisted for a moment in an intensity of white light, and then slumped to the ground.

The Black Dalek turned to Zeno as Ogron guards dragged the body of the Controller from the room. 'You have proved yourself worthy to be the new Controller. But be warned: the Daleks expect total loyalty from those who serve them!' Zeno bowed and walked from the room.

The Daleks began to talk amongst themselves in grating metallic voices. It was not so much a conference: since all Daleks think alike it was more a chorus of agreement. The Golden Dalek spoke first.

'The Doc-tor is a Time Lord. His intervention may be able to return the course of history to its original path.'

Then the Black Dalek: 'We must follow him to the twentieth-century time zone and destroy him.'

'The war amongst the humans must break out,' pronounced the Golden Dalek.

'The Dalek conquest of the planet Earth must not be reversed,' agreed the Black Dalek.

The Daleks left the room to prepare for their expedition. This time they would invade the twentieth century in force.

In spite of the early hour there was a little crowd of spectators around the gates of Austerly House. They watched with interest as one by one the diplomats arrived in their long black limousines. There was even a television news team. The commentator was working very hard to make a series of pictures of middle-aged men getting out of cars sound exciting.

'And it is no exaggeration to say that the peace of the world may well depend on what happens here today. On the steps you can see Sir Reginald Styles greeting the Chinese delegate as he steps from his car. The last-minute agreement of the Chinese to attend has given this conference its greatest chance of success. That agreement is due almost entirely to the efforts of Sir Reginald himself. Beside Sir Reginald on the steps is Brigadier Alastair Lethbridge-Stewart. The Brigadier is, of course, head of the British section of UNIT, the United Nations Intelligence Taskforce, and he is in charge of security at the conference.'

The commentator paused, racking his brains for something else to say. He was wishing that something, anything, would happen when his wish was suddenly granted. A jeep, driven very fast, suddenly shot up the drive and came to a screeching halt at the front steps. A very tall man in rather tattered clothes leaped out, followed by a very small young lady. The tall man rushed up to Styles and the Brigadier and hustled them inside the building.

The commentator caught a protesting cry of 'Doctor—what do you think you're . . .' and then the trio disappeared inside the hall.

Inside the Doctor was saying, 'Never mind where I've been. You must evacuate this house at once!'

Styles said furiously, 'Is this man mad?'

'Please, do as he says,' said Jo. 'If you don't you'll all be blown up!'

'That's right, Brigadier,' said the Doctor. 'Somewhere in this house there's a bomb.'

'Impossible,' the Brigadier said flatly. 'Whole place has been searched.'

'Then search again' replied the Doctor, 'but clear this building first!'

Styles said, 'I flatly refuse to leave, Brigadier. And I insist this man be removed.'

In the cellar beneath the house Shura was priming his

Dalekenium bomb. By lifting the lid of his manhole a little earlier he'd been able to hear the noise and bustle of the arrivals. He'd even heard a passing sentry calling, 'Smarten up, there. Old Styles is just arriving.' For Shura that was evidence enough. He'd waited a little longer, finished the last of the bread and wine, and now the bomb was primed. Little figures began to click over on the dial of the bomb. Then they stopped. Shura peered at them muzzily with his light-cell but they seemed blurred. The timing mechanism had jammed. But it didn't matter. He could easily do without it!

On the road near the tunnel Sergeant Benton leaned against a wall and stretched. He wondered how much longer he'd have to go on guarding this rotten tunnel. Nothing had happened there for ages. He peered into the darkness of the tunnel mouth. Something seemed to be moving.

In the hall of Austerly House time was ticking away and the argument still raged. Styles was adamant and finally the Doctor gave up. 'Brigadier, get Styles and the rest of them out of this house at once. Use force if you have to!'

The Doctor dashed to the wine-cellar door and opened it. He switched on the light. The cellar was empty.

'Cellar, the book said a cellar,' he muttered to himself. Rejoining the group in the hall, he said abruptly, 'Sir Reginald, is the wine cellar the only cellar in the house?'

Sir Reginald looked at him in amazement, convinced by now that the Doctor was quite mad. 'Yes, of course!' he snapped.

The Doctor shook him by the shoulder. 'Think, man, think . . . there must be another!'

'There's a little coal cellar by the back kitchen,' said Styles after a moment. 'Never used now, of course.'

As the Doctor was about to rush away the Brigadier's walkie-talkie crackled into life. The Brigadier listened to the agitated voice and said, 'Do your best to hold them, Benton. If you can't, fall back slowly. I'll reinforce you as soon as I can.'

He turned to the Doctor and said, 'Some kind of attacking force is coming out of the tunnel. Those ape-things and something else. Some kind of robots . . .'

'Daleks,' whispered Jo. 'Daleks and Ogrons!'

The Doctor nodded. 'They're coming to blow up the house and kill Styles—make sure that history goes their way.'

The Brigadier understood none of this but he was at his best in a military situation. The attack from the tunnel gave him the excuse he needed. He turned to Styles and said crisply, 'You, Sir Reginald, the diplomats and all their staff will evacuate this house at once! Don't argue, man, you can make your protest later. Captain Yates, get them moving!'

Seconds later the television commentator saw the extraordinary sight of a number of distinguished foreign diplomats being practically thrown into their cars by UNIT troops and driven away at speed. He had no chance to describe this for the viewers, however, for minutes later he and his team were being bustled into a jeep and driven away likewise.

In the now rapidly emptying house the Doctor ran to the little coal cellar. He burst open the door and saw Shura, lying on the coal, covering him with a pistol. On the coal beside Shura was the stubby little bomb. The Doctor drew a deep breath. 'Shura,' he said quietly. 'You've got to listen to me.'

The invaders from the tunnel advanced remorselessly upon the house. The UNIT troops fought bravely but could not hold them back. The Ogrons could be killed, though with difficulty. But the Daleks—they seemed invincible. Nothing stopped them as, flanked by their Ogron guards, they glided effortlessly forward. They swept up the drive and were now very close to the house. The Brigadier blazed away from the front steps. Men were being shot down all round him and he knew that it was only a matter of time . . .

Jo Grant looked from a window with horror at the advancing Dalek army. Instinctively she ran to warn the Doctor.

In the coal cellar doorway the Doctor, still covered by Shura's gun, was saying persuasively, 'Shura, if you set off that bomb you'll be sacrificing yourself for nothing. Styles has gone now—he isn't in the house, I tell you.'

Shura's hand was resting on the little black plunger. He said dreamily, 'Must kill Styles, must stop the war . . .'

The Doctor looked at him sadly. Shura's face was gleaming with sweat, his eyes unnaturally bright. The Doctor recognised the signs of high fever. There was little chance of getting through to Shura now.

Jo Grant ran and joined him in the doorway. 'Doctor, come away! The Daleks are attacking from the tunnel! They're almost in the house . . .'

She stopped talking as she saw the grim figure of Shura, crouched on the coal, the bomb beside him.

Shura reacted to Jo's voice. 'Daleks? Daleks . . . here?'

'That's right,' said the Doctor. 'They've come to make sure their version of history isn't changed. Shura, *please*, won't you come with us? We can save you.'

Shura seemed to become suddenly rational. An attacking force of Daleks was something his fevered mind could grasp. 'You two get out of here. Leave them to me. Just let them get into the house . . .'

Jo said, 'Shura, no! Make him come with us, Doctor.'

'This is Dalekenium,' said Shura. 'The only stuff that will deal with the Daleks—their own bomb!'

'We could rig up a time fuse,' said the Doctor desperately. 'Shura, there must be some other way . . .'

'The time mechanism is broken,' said Shura. 'Anyway this stuff's too unstable. I'll use the contact plunger. Only way to be sure.' His hand hovered over a black plunger in the side of the bomb. 'Now are you getting out, Doctor? Or do you both want to be here when I press this?'

The Doctor gave him a last look, then said, 'All right, Shura. Come on, Jo!'

The two ran through the empty house to the front steps where the Brigadier and what was left of his men were fighting a last desperate rearguard action. Some of the Ogrons had fallen but most of them were still advancing, the apparently invincible Daleks at their head.

The Doctor ran up to the Brigadier and yelled, 'Fall back! Everyone fall back! Let them into the house. It's the only way.'

The Brigadier shouted, 'You heard the Doctor! Everybody pull back! Regroup on the hill behind the house.'

Led by Jo and the Doctor, the Brigadier and his few remaining troops turned and ran. Triumphantly the Daleks and their Ogron army came on.

From the little hillside behind the house the Doctor and the others watched as a triumphant flood of Ogrons, led by the Black Dalek and the Golden Dalek swept up the drive and swirled into the house. Softly the Doctor muttered, 'Now, Shura, *now*!'

Inside the house the Daleks and their Ogron guards milled about the empty rooms. From his hiding place in the cellar Shura could hear the angry Dalek voices.

'Where are the delegates?'

'Where is the man Styles?'

'They must be found and exterminated.'

'The Dalek conquest of the planet Earth must not be reversed.'

'The Daleks will be victorious!'

Shura said softly to himself, 'Oh no, not this time. This time it's going to be different.' With that he pressed the black plunger on the bomb.

From the hillside the Doctor and his group saw the tremendous eruption. It destroyed the house in a single, savage blast. The noise was shattering. As the black smoke drifted away they saw that the house had completely vanished. No ruins, no debris, just a gaping black hole in the ground . . .

The Doctor turned to Styles, who was standing nearby. 'Your conference has been saved, Sir Reginald. I hope you make sure it's a success. You still have a choice of futures.'

Styles looked at him wonderingly. 'Don't worry. We all know what will happen if we fail.'

'So do we,' said the Doctor. 'We've seen it, haven't we, Jo?'

Ignoring the puzzled looks from Sir Reginald and the Brigadier, Jo and the Doctor walked down the hill.

14

All Kinds of Futures

'I'm sorry, Doctor,' said Jo obstinately, 'I still don't understand.'

They were walking along the corridor towards the laboratory.

'It's quite simple, Jo. Somehow the Daleks managed to pervert the course of history so that they could conquer the Earth. The guerillas tried to change things back but because they were a part of history their intervention just repeated the pattern. I was able to intervene and put history back on its proper tracks.'

'I know,' said Jo impatiently, 'because you're a Time Lord. But that still doesn't explain how—' she stopped in amazement as the Doctor flung open the laboratory door. Another Jo Grant was standing there, looking at her with equal astonishment.

The Doctor said, 'Good grief, yes, of course, I remember now.' He looked at the second Jo Grant. 'Now don't you worry, my dear. I know you're alarmed but—'

To Jo's astonishment a second Doctor came out of the TARDIS. He frowned at them. 'Oh no, what are you doing here?'

Jo heard the Doctor reply. 'Don't worry, I'm not here, that is . . .well, in a sense I am here but you're not there . . . It's a bit complicated to explain.'

'Well, this won't do at all, will it?' said the second Doctor severely. 'Can't have two of us running about.'

'Don't worry, old chap,' said the Doctor. 'It'll all be . . .'

Suddenly the second Doctor and the second Jo disappeared. Calmly the Doctor walked into the lab and took off his cloak.

'Wait a minute,' said Jo, 'that all happened before. Only they were us and we were them.'

The Doctor smiled, 'Don't worry about it, Jo. I told you Time was a very complicated thing.'

The Brigadier entered looking a little shaken. 'I think I've been having hallucinations. For one ghastly moment I thought I saw two of you.'

'Nothing for you to worry about, old chap,' said the Doctor soothingly.

'Ah well,' said the Brigadier. 'Now then, what did I come in for? Oh yes, good news from the conference. Seeing that explosion seems to have done 'em all good. According to old Styles they're all co-operating beautifully.'

'I'm glad to hear it,' said the Doctor. 'Now if you'll excuse me I've got work to do.' He opened the door of the TARDIS.

Jo saw that he was about to plunge back into wrestling with the problem of the grounded TARDIS. Before he could disappear she said, 'Doctor!'

The Doctor paused. 'Yes, Jo,' he said patiently.

'That future we saw—with the Daleks ruling the Earth—is it going to happen, or isn't it?'

'It is and it isn't,' said the Doctor not very helpfully.

'Oh come on, Doctor,' said the Brigadier, coming to Jo's support. 'What sort of answer is that?'

'I meant exactly what I said,' protested the Doctor. 'First it is—and then it isn't. There are all kinds of futures you know.'

'Futures with Daleks in them?' asked Jo.

The Doctor said, 'It's possible, Jo.'

'But surely those Dalek things were all destroyed?' said the Brigadier.

The Doctor said. 'That was a mere handful. The Daleks exist in many places and many times. I thought I'd destroyed them once before but I was wrong.'

The Doctor stood for a moment, gazing into the distance, as if he were looking through Time itself, thought Jo, wondering when and where his old enemies would attack again.

The Doctor came out of his daydream and gave her a smile. 'I've just *got* to get the TARDIS working again, Jo,' he said. 'I've got a feeling I'm going to need it.'

With that he disappeared inside the TARDIS and closed the door.

THE PLANET OF THE DALEKS

1

Jo Alone

The tall white-haired man lay still as death. The girl leaning over him could find no pulse, no beat from either of his hearts. His skin was icy cold to the touch.

She perched on the end of the couch and hid her face in her hands. All around her the machinery of the mysterious space/time craft called the TARDIS hummed gently and contentedly, as if unconcerned with its owner's fate. The column in the many-sided central console rose and fell. The TARDIS was in flight through the space/time vortex.

The girl, who was very small and very pretty, rubbed her eyes and stood up. She opened a locker in the base of the control console and took out a small black box. It was very much like one of the tape-recorders common on twentieth-century Earth, although its power source was eternal and its recording capacity unlimited. This was the log of the TARDIS, used only in emergencies. The girl switched it on and began to speak.

'My name is Jo Grant. For some time I've been the Doctor's assistant in UNIT—the United Nations Intelligence Taskforce. Recently the Doctor took me for a trip in the TARDIS. We travelled far into the future and became involved in a plot to cause a space war. The Doctor discovered his old enemy the Master involved in the plot—and behind the Master were the Daleks. Although the Doctor managed to defeat the Master and prevent the war, he was seriously wounded in a Dalek ambush. I managed to get him into the TARDIS.'

Jo's voice faltered as she remembered the dangers they had escaped. She steadied herself, and went on. 'The Doctor had a serious head-wound . . . he was barely conscious. He managed to get the TARDIS to take off, then used something he called a telepathic circuit to send a message to his own people, the Time Lords. After that he started slipping into a coma. He said he might sleep for a very long time. He asked me to record what happened in this log.'

Jo switched off the log, and went to examine the Doctor again. When she'd finished, she picked up the machine. 'The Doctor's breathing seems to have stopped. There is no pulse or heartbeat, and his skin is icy cold.'

Jo Grant paused, and took a deep breath. She was well aware that in any human being these symptoms could have meant only one thing—death. What gave her hope was her knowledge that the Doctor was *not* human. She had seen him in this kind of coma before; it had been part of the mysterious process by which his Time Lord body was able to heal itself after exceptional damage and stress. Jo hoped this was happening now. The alternative, that the Doctor was dead or dying, was too terrible to contemplate.

Suddenly she became aware that something was happening. The sound of the TARDIS had altered. The central column was slowing down. On the control panel, lights flickered, switches and controls moved of their own accord. She switched on the recorder. 'The TARDIS seems to be landing—the Time Lords must be operating it by remote control. I hope they've brought us somewhere we can get help for the Doctor.'

She glanced at the Doctor again, then ran over to him in shock. His whole face was covered with a glistening white frost. Carefully, Jo wiped the frost from the

Doctor's face with her handkerchief. For a moment she feared the Doctor really *was* dead. Then his eyes flicked open. They stared unseeingly at her for a moment, and closed again. Jo gasped with relief. 'Doctor . . . oh Doctor, you're alive!' The Doctor gave no sign that he had heard her. He seemed to have sunk back into his coma.

Jo became aware of a squelching, slapping sound. It was coming from outside the TARDIS. She went to the control console and after some fumbling managed to find the scanner switch. Slowly, a dim picture appeared on the little screen.

It showed a stretch of dense jungle, vines, trees, creepers and strangely shaped plants jostling each other for room. She knew at once she was not on Earth. The vegetation was alien, with a sinister fleshy quality, as though this jungle was really one enormous beast. Through a slight gap in the foliage, Jo could see part of some crumbling ruin, eroded and overgrown. Something blobbed onto the screen, accompanied by the now-familiar squelching sound. Another blob appeared, then another. Jo looked hard. Rain? No, something thicker—and more alive. Jo switched off the scanner and stood thinking. Conditions looked nasty outside. It seemed to be night-time, and it would probably be cold. She went to a clothing locker in the wall and took out a long-sleeved, hooded coat, and a pair of thick gloves. As she put them on she went back to the Doctor. 'I don't know if you can hear me, Doctor. I'm going to look for help. I'll be back as soon as I can.' With a last look at the still figure on the couch, she slipped the little recorder into her pocket, operated the door-control and went out into the jungle. The door of the TARDIS closed behind her.

Stretched out on the couch, the Doctor was as cold and still as the stone effigy on a Crusader's tombstone.

Outside the TARDIS, the light was murky-green and the

air chill. Jo was glad of her warm coat. The TARDIS had landed in the middle of a thicket of spongy, fleshy plants, which seemed to give out a sinister hissing sound. The police box, the TARDIS's exterior form, was covered with blobs of some thick white substance. Even as she watched, one of the spongy plants swayed forward and 'spat' another blob onto the side of the TARDIS. It was as though the arrival of the police box had trigggered off some defence mechanism, and the plants were blindly attacking this new enemy. Jo had often heard the Doctor say that the TARDIS was invulnerable to outside attack. Deciding it wasn't likely to be harmed by a few messy plants, she turned to go.

As she moved, something struck her shoulder. One of the plants had registered her as an enemy and shot a stream of the viscous liquid at her. Shuddering, she wiped if off with her gloved hand. Hurrying out of range of the sponge-plants, Jo pushed her way through the jungle to the ruined structure she had seen on the scanner.

There wasn't much to see when she got there. Crumbling stone pillars, broken walls, a slab of stone that might have been an altar . . . Jo guessed she was looking at the ruins of some ancient temple—proof that there had once been intelligent life on this strange planet, though it could have died out thousands of years ago. On the other hand, reflected Jo, you could probably find just such a ruin in the jungles of Brazil—with a modern super-city only a few miles away. Cheering herself with this reflection, she moved on.

To her great relief, the jungle soon became less dense, giving way to a stretch of sandy ground in which the plants grew more sparsely. She became aware of a change in the quality of the light. The dull green murk was giving way to a yellow glare.

The temperature rose dramatically, and it was dawn, just as if someone had switched on a light. A great yellow sun blazed down from the sky, and Jo found it intolerably hot in the hooded coat. She took it off, noticing with distaste that the splash of fluid from the sponge-plants had turned itself into a thick green mould, which actually seemed to be growing on the coat. She threw it to one side and carried on without it.

Dotted among the other plants were taller reed-like growths, surmounted with a small round pod, fringed with leaves. In the centre of the pod was an opening, uncannily like the pupil of a human eye. As she passed a clump of these plants, Jo was amused to see the stalks sway towards her, and the eyes of the plants open wide as if in astonishment. But her amusement soon vanished. She heard strange rustlings and weird cries from the thick jungle behind her. Jo hurried on, unable to shake off the uncomfortable feeling that *something* was following her . . .

The Doctor's eyes flicked open. He swung his long legs to the ground, stood up and looked round. 'Jo?' he called. 'Jo, where are you?' He listened. All he heard was a continuous slap, slap, slap—as though something was splashing onto the outside of the TARDIS. The Doctor sniffed. Something else was wrong. He went to the console. The instruments showed a breathable atmosphere outside—the TARDIS should have been drawing on that for air, first filtering out any undesirable elements. But there was a faintly musty smell in the air. The TARDIS was using its automatic air-supply. For some reason, no air was reaching the TARDIS from outside.

A warning light began to blink on the console. The Doctor looked. A tiny screen was flashing a message. 'AUTOMATIC OXYGEN SUPPLY EXHAUSTED.'

The Doctor shook his head. He was still feeling muzzy and confused. Everything seemed to be going wrong. 'Just have to use the emergency supply,' he muttered. He touched a control and a wall panel slid back, revealing three large oxygen cylinders, each surmounted with a glass dial. The Doctor switched on the first one. There was a brief reassuring hiss of oxygen—then silence. The Doctor peered at the little dial—the needle read 'EMPTY'. He tried the second cylinder. The result was the same. The Doctor turned on the third cylinder, and this time the hiss was steady and continuous. He gave a sigh of relief and looked at the dial. The needle wasn't at the EMPTY mark, but it was hovering perilously close. 'Less than an hour's supply,' said the Doctor thoughtfully. He knew he had only himself to blame. It was bad enough letting one back-up system run low, but two . . .

Registering a mental vow to top up *all* the TARDIS oxygen systems as soon as possible, the Doctor decided that, since air wasn't getting in, he would have to go out. He took a cloak from the wardrobe locker and operated the door control. Nothing happened. The Doctor frowned, re-checked the control circuits, then tried again. Still nothing. He was trapped in the TARDIS.

In the silence the Doctor could hear the steady slap, slap, slap, from outside. The oxygen cylinder hissed away, the needle on its dial flickering steadily closer to the empty mark. When the oxygen was exhausted, he would die . . .

2

The Invisible Menace

Jo hurried on, making better progress now that the jungle had thinned out. She noticed something in front of her and dropped to one knee. In a patch of soft sand she saw the clear imprint of a foot. A little further ahead she could see another footprint, and then another . . . She slipped off her glove to feel the ground, wondering if the footprint was recent or very old. She crumbled the sand between her fingers, not noticing how close she had come to the base of one of the sponge-plants. Suddenly the plant spat milky liquid at her. Jo jumped back, but a few drops of the fluid caught the back of her hand. She fished out her handkerchief and scrubbed the stuff off, throwing away the handkerchief when she'd finished. Pulling her glove back on she followed the line of footprints. They led her through a patch of thicker jungle and into a clearing. In the centre of the clearing stood the wreck of a small spacecraft, its hull picked out in blue and gold.

Jo moved cautiously towards it. The ship was small and stubby, vaguely cigar-shaped. Hull and fins were badly damaged, and the door hung open. Already a tracery of jungle vines was growing across the gap—which didn't necessarily mean the wreck wasn't a recent one, thought Jo. Everything probably grew with frightening speed in a jungle like this.

Jo called through the doorway. 'Hello, anybody there?' No reply. Gathering her courage, she climbed inside.

The interior was cramped and gloomy, dimly lit by the greenish light filtering in from the jungle outside. In the nose-cone of the craft, Jo could see a tiny flight-deck. A space-suited figure was sitting in the pilot's seat. Jo moved towards it. The man showed no sign of being aware of her presence. Timidly she tapped him on the shoulder. The swivel chair creaked round, and the body of the spaceship pilot slid gently to the floor, the face behind the helmet-visor stiff and dead.

Jo screamed and backed away . . . and a hand came firmly down on her shoulder. Two men stood looking at her. Both were tall and fair-haired, dressed in simple uniforms with a sensible workman-like look about them. They had wide webbing belts round their waists, from which hung a variety of tools and weapons, and small packs on their backs. The man holding her was very big with a long bony face, at once kindly and stern. The man behind him was smaller, thin-faced and younger, with a fierce angry look about him. In his hand was a blaster, aimed steadily at Jo.

Jo looked fearfully at them. 'Who are you?'

'My name's Taron,' said the big man. 'This is Vaber.'

Vaber holstered his gun. It was clear that he didn't consider her much of a menace. 'Where do you come from?' he demanded. 'What planet?'

'I come from Earth.'

Jo's simple statement brought a surprising reaction. Both men stared incredulously at her. 'There's no such place as Earth,' Vaber said roughly. 'It's just a name in the old legends.'

'How did you get here?' asked Taron.

'In the TARDIS. It's a kind of spaceship.' To Jo's relief they accepted this without question. 'I've a friend with me,' she went on. 'He's desperately ill, he may even be dying. Please, can you help me?'

'Look, we've no time for—' Vaber began speaking

roughly, but Taron interrupted him.

'I'm qualified in space medicine. I'll do what I can for your friend. Where is this TARDIS?'

'Back through the jungle, close to a sort of ruined temple.'

Taron nodded. 'I think I know the place.'

A third man ran into the spaceship. Like the others he was uniformed and fair-haired. He was very tall and thin, more openly frightened than his two companions. 'Patrol approaching,' he gasped. 'Three or four of them.'

Taron took command. 'All right, Codal, we'll move out.' He turned to Jo. 'You stay here and hide. If we try to take you, you'll only slow us down. We'll lose them in the jungle and come back for you when we can.'

Before Jo could protest all three had fled from the spaceship, leaving her full of unanswered questions. What was this unknown 'patrol' that caused such alarm?

She went to the door and looked out, but the three men had already vanished. Jo heard a sudden rustling sound from the patch of dense green jungle at the edge of the clearing. *Something* was forcing its way through it, and it was coming towards her . . . Jo ducked back inside the ship and looked quickly round for a hiding place.

She found a tall wardrobe-like wall locker which held spare uniforms and space-suits. Jo slipped inside, huddling behind the rack of garments, and pulled the door closed. There was a slatted ventilation panel in the door, so she could still see out.

The ship rocked a little and the vines over the door were pushed aside. Jo peered through the panel, and saw—nothing! Yet obviously *someone* had entered the cabin. She could hear hoarse breathing and stealthy, padding footsteps. A plastic beaker rose in the air of its own accord, then dropped to the floor. On the flight-deck a pen, a plastic notebook, various navigational instruments rose and fell in the same eerie way. Lockers opened and closed, their contents floating through the air and falling to the ground as the invisible searcher dropped them. The activity was coming nearer. Jo held her locker door tightly closed from the inside. Sure enough, a few minutes later, she felt the unseen something on the other side of the door trying to turn the handle. She clung on desperately. After a moment the pressure stopped and the hoarse breathing moved away.

Jo peeped out. Close to the door, a plastic carton jumped, as though suddenly kicked aside. The little craft tilted, the vines over the door were brushed aside by the unseen form, the craft lurched and then resumed its former position. Jo crept out of hiding and went to the door, peering through the curtain of vines. On the marshy ground before the ship a line of footprints was appearing, footprints completely alien in shape. They moved towards the edge of the clearing, the plants rustled and waved, and the invisible intruder was gone.

The Doctor checked all the door-opening circuits and found them in perfect order. Abandoning the control panel console, he tried opening the doors manually. For some time he struggled without success. The doors were held from the outside with a grip that was rubbery yet firm. It yielded, but would not give way.

The hiss of the oxygen cylinder faded and died. A warning light flashed on the centre console. Wearily the Doctor staggered across to it. This time the message on the screen read, 'CABIN ATMOSPHERE SHORTLY UNABLE TO SUSTAIN LIFE.' The Doctor went back to the door and resumed his desperate struggle.

Already he felt consciousness beginning to slip away.

Vaber and Codal crouched in a clump of thick jungle, blasters at the ready. They spun round at the sound of approaching movement. It was Taron. 'I think we've lost them. There were just a few scouts, and they're moving off that way, away from the ship. The girl should be all right. We'd better try to find this friend of hers.'

Vaber looked incredulously at him. 'You don't mean to say you meant it? Why should we waste time on some stranger?'

'Because he's ill. I'm still a doctor, Vaber. Even here.' Taron led the way into the jungle, and the others followed.

When they reached the ruined temple, it took them quite a time to find the TARDIS. They had been looking for some kind of conventional spaceship, until they realised that the tall, oblong shape was the 'spacecraft' they were seeking. The fact that the TARDIS was coated with the rubbery fungus spat out by the sponge-plants didn't make things any easier.

Tron scratched his head. 'Well, whatever it is, it's the only *new* thing here—so it must be what we want!'

From a belt-pouch he took a tiny square of transparent plastic, which unfolded into a complete protective suit—cape, hood and gauntlets all in one. From his pack he produced a spray which dissolved the rubbery growth covering the TARDIS. When an area was cleared, Taron started to pull the fungus away with his gloved hands. The others joined him, the sponge-spores splashing harmlessly on their protective clothing.

When they'd freed the area around the door, it swung suddenly open, and the Doctor toppled out. They grabbed him and dragged his body clear. The TARDIS door swung closed behind him, and the sponges resumed their mindless attack.

The Doctor was sucking great whooping breaths into his lungs. As soon as he could speak, he gasped, 'Thank you . . . thank you very much indeed. How did you find me?'

Taron briefly told him of meeting Jo in their wrecked spacecraft. The Doctor was relieved to hear that, until recently at least, Jo was still all right.

Taron turned to Codal. 'Better circle the area, see if

there's any more activity.' As Codal slipped away, Taron saw the Doctor staring intently at him. 'Well, what is it?' he said brusquely.

The Doctor said, 'Forgive me. It's just that I seem to know you—all of you! Or rather, I know your people.'

'That's scarcely likely.'

'Oh you never know,' said the Doctor airily. 'I travel quite a bit. Where *are* you from?'

'A planet many systems from here. It's called—'

'Skaro!' said the Doctor triumphantly, answering his own question. 'Of course—you're Thals!'

Taron stared at him. 'How could you possibly know that?'

'I've visited Skaro. I was there at the time of the first Dalek war.'

Taron looked at the tall shape of the TARDIS, now once more obscured by the rubbery spitting of the sponge-plants. 'In our legends, there is a being from another planet, who came to Skaro at our time of greatest peril. He travelled in something called—'

'The TARDIS,' confirmed the Doctor. 'That's it over there.'

'He had three companions,' said Taron slowly.

The Doctor supplied the missing names. 'Barbara, Ian and Susan.'

'Are you trying to tell us that *you* are the Doctor?' demanded Vaber.

'That's right, old chap.'

'That's impossible. The First Dalek War was generations ago, before any of us were born. No one lives that long.'

'Ah, but I'm not a Thal. Besides, don't your legends tell that the TARDIS could also travel through time?'

Vaber came closer, hand steady on the blaster in his belt. 'And now you turn up here—of all the planets in the galaxy! Well, I don't believe you. You've come to spy on us. Who are you? What are you really doing here?'

The Doctor looked calmly at him, trying to make allowances for the fact that Vaber was obviously frightened and exhausted, ready to lash out at any target. 'Now see here, young man,' he said mildly. 'You helped to save my life and I'm grateful, but that doesn't give you the right to interrogate me.'

They were interrupted by Taron. He whipped another aerosol from a belt-pouch and sprayed the Doctor's cheek. The Doctor jumped back. 'What do you think you're doing?'

'There was a splash of that white fluid on your face. It contains the growth-spores of the sponge-plants. The fungus grows very quickly. Without treatment it would have spread all over your body.'

The Doctor shuddered. 'It seems I must thank you for saving my life a second time.'

Jo grew bored waiting for the Thals to return, but she didn't dare venture outside the spaceship. Hunting round the little cabin she found a plastic box of food concentrates, rubbery cubes in several different colours. She ate a couple and found them odd-tasting but satisfying. In a recess she discovered a wash-basin. After a certain amount of fiddling with taps, she managed to produce first drinking-water, and then a stream of warm soapy water in the little basin.

Jo decided on a quick clean-up. It would not only make her feel better, it would help to pass time till the others returned. She pulled off her gloves and started to roll up her sleeves. Then she stopped, gazing in horror at the back of her right hand. A spreading blotch of fungus had grown all over it . . .

The Doctor listened as his rescuers argued between themselves. It seemed to be a question of whether they should move off at once, or wait for the return of Codal. Eventually it was decided they should wait.

The Doctor thought he might as well use the time in gathering some information about his new surroundings. 'What's the name of this planet?' he asked.

It was Vaber who answered, speaking with the harsh bitterness that seemed habitual to him. 'Spiridon—one of the nastiest pieces of planetary garbage in this galaxy.'

The Doctor raised his eyebrows. 'Indeed! Is it inhabited?'

'Oh yes! Vegetation with all the more unpleasant characteristics of animal life. Animals that eat everything that moves, including each other. And a climate changing from tropical in the day to freezing at night.'

'Any *intelligent* life-forms?'

'Only the Spiridons. They had a civilisation once, but it's in ruins now.'

'I'd very much like to see one of them.'

Vaber grinned sourly. 'You'll find that difficult. They happen to be invisible.'

There was another important question in the Doctor's mind. He spoke cautiously, feeling his way. 'I gather you're on some kind of special mission here—that you have dangerous enemies?'

The Thals looked suspiciously at him, but didn't answer.

'I'm on something of a special mission myself,' continued the Doctor. 'Perhaps we can help each other?'

Taron shook his head. 'I'm sorry, we don't know enough about you to trust you like that.'

'Oh, why don't you tell him?' snarled Vaber. 'We're none of us going to get off Spiridon alive. This is a suicide mission.'

The Doctor looked sharply at him. 'What makes you say that?'

'We crash-landed. Our Commander was killed on impact, so Taron here took command. The sub-space radio was wrecked on landing, and the ship's so badly damaged we can never take off again.'

'You volunteered, Vaber,' said Taron harshly. 'No one forced you to come.'

For men sharing a desperate mission, they didn't get on very well, thought the Doctor. Quietly he asked. 'How many of you are here?'

'We were seven,' said Taron slowly. 'The Commander was killed—and we've lost three more since then.'

'But you still won't accept my help?'

Taron shook his head. 'We'll take you back to your friend, then you're on your own. Our mission is too important to risk on unknowns.'

'You may not trust me yet, Taron, but I have a feeling there's already a very strong link between us. To quote an old Earth proverb—"My enemy's enemy is my friend."'

The lanky Codal suddenly appeared from the jungle. 'Everything's quiet now.'

Taron stood up. 'Let's get moving. Doctor, if you see me signal get under cover fast. And don't make a sound.'

'I have been in jungles before,' the Doctor said rather huffily.

'Not like this one,' said Taron grimly.

As they made their way through the jungle, Taron saw that the Doctor could move as silently as any of them. He seemed unaffected by the blazing heat, and showed no signs of tiring as they forced their way through the tough vegetation.

They came to a broad path cutting across the jungle. It had obviously been cleared by some advanced technological means. Touching the severed ends of a vine the Doctor guessed at a wide-beam heat-ray. Taron held up his hand for silence. Something was moving towards them. Curiously enough, they could hear it but not see it. It made a strange clanking, grinding noise, suggesting some complex mechanical device on the point of complete breakdown. A blurred trail crept towards them along the charred surface of the path. It wavered and stopped, and the harsh grinding sound died away. Codal looked at Taron. 'What do you think?'

'Sounds like light-wave sickness. That's what the others had.'

'Shall we risk it then? Show our new friend what we're up against?' Vaber had swung into a mood of hysterical cheerfulness. He ran out on to the path, and up to the point where the mysterious tracks ended. He pulled a couple of sprays from his belt pouch, and tossed one to the Doctor. 'Here you are, join in the fun!'

The Doctor looked at the spray. 'Is this some kind of weapon?'

Vaber laughed. 'It's *paint*, that's all. A paint-spray from the ship's stores.'

Vaber touched a nozzle on the top of the little spray, and a mist of bright blue paint shot out. He waved the spray to and fro in front of him, and after a puzzled look at Taron, the Doctor did the same. His spray produced a fine mist of gold.

Slowly a shape apeared in the empty air ahead of them. The effect was rather like a 'magic' drawing book where a pencil rubbed across an apparently blank page produces a hidden picture.

This picture, however, was solidly three-dimensional. Standing in the middle of the path, its shape picked out incongruously in blue and gold, was the menacing form of a Dalek.

3

The Deadly Trap

Vaber looked at the Doctor, wondering how he would react. If he expected fear or horror, he was disappointed. The Doctor himself had come to Spiridon in pursuit of the Daleks. Moreover, he had realised from the first that the presence of Thals confirmed that there were Daleks on the planet. Taron's 'special mission' could only be some operation against the hereditary enemies of the Thals. The Doctor started examining the Dalek with an air of brisk competence. He waved a hand in front of the eye-stalk. 'Total loss of vision, motive power nil, weaponry de-activated too—luckily for us!'

Taron was watching him curiously. 'You seem to know a good deal about Daleks.'

'I've had cause. But I've never come across invisible ones before. How do they do it?'

Codal seemed to be the scientist of the party. 'They discovered it by studying the Spiridons. That is the reason they came to this planet. It's some kind of anti-reflecting light-wave.' Recognising a fellow spirit, Codal was talking as one dedicated scientist to another. 'Their problem is that to create the energy needed they use enormous amounts of power. They can't sustain it for long. Either they revert to visibility, or they fall victim to light-wave sickness, like this one. Let's take a closer look, shall we?'

Codal was all set to dismantle the Dalek on the spot,

but the Doctor held him back. 'Most Daleks have an automatic distress-call. Even when the Dalek is de-activated the transmitter might still go on functioning for a while. We'd better keep moving.'

Some time later Taron halted in a small clearing. 'Codal and I know this area best. We'll scout ahead. Vaber, you stay here with the Doctor.'

Taron and Codal moved away. The Doctor, as always making the best of things, settled himself with his back to a curiously gnarled tree trunk, long legs stretched out before him. 'Your Taron's a cautious fellow.'

'Too cautious,' Vaber muttered protestingly. 'Things would be different if Miro was still alive.'

The Doctor was examining a clump of oddly shaped plants growing near his tree. 'Miro?'

'Miro was our Commander—he was killed when we landed. Taron is the expedition's doctor. I was Miro's number two, but technically Taron outranks me. He took command—and a fine mess he's made of it. He'll go on being cautious till we all get killed.'

The Doctor nodded thoughtfully. Vaber's story accounted for the tensions within the small group of Thals. Taron was a doctor, unaccustomed to active command. Now that the responsibility was his, he might well be ultra-careful, fearful of making some mistake. On the other hand, his attitude might be amply justified. As yet the Doctor knew too little of the situation on Spiridon to form a proper judgement. 'What do you think Taron should do?' he asked casually.

Vaber was eager to tell him. 'Attack the Daleks and wipe them out. There are no more than a dozen of them on the planet, just a small scientific party studying invisibility techniques. One determined attack could destroy them all.'

The Doctor nodded thoughtfully. It sounded a very attractive plan. But could things really be that easy? With the Daleks you could never be sure. 'Tell me about the

Spiridons,' he said. 'Are they always invisible?'

Vaber abandoned his prowling and sat down at the edge of the clearing. 'Codal says so. According to him, this planet is so hostile they had to develop invisibility—he calls it the ultimate in survival techniques.'

Although neither the Doctor nor Codal realised it, the hostility of Spiridon was being demonstrated at that very moment. In the dense jungle behind Vaber, a thick hairy tentacle, about the size of a full-grown python, was stirring. Typically enough for Spiridon, the tentacle belonged not to an animal but to a plant. At the centre of the plant was a fleshy orchid-like growth some twenty feet across. The plant, like many on Spiridon, was carnivorous, and the long tentacles growing out from the centre were designed to capture its prey.

The Doctor was still intent on his clump of plants. He had discovered that if he moved his hand to and fro, an 'eye' opened on the pod, and the plant swayed to and fro as if watching him. 'Fascinating,' he murmured.

Vaber saw what he was doing. 'Useful, too. The plants react whenever one of the invisible Spiridons approaches. We use them as a kind of early-warning system.'

Unseen, the tentacle slipped closer.

'The Spiridons co-operate with the Daleks, then?' asked the Doctor.

'I don't think they have any choice. The Daleks saturated the jungles with killer rays. Invisibility didn't protect the Spiridons against that kind of thing. The survivors were too terrified to do anything but surrender and co-operate.'

The tentacle was close enough now. It reached out like a whiplash, winding round Vaber's waist and dragging him towards the jungle. Alerted by the screams, the Doctor sprang across the clearing and grabbed Vaber's legs, trying to haul him back. But the tentacle was appallingly strong. The only result was that both of them were hauled remorselessly into the jungle. The Doctor heard Vaber gasp. 'Knife . . . get knife . . .'

A heavy jungle knife was sheathed at Vaber's belt. The Doctor grabbed it and hacked savagely at the tentacle. Thick green ichor spurted out. The tentacle unwound from Vaber, lashed about wildly and snaked back into the jungle. Vaber crumpled to the ground, and the Doctor was kneeling over him when Taron rushed in from the other side of the clearing. 'What happened?'

The Doctor waved towards the jungle. 'Something rather nasty was planning on having us for breakfast.'

Vaber struggled to his feet, as if unwilling to show weakness in Taron's presence. 'I'm all right now . . .' He winced as the effort of speaking sent a stab of pain through his bruised ribs.

Taron looked anxiously at him. 'If you'd like to rest for a while . . .

'I said I'm all right!' He looked at the Doctor and muttered, 'Thanks.'

The Doctor cleaned the knife in the ground and tossed it back to Vaber. 'Let's call it a useful lesson—on the need for caution at all times! Perhaps Taron is right after all.'

Taron looked puzzled. 'What about?'

The Doctor was looked at Vaber. 'About not rushing headlong into an attack on the Daleks.'

Vaber flared up again. 'If I'm going to die, I want it to be for a better reason than providing nourishment for some flesh-eating plant . . .'

The quarrel was interrupted by the arrival of Codal. 'What are you all doing? Look at the eye-plants!'

The plants were lashing about in agitation, their fringes of leaves curling closed over the central pods.

'Spiridon patrol,' Taron said curtly. 'We'd better hide.'

He led them into the centre of a clump of low-lying plants, rather like dwarf palm trees. There was space to hide between the thick trunks, and the wide leaves gave good cover. From their vantage-point they could see the jungle all around being thrashed by the movement of an unseen presence.

The Doctor studied the pattern of movements. 'The sweep's moving this way. They'll find us if we don't change position soon.'

Vaber reached for his blaster. 'Why don't we attack first? We can ambush them.'

Taron's hand closed on his arm. 'We don't know how many there are! And what do we use as a target if we can't see them?'

Codal said, 'I'll lead them off. You can all get away while they're following me.' Before anyone could stop him, he had left his cover. He started to run through the jungle, making no attempt to conceal himself and generating as much noise as he could.

The others watched him crash away. Soon there was a quick ripple of movement in the thick green vegetation, a ripple that went off after Codal.

'It's working,' said Taron. 'They're following. Codal's given us our chance. Let's not waste it.'

Wriggling from their hiding-place, they began to run in the opposite direction.

Codal came panting to a halt in the middle of a jungle trail. The Spiridon patrols were a long way behind. With any luck he'd led them far enough to give the others a chance of escape. It was time to begin circling round to re-join them. His thin chest heaving as he gasped for breath, Codal felt astonished at his own audacity. He'd been on the move before he'd realised what had come over him. Maybe he wasn't such a wash-out after all. Codal was the youngest and least experienced of the Thal party, and the question of his own courage was something that preoccupied him constantly. But his moment of self-congratulation was brief. He saw a clump of eye-plants beside the trail, and realised with a feeling of sudden dread that they were all tightly closed. Suddenly, invisible hands gripped him tightly. He struggled wildly, kicking and punching at his unseen captors, hearing grunts as the wild blows landed. But the struggle was hopeless. The invisible hands tightened their grip, Codal watched helplessly as a chunk of dead wood rose from the side of the trail and flew straight for his head . . .

Jo Grant was feeling very weak by now. The blotchy fungus had spread half-way up her arm, and seemed to be draining her strength. Her temperature had rocketed, and she was sick and giddy. She felt she ought to keep her log up to date, though there was little enough to say. Fumbling with her left hand, she took the recorder from her pocket and touched the control. 'My hand and arm have become infected by some plant from the jungle. The infection is spreading very rapidly. I don't think the men I met here are coming back, so I'm going to try to get through the jungle and find help.' She switched off the recorder and thrust it clumsily back in her pocket, not noticing that it was only part-way inside. She got to her feet, staggering as a wave of dizziness came over her, and made for the door.

She was attempting to climb down from the spacecraft when she heard a thrashing movement in the jungle. The invisible creature was returning! Terrified, Jo turned and went back inside, intending to return to her hiding place in the locker. She didn't realise that the recorder had dropped to the ground outside the ship. The effort of moving was too much for her. The cabin spun round and everything went black.

The jungle rustled as the Spiridon forced its way through the vegetation. It paused at the edge of the clearing, moved across to the little spacecraft and climbed aboard. Jo's body was sprawled in plain sight in the centre of the cabin. The Spiridon moved curiously towards her . . .

Safe in a new hiding place, Taron, Vaber and the Doctor

waited as long as they dared for Codal to reappear. Finally Taron stood up. 'We'd better make for the spaceship. Maybe he'll rendezvous with us there.'

'Or maybe we're down to two, now.' Vaber spoke sourly.

Taron said nothing. He led the way through the jungle, and the Doctor followed, Vaber trailing sulkily behind. It took them a long time to reach the spaceship. Taron moved with his usual caution, insisting on a wide detour to avoid further patrols.

But at last they came to the edge of the clearing. The wrecked spaceship was still sitting in the middle of it. The Doctor pressed forward, eager to be reunited with Jo, but Taron held him back. 'Wait—there's movement on the other side of the clearing.' To the Doctor's horror, four Daleks glided out of the jungle, grouping themselves in a semi-circle around the little ship. The Doctor heard the familiar, hated voice cutting through the jungle air.

'Dalek patrol calling Command Centre. Thal spacecraft has been located. We shall destroy according to instructions.' The Daleks widened their semi-circle. The patrol leader ordered, 'Prepare to fire.'

The Doctor started to get up. Taron tried to stop him. 'There's nothing you can do.'

The Doctor threw off his grip. 'Jo's inside there! I've got to stop them.'

The Dalek voice ordered, 'Fire!' Before the order could be carried out, the Doctor ran forward, placing himself between the ship and the Dalek guns. 'Wait! You mustn't shoot, there's someone inside.'

For a moment the Daleks froze, as if stunned by the audacity of the interruption. Then the patrol leader spoke. 'Disable prisoner. Save for interrogation.' Instantly a Dalek fired and the Doctor's feet were smashed from under him by an agonising blast of pain. As he crashed to the ground he heard the Dalek voice again. 'Proceed as ordered. Fire!'

His legs numb and useless, the Doctor called, 'No, you mustn't . . .'

Above his head the Dalek guns blazed in unison. The little spaceship glowed cherry red and exploded in a blast of flame.

4

In the Power of the Daleks

Unable to bear the sight of the blazing spacecraft, the Doctor lowered his eyes to the ground. A few feet away he saw a familiar black shape—the TARDIS log-recorder. Automatically he reached out for it and thrust it in his pocket. A Dalek loomed over him. 'Stand up.'

The Doctor tried. Agonising pins-and-needles shot through his legs, and he stumbled and fell.

'Stand up or we will exterminate you now.'

Painfully the Doctor got to his feet. The Dalek herded him forward. 'Walk!'

The Doctor stumbled slowly away between his captors. At the edge of the clearing he stopped to look back at the still-blazing ship.

'Move.' The Daleks ordered him forward.

As the Dalek patrol and its prisoner disappeared into the jungle, Taron and Vaber came out of hiding.

Vaber looked after the departing Daleks. 'We should have helped him.'

Taron shook his head, gazing into the flames. 'There was nothing we could do . . . nothing.'

Feeling gradually came back to the Doctor's legs during the long march through the jungle, but he was glad when their destination came in sight. It was nothing more than a small, squat blockhouse. The door slid open to reveal a lift, and the patrol passed inside.

The Doctor was quite unsurprised by this development. It was normal Dalek practice to install their bases underground whenever possible. Daylight and open air meant nothing to them, and they flourished best in a controlled underground environment.

The lift plunged down and down, and the Doctor cupped his hands over his ears as they popped under the changing pressure. At last the lift shuddered to a halt and they all filed out. They were in a long straight corridor, apparently cut from solid rock. At intervals in either direction other corridors intersected across their one.

The Doctor was taken to a heavy metal door. A Dalek touched a control, the door opened and the Doctor was thrust inside. The door closed behind him.

It was no surprise to the Doctor to find himself in a bare, metal cell. What did surprise him was to see Codal crouched in one corner, his head in his hands. The young scientist looked up in astonishment. 'Doctor!' Then his face fell. 'So it was all for nothing. They got you after all.'

'Not all of us. Taron and Vaber are still free.'

Briefly the Doctor explained how he'd been captured, then Codal told the Doctor of his own capture. 'I don't understand why they didn't kill me,' he concluded.

'I'm afraid they're saving us both for interrogation,' said the Doctor. 'They'll want to know what we're doing on this planet.'

Codal shuddered, terrified at the thought of Dalek questioning. The Doctor could see he needed cheering up. 'I haven't thanked you for giving us that chance to escape. It was very brave of you.'

Codal laughed bitterly. 'Brave? Me? I've been in terror since we landed on this planet.'

The Doctor nodded. 'That's natural enough. We're all afraid at times.'

'Taron and Vaber know how to deal with fear. I'm a scientist, not a soldier. I'm not used to danger.'

'I thought all your force were volunteers?'

'We were!' said Codal gloomily. 'I was the only scientist young and fit enough to come on the expedition. Everyone expected me to volunteer, so I did. I didn't even have the courage to be the odd man out.'

The Doctor chuckled. 'Courage isn't a matter of not feeling frightened, you know.'

'Then what is it?'

'It's being afraid, but doing what you have to do anyway. Just as you did. You're a very brave man, Codal.'

Codal smiled wryly. 'I'm not convinced. But thanks anyway. Well, what do we do now?'

'We start trying to find a way out of here. Now let's see if we've got anything useful. Did they search you?'

'No, not really. Just took away my blaster and my knife.'

'Then turn out your pockets. You never know.' The Doctor began searching his own pockets, but the first thing he found made him pause in sorrow. It was the log-recorder Jo had taken from the TARDIS. He switched it on playback, listening to Jo's voice. 'The Doctor appears to have fallen into a deep coma . . .' He played the tape through, learning of Jo's leaving the TARDIS, her meeting with the Thals. He shuddered at the description of her infection by the fungus. But now it seemed she hadn't been inside the ship. Perhaps she had survived after all.

Jo Grant awoke from a nightmare-haunted sleep to find herself lying on a pile of skins in a tiny cave. She could see a greenish glow of jungle light coming from the vine-covered entrance. She became aware that her temperature had gone down, and the throbbing in her arm had almost vanished. She looked at her hand and arm. They were covered with a thick yellowish paste, and beneath it the stain of the fungus had receded.

Jo blinked and looked round the cave. A wooden bowl

was hovering in the air, and a bunch of brightly coloured berries was squeezing itself into it. One of the invisible creatures from the spaceship was in the cave with her. Jo kept perfectly still. The bowl floated towards her. She heard the sound of hoarse breathing, and then a whispering voice. 'Do not be afraid. I want only to help you.'

Since there was no one else to talk to, Jo spoke to the wooden bowl. 'Who are you?'

'My name is Wester. I am a Spiridon. Drink this juice. It will help you to cast off the effect of the fungoid infection.'

The bowl bobbed nearer. Jo took it and drank the juice, which seemed tart and sweet at the same time. She felt a glow through her body.

'The infection is almost gone,' whispered the ghostly voice. 'This will clear it completely.'

Jo drained the bowl and an unseen hand took it and put it to one side. 'What's happened?' she asked confusedly. 'Where are we?'

'We are in a cave near the Dalek city. I found you unconscious in a spacecraft and brought you here. Soon after, the Daleks destroyed the ship.'

'Why did you help me?' asked Jo. A wave of dizziness came over her. 'There's so much I want to ask you,' she said faintly. 'I don't know where to start.'

'You must rest while the juice takes its full effect,' said the Spiridon voice. 'Afterwards we shall talk . . .'

Jo nodded sleepily, letting herself drift away.

When she awoke some time later, she was fresh and alert. To her delight, all traces of the infection were gone from her hand and arm. Wester fed her on strange-looking fruits, and as she ate he told her of the sad state to which the Daleks had reduced his planet. 'They bombarded our world with bacteria and deadly rays. Spiridon became a planet of the Daleks. Only a handful of my people survived, and they were forced to co-operate with the Daleks in their attempt to discover the secret of invisibility.'

'But *you* don't co-operate?'

'A few of us do what we can to resist them . . . it's little enough. I hoped the aliens might help us, but they are being killed one by one. Another was captured today—though he looked different from the others.'

Jo's interest was aroused. 'What did he look like?'

'Tall with white hair. His clothes were different.'

'The Doctor!' said Jo excitedly. 'He must have recovered after I left the TARDIS. Trust him to get straight into trouble. I've got to help him.'

'That is not possible,' whispered the Spiridon sadly. 'The Daleks will interrogate him, then use him in their light-wave experiments. He would be better dead.'

The Doctor put away his sonic screwdriver with an angry frown. 'Hopeless. If there's one thing the Daleks are good at, it's making locks!'

Codal shook his head sadly. 'Well, if we can't get the door open . . .'

The Doctor took up the thought. 'Then we must make our escape when the door is already open.'

'By which time there'll be at least one Dalek standing there.' Codal spoke with gloomy relish.

The Doctor was not discouraged. 'Exactly. We've been looking at the problem in the wrong way. We're not trying to deal with a door—we're trying to deal with a Dalek!'

'How?' asked Codal simply.

The Doctor rubbed his chin. 'I'm not sure yet.' He poked irritably at the pile of objects they'd unearthed from their pockets. 'There must be something useful here . . .' He picked up the little recorder. 'A small but very efficient electric motor—with a built-in atomic power source . . . Now if I dismantle the circuitry, reverse the polarity and convert it to a receiver–transmitter with positive feedback . . '

He looked expectantly at Codal, who said, 'I see! The Dalek guidance system functions by means of high frequency radio-impulses . . .'

'. . . and if I can jam those impulses, the Dalek should develop a nice little brain-storm.' Eagerly the Doctor set to work.

In the central control area, the Dalek Commander, military leader of the expedition to Spiridon, was listening to the report of his second-in-command. 'Scientific section request that after interrogation, prisoners should be transferred to their laboratory for light-wave experiments.' The Commander looked across at the laboratory, a sealed-off section separated from the control area by a glass wall.

'Agreed. What of the rest of the Thal expedition?'

'Two Thals estimated still at liberty. Their capture is inevitable.'

In a secluded jungle clearing, Vaber and Taron were digging furiously. As he worked, Vaber thought grudgingly that for once Taron's obsessive caution had paid off. As soon as they had crash-landed, Taron had decided that the Daleks were certain to discover the spaceship sooner or later. Almost his first action had been to order the transport of their precious explosives to this cache in the jungle.

Taron grunted as his fingers touched plastic wrapping. After a little more digging he lifted out a large bundle and set it on the ground.

Exultantly Vaber helped him to unwrap it, and looked in satisfaction at the stubby cylindrical bombs with their attached timing and detonating devices. 'There's enough explosive here to wipe out fifty Daleks. We can rush the blockhouse, blow the lift-shaft and bury the lot of them for ever.'

'Suppose we don't make it to the lift-shaft? I won't take unjustified risks, Vaber. There are only two of us now, and you know what it means if we fail. We'll move when we have a plan that I think has a chance of succeeding, and not before.'

Vaber looked on appalled as Taron started to re-wrap the explosives. He drew his blaster. 'Hand over those bombs.'

Taron glanced up, saw the blaster and went on working. 'No.'

'Give them to me. I'll kill you if I have to.'

Taron finished wrapping the bundle and started to bury it. 'Then you'll have to kill me.'

Vaber glared helplessly at him, unnerved by Taron's calm.

There was a sudden roar, a blast of heat, and something shot over their heads to vanish behind a nearby hill. Vaber looked after it. 'That was a spacecraft,' he said. 'Coming in to land too low and too fast. Come on!' He ran towards the little hill. Taron, cautious as ever, finished burying the explosives then ran after him.

It didn't take long to find the wrecked spacecraft—the plume of black smoke soaring above the jungle made an excellent guide. They were almost in sight of it when there came a dull roar, and a blast of heat that knocked them off their feet. 'It's blown up,' said Taron, as they picked themselves up.

'Let's hope they got out in time.'

They heard someone pushing through the jungle towards them and waited. A tall, fair-haired girl in Thal space uniform staggered out of the jungle, her face blackened with smoke.

Taron recognised her at once, and ran to her. 'Rebec! What happened?'

The girl looked at him dazedly. 'Our glide angle was too steep. We overheated coming through the atmosphere. The ship blew just after we landed.'

'Any other survivors?'

'Marat and Latep . . . just behind me.'

Vaber came forward. 'Why did you come? How did you know we needed help?'

The girl shook her head as if to clear it. 'When you didn't report by sub-space radio, we guessed you must be in trouble. Then Communications intercepted another Dalek space signal. This time they managed to crack the code. Once we'd read it, we had to warn you . . .'

'Warn us? What about?'

'About the Dalek force on Spiridon.'

'We know that already,' said Vaber impatiently. 'There are about a dozen of them.'

Rebec shook her head. 'That's what we thought when we sent you. But we were wrong. The signal we intercepted was to Dalek Supreme Command. It said the Dalek force on Spiridon was now complete. Somewhere on this planet are ten thousand Daleks!'

5

The Escape

Even Vaber had to admire the stolid calm with which Taron took this shattering news. He nodded and said, 'This means we must act immediately.' He turned to Rebec. 'Are you fit enough to move? The Daleks will send a patrol very soon to investigate the crash.'

Rebec said, 'I'm all right—just a bit shaken.'

Two more Thals came out of the jungle, one a tall muscular man with a fresh open face, the other scarcely more than a boy. Taron greeted them calmly. 'Marat, Latep, are you all right? We can talk later. Right now it's important to get out of the area.'

With a cheeky grin, young Latep answered for both of them. 'We're fine. Came down with a bit of a bang, that's all. Marat always was a terrible pilot.'

Marat grinned, aiming a playful mock-punch at his smaller friend. 'No one else would have got you here at all!'

Taron spoke seriously. 'It's good to see you—all of you. We'd better be moving.'

The small group of Thals disappeared into the jungle.

Just outside the city, Jo Grant crouched in hiding, Wester beside her. Not that Wester needed to hide, she thought, since he was invisible anyway. By now Jo was quite accustomed to the unseen presence of the Spiridon, and to the ghostly whispering in her ear. She parted the leaves and peered through the gap. She could see the blockhouse, Dalek guards patrolling all round it. Figures in furs and skins were carrying great basket-loads of vegetation through the blockhouse doors. 'Who are they?' she asked.

'They are Spiridons, enslaved by the Daleks.'

'But I can see them.'

'You see the robes they wear. The Daleks have ordered our people to wear such robes. They must be visible at all times.'

'What's that stuff they're taking into the city?'

'Samples of our vegetation. The Daleks are experimenting with plant-destroying bacteria.'

Jo looked at the baskets. They were really enormous wire crates. It took two of the Spiridon slaves to carry one. 'If I could get into one of those baskets, I'd be carried straight past the Dalek guards.'

'It is too dangerous,' hissed Wester.

Jo ignored him. 'Whereabouts would they be likely to take the Doctor?'

'Prisoners are always held on the lower levels. He is probably on level seven.'

'I'm going to try it,' said Jo. 'Come on, let's work our way round to that patch of jungle.'

Getting into one of the baskets proved surprisingly easy. They made their way to the edge of the jungle and crept up on a party of Spiridon slaves working under the supervision of a Dalek guard. Jo edged as near to the baskets as she dared, while Wester moved noisily about in the jungle on the other side of the clearing. The Dalek guard registered the noise and moved to investigate. The slaves watched the guard, chattering excitedly together in their hissing voices. Jo slipped unobserved into a nearly-full basket, burying herself under the thick vegetation. The Dalek guard, finding nothing, herded the Spiridon slaves back to work. Soon two of them picked up her basket and started carrying it towards the city.

Jo lay under the vegetation, her heart pounding. She hoped that getting out of the Dalek city would prove as easy as getting in.

Taron and the other Thals stood shivering in the middle of a strange, icy landscape. They had climbed a range of low, rocky hills covered with a thick coating of icy slush. They were dotted with gaping, cavernous openings rather like giant pot-holes, and it was to the edge of one of these sinister apertures that Taron had led them. The edge of the hole was rimmed with ice and snow.

Rebec crumbled a piece of the ice between her fingers. 'There's something odd about this stuff—it's well below freezing point, but it's still *soft* . . .'

Taron nodded. 'Codal called it an allotrope—ice in a different form from the kind we know. He says the core of this planet is a solid mass of the stuff. Every so often, the pressure builds up and the ice pours out of these holes.'

Marat peered into the hole. 'Sort of a cold volcano?'

'That's right. Codal calls it an "icecano".'

'Very interesting, Taron,' said Marat. 'Now tell us why you brought us here—and why you sent Vaber and Latep back for the explosives?'

'When we first landed on this planet, I ordered a full reconnaissance of the area around the Dalek city. I formed a plan to destroy it. But things went wrong. First we lost three men in an ambush, then Codal was captured. That left myself and Vaber. My plan wouldn't work with just two men so I abandoned it, started looking for another. Now you're here we can revert to the original idea.' Taron drew a long breath after what, for him, had been a very long speech. He went on, 'When the Daleks built their underground city, they used this icecano to provide a cooling system. Apparently they needed very low temperatures for their experiments.'

'I wonder why,' Rebec said thoughtfully. 'Invisibility is

a problem of light-waves, temperature's got nothing to do with it.'

Taron ignored the interruption. 'The Daleks drove shafts out to meet the natural fissures. If we go down one of these outlets and work our way along to the junctions, we could reach the heart of their city unseen, plant charges at strategic spots and blow the whole place up.'

Rebec looked into the dark icy hole and shivered. 'And suppose this icecano thing erupts while we're down there?'

Taron said nothing. The answer was obvious enough.

Marat was looking down the icy slope. 'Vaber and Latep are coming,' he called.

Slipping and sliding on the icy rock, the two Thals toiled up to rejoin their friends. Vaber was carrying a plastic bundle. He unwrapped the bombs and shared them out. The Thals stowed them away in their back-packs. Vaber looked alert and eager, his normal sulkiness transformed by the prospect of action. 'I've changed the hiding place of the rest of the explosives, as you ordered, Taron,' he said. 'I've marked the position on this map.' He showed Taron a crumpled piece of paper. 'X marks the spot!'

Taron took the paper and studied it. 'I know the place. Here, Marat, you take this—just in case.' He turned to the others. 'We'd better get started. The fact that there's an army of Daleks in that city makes its destruction a matter of top priority. Vaber, you and Latep take your bombs and find another opening, closer to the main entrance of the city. Blow up the main lift-shaft and the whole place will be buried. The rest of us will attack from this end.'

Taron produced a coil of fine plastic rope from his pack and slung it over his shoulder. He touched a control in his belt. 'Switch on your heating units, all of you, it's going to be cold down there.' Poised on the edge of the hole, Taron looked round the little group, his eyes lingering on

Rebec for a moment. He swung a leg over the edge, and Vaber went to help him.

'Taron,' he whispered, 'I'm sorry—about what happened.'

'Forget it.' Taron scrambled over the edge and slid down into the darkness. Vaber and Latep helped Rebec and Marat to follow him down. Then they turned and ran, looking for the hole that would provide their own entrance to the Dalek city.

The Doctor finished his work on the reassembled recorder, fitting the parts tidily back into the box. He looked up at Codal. 'Well, that's the best I can do. Only one thing we need now—a Dalek to try it on!'

Codal said nervously, 'I think you're going to get your wish. I can hear the lift.'

A few minutes later the door opened and a Dalek entered the cell. Codal and the Doctor were sitting innocently in the corner. The Doctor's hands were behind him.

'Prisoners will stand,' ordered the Dalek. Slowly they got up. 'You will be taken for interrogation. Move!'

The Dalek stood waiting just inside the door. The Doctor and Codal moved forward. When they were close enough, the Doctor shouted, 'Now!'

Codal leapt on the Dalek, jamming it against the wall. His shoulder to the metal casing, he grabbed the Dalek's gun-stick, forcing it upwards. At the same time the Doctor jumped behind the Dalek and pressed the re-built recorder to its headpiece.

The Dalek struggled violently in Codal's grip. It was amazingly strong and he knew he couldn't hold it for long. 'Surrender immediately, or you will be exterminated,' grated the harsh voice. Then almost immediately it changed its sound. The pitch became higher and there was a note of hysteria. 'Surrender, surrender . . . I am losing control, I am losing control . . .' Suddenly the words garbled together in a agonised electronic shriek. Wrenching free of Codal's grip, the Dalek began hurling itself about the cell, crashing and rebounding from one wall to another like a bee trapped in a bottle. Codal and the Doctor jumped desperately about in the confined space, trying to avoid being crushed. The recorder was knocked from the Doctor's hand. At last the Dalek zoomed straight at the wall, crashed into it, rebounded, spun round and was still.

Gasping, Codal looked at the Doctor. 'That's a very effective little machine.'

'Not any more,' said the Doctor sadly. He picked the crushed recorder from the floor. In the confusion it had been stepped on by the Doctor and run over by the Dalek. It tinkled when the Doctor shook it, 'Still it's served its purpose.' He glanced at the inert Dalek. 'Much as I abhor violence, I rather enjoyed that.' He went to the still-open door. 'Come on, Codal. We can get out of this cell now—but we're a long way from being free.'

The basket was put down with a thump, and Jo peered cautiously out. She was in a long, wide corridor. Fur-clad Spiridon slaves were emptying the baskets into metal bins and pushing them into what seemed to be a huge laboratory. Others were carrying the empty baskets away. Clearly, it wouldn't do for Jo to be still in her basket when it was tipped out. She slipped out of the crate, keeping the stack between her and the Spiridons, and ran off.

She obviously couldn't stay in the open—Daleks or Spiridons were bound to spot her. Jo decided to look for a hiding-place while she thought out her next move, and crept cautiously through the next door in the corridor.

It took her into a huge rock-walled area, packed with various kinds of Dalek scientific equipment. Jo guessed it was their control centre. Behind a glass wall dividing the area, they were moving about on various mysterious tasks. There were more Daleks in the control area but they were all some distance away with their backs to her.

Jo looked round for a hiding place. Like most of the Dalek underground city, the room seemed to have been carved from solid rock, and the walls weren't quite regular in shape. Huge gleaming instrument consoles had been lined up against the rock walls but they weren't completely flush with it. There was a gap, rather like that between a sofa and a wall, into which a very small person might squeeze. Thankful, not for the first time, for her lack of size, Jo slipped behind the nearest console and worked her way along the gap until she was completely concealed.

Suddenly, a dial close to her hiding-place began to give out a sharp pinging sound. Two of the Daleks moved across to it, and Jo could hear their voices on the other side of the bank of instruments. 'Sensors detect ice eruption imminent.'

'Prepare to close all cooling ducts. Activate closure when warning dial reaches red alert.'

'I obey.'

One of the Daleks returned to its place on the far side of the room. But the other stayed where it was, evidently watching the warning dial. In its present position it would certainly see Jo if she tried to get away. Her hiding placc had become a trap.

The news of the ice eruption, meaningless to Jo, was a deadly threat to Taron and his party. They were working their way along the ice fissure, which by now had broadened out into a sizeable tunnel, hoping it would lead them to the Dalek city. An icy wind sprang up, accompanied by a low rumbling noise. They struggled forward against it as long as they could, until they came to a point where the tunnel branched. They stopped and the Thals looked at Taron in enquiry. The noise of the wind was too great to allow talking, but Taron made a gesture that they should wait. He ran a little way down the right-hand tunnel, then stopped in horror. A wall of ice completely blocked the tunnel—and it was moving towards him.

Taron turned and ran back to the fork, making signs to his little group that they should turn down the left-hand path. Rebec shook her head, pointing back the way they had come, obviously suggesting that they should give up and go back. But even as she pointed, the wall of the fissure cracked open and more ice flooded through, blocking their retreat. There was only one way they could go. As they ran down the left-hand fork the ice appeared behind them, pursuing them down the tunnel.

The Doctor and Codal had almost succeeded in reaching the lift when a Dalek appeared round a corner. Luckily it was as surprised as they were. They turned and ran, disappearing round a corner as the Dalek fired. The Dalek's lights flashed agitatedly and it began screeching, 'Alert! Alert! Alert!'

The message was received in the central control room where Jo crouched in hiding. Again she heard Dalek voices.

'Level seven reports prisoners are at liberty.'

'Instigate condition of maximum alert. Normal operations will cease until prisoners are recaptured.'

'I obey.'

A moment's pause and then another voice, speaking over a public-address system: 'All Daleks will report to lower levels. Maximum security search to commence immediately. Locate and destroy prisoners. Locate and destroy!'

In her hiding place, Jo Grant listened excitedly to the Dalek voices. She was sure the Doctor was one of the escaped prisoners. Trust him to get away without her help. Jo desperately wanted to make her way to the lower levels to find him, but she couldn't—not while the Dalek maintained its stand. Ironically, positions had reversed. Somewhere in the Dalek city the Doctor was free—but Jo herself had become the Dalek's prisoner.

6

Danger on Level Zero

Codal and the Doctor pelted frantically along the complex of corridors, dodging round corner after corner as more and more Daleks appeared. The Doctor, however, was not running completely at random. He led them round three sides of a square back to the lift for which they had originally been heading. At last the lift door came in sight, the doors standing invitingly open. The Doctor and Codal hurled themselves inside—and a Dalek appeared in the lift corridor.

The Doctor stabbed frantically at the lift controls. It took the astonished Dalek a moment to register their presence. By the time it had raised its gun-stick to fire, the lift doors were already sliding closed. They came together just as the Dalek fired, the blast of its gun scorching the metal doors.

Inside the lift the Doctor was stabbing at the up control. Nothing happened. 'They must have operated the master control,' he said. 'Well, what won't go up, must go down.' He touched the down control, and the lift began its smooth descent.

The Doctor let it take them down a few stages, stopped the lift and opened the doors. They slid back to reveal a waiting Dalek. It had time to fire only once before the Doctor closed the doors and sent the lift on its way. Codal looked at the scorch-mark on the back wall of the lift. 'They want to force us down to the lower levels, Doctor.

They'll be waiting for us!'

The Doctor rubbed his chin. 'Well if we've got to go down to the basement, we must try and get there before them.' He ripped off the panel by the controls, made a few adjustments with his sonic screwdriver. 'Hold tight, Codal, we're dropping to level zero—non-stop!'

He touched a control, there was a shower of sparks, and the lift dropped like a stone. Codal sank to the floor, hands over his ears, which were popping with the rapidly changing pressure.

The lift stopped with a jarring thump, and the Doctor opened the door. They saw a gloomy, dimly lit area with rock-walled corridors stretching off in several directions. The whole place looked primitive and functional, less finished than the higher levels. The Doctor guessed that this would be where the basic maintenance machinery of the Dalek city was kept. He led the way along a corridor, more or less at random. The first priority was to find a safe hiding place. After that they would just have to take things as they came.

He had chosen a corridor that seemed dark and deserted, hoping that it would lead well away from the main centres of activity. Although the Doctor didn't realise it, the corridor ran along the outer edge of the city. It was empty because it had been evacuated. It was part of the area most endangered by icecano eruptions. Along the corridor at regular intervals were metal grilles flanked with heavy metal shutters. At the moment the shutters were drawn back, and an icy blast of cold air streamed through each grille. The Doctor shivered, wondering why the Daleks needed to keep this area so cold. As they passed yet another of the grilles, he heard a grinding, rumbling sound. It seemed to be getting closer.

The sound was very close indeed for Taron, Rebec and Marat. They were crawling along a rapidly narrowing ice fissure, with the wall of ice rumbling steadily in pursuit. It was hard to move quickly in the confined and slippery space, and Taron had a terrible feeling that the ice was gaining on them. Above the steady rumbling of the moving ice he heard Rebec shout, 'Look, up ahead. It's the shaft . . .'

Ahead on the left, a square-cut shaft, obviously Dalek-made, led off from the natural fissure at right angles. They reached it just in time. The ice wall surged forward with unexpected speed, and it was almost on their heels when they entered the shaft.

They were in a small square tunnel, fairly short, which ended in a heavy metal grille. Taron peered through. On the other side was a dimly lit, rock-walled corridor—and someone was coming along it. Taron peered through the grille in astonishment as two figures approached. 'Doctor! Codal,' he called.

The Doctor was equally astonished to hear the voice of Taron floating out of the air. He ran to the grille and was just able to make out Taron crouching on the other side. 'I don't suppose this is the moment to ask how you got in there,' he said mildly. 'All the same, I'd be fascinated to know . . .'

'Doctor, help me free the grille,' interrupted Taron. 'We're trapped in this shaft and the ice is moving up behind us.'

In the Dalek control room on the upper levels, the Dalek watching the ice monitor saw the dial creep into the danger area. From her hiding place Jo heard it say, 'Ice eruption endangering perimeter corridors. Cooling duct shutters now being closed down.' The Dalek touched a control.

With the Doctor and Codal tugging on one side, and Taron and Marat pushing from the other, the metal grille didn't stand a chance. It gave way with a shriek of rending metal. The Doctor threw it to one side—just as the heavy, electrically operated shutters started to close.

The Doctor and Codal acted together, each seizing the edge of the shutter and struggling to hold it back. Taron wedged himself longways between the closing shutters, shoulders against one, boots against the other.

The cooling shaft was almost filled with ice now, and Marat could feel its clammy bulk pressing against him. 'Hurry,' he yelled. 'it's going to crush us!'

Despite the effort of all three men, Taron's powerful body was slowly being folded in two by the pressure of the twin shutters. Quickly Rebec clambered over him. Marat followed. Codal and the Doctor gave a final heave, the Doctor shouted, 'Now Taron!' and Taron rolled out into the corridor. Thankfully the Doctor and Codal let go, and the shutters slammed closed, a thin trickle of ice trapped between their edges.

The Doctor helped Taron to his feet. There was a babble of greetings and explanations. Suddenly Codal yelled, 'Daleks! Run, everybody!'

Two Daleks had appeared in the corridor. The Doctor led his party at a run in the other direction, dodging and weaving to escape the blast of Dalek guns.

The two Daleks followed in pursuit. As they reached the shaft through which Taron and the others had escaped, the metal shutters buckled inwards. A gushing flood of ice poured into the corridor, burying the Daleks.

The Doctor paused, looking back over his shoulder. 'Now there's a bit of luck,' he said cheerfully. 'Let's get away from here.'

Once again, news of the Doctor's progress was relayed to the Dalek control room. 'Prisoners have been driven to level zero. All ascent areas sealed off. All units proceed to level zero immediately.' Daleks began gliding from the room, but the one near Jo remained in his place. She was still trapped.

The Doctor and his friends got quite some way before they ran into the next Dalek patrol. The corridor behind them was sealed off by the ice, but Daleks had meanwhile been pouring in from the upper levels, and it was inevitable that the fugitives would eventually be discovered. They turned a corner to find half a dozen Daleks waiting in ambush.

Spinning round they ran desperately down the nearest side corridor, dodged down another, and found themselves trapped. This corridor ended in a pair of massive metal doors. Another, smaller door, also closed, stood just to the left of them.

The Doctor looked at the control panel beside the doors. 'Both locked,' he said. 'This is some kind of security area.' Working with amazing speed he unscrewed the control panel, and began using his sonic screwdriver. 'If I can over-ride the security seal . . .' With agonising slowness the larger doors started to slide apart. The gap widened until it was almost big enough to admit a body.

Daleks appeared at the far end of the corridor. Their harsh voices rang out. 'Surrender immediately or you will be exterminated!'

Marat, at the rear of the little group, glanced nervously at the slowly opening doors, then at the advancing Daleks. Five people had to get through those doors, *and* close them again, before the Daleks were near enough to fire. There wasn't enough time. Before anyone could stop him, Marat yelled, 'Get inside, all of you!' Drawing his blaster he began running towards the Daleks.

As if astonished, the Daleks halted their advance. Marat had time to fire only once. A Dalek spun round under the effect of his blaster and immediately the rest of the Daleks fired in unison. Marat's smoking body was slammed across the corridor.

By now Rebec, Codal and Taron were through the gap. The Doctor sent an anguished look after Marat, realised he was beyond help and went through the doors himself. On the other side he worked quickly on the controls and the heavy doors began sliding closed again. The edges touched just as the first Daleks reached them and opened fire. The Doctor made a few more adjustments, and leapt back as there was a shower of sparks and a bang. 'Fused solid,' he said with satisfaction. 'They won't open them with the controls, that's for sure.'

Rebec was sobbing in Taron's arms. He patted her awkwardly on the back. 'There's nothing we can do for him now,' he said gruffly.

The Doctor came over to them. 'Oh yes there is! Marat sacrificed himself to buy us a little more time. We owe it to him to make good use of it.' Rebec nodded, stifling her sobs. The Doctor looked round. 'Now what sort of a place is this, I wonder?'

They were in a huge, circular, rock-walled chamber, with a domed roof. Massive Dalek machines hummed and throbbed around them. The Doctor crossed to examine them, looking at the rows of dials and switches. 'It's some kind of refrigeration unit,' he said. 'This must be the cooling chamber. Now, with all that ice around, why do the Daleks need to make it colder still? You could freeze an ocean with a unit this size.'

'Well, at least we're safe for a while,' said Rebec shakily. 'There's no other door, and if that one's really sealed . . .'

'Don't underestimate the Daleks,' warned the Doctor. 'They won't let a little thing like a solid metal door deter them for long.'

Codal was examining the far side of the room, where a big metal cowl like a chimney-piece projected out from one wall. 'Look at this,' he called. They crossed to join him. He was standing directly under the cowl, pointing upwards. A huge circular chimney with gleaming metal walls stretched up above them. It went up and up until it ended in a tiny dot of blue, almost out of sight.

'Some kind of ventilation shaft,' said the Doctor. 'Seems to go clear up to the surface!'

Taron grunted. 'No use to us. Too wide and too smooth to climb.'

The Doctor nodded absently, the tiny spark of an idea glowing somewhere in his mind. He ducked out from under the cowling, and wandered across the room. Some of the machinery in one corner was evidently under repair. It was covered with huge protective sheets of transparent plastic. The Doctor tested it between his fingers. It was fine, but seemed very strong. He looked at the coils of plastic rope slung over the shoulders of the Thals. The Doctor ran his fingers through his hair, his mind full of calculations about weight,lift and gravity. A scream from Rebec interrupted him. 'Doctor, look at the door!'

A tiny glowing, smoking point had appeared in the metal of the door. As they watched the point started to move downwards, forming the beginnings of a line . . .

'They're cutting through the door,' said Taron.

The Doctor shot him a look. 'Well, it was pretty obvious they'd do something of that sort. You've got to admire their technology, haven't you?'

Taron looked at him as if he were mad. 'Doctor, it's only a matter of time before they're in here. What are we going to do?'

The Doctor's voice was almost apologetic. 'Well, as a matter of fact I do have an idea. But I'm afraid it's rather bizarre . . .'

Outside the heavy metal doors, the leader of the Dalek security squad looked on in satisfaction as the cutting equipment gradually extended the glowing line. Another Dalek approached. On the end of its sucker arm was a crumpled scrap of paper. 'The dead Thal was carrying this paper.'

The squad leader studied the paper. It was the map

Vaber had given Marat, after shifting the hiding place of the explosives. 'It may contain information of importance. Send it to central control for analysis.'

'I obey.'

Inside the cooling chamber, the Doctor was showing the Thals how to tie lengths of rope to the corners of a huge square of plastic.

'I wish you'd tell us the point of all this,' grumbled Taron. 'Just what are we making?'

'Well, on Earth they'd call it a parachute—but it's a parachute for going up, not coming down. A parachute-balloon, say.'

'You're not trying to tell me we're going to fly up the chimney?' ask Codal incredulously.

'It's the only way we can get out,' said the Doctor. 'There's a powerful updraft in that chimney. If we can trap a big enough pocket of it in this—all we have to do is hang on.'

Taron said, 'That's ridiculous, Doctor. It'll never work.'

'It had better,' the Doctor said grimly. 'Look!'

While they had been busy, the line on the door had enlarged itself to form two sides of a square arch. Once the third side was cut, a huge chunk of the doors would simply fall away, leaving a gap through which Daleks could enter.

The knots completed, the Thals manhandled the unwieldy sheet of plastic across the room and began to stuff it up the cowling. They disappeared underneath, and after a moment Codal emerged. 'It's no good, Doctor. It's forming a pocket, but the updraft isn't strong enough.'

The Doctor rubbed his chin. 'Hold on, I'll switch the unit to maximum. That'll boost the updraft.'

The Doctor ran to the refrigeration unit and adjusted controls. Under the cowling, Taron and the others felt the updraft increase to a steady gale. The Doctor was crossing the room to join them when his attention was caught by something on the wall near by. A short ramp ran up to a little platform. Set in the wall just above the platform was a metal-shuttered window. The general effect was of a kind of viewing gallery. But a viewing gallery to what? Even under such dangerous circumstances as these, the Doctor was unable to resist it. Curiosity had always been his strongest characteristic. He ran up the ramp, pulled back the shutter and looked through.

From the other side of the room, Codal called, 'It's working, Doctor, the balloon's lifting.'

The Doctor scarcely heard. He was staring, in sheer amazement, at one of the most astonishing sights he had ever seen. The window looked out on to an enormous dimly lit cavern, metal catwalks round its walls. The cavern was so vast that its furthest walls were lost in shadow, and it was completely filled with row upon row of Daleks, thousands of them, rank after rank, standing completely still, wisps of icy vapour drifting about their bodies. A whole army of Daleks, silent, motionless, waiting . . .

Another shout from Codal broke into the Doctor's trance. 'Doctor, they're nearly through. Hurry!'

The Doctor looked at the metal doors. The third side of the arch was almost cut through. He ran to the cowling. The plastic 'parachute' had risen far up the chimney, and the Thals were hanging on to the ropes. Taron tossed one to the Doctor and he caught hold, wrapping it round his fists. The ropes were tugging hard now, trying to lift them up but not quite making it. The Dalek cutting machine was on the last few inches of the arch. 'It's no use,' yelled Codal. 'There's not enough lift to take all our weights.'

'Give it time,' said the Doctor steadily. 'It'll take us up.'

'It isn't going to work,' said Rebec desperately.

The leader of the Dalek security squad watched the cutting machine complete the last section of its arch. A Dalek gripped the cutaway section with a magnetic clamp and pulled. The section lifted out, and the Dalek dragged it clear, leaving a cut-out archway in the metal doors.

'Attack force prepare,' ordered the squad leader. 'Maximum fire power. All prisoners to be exterminated.'

Gun-sticks at the ready, the Daleks swept into the cooling chamber.

7

Ascent to Peril

The cooling chamber was empty.

The astonishment of the Daleks was almost ludicrous. They crowded into the room, spinning round wildly in search of the fugitives. There was a note of hysteria in the leader's voice. 'Escape from this section is impossible. There are no other exits. The prisoners are hiding. Locate and destroy. They are to be exterminated.'

The orders sounded logical but they were impossible to carry out. There was nowhere for the prisoners to hide, nowhere to search. The Daleks milled about the room in a state of utter confusion.

The Doctor and his friends meanwhile were floating slowly up the great metal chimney, the plastic sheet billowing above them like the sail of some great yacht. As the doors finally gave way they had achieved lift-off, disappearing up the chimney seconds before the Daleks had entered the room. Once they were under way the ascent seemed to go easier, and now they were rising slowly but surely upwards. Quite a pleasant sensation, the Doctor was thinking. He really must try hot-air ballooning some time.

Rebec glanced down and shivered, closing her eyes. 'How far have we climbed?'

The Doctor looked at the drop beneath them. 'Hard to tell. I just hope we're high enough to be out of range. One of them's bound to look up here sooner or later.'

Even as the Doctor was speaking, a Dalek had glided beneath the cowling. Its eye-stalk swivelled casually upwards, then it let out an astonished squawk. 'Prisoners located.' It raised its gun-stick and fired.

They heard the roar of the blast as it echoed round the chimney, and even felt the heat, but they were quite unharmed. 'That's a relief,' said the Doctor. 'It seems we are out of range!' He saw Rebec twisting on her rope, sobbing with fear. 'Just keep your eyes closed, my dear, and hang on tight. You'll be all right.'

He looked at the two others. Taron was hanging on in grim silence, but Codal was looking about him keenly, scientific interest overcoming his fears. 'How long before we get to the top, Doctor?'

'Quite a while. We're coming right up from the lowest level, remember. It's going to be a long, slow climb.'

In the cooling chamber below, the Dalek leader was giving orders to retrieve the situation. 'A patrol will be sent to the surface immediately, to the point where the shaft emerges. They must reach the area before the prisoners can escape. Order an anti-gravitational disc to be brought here immediately.'

'I obey.' The second-in-command glided from the room. The leader moved under the cowling and swivelled his eye-stalk upwards.

The prisoners were scarcely visible now, just slowly ascending dots. But they had not escaped. Soon Daleks would be waiting at the head of the chimney, and a Dalek pursuing them up it. They had simply entered a trap, with no escape.

Jo Grant wondered if she was doomed to spend the rest of her life hiding in Dalek control like a rat in the wainscotting. There was only one Dalek in the area now, but it was still too near her. Her heart sank when two more entered and crossed to 'her' Dalek. 'You will come with us. The ice eruption is under control. We have discovered where the Thals have hidden their explosives. We must find and destroy them.' The new arrival carried a crumpled scrap of paper on its sucker-arm.

'I obey.' The three Daleks left the control room—and the way to Jo's escape was clear. After a moment's reflection, she decided to follow the patrol. For one thing, they would presumably lead her out of the city. For another, perhaps she would find some way of preventing them from finding the Thal explosives. There was no way she could help the Doctor directly, now; the next best thing was to help the Thals.

Jo slipped along the corridor after the three Daleks. They passed the laboratory area where slave Spiridons were still unloading endless baskets of vegetation. Tossed over a crate, Jo saw one of the voluminous fur robes worn by the Spiridons. Presumably its invisible owner had abandoned it in defiance of regulations. Hoping he was nowhere near, Jo snatched up the robe and pulled it on. Grabbing an empty basket, she set off boldly after the Dalek patrol.

The robe was far too big, but that was all to the good. It covered her entire body from head to foot, and the loose sleeves concealed her hands. It didn't seem to bother the Daleks that they were being trailed by a very small Spiridon. Presumably Spiridon slaves were beneath their notice.

Jo followed the patrol along the corridors, into the lift, up to the surface and out into the jungle, without being stopped or checked. As soon as she was clear of the blockhouse, she dropped behind the patrol and dumped her disguise and the empty basket in a clump of bushes. Using the jungle for cover, she hurried after them.

The Daleks led her through the jungle across an area of rocky hillside, and finally into a sort of quarry. Watching from a distance, Jo felt the ground beneath her vibrating. She could see the Daleks moving to and fro along the bottom of the quarry, a rock wall rearing up above them like a cliff-face. The rock was loose and crumbly. Occasionally chunks rattled down onto the patrol, dislodged by subterranean vibrations from the icecano. Eventually one of the Daleks paused by a large rock. The others joined it, and between them they pushed the rock away, revealing the entrance to a tiny cave. Inside the cave mouth lay a plastic bundle.

Jo crept closer, until she was near enough to hear what the Daleks were saying. 'Explosives are equipped with detonating mechanisms. We will explode them here. Activate mechanisms.' One of the Daleks glided closer to the bomb cache, its sucker-arm reaching out. 'All mechanisms now primed. The bombs will self-detonate when we have left the area. We shall return to the city and assist in recapturing the escaped prisoners.'

The three Daleks wheeled and filed away. Jo waited until they were out of sight, then made her way towards the bombs. Acting on the general principle that whatever the Daleks wanted, she was against, Jo was determined to switch off the bombs if she possibly could. Maybe the Thals or the Doctor would get a chance to pick them up later and use them against the Daleks.

The bombs lay in the cave mouth, ticking away quietly. They were stubby metal cylinders, silvery in colour, each surmounted with a small clock face. The single hand on each clock was moving slowly from the 'one o'clock' to the 'twelve o'clock' position. It was easy enough to work out that when the hand reached twelve the bombs would blow up. Beside the clock face was a button, like that on a stop watch. Bracing herself, Jo reached out and pressed the button. The hand stopped moving. She gave a sigh of relief and switched off the second bomb, ignoring the dirt and small stones rattling down from overhead.

A further shower rained down as Jo moved over

to the third bomb. Unfortunately this contained a few larger stones and one of them struck Jo behind the ear as she leaned over the third bomb. It wasn't very big, only slightly larger than a tennis ball, but the impact was enough to knock her out. She slumped forward over the third bomb. Since she hadn't managed to turn it off, this third bomb was still ticking. The hand on its clock moved steadily towards detonation point.

Dangling from their parachute-balloon, the Doctor and the Thals were now near the top of the enormous chimney. The round disc of blue sky was getting bigger and nearer, and they were beginning to hope they might actually reach it. The Doctor seemed to be enjoying himself. 'You must admit,' he said chattily, 'it really is rather an exhilarating sensation.'

Rebec, her eyes tight shut, spoke through clenched teeth. 'The only time I ever want to leave the ground again, is in the rocket that takes me away from this planet.'

'Now don't *worry,*' said the Doctor reassuringly. 'As long as you hold on tight, you're perfectly safe.'

Above the Doctor's head, at the point where his rope was attached to the plastic sheeting, a tiny tear had appeared. Slowly, very slowly, it began to spread.

A long way below, in the cooling chamber at the bottom of the chimney, a squad of Daleks was manoeuvring a flat metal disc into position beneath the cowling. It was about a foot thick, and just big enough for one Dalek to stand securely in the centre. The squad leader glided up a little ramp and took his position on the disc. A Dalek scientist reported, 'Anti-gravitational disc now in position. Energy building up to full lift-off capacity.'

Even as he spoke, a hum of power came from within the disc. It built up to a throbbing crescendo and then stopped. The squad leader ordered, 'Prepare for lift-off!'

The energy hum started again, this time with a steady throbbing note. 'Lift-off!'

The anti-gravitational disc rose slowly in the air, carrying the Dalek up the long chimney in pursuit of the fugitives.

Meanwhile, another Dalek patrol was moving swiftly through the jungle on its way to intercept the prisoners at the top of the shaft. A report from central control had informed them that the prisoners were still in the chimney, and they were confident of arriving in time to exterminate them as they emerged. The patrol's route took it into the rocky area where the hills rose out of the jungle. They were passing along a trail that led through a kind of quarry when their leader spotted a suspicious sight on the rock slope ahead. A small figure was crouching over some silvery objects. The patrol leader halted. 'We have discovered a Thal saboteur with hidden explosives. The Thal must be captured and interrogated.' They began gliding along the path towards the cave.

Jo Grant was just recovering consciousness. Muzzily she climbed to her hands and knees, shaking her head to clear it. Suddenly she became aware of double danger. The clock-hand on the third bomb had almost reached detonation point. And several Daleks were advancing towards her along the trail.

Jo grabbed the two switched-off bombs and scrambled up the rocky slope. The Daleks increased their pace. 'Halt. Halt and surrender or you will be exterminated!'

Ignoring the order Jo stumbled on. The Daleks followed after, confident they could stun her with their blasters when they were close enough.

As the Dalek patrol came level with the little cave, the third bomb exploded. There was a tremendous explosion and a huge avalanche of earth and rocks poured down. Jo flung herself to the ground, still clasping the two bombs. Earth and stones rumbled past her, but this time her luck was better, and she survived unharmed. When the noise died away she looked up.

Where the Daleks had been was a huge pile of rubble, burying them completely. A bomb under each arm, Jo stumbled towards the shelter of the jungle.

The parachute-balloon had almost reached the top of the shaft by now. The Doctor peered upwards. 'The chimney narrows near the top and the sides are ribbed. The parachute may jam, but we should be able to climb up. Be ready to grab a hand-hold.'

Taron was looking downwards. 'There's something coming up after us!'

The Doctor glanced down and saw the tiny dot of the anti-gravitational disc moving steadily up the chimney. 'It's all right,' he called. 'It isn't climbing any faster than we are—and we've got a big start. We'll be at the top before it gets in range.'

Suddenly he heard Rebec scream, 'Look, Doctor, the parachute! It's tearing!'

The little tear by the Doctor's rope had become a huge rip, spreading rapidly across the plastic sheeting. 'The whole thing's going,' he yelled. 'Jump for the sides—we'll have to climb.'

One by one, Rebec, Codal and Taron jumped for the metal ribbing, scaling it like a ladder. They climbed up and up, arms and legs aching, for what seemed an incredibly long way. At last, one by one, they were able to scramble over a low stone parapet that bordered the chimney outlet and into the open air. Taron was the last to climb out. He leaned over the parapet and looked down the chimney. 'The Doctor's still inside!' he yelled.

Last to leave the falling balloon, the Doctor had

succeeded only in catching the very lowest rung of the ribbing ladder. With no foothold to help him climb, he was dangling from it by both hands.

Lower down the chimney, the crumpled mass of plastic, its supporting air-pocket dispersed, was drifting slowly downwards.

Lower still, the anti-gravitational disc, the Dalek passenger clearly visible by now, rose steadily towards the helpless Doctor.

8

The Enemy Within

Swiftly Taron uncoiled the length of plastic rope from his shoulder and lowered it into the shaft. It was almost long enough, but not quite. The end of the rope dangled less than a foot from the Doctor's hands. He gave a worried glance below him. The Dalek on its anti-gravitational disc was rising steadily higher. It would soon be near enough to fire. The falling plastic threatened to smother it, and the Dalek blasted it into flaming fragments.

At the top of the shaft Taron called, 'He can't reach it. Rebec, Codal, hold my legs.' He lowered the upper half of his body into the shaft, straining to bring the rope within the Doctor's grasp. Taron stretched dangerously forward, the Doctor let go with one hand and reached out—and the end of the rope brushed the tips of his fingers.

The pursuing Dalek was very close now. The rescuers made one final effort. Taron leaned full-length into the shaft, secured only by Codal and Rebec's grip on his ankles. The Doctor lunged desperately upwards and managed to catch the end of the rope with his left hand. Just as he did so, his right slipped from the smooth metal of the ribbing. He dangled spinning in mid-air, clasping the rope with one hand.

Rebec and Codal gripped Taron's legs, helping to brace him against the Doctor's weight on the rope.

The Doctor, meanwhile, grabbed the rope with his other hand, and started to climb it hand over hand, even as the three Thals were pulling it up. Taron fell back outside the parapet, then the Doctor shot out of the chimney like a cork out of a bottle, and scrambled over the parapet.

'Dalek,' he gasped. 'Still coming up.' He looked round for a weapon. Embedded in the ground near the parapet was a huge round boulder. The Doctor ran to it and started heaving with his shoulder. The boulder tilted a little. 'All of you, help me,' he ordered. Even with four of them it was a tremendous effort to roll the boulder up the hillside and then to lift it up onto the parapet. Heaving and panting they managed it at last. For a moment the boulder was poised on the parapet. Then the Doctor yelled, 'Heave!', and with a final shove, they tipped it over.

They crowded round the parapet to see the result. The boulder whistled down the shaft and struck the disc's edge, spinning it like a coin and wrecking the anti-gravitational mechanism. Boulder, disc and Dalek tumbled down the shaft together, gathering speed as they fell.

At the bottom of the shaft the squad of Daleks was gathered round waiting. The hurling objects shot out of the shaft all together. There was a tremendous roar as the disc exploded, and the Daleks were blown in all directions.

At the top of the chimney, the Doctor and his friends heard the noise. The doctor smiled in satisfaction. 'That should hold them for a while. Let's get away from here, before their patrol arrives.'

Taron said, 'We must get to the quarry where Vaber left the explosives. If the Daleks find that map they'll try to destroy them.' They set off down the hillside.

As they were approaching the quarry, Jo Grant was leaving it. She met them crossing a jungle clearing.

Scarcely able to believe her eyes, Jo flung herself into the Doctor's arms. 'Doctor, I thought you were still in the TARDIS. I thought you were dying . . . oh I don't know what I thought.'

The Doctor was just as delighted, and even more surprised. 'But I was afraid you were dead. I thought you might have been in that Thal spaceship when the Daleks blew it up . . .'

Jo began pouring out a confused account of her adventures, but the Doctor stopped her. 'There'll be plenty of time for explanations later. You've already met Taron and Codal. This is Rebec.'

Jo gave them a polite hello, and turned back to the Doctor. 'I heard you'd been taken prisoner by the Daleks. I went into the city to rescue you . . .'

'You did what?'

Taron interrupted them. 'It'll be dark soon. I think we'd better pick up those explosives.'

'If you're talking about some bombs hidden in a quarry—don't bother,' said Jo. 'One of them went off, and I've hidden the others in a clearing near by.' She told them what had happened at the quarry.

Taron shook his head wearily. 'So much has been going on that it's hard to think straight. We'd better rest here for a while.'

The Thals set up camp. Their seemingly inexhaustible back-packs produced supplies of concentrated food, and tiny atomic-powered stoves with which to heat it. Soon they were all washing down the tough, chewy food-concentrates with delicious hot soup, and Jo felt strength flooding back into her body. As they ate, Jo and the Doctor brought each other up to date on their adventures. Both realised how lucky they were to have come together again unharmed.

The Doctor took a swig of soup. 'But why didn't you just stay inside the TARDIS, Jo? We'd have been safe there—while the air lasted.'

'You didn't look very safe. I thought you were dying, so I went fo find help.'

'On a planet occupied by the Daleks? Surely I warned you.'

'You didn't warn me about anything, Doctor. You rushed into the TARDIS, rattled off a quick telepathic telegram to the Time Lords and then collapsed.'

The Doctor looked crestfallen. 'I'm sorry, Jo. I wasn't quite myself! I asked the Time Lords to send us after the Daleks, then I blacked out.'

'What are the Daleks doing on this planet, anyway?'

'I thought they were just studying the secret of invisibility, but there's more to it than that. They've got an enormous army concealed here, I saw it myself. It's obviously part of some plan to conquer the galaxy . . .'

While the Doctor and Jo were talking, Rebec and Taron sat together near by. It was their first chance to be alone since they had met again on this planet. Back home on Skaro they had been close friends, with an understanding that they would eventually marry. But here on Spiridon, Rebec had found Taron a different man, his manner strained and almost hostile.' 'You might at least say you're glad to see me,' she said lightly.

He looked coldly at her. 'I might. Why did you come?'

'Because I wanted to be with you.'

Taron was silent for a moment, then he burst out, 'Don't you understand what you've done? Even if Vaber and Latep are alive, there are still only five of us. Five survivors from two missions, to destroy an army of Daleks.'

'How does my being here make things any worse?'

In a level voice Taron said, 'Because I love you. And that will cloud my judgement. I may hesitate to take risks, necessary risks, because I'll be worrying about you. And if my judgement fails, then the Daleks will win!' He got quickly to his feet and crossed to the other side of the clearing. Rebec began sobbing quietly to herself.

The Doctor looked up from his conversation with Jo. As always, he was very well aware of what was going on around him. Casually he got up. 'I think I'll have a quick word with Taron. Rebec might appreciate a feminine shoulder at the moment.'

While Jo went to console Rebec, the Doctor joined Taron on the other side of the clearing. He was staring morosely into the thick green jungle, its leafy depths shadowed with the approaching darkness. 'Load getting a bit heavy, old chap?' asked the Doctor.

Taron couldn't help responding to the sympathy in his voice. 'I'm not sure I can handle things any more.'

'Because you're not made of stone?'

'I have to lead this expedition, Doctor. It's a job that doesn't allow for human weakness.'

'Perhaps they should have sent a machine.'

'I thought I could act like one,' said Taron grimly. 'I was wrong.'

'Good!' said the Doctor heartily. 'The business of command is not meant for machines. Forget you're dealing with people's lives and you're no better than the creatures we came to destroy. Once we start acting like Daleks—the battle's already lost!'

Taron was about to reply when he heard movement in the jungle. He drew his blaster and waited, calling a warning to the others. 'Look out, someone's coming.' They waited tensely—and Vaber and Latep came out of the jungle. There was a joyful reunion among the Thals. Vaber and Latep had been about half-way along their chosen ice-fissure when they had heard the icecano beginning to erupt. Not daring to go on they had set their bombs to explode, only to see them engulfed by a surge of ice which had absorbed the effects of the explosion. 'We were lucky to get clear and survive,' concluded Latep. 'We went to the quarry to get the other bombs, but they'd already been exploded.'

Jo couldn't resist joining in. 'Not all of them. I rescued two and buried them not far away.'

'Then we've still got a chance,' said Vaber eagerly. 'We can attack again in the morning.'

'Maybe,' said Taron, 'but meanwhile we've got to get through the night. We can't stay here, it's too near the main Dalek trails. Besides, we'd never survive the cold. We'll have to go to the Plain of Stones.'

The Doctor looked puzzled. Codal came forward and explained. 'It's an area scattered with huge boulders. They're made of a stone that soaks up the sun's heat during the day and releases it at night.'

'Sort of night storage heaters,' suggested Jo. 'It'll be nice to be somewhere warm for the night.'

'It's a dangerous place,' warned Codal. 'A lot of wild animals go there for the warmth.'

Taron said, 'Jo, will you take Latep to the place where you hid the bombs? The rest of us will pack up camp.'

Jo turned to Latep, who smiled at her. She decided she quite liked the look of him. He had a cheerful open face, and as the youngest and smallest of the Thals, he was the only one anywhere near her own age and size. All the rest of them towered over her, and seemed terribly serious about everything. Jo held out her hand. Latep looked at it in amazement. She realised he didn't know what she meant. 'It's an old Earth custom,' she explained. 'We clasp hands like this to show we're pleased to meet each other.'

Latep took her hand and shook it vigorously. 'Come on,' said Jo. 'Let's go and get those bombs.'

With the bombs collected and the camp packed up, they all set off through the jungle again. It was almost dark now, and getting very cold. Codal was moving ahead of the main group, acting as scout. Suddenly he called back, 'Down everybody! It's a Dalek patrol.'

The Doctor dropped to the ground, and wriggled forward on his elbows to lie beside Codal. On the trail just ahead, a Dalek patrol was gliding through the dusk. Accompanying them were Spiridons in their furry, all-concealing robes.

As the patrol disappeared into the darkness, the Doctor tapped Codal on the shoulder. 'Did you notice how slowly that patrol was moving? Almost as though their reflexes weren't functioning properly.'

Taron joined them. 'They're still fast enough to kill us on sight, Doctor. I think we can chance moving on now.'

An indignant voice floated forward to them. 'Let's get on with it then, I'm freezing!' It was Jo. Taron waved them on, and they all moved forward.

The Plain of Stones was exactly what its name suggested, a bleak plain littered with huge boulders. Their fantastic, twisted shapes loomed up out of the darkness. From all around came the growling, chattering and howling of Spiridon animal life. They found a circle of boulders grouped together, a kind of miniature Stonehenge, and decided to make camp between them. As they were settling down, there came a sudden hoarse scream, and a great black shape swooped over their heads, with a flapping of enormous wings. Jo gripped Latep's arm. 'What was that?' The boy shrugged and it was Taron who answered.

'Some kind of pterodactyl, I think. They only come out at night.' He turned to the Doctor. 'Will you take the first guard with Latep, Doctor?'

'Yes, of course. Maybe you'll keep us company for a while, Jo?'

They became aware of angry voices. Vaber was helping Codal to set up camp, and indulging in his usual complaints. Since the failure of the attack on the Dalek city, his old moroseness had returned. 'I'm sick of all this running and hiding, Codal,' he was saying. 'We need to attack, and soon.'

Taron crossed over to them. 'I'll decide that, Vaber.'

'You—you've already bungled one attack. You missed your greatest opportunity.'

Taron sighed. 'And what was that?"

'The refrigeration plant. Codal's been telling me about it. Obviously it's vital to the success of the Daleks' plans.'

'We still don't know why the Daleks need such low temperatures,' said Taron mildly.

'Who cares about why? The fact is they do. Destroy that refrigeration plant and we ruin the Daleks' plans. We can go back down the shaft you came up. Better still we could just lower the bombs down . . .'

Taron shook his head. 'The Daleks won't have left that shaft unguarded. We'll attack again, but the whole thing has to be properly planned. Until then, we wait.'

The word might have been chosen to enrage Vaber. 'Wait!' he sneered. 'That's all we hear from you. I suppose you're scared to take any action with her round your neck.' He nodded towards Rebec, who was standing listening to the argument in distress.

Taron's big hands flashed out and gripped Vaber round the throat, shaking him savagely. Vaber kicked Taron's feet from under him, and the two men rolled struggling on the ground. The Doctor's voice cracked out like a whip. 'Stop that, both of you. Get up at once!'

Shamefacedly the two Thals got to their feet. For all their size and strength they looked like children caught brawling in the playground. The Doctor spoke more gently. 'We'll never defeat the Daleks unless we stay united. We're letting the strain make us suspicious and hostile. That's the real enemy, the enemy within—not the Daleks but our own fears.'

For a long moment Taron and Vaber glared at each other. Then Taron said slowly, 'I'm still in command here, Vaber. We'll attack when I say so, and not before.

Like it or not, you'll obey orders. If you don't—I'll kill you!'

In the control room, the Dalek Expedition Commander was addressing his aides. Grouped around him in a semi-circle, they listened meekly to the arrogant voice. 'One Patrol is missing. Others report no contact with the prisoners. Supreme Command are gravely displeased with the progress of this operation.'

No one replied, or attempted excuses.

The Expedition Commander went on, 'Supreme Command has decreed we prepare a bacteriological weapon. It will destroy all living tissue on Spiridon. Daleks and Spiridon slave workers will be given immunity to the disease.'

Again there was no reply. It did not occur to any Dalek to protest at this ruthless proposal to wipe out the life-forms of an entire planet. Massive retaliation to opposition had always been the Dalek way.

The Commander turned to a Dalek scientist. 'Report progress on the bacteriological weapon.'

The Dalek scientist indicated a metal trolley inside the laboratory. Through the glass wall they could see that it contained a number of jars. 'The bacteria are now multiplying. After release into the atmosphere, the culture will totally contaminate the planet. All plant life will wither and die. All un-immunised animal life will be exterminated. The culture will be ready for release in one Spiridon day.'

'Approved. Continue preparations.'

Another Dalek entered and stood waiting to speak. The Commander swung towards it. 'Report.'

'Spiridon slave-spies report aliens in hiding at Plain of Stones.'

'Order all search units to concentrate on that area.'

'I obey.'

Her back against one of the boulders, Jo Grant was dozing comfortably. The huge rock gave out a steady warm glow, and she was having a confused dream about holidays on the French Riviera. Gradually she became aware of an agitated voice breaking into her dream and bringing her awake. It was Taron, shaking the Doctor who lay dozing beside her. 'Doctor, wake up. It's Vaber. He's cleared off and taken the bombs. He left this note.'

Taron held out the note and the Doctor read it aloud. 'I'll do what has to be done on my own.' He tossed the note back to Taron. 'Of all the melodramatic nonsense. He doesn't stand a chance on his own.'

'Neither do we now,' said Taron grimly. 'He's taken the last of the explosives. I'm going after him.'

The Doctor rose. 'I'll come with you.'

'I'd prefer you to take charge here.'

The Doctor was pleased by Taron's trust. 'All right. If that's what you want.'

'Codal, you come with me,' ordered Taron. 'The rest of you stay here. The Doctor's in command till I get back.'

Codal and Taron slipped away into the darkness. Jo drifted back to sleep, only to be awakened by the Doctor. 'I think we'd better build a fire,' he said.

Jo was still drowsy, disinclined to move. 'Why, Doctor? It's warm enough with these boulders.'

'Not for warmth, Jo, for safety. Look!' The Doctor pointed. A circle of fiercely glowing eyes ringed the camp. The wild-life of Spiridon was moving in for the kill.

Vaber didn't stand a chance. A bomb clutched under each arm, he stumbled towards the Dalek city, blind to everything except the need to justify himself against Taron—Taron who'd taken away the command that was rightfully his own. A bulky shape loomed out of the darkness—a fur-clad Spiridon. Vaber turned to run, but other shapes surrounded him. They threw themselves upon him, and claw-like hands gripped him so that he could not move. He heard a throaty whisper. 'Take him to the Daleks!'

9

Vaber's Sacrifice

Hiding near by in the jungle, Taron and Codal looked on appalled. They had been close behind Vaber, about to seize him themselves and recover the bombs, when they had witnessed his capture by the Spiridon patrol. There was no chance of a rescue. The Spiridons were too numerous. The two Thals watched helplessly as Vaber was hurried away. Taron tapped Codal's shoulder. 'We've got to recover those bombs. Come on.' Silently they began to follow the Spiridons and their prisoner.

The Doctor, Jo, Rebec and Latep huddled around the little fire. Already it had proved a problem to keep it going. There wasn't much fuel in the immediate area, and to go out into the darkness would have brought them within range of the creatures with the glowing eyes. Despite the fire, those eyes seemed to be moving closer. Rebec drew her blaster. 'I'll try a shot at them.' She fired at random into the darkness. There was a crackle of energy and a howl of pain. The eyes retreated. Then after a moment they returned, creeping even closer.
'They don't stay scared for long, do they?' the Doctor said grimly.

Rebec fired again. This time the energy-crackle suddenly fizzled out. 'The charge is exhausted.' she explained.

The Doctor looked at Latep who shook his head. 'I'm

sorry—I lost my blaster in the crash.'

The Doctor sighed. 'We'd better find more wood for the fire.' They began to search. Behind one of the near by boulders the Doctor found a kind of stunted tree. Wrenching it from the thin soil, he carried it over to the fire. 'This should keep us going for a time.' While the others broke off twigs and threw them on the fire, the Doctor trimmed a couple of larger branches to use as clubs. He lit the end of one in the fire and advanced towards the threatening eyes, waving the blazing torch in front of him. With angry roars the unseen creatures retreated. 'Get yourselves torches, all of you,' he ordered. Jo and the others obeyed, and a vigorous advance with blazing branches soon sent the creatures scurrying away. 'They'll come back of course,' said the Doctor cheerfully. 'But at least we've given ourselves a respite.'

Exhausted by their efforts, they sat silently round the fire. Eventually the Doctor said, 'What possessed Vaber to go rushing off like that?'

Rebec sighed. 'Once he'd worked out his plan, he couldn't bear to wait.'

'What plan?'

'To blow up the Dalek refrigeration unit. He thought if he destroyed that, he'd destroy the Daleks.'

The Doctor looked at her in horror. 'On the contrary—he'd be bringing their army to life.'

'Doctor,' said Jo, 'if you'd only remember to explain things occasionally . . .'

The Doctor took a deep breath. 'All right, I will. The Daleks I saw in that arsenal place, next to the cooling chamber, were in a state of suspended animation. No ageing process, no degeneration, no maintenance needed. An army of Daleks, in cold storage until it's needed. That's why the Daleks came to this planet. To use it as a base. The invisibility business is only a side-line. What they were really after was the planet's core of ice.

But they found the icecano was too unstable, so they built the refrigeration unit.' He looked round at the others. 'The minute the temperature rises, all those Daleks will come to life.' He was interrupted by a hoarse voice from the darkness.

'Jo! I have found you.'

The Doctor leaped to his feet. A bulky figure moved into the circle of firelight, fur-clad and carrying an ugly-looking club. The Doctor grabbed for a club of his own, but Jo spoke up, 'It's all right, Doctor. It's Wester—the Spiridon who helped me when I was ill.'

The Doctor lowered his club. 'Then I owe you a great debt. Please accept my thanks.' He held out his hand and felt it gripped by another invisible one, emerging from the wide sleeve of the furs.

The whispering voice said, 'I have news from the city. The Daleks have prepared a bacteriological weapon. It will destroy all life on this planet, except for the Daleks and their servants. I wanted to warn you. Now I shall go back to the city to try and prevent them.'

The Doctor's voice was grave. 'We'll do all we can to help. Thank you for warning us.'

Jo started to say, 'Wester, be careful . . .' But the Spiridon had already vanished.

The Doctor said decisively, 'We'll move out at full light.'

'What about Taron and the others?' Rebec protested.

'We'll wait till dawn. If they're not back by then—we must go without them.'

The Spiridon patrol moved swiftly down the trail. A nucleus of them stayed tightly clustered around their prisoner. Others ranged in a wider group, acting as scouts and rearguards. The last Spiridon of the patrol was some way behind the others. The patrol heard nothing as suddenly Codal and Taron leaped from hiding and bore the rearguard Spiridon to the ground, stunning him with swift blows. Taron stripped the fur robes from the invisible creature and pulled them on himself. 'I'll try to get close to Vaber,' he whispered. 'Be ready to move in when I jump the guards.'

Codal nodded, and Taron ran to join the rest of the patrol. Codal followed at a distance, keeping under cover.

Taron caught up with the patrol, indistinguishable from the Spiridons in his furs. The patrol moved on for quite some way, and still Taron made no move. Codal began to worry. Surely they'd be at the Dalek city before very long. Dodging through a clump of bushes he crept closer to the last figure in the patrol, tapping it on the shoulder. 'Taron,' he whispered, 'surely it's time we . . .' The figure swung round. To his horror Codal saw there was no face beneath the hood, just emptiness. He was talking to a genuine Spiridon.

The creature jumped him, invisible hands reaching out. Codal struggled desperately but the Spiridon was very strong. Suddenly his opponent jerked and went limp. Yet another fur-clad figure had appeared and stunned it, and this one was Taron. 'What do you think you're doing?' he whispered angrily.

Codal laughed hysterically. 'I spoke to him. I thought he was you!'

'Nearly got yourself killed,' muttered Taron. 'Still, it's provided us with another disguise. Get these furs on and follow me. I've marked out the one carrying the bombs. When I jump him, you grab the bombs and run. They're first priority.'

'What about you?'

'As soon as you're away I'll free Vaber. We'll make a run for it.'

Codal nodded, glad they were not abandoning Vaber, despite all the trouble he had caused them. Soon the two fur-clad figures were hurrying to rejoin the Spiridon patrol.

Taron was just about to make his move when ill-fortune struck. The Spiridons encountered a patrol of Daleks, and came to an immediate full stop. A Dalek voice rasped, 'Halt. What is happening?'

Eager for praise, a Spiridon whispered, 'We have captured one of the aliens. He was carrying explosives.' The Dalek patrol leader glided forward to where Vaber was held by two Spiridons.

'Where are your fellow Thals hiding?'

Vaber's voice was defiant. 'No idea. You want them, you find them.'

'Release him. Move away.' The Spiridons holding Vaber let go and stepped back. The Dalek's gun-stick swung to cover Vaber's isolated figure. 'Answer or I will exterminate you.'

Vaber seemed to wilt beneath the threat. 'No . . . don't fire. I'll take you to them . . .'

There was satisfaction in the Dalek's voice. 'We will start at once.'

Vaber turned as if to lead the way. Suddenly he ducked between the two Spiridons and sprinted for the cover of the jungle. An outlying Spiridon grabbed him and they grappled desperately. Vaber managed to swing the Spiridon round, using him as a shield. But the death of one of their servants was of little concern to the Daleks. The patrol leader ordered, 'Open fire!' Dalek guns blazed and Vaber and the Spiridon were blasted down together.

As the Daleks moved towards the bodies, Taron and Codal acted. Moving in on the Spiridon with the bombs, they clubbed him to the ground, grabbed one bomb each and made off into the jungle. Confused by the flurry of movement the Daleks swung round and opened fire. But they were too late. Taron and Codal had disappeared. With angry cries of 'Pursue! Pursue and exterminate!' the Daleks followed after them.

A Dalek technician was reporting to the Chief Scientist. 'The antidote is prepared and ready to be administered.'

'Demonstrate.'

The technician produced a square, gun-shaped device mounted on a trolley, and touched a control. There was a fierce hiss and a fine cloud of mist covered them both. 'Synthesised anti-bacteriological elements have been released. The elements provide immunity on contact.'

'Approved. I will order all Dalek units and Spiridon slave workers to assemble for treatment. Are the bacteria now ready for release?'

Proudly the Dalek technician gestured towards the other trolley. 'The growth process is complete. Removal of the container tops is all that is required to allow bacteria to enter the atmosphere.'

Dawn came at last, with a sudden blaze of light and heat. Thankfully the Doctor let the fire die down. The creatures of Spiridon had returned to their lairs. The Doctor disappeared on a brief scouting expedition, while Latep scanned the plain from on top of a high rock. Jo heard him call out, 'Someone's coming. It's Codal and Taron!' Codal and Taron hurried into camp, the Doctor close behind them.

There was time only for the quickest of reunions. A saddened silence fell as Taron told them of Vaber's fate. The Doctor said, 'He was rash and impulsive, poor fellow, but he was right about one thing. It is time we went over to the attack.'

Defensively Taron said, 'If you can provide me with a workable plan . . .'

'I think I can,' the Doctor said gently. 'I've been thinking it out for most of the night. Will you trust me?'

Taron nodded wearily. 'I'll leave it to you, Doctor. You can't do worse than I've done.'

'Nonsense,' said the Doctor briskly. 'We gathered invaluable information on that first attack. Now it's time to put our knowledge to good use. We need to get back inside the city, undetected this time.'

'And how do we do that?'

'Well, the first thing we must do,' the Doctor said cheerfully, 'is to get ourselves spotted by a Dalek patrol!'

There was an astonished silence. The Doctor smiled, and added mysteriously, 'Come with me, will you, Taron? The rest of you wait here.'

The Doctor led Taron a little way into the hills that bordered the Plain of Stones. They stopped by a small round pool in the rocky ground. 'There!' announced the Doctor triumphantly. 'Found it this morning when I was having a scout around.'

Taron was unimpressed. 'The planet is full of these pools, Doctor. They're liquid ice, fed from the icecano.'

'Exactly. It's odd, but water on this planet seems to sustain sub-zero temperatures and still remain liquid.'

Taron said, 'I'm sorry, Doctor, but I still don't see . . .'

Patiently, the Doctor explained. 'Daleks are vulnerable to extremely low temperatures. At sub-zero levels, they wouldn't be able to function at all. Now do you see?'

A slow smile spread over Taron's face. 'Yes . . . yes, I do see.' He started scanning the landscape around them. 'Let's look round and plan a way to make it work.'

The Doctor was smiling too. 'It's a good feeling, isn't it—when the hunted become the hunters?'

10

Return to the City

After the death of the captured alien, and the escape of two others with their recovered bombs, the Dalek Commander ordered an intensified search of the Plain of Stones. The searchers worked in twos, not threes, to maximise the number of patrols. The leader of the first patrol knew that the aliens were cunning and desperate, and he was surprised when they found two of them almost immediately. Perhaps tiredness was making them careless.

The two aliens, both young and small, were standing in the middle of the track that led to the Plain of Stones, almost as if they wanted to be seen. When the patrol spotted them, they turned and ran off between the rocks. They moved slowly, as if very tired, and the patrol soon began to overhaul them. 'Pursue and exterminate,' ordered the patrol leader. 'Supreme Command advise no prisoners to be taken. They must be exterminated!'

The aliens disappeared once they were among the rocks, and the Daleks were forced to hunt for them. Although there were only two of them, they moved confidently forward, quite sure of their ability to deal with aliens.

Jo and Latep collapsed panting behind a rock. 'Are you all right, Jo?' gasped Latep.

'Just about. Never run so fast in my life!'

Latep peered from behind the rock. 'They're coming.

Ready?' Jo nodded. They sprang from the rock and sprinted off.

The Daleks saw them and set off in pursuit.

Taron, Codal, Rebec and the Doctor were crouched behind a giant boulder beside the trail to the ice pool. The place was carefully chosen. The path was narrow here, and the Daleks would have to move in single file. Jo and Latep dashed along the path and joined them in hiding. Panting, Jo said, 'The Daleks are just behind us.'

'Right,' ordered the Doctor. 'Scatter, I'll take over.' Jo, Latep and Rebec took cover near by. Taron and Codal ran down the trail to the pool, to their pre-arranged positions. The Doctor waited. When the two Daleks came in sight, he stepped from hiding, then instantly ducked back. Even so, he moved only just in time. The blast from a Dalek gun charred the rock above his head.

The patrol leader ordered, 'Give protective fire,' and moved off alone. The second Dalek followed more slowly, its gun-stick swivelling suspiciously all around.

The patrol leader rounded the boulder and moved cautiously along the trail that bordered the ice pool. Suddenly the Doctor appeared from behind one of the rocks, disappearing again almost immediately. The patrol leader moved forward. Another blast from its gun seared the rocks, very close to the Doctor. The Dalek was near to the edge of the pool now. Suddenly Taron appeared from hiding. He charged the Dalek, gripping it from behind so the gun could not bear, and started shoving it by main force towards the ice pool. Circling behind the Dalek, the Doctor ran to help.

Slowly they edged it towards the pool. The Dalek resisted with all its strength. All the time it was calling, 'Assist! Assist! I am being attacked!'

Further down the trail, Jo saw the second Dalek speed forward to answer the call, and realised that she had to delay it. She dashed across the trail and the Dalek swung round in pursuit. Jo's foot turned on a small rock and she crashed to the ground, sprawled helplessly on the path as the Dalek bore down on her.

As the Dalek was about to fire, Latep jumped on it from the top of a near by boulder. He had a Spiridon robe in his hands which he threw over the Dalek, covering the eye-stalk completely.

The Dalek spun round helplessly, shrieking, 'Vision circuits impared. I am losing control.'

Somehow Latep stayed perched on top of the Dalek, holding the robe firmly in place. Codal ran from hiding, grabbed the Dalek's gun-stick and jammed it upwards, so that the blast of its firing exploded harmlessly in the air. Rebec and Jo came to help him, and between the three of them they shoved the helpless Dalek along the path taken by the patrol leader.

As they rounded the boulder, the Doctor and Taron gave the patrol leader a mighty shove that sent it splashing into the ice pool. The waters bubbled and hissed, and the leader's cries ended abruptly. The Doctor and Taron ran to help with the second Dalek. Latep leapt from its back and joined them. Propelled by six pairs of arms, the Dalek shot off the path like a rocket and splashed into the ice pond beside its leader.

There was a chorus of shouts and hurrahs from the bank. Jo and the Doctor joined the jubilant Thals in an orgy of hand-shaking and back-slapping. Then the Doctor held up his hand for silence. 'Well done, all of you. But remember, we still have work to do!'

Taron and Latep switched on their heat units and waded into the icy water. 'Don't get directly in front of their guns,' warned the Doctor. 'They may still be dangerous. Pull the top sections clear.'

Taron and Latep did so, shuddering at the sight of the hideous creatures housed inside. 'Are they dead?' called the Doctor.

Latep swallowed as he answered, 'I think so. The cold

must have killed them instantly.'

'You'll have to get the bodies out and throw them in the pond.'

Thankful for their thick space-gauntlets, Taron and Latep groped inside the machine-casing, and threw the twisted bodies into the pool. There was a general sigh of relief as they vanished beneath the surface. 'Now,' said the Doctor more cheerfully, 'let's get the machines on to the bank.'

They began heaving the machines out of the pond and on to the path.

A long file of Spiridon slave workers was moving slowly into the Dalek city, reporting for their immunisation treatments as ordered. No one noticed when Wester slipped from the jungle and joined the line. No one was concerned about one extra slave worker.

Inside the city a Dalek was waiting to direct them. 'Spiridon workers will proceed to level four to await treatment.' The file of docile slaves did as they were ordered. Except for Wester, who slipped away from the line and made his way towards the Dalek laboratory. He knew from other Spiridons in his resistance group that this was where the bacteria containers were being kept.

No one stopped him on his way there. There was a feeling of great excitement in the Dalek city, with Daleks bustling in all directions. But at the door to the control room, he was halted by a Dalek guard. 'Stop. What are you doing here?'

'I have a vital message for the Chief Scientist.'

'The Chief Scientist is occupied. You may enter the laboratory and report when he is free.' Scarcely able to believe his luck, Wester crossed the control area and waited by the sealed door to the laboratory. It hissed open to admit him, hissed closed behind him once he was inside.

Wester saw a group of Daleks gathered round a

bulbous, gun-shaped device which was mounted on a metal trolley. Beside it on another trolley stood a number of transparent jars, their lids firmly sealed.

Wester made no attempt to approach the group of Daleks. Instead he slipped into the farthest corner of the laboratory. The Daleks seemed to be arguing among themselves.

The Chief Scientist asked angrily, 'Why are you not ready to administer the protective treatments as ordered?'

'There is a minor fault in the mechanism. I shall rectify it immediately.'

'Make all speed. Dalek units and Spiridon workers are assembled and waiting.'

The Dalek technicians clustered busily around the immunisation machine.

Wester slowly slipped the fur robes, symbol of slavery, from his body and stuffed them under a machine. Protected by his invisibility, the only weapon of his people, he waited for his opportunity.

Close to the entrance to the Dalek city an oddly assorted group was assembled. One Dalek, three fur-clad Spiridons, a Thal and a human female. Only the last two were actually what they seemed. Inside the machine casing of the Dalek crouched Rebec, ready to act as their passport into the city. The three Spiridons were Codal, Taron and the Doctor . . . another unfortunate Spiridon had been ambushed to provide a third set of robes. The Doctor leaned towards the Dalek. 'Are you all right in there, Rebec?'

There came a muffled 'Yes' in reply. As the smallest, Jo would have been the logical choice to go inside the Dalek, but she had been so obviously unwilling that Rebec volunteered.

The Doctor turned to Jo and Latep. 'Are you sure you can find the right ventilation shaft?'

Latep nodded. 'Taron's given us a map.'

Jo said, 'I wish we could all go in together, Doctor.'

'A two-pronged attack doubles our chance of success. I want you to detonate your bomb in the tunnel near the cooling unit—but whatever you do, don't damage the unit itself. That must go on functioning.'

'We understand, Doctor.'

'Off you go then—and good luck!'

Jo and Latep moved away into the jungle. The Doctor looked anxiously after them for a moment, then gave Rebec's Dalek a hearty slap. A little jerkily she propelled it forward. The Doctor, Taron and Codal followed, three Spiridon slaves being escorted back to the city by their Dalek master. Codal hugged the remaining bomb, concealing it under his fur robes.

All went well until they reached the entrance itself. A Dalek guard glided forward to challenge them. 'All units were ordered back to base some time ago. You are late.'

Rebec's Dalek naturally enough said nothing. The guard spoke angrily. 'Report to central control immediately.' It moved aside, and all four entered the city.

When they emerged from the lift, it was easy enough to lose themselves in the general bustle of Daleks. There was a crowd assembled outside the control area, all with an air of expectant waiting. The Doctor and his party edged their way across until they were at a point where they could look through the glass wall into the sealed-off laboratory. They saw a small group of Daleks clustered round a trolley, apparently working on a gun-like device. Near by stood another trolley, holding sealed containers.

'What are they doing?' whispered Taron.

'I imagine they're preparing to immunise this lot,' said the Doctor quietly. 'Those sealed jars must be the bacteria culture. If we can get close enough to the immunisation machine to wreck it, they won't be able to release the bacteria without killing themselves.' The

Doctor became silent, trying to work out a feasible plan of attack.

The leading Dalek technician moved back from the immunisation-gun. 'Fault rectified. Equipment now fully operational.'

The Chief Scientist ordered, 'Start to administer protective treatment to all units immediately. When that is done, the jars of bacteria culture will be opened at selected points on the planet. All non-immunised life will be exterminated.'

The technician began pushing the trolley towards the door. Suddenly the immunisation-gun rose in the air of its own accord and crashed down on to the trolley of bacteria cultures, smashing most of the jars.

Taron gripped the Doctor's arm. 'There's an invisible Spiridon in there.'

'It's Wester,' said the Doctor, 'It must be. He said he was going to stop them. He's better qualified for sabotage than we are.'

By now there was pandemonium in the laboratory. Those jars still unsmashed were flying through the air, breaking open against the walls. The Dalek scientists milled about, trying to find their invisible opponent.

'He's released the bacteria while he's still in there,' said Taron. 'He's committed suicide.'

The Doctor's voice was sad. 'I know. Listen!'

The Dalek Chief Scientist was speaking over some kind of public address system. 'The door to this laboratory must never be opened. No one can enter. We can never leave here.'

'Don't you see?' whispered the Doctor. 'The Daleks still aren't immunised. If they open that hermetically sealed door, the bacteria will escape and destroy *them*. Wester's done our job for us, better than we ever could . . . but it's cost him his life.' Saddened they turned away.

Daleks and Spiridons were milling about in confusion, and it wasn't difficult to slip away to a side corridor.

'We must find a lift and reach the lower levels,' ordered the Doctor.

They were almost up to the lift doors when a voice grated, 'Halt!' A Dalek had appeared at the end of the corridor. It glided towards them. 'Spiridon slave workers were ordered to wait on level four. Move!'

Rebec, inside her Dalek, stayed motionless. The Doctor, Taron and Codal huddled inside their furs, and slowly turned. As they came level with the Dalek it ordered, 'Wait!' Its eye-stick swivelled downwards. The Doctor followed the direction of its gaze. Taron's booted foot had emerged from his concealing robes. Suddenly the Dalek shrieked, 'You are not Spiridons. You are alien intruders. Emergency! Emergency! Emergency!'

11

An Army Awakes

The Doctor made no attempt to bluff. He whipped off his furs, flung them over the Dalek's eye-stalk and gave it a shove that sent it reeling down the corridor. He and Taron grabbed Rebec's Dalek and shoved it along at full speed. Behind them they could hear a Dalek voice screeching out over the loudspeaker system. 'Alert! Alert! Alert! Aliens at liberty in city. Instigate maximum security conditions. Alert! Alert! Alert! Aliens accompanied by impostor Dalek. Find and exterminate!'

A Dalek patrol came round the corner to find itself facing two aliens, one each side of a Dalek. The aliens dodged back out of sight, but the Dalek did not move. Realising that this must be the impostor, the patrol opened fire.

The Dalek spun round, smoke and flames belching from its top-section. 'Impostor Dalek destroyed,' reported the patrol leader.

Just around the corner the Doctor, Taron, Codal and Rebec were running for their lives. The Doctor yelled to Rebec, 'You stopped being a Dalek just in time!' Rebec smiled back, too breathless to talk.

They found a lift at last and dashed inside. The Doctor adjusted the controls to take them directly to level zero. 'We've got to get to that arsenal,' he explained.

'Then what?' demanded Codal. 'You still haven't told

us all your plan, Doctor. What use is one bomb against an army of Daleks?'

'A great deal of use—in the right place,' said the Doctor mysteriously. 'We can't destroy that army—but we can stop it ever going into action.'

The lift door opened and they emerged on the lowest level. They ran to the cooling section from which they had escaped such a short time ago. The remains of the anti-gravitational disc still littered the area beneath the wrecked cowling, and they passed through the arch that the Daleks had cut in their own door. Rebec shuddered, remembering the nightmare journey up the chimney. Now they were back again. The only difference was that they had a bomb—and the Doctor's plan.

The Doctor himself seemed cheerful and confident. 'See what you can find to make a barricade and seal off the end of that corridor,' he ordered. 'The Daleks are bound to arrive soon. We've got to delay them as long as we can.'

He ran up the ramp and looked through the hatch that gave on to the arsenal. His face clouded as he looked at the Daleks in their motionless ranks. Rebec came up the steps and joined him. She gasped at the sight of the Dalek army. 'The greatest Dalek invasion force ever assembled,' said the Doctor. 'Equipped with the Spiridons' power to become invisible. Nothing could stop them!' He slammed the hatch closed. 'Let's give the others a hand with that barricade.'

Taron and Codal had ripped up work-benches and shoved pieces of machinery into quite a formidable barrier. The Doctor and Rebec helped them to add the finishing touches.

All their lives depended on the strength of the final result.

In the control centre the Expedition Commander was

listening to a report from his second-in-command. 'Message from Supreme Command spacecraft. The Dalek Supreme will shortly arrive on Spiridon. He will assume total command of all operations on this planet.'

The Commander accepted the news without complaint. 'Understood. Continue.'

'Supreme Command have identified the alien who is not of Thal origin. He is the one known as the Doctor, the greatest enemy of the Daleks.'

The Commander considered. 'He will have much valuable knowledge. He must be captured and interrogated.'

Jo and Latep were still quite close to the Dalek city when they saw the little spacecraft come in to land. Sinister and saucer-like, it glided into an open space near the city entrance. Crouched at the edge of the jungle, Jo and Latep watched.

A ramp appeared silently from the body of the ship. A door opened and two Daleks glided down, taking up a position at the bottom, one either side. A third Dalek appeared at the top of the ramp. Its body-colour was not the usual silver but a gleaming black, and its dome shone brightly in gold. This Dalek glided smoothly down the ramp and set off towards the city, followed by the two aides.

Latep's voice was full of awe. 'That was the Dalek Supreme, head of the Supreme Council. Second only to the Emperor himself.'

Jo was staring thoughtfully at the spaceship. 'That doesn't look too different from your own craft. Could you fly it?'

Latep nodded. 'Any of us could. We've studied captured Dalek ships.'

'Then you could use it to get back to Skaro! Don't you see, you're not marooned here any more. I wish we could tell the others.'

'Maybe it's as well we can't.' Latep spoke seriously. 'There's something to be said for thinking you're on a suicide mission. You've got nothing to lose.'

Jo looked at him in exasperation. 'I thought you'd be pleased there was at least a hope of getting away.'

Latep smiled. 'Believe me, I am. I think I've found a very good reason for wanting to stay alive.' He looked directly at Jo as he spoke.

Jo turned quickly away. 'We'd better get moving again. There's still a long way to go.'

The Doctor stared at the machinery in the cooling chamber and cursed fluently in an obscure Martian dialect.

Taron couldn't understand the words, but the meaning was plain enough. 'What's the matter, Doctor?'

'I was hoping to find a way to lock these controls in the on position. As soon as the refrigeration's switched off, the Dalek army is going to start coming to life. Won't work though, the main switches must be in the central control area. We'll have to use my other plan. Taron and Rebec, keep an eye on the barricade, Codal, you come with me.'

He led Codal out into the corridor and used his sonic screwdriver to open the smaller door that led into the Dalek arsenal. Codal stopped short at the sight of the immense army of Daleks, but the Doctor said cheerfully, 'Don't worry, they're all fast asleep.' He pointed to a ramp leading up to the metal catwalks surrounding the huge cavern. 'We're going up on to those catwalks, Codal, you one way and me the other. We're looking for a nice large fissure in those walls . . .'

The Dalek Supreme, flanked by his aides, stood in central control. The area had been cleared. The Dalek Commander and his second-in-command stood before him. Harshly the Dalek Supreme addressed the second-in-command, ignoring the Expedition Commander. 'Report on invisibility experiments.'

'Daleks can achieve invisibility for two work periods only. In excess of this period, breakdown from light-wave sickness occurs.'

'Satisfactory. The Supreme Council has ordered our army to be activated immediately. The invasion of the galaxy will begin at once. Close down refrigeration unit.'

'I obey.' The second-in-command moved away.

The Dalek Supreme turned his attention to the Expedition Commander. 'The action of hostile aliens has caused disruption of our operations on this planet.'

'The matter was beyond my control.' The Commander spoke without hope, knowing he was already condemned.

'Your orders were to exterminate them.'

'It has not been possible. Because of Spiridon sabotage we could not use the bacteria.'

The Dalek Supreme paused for a moment and then delivered judgement. 'The responsibility was yours. You have failed. The Supreme Council of the Daleks does not accept failure.'

The Expedition Commander stood quite still, accepting his fate. The guns of the Dalek Supreme and his aides blazed together, and the Commander exploded in smoke and flames.

Latep and Jo stood at the top of the chimney-shaft. Latep had rigged up a kind of derrick made from tree branches gathered on the way. One end of an immense coil of rope was secured to it, and he was paying the other down into the shaft. Jo looked on full of misgiving. 'Suppose that contraption doesn't hold?'

Latep grinned. 'It'll hold.'

'Well, suppose the rope isn't long enough?'

'Jo, we've got every piece of rope in the entire expedition fastened together. Believe me, it'll be long enough. Your friend the Doctor worked it out.'

Jo smiled wanly. 'It's not only the trip down that worries me: it's what we'll find at the bottom.'

Latep grinned encouragingly. 'We'll find the Doctor and the others, just as arranged. I'm off. Follow me when I call.' He swung his leg over the parapet, gripping the rope with his hands and feet.

Jo leaned forward and kissed him quickly on the cheek. 'Good luck, Latep.'

'And to you, Jo.' He slipped down out of sight. Jo waited anxiously until she heard his voice booming up the chimney. 'It's all right, Jo, come on.' She climbed the parapet, gripped the rope in the way he'd shown her and started following him down.

The Doctor was still searching when he heard Codal call, 'Doctor—I think I've found what you need.'

The Doctor ran along the catwalk to join him. Codal, the precious bomb at his feet, was standing by a jagged hole in the rock walls.

The Doctor examined it with interest. 'Now that looks promising. How deep is it?'

'Pretty deep I think, I can get my arm inside.' Codal demonstrated.

Taron appeared in the doorway of the arsenal. 'Doctor, the Daleks have reached the barricade—they're attacking it now! And the cooling unit seems to have been switched off. The temperature's rising.'

The Doctor paused. 'So it is. It'll only take a very small rise for these Daleks to start moving. We've got to work fast, Codal.'

Codal wasn't listening. He was staring in fascination down into the arsenal itself, his eyes wide with horror. 'Look, Doctor.' he pointed. The Doctor looked. In the ranks of Daleks below him, gun-sticks were swivelling uncertainly, eye-stalks waving in unfocused menace. Some of the Daleks were shifting a little, bumping gently against their neighbours. Sluggishly, reluctantly, but quite unmistakably, the army of Daleks had started to come to life.

12

The Last Gamble

Taron and Rebec looked down the corridor from the cooling chamber towards the barricade at the far end. It was shuddering rhythmically as Daleks hurled themselves against it. At first they'd tried blasting it aside, but that had simply melted the metal and welded it together more strongly. Now they were using brute force, hurling themselves against it in relays like battering rams. It was a slow and clumsy method, but effective. Already parts of the barricade were beginning to fall away.

'A couple more tries and the whole lot will come down,' said Taron. 'Time we pulled back.'

They went through into the Dalek arsenal, and Taron touched the controls to close the door. There was no response. Taron shook his head. 'It's no good, the Daleks have cut off the power.' They climbed the ramp to the catwalk, joined the Doctor and Codal, who were busily enlarging their fissure by clearing out the rubble.

'The door won't shut, there's still no sign of Jo and Latep and the Daleks are nearly through the barricade,' reported Taron briskly. 'What now?'

The Doctor considered for a moment. 'They must have got all these Daleks in here somehow, and presumably they've provided a way to get them out. I don't suppose they're planning to take them up in the lifts, one by one! My guess is that one of these catwalks will lead to an exit, probably some sort of ramp. See what you can find.'

Taron and Rebec raced away, and the Doctor stretched a long arm inside the fissure. 'That seems to be clear enough. Pass me that bomb, Codal.'

Codal swung round to pick up the bomb—and caught it with the side of his foot as he turned. The bomb rolled slowly towards the edge of the catwalk. Codal dived for it, but just too late. Eluding his fingers by inches, the bomb rolled off the edge and fell to the area below.

The Doctor and Codal braced themselves—but nothing happened. Codal peered over the edge. 'There it is, down there.' He pointed. The bomb had rolled a few feet and lodged against the base of one of the Daleks. The Doctor looked. The drop was only about ten feet. Without hesitation he lowered himself over the edge, hung by his hands for a moment and dropped.

For a moment the Doctor stood still, gazing around him. Talk about Daniel in the lions' den, he thought. Here he was in full view of an entire Dalek army. The Daleks seemed dimly aware of his presence, but were still too dormant to do anything about it. Eye-stalks swivelled slowly in an attempt to follow his progress as he picked his way between the stirring forms. Sucker-arms and gun-sticks waved erratically at him, and the slow-moving bodies of the Daleks jostled him as he walked. Working his way through the crowd of Daleks, the Doctor moved towards the bomb. The Dalek against which it was resting started moving too, and the bomb rolled further away, to be knocked further still by yet another Dalek. It was like a ghastly slow-motion football game, thought the Doctor, with thousands of players on the other side.

Dodging through the obstructing Daleks he reached the bomb at last and scooped it up. Codal was watching anxiously from the catwalk when the Doctor called 'Here!' and tossed him the bomb. With a gasp Codal caught it. The Doctor worked his way back to the catwalk. He jumped to swing himself up, but it was too high—he couldn't get a good enough run in the crowded space. The Daleks were pressing in on him now, as if trying to crush him. The Doctor climbed nimbly on top of the nearest Dalek and used it as a launch-pad for a flying leap to the catwalk.

Codal was examining the bomb anxiously. 'I think it's all right, but the timing mechanism's damaged. It'll take me a few minutes to fix it.' He produced tools from his belt and got to work.

Taron and Rebec came running back along the catwalk. 'You were right, Doctor,' said Rebec excitedly. 'There's a huge spiral ramp over on the far side. It must lead right to the surface.'

'Excellent. That's our way out, when the time comes.'

'Isn't it about time you explained the rest of your plan?' asked Taron.

The Doctor smiled. 'I'm sorry—you've been very patient. Well, as you know, this arsenal is right on the edge of the icecano. The Daleks built it there deliberately so they could use its cooling power. This whole area is honeycombed with ice tunnels—and the icecano is unstable. If we explode our bomb in exactly the right place, it could make the icecano erupt *and* weaken the walls. The ice will break through and flood this entire cavern. That's the theory, anyway. We'll just have to hope it works.'

'The ice won't destroy them,' Rebec pointed out. 'It will just put them into suspended animation again.'

'With only one bomb that's the best we can hope for. Besides, once the chambers are flooded it will take centuries to seal off the icecano and get the Daleks out.'

The Doctor was interrupted by an explosion from outside the chamber. He turned to Codal. 'You'd better hurry, old chap. That sounded like the last of the barricade—they've used explosives!'

Back in the cooling chamber, a pair of legs appeared beneath the shattered cowling. Latep dropped to the ground, followed by Jo.

He helped her up. 'You all right?'

'I think so,' she gasped. 'What's that noise?' From the corridor outside came a tremendous banging and clattering. They crept to the door and peered out. Daleks were pushing aside the remains of the shattered barricade. Jo looked anxiously at Latep. 'We've got to stop them!'

Latep unslung his bomb from its holder, made a quick adjustment to the timing mechanism. He stepped boldly into the corridor and bowled the bomb at the Daleks. A Dalek fired the moment he appeared. Latep threw himself backwards, the blast missing him by inches. For a moment the gleaming cylinder sat harmlessly in the middle of the Daleks. Then it exploded, shattering the nearest Daleks and bringing down a pile of rubble that blocked off half the corridor.

Jo and Latep strained to see through the dust and smoke. At the far end of the corridor, Daleks were already beginning to push aside the rubble.

'They don't give up, do they?' said Jo. 'Let's go and find the Doctor.' They ran into the arsenal and along the catwalk. Rebec, Taron and the Doctor, still waiting for Codal to finish his repairs, greeted them enthusiastically. 'The Daleks are nearly here,' warned Jo. 'We used our bomb to try and stop them, but it didn't work.'

Codal looked up. 'All right, I've finished.'

The Doctor gave a sigh of relief. 'Taron, you lead the others to the surface. Codal and I will set the bomb and follow you. Codal, set the bomb to detonate in thirty seconds.'

Taron, Rebec, Latep and Jo ran along the catwalk towards the ramp.

The Doctor watched Codal touch a control on the bomb. 'Detonator running,' said Codal, and passed the bomb hurriedly to the Doctor. The Doctor thrust it deep inside the rock-fissure, groping to wedge it in a good position.

In the corridor, the Daleks pushed aside the last of the rubble and glided towards the arsenal door.

The Doctor withdrew his arm from the fissure. 'Right, that should do it. Come on!' They started running along the catwalk, just as the first Daleks glided through the arsenal door. The Daleks moved cautiously up the ramp, and on to the catwalk.

The Doctor and Codal tore along the catwalk, leaving the Daleks behind. On the far side of the arsenal, the other four were waiting. Behind them a huge spiral ramp led upwards into darkness.

The little group anxiously watched the Daleks move slowly along the catwalk. The Doctor could hear Codal counting under his breath. 'Seven, six, five, four, three, two, one . . .'

As the leading Dalek drew level with the fissure, the bomb exploded. There was a blast of flame and smoke from the fissure, and the Daleks were blown clear into the arsenal, crashing down upon the waking army. The catwalk was twisted and wrecked. For a moment it seemed that was all. 'It hasn't worked,' breathed Codal. 'They'll repair that damage in no time. We've failed.'

'Wait,' said the Doctor quietly.

The heard a low rumbling. Cracks were appearing in the rock wall by the fissure, like the cracks made by dropping a stone on to thin ice. The cracks lengthened, spread . . . Suddenly a whole section of wall burst inwards and a river of liquid ice began flooding through. The huge cavern was flooding as they watched. As the searing cold of the liquid ice rose around their bodies, the army of Daleks froze into immobility, resuming the long sleep from which they had so briefly awakened. From outside the arsenal came a threatening roar as ice broke through to other parts of the city. The icecano had erupted.

The Thals were already running up the spiral ramp. Jo tugged at the Doctor's sleeve. 'Come on, Doctor!'

The Doctor paused for a last look. The huge cavern was more than half-filled with ice by now, the helpless Daleks disappearing beneath the flood. 'Most satisfactory,' said the Doctor with a smile. He and Jo ran after the others.

There were only three Daleks left in central control, the newly arrived Dalek Supreme, and his two aides. All members of the Dalek expedition to Spiridon had been involved in the final attempt to capture the Doctor, and were now trapped by the erupting ice.

The leading aide was calmly reading the instruments in the control room, relaying a story of unmitigated disaster. 'Arsenal and all lower levels inundated. Molten ice rising rapidly through all levels. No response from any Dalek unit.'

The Dalek Supreme spun round. A trickle of molten ice was flowing through the door of central control. 'Advise Supreme Command. Attack force totally immobilised. No survivors. Set self-destruct on all instruments. We are abandoning.'

The Doctor and his friends were gathered round the ramp that led to the Dalek spacecraft. Codal had opened the door with ease, and was happily checking the controls. They heard a low hum of power as the ship was readied for take-off. 'Time to go,' said the Doctor cheerfully.

Rebec was holding Taron's hand. 'And now we can go back home, to Skaro. That's something I never expected.'

Taron turned to the Doctor. 'There's no adequate way of thanking you, Doctor, but if there's ever anything we can do?'

Vastly embarrassed, the Doctor shook his head. Then he said, 'Wait, perhaps there is something. The Thals have always been peace-loving people. I'd like to think they'll remain so. When you get back home, you'll be heroes. But don't glamorise your adventures. Don't make them think war is an exciting game. Tell them about the fear and the danger, the friends who won't be coming back.'

Taron nodded gravely. 'You can depend on us, Doctor. Goodbye.' Taron and Rebec hurried into the ship.

The Doctor looked for Latep and Jo, who had been talking a little apart from the others. They came up to him, Latep holding Jo's hand. He looked nervous but determined. 'I've been trying to persuade Jo to come back to Skaro with me, Doctor. Would you object?'

The Doctor looked down at Jo. 'Not if that's what she wants. Is it, Jo?'

Jo smiled tearfully at Latep. 'I'm sorry, Latep, I'm afraid it isn't. I like you very much—but I've got my own world and my own life to get back to.'

Latep nodded. He held out his hand. Jo shook it, then kissed him on the cheek. He hurried up the ramp.

Taron appeared in the doorway. 'You'll need these to get back into your ship, Doctor,' he called, and tossed down a plastic-wrapped bundle. 'Goodbye, and thanks again!'

They heard a chorus of goodbyes from inside the ship, then the door closed and the ramp retracted. Jo and the Doctor ran to the edge of the jungle, then turned to watch the take-off. With a roar of its booster-rockets the ship blasted-off, disappearing into the sky on its way back to Skaro.

The Doctor examined the bundle Taron had thrown him. It held two sets of plastic protective clothing and a spray. 'Very thoughtful of him,' he said. 'We'd have had a job getting back in the TARDIS without these.'

Jo wasn't listening. She pointed to the blockhouse guarding the entrance to the Dalek city. From it were emerging the Dalek Supreme and his two aides. 'Oh dear,' said the Doctor. 'I don't suppose they'll be too happy about the Thals taking their spaceship.'

'No.' Jo smiled. 'I don't suppose they will.'

Jo and the Doctor turned and ran. A blast from a Dalek gun set fire to the jungle beside them. As they hurried through the undergrowth they heard the outraged voice of the Dalek Supreme, 'Aliens! Pursue and exterminate!'

Fortunately for Jo and the Doctor, the Dalek Supreme and his aides were strangers on Spiridon, and knew far less about the planet than they did themselves. It didn't take long to lose them in the dense jungle. After that, it was just a matter of enduring the long trek back to the point where the TARDIS had first landed.

When they reached the ruined temple it took them quite a while to recognise the TARDIS. The sponge-plants had been unable actually to eat it, but they'd covered it so thoroughly with their fungus that it looked rather like a large, square sponge. The Doctor and Jo put on the protective plastic garments and the Doctor sprayed the TARDIS until he found the door. Once it was located, he concentrated on clearing the fungus with the spray so that he could open the door.

Jo looked on as he worked. The sponge-plants, aroused by their presence, were spitting angrily. Jo shuddered as she saw the white blobs spattering on the Doctor's plastic coat, remembering her own infection before she'd been cured by Wester. Poor Wester, she thought. The Doctor had told her of his self-sacrifice . . .

Suddenly Jo saw three gleaming shapes approaching through the jungle. With incredible persistence, the Daleks had found them again.

She tapped the Doctor on the shoulder and pointed. The Doctor nodded unperturbed. 'Nearly done, Jo. The lock's bunged up with this stuff, and the key won't turn.'

The Doctor worked unhurriedly. The Daleks moved steadily closer.

'Hurry, Doctor,' said Jo. 'They'll spot us any minute now!'

She was right. Seconds later the leading Dalek registered the figures standing by the TARDIS. It fired at once, and the blast scorched a patch of fungus from the TARDIS's side. But the Doctor had the door open now. 'Hurry, Jo,' he yelled. Running past the gauntlet of the spitting sponges, Jo dashed inside, and the Doctor slammed the door behind them.

By now all three Daleks were approaching the TARDIS, gun-sticks blazing. But they were too late. The Daleks watched helplessly as the TARDIS dematerialised, fragments of fungus dropping to the ground. Their greatest enemy had defeated their plans and escaped their vengeance once again.

The Dalek Supreme turned arrogantly to his aides. It had been a day of total catastrophe, the army buried, the Spiridon expedition wiped out, the city destroyed. Any other life-form would have been crushed by despair. But Daleks do not recognise defeat. They ignore it and carry on their chosen path of conquest and destruction.

There was utter confidence in the voice of the Dalek Supreme. 'Supreme Command will dispatch a rescue craft. Immediately on arrival, preparations will begin to free the army from the ice. We have been delayed, but not defeated.' The harsh voice rose triumphantly. '*The Daleks are never defeated!*'

Jo was feeding the protective garments into a disposal chute. 'Spiridon is one planet I never want to see again,' she said.

The Doctor finished his in-flight check, and moved to a monitor screen. He adjusted controls until the screen filled with stars, and then narrowed the focus down to one particular planet. 'What about this one, Jo?' he asked mischievously. 'That's Skaro. Any regrets?'

Jo smiled a little sadly, thinking of Latep's earnest

pleas. But she shook her head. 'No, Doctor. Skaro's not for me.'

The Doctor adjusted controls again. Another galaxy, and then another planet swam up on the screen. 'What about this little world?'

Jo looked at the planet floating peacefully in space. 'That's Earth, isn't it?'

The Doctor nodded.

'Then that's the one I want to see,' Jo said firmly. 'Home please, Doctor!'

The Doctor smiled. 'Very well, Jo. Home it is.'

He leaned over the control console and set the co-ordinates for Earth.